1

SUN AT MIDNIGHT

Alice Peel is a geologist. She belives in observation, thesis, analysis and proof. But now, standing alone on the deck of a rickety Chilean ship as a stark landscape reveals itself, everything that lies ahead of her is unknown and unpredictablc. Six weeks earlier her comfortable, ordered life was suddenly up-turned by the end of her relationship, prompting Alice to accept an invitation to join an expedition group working at the end of the earth: Antarctica.

Nothing has prepared Alice for the harsh beauty of the ice-blue and white and silver world, or the claustrophobia of a tiny base shared with eight men and one other woman. The isolation wipes out everyone's past, and tension crackles in the air. But there is a jolt of recognition between Alice and James Rooker, a man on the run, a man who has been running since his childhood in New Zealand. It is unlike anything she has ever known.

And it is in Antartica that she discovers something else that will change her life forever . . . if she survivies.

SUN AT MIDNIGHT

Rosie Thomas

WINDSOR
PARAGON

First published 2004
by
HarperCollins Publishers
This Large Print edition published 2004
by
BBC Audiobooks Ltd by arrangement with
HarperCollins Publishers Ltd

ISBN 1 4056 1030 1   (Windsor Hardcover)
ISBN 1 4056 2023 4   (Paragon Softcover)

British Library Cataloguing in Publication Data available

Printed and bound in Great Britain by
Antony Rowe Ltd., Chippenham, Wiltshire

Acknowledgements

Andrew Prossin of Peregrine Adventures generously enabled me to make two unforgettable trips to Antarctica aboard the *Akademik loffe*. I am grateful to Bill Davis, Aaron and Cathy Lawton, David McGonigal and all the expedition staff and ship's crew in the 2000 and 2003 seasons. Andrew Prossin also introduced me to Professor Christo Pimpirev of the Department of Geology at the University of Sofia, who immediately invited a stranger to join his team for part of a season at St Kliment Ohridski Base, Livingston Island, South Shetlands. Without the opportunity to live and work alongside the members of the Eleventh Bulgaria Antarctic Expedition I could not have written this book. Nor would I have enjoyed the experience of a lifetime.

I am also indebted to Captain Rod Wood, CabAir Helicopter Training Schools, Elstree Aerodrome, Borehamwood; Dave Taylor, Helicopters Cambodia Ltd; Mr Anthony Silverstone; Phil Bowen and Exodus; and to Sara Wheeler.

*For the members of the XIth
Bulgaria Antarctic Expedition—Christo, Dimo,
Dany, Elmira, Koko, Milcho, Murphy, Niki, Roumi,
Stanko and Valentin—with love and grateful thanks.*

'always on our team'

CHAPTER ONE

The wind blew straight off the frozen bay. It was thickened with sleet but the man working on the skeleton roof didn't seem to notice the cold, or the way the flecks of ice drove into his eyes. He had climbed the raw wood truss at one end of the building and now he straddled the main beam high above the mud- and snow-smeared mess of the site. The hotel had been due to open at the beginning of the short summer season, but the weather had been bad even by local standards, and the work had been slow and dogged with problems. Now the job was way behind schedule. The first fix wasn't even finished, a month before the completion date. The site crew were mostly Mexican, the main contractor was from Buenos Aires and they all hated the cold. The architect worked for a big commercial practice in Portland, Oregon, and he flew into town and found fault for a couple of days before flying right out again. The hotel company was German-owned, with an aggressive development programme and a policy of cutting construction costs right to the bone.

All of this was routine, however. It was work, life's usual shit. James Rooker didn't even bother to think about it.

He vaulted along the beam, squinting against the wind and snow, checking the bolts that secured the plates that held the trusses in place. The wood was split and some of the bolts were missing. This was Juan's and Pepito's work, of course.

Down below, the whistle sounded for the end of

the day. Instantly a trail of men straggled across the site to deposit their tools and pick up their coats.

Rooker looked across to the bay and the snow slopes lining the Beagle Channel. It was September and the only ship in the harbour was an ugly Russian ice breaker waiting to head south, but in a few more weeks it would be summer and the cruise ships would be moored up on either side of the main jetty. The town would be full of tourists in fleeces and hiking boots, coming and going from their sea voyages and their glacier hikes and waterfall sightseeing trips and treks in the National Park. There would be a little blue-painted funfair train running through the streets, and an employee of the tourist company dressed in a giant penguin suit would spend five hours of every day posing for photographs and using his flipper to shake hands. It would soon be time to be somewhere else. As this occurred to him, Rooker noticed that the snow had stopped. A slice of sky showed through the clouds and an oblique shaft of silver light fell across the sea ice.

He swung down from his beam and clambered down a series of ladders to the ground. The finished hotel would have sympathetic wood cladding, but as yet it was a grey breeze-block slab with holes poked in it for windows. A pair of men had started work today on the ground-floor door and window frames.

He caught sight of Juan in a group making tracks towards the site gate through the skim of wet snow.

'Hey!' Rooker yelled. 'You, Juan, I want you.'

The man stopped and waited. He was small, dark-skinned and hopeless. '*Sí?*'

Rooker towered over him. He jerked a thumb

towards the roof timbers. 'What's that crap up there?'

The carpenter shrugged. He was used to the foreman's ways. 'Weather bad,' he muttered routinely.

'Then let's get the fucking roof on straight, Mex, so we can all have some shelter. Okay?'

'*Sí.*'

'Bad work, no *pesos*. *Comprende*?' Rooker rubbed his thumb and forefinger together.

The man nodded and hitched his canvas bag over his shoulder. It was Wednesday and the crew got paid on Thursdays, so there would be no drinking tonight. Juan just wanted to get back to his lodgings for some food and warmth and a night's sleep.

'Get on, then,' Rooker said, losing patience. Everyone else was already gone, Pepito presumably amongst them. The grey light was fading fast. The roof and its correct fixing would have to wait for tomorrow, yet another day. Juan trudged away and Rooker locked up the metal cabin that served as the site hut and tool store. By the time he was padlocking the gate in the metal fencing it was fully dark. Night fell swiftly at this latitude.

He walked quickly down the hill towards the centre of town. Up here, on the outskirts, the roads that bisected the main streets were still unmade. There were mounds of filthy snow beside the steps up to narrow front doors. The houses were corrugated metal boxes not much more elaborate than the site hut, but they were brightly painted and the curtains were already snugly pulled at most of the windows. A couple of dogs reared and snarled at the end of their chains as he passed. It was bitterly cold now. As he turned right under the dirty orange glare of a street lamp he saw the lights of a plane low in the sky. It was the evening flight from Buenos Aires, coming in to land at the new airport.

The bar he was heading for wasn't one of the brightly lit ones in the main street parallel to the harbour wall. Those places had check tablecloths and pictures on the walls, and they served fancy-priced beer or coffee or even cocktails to tourists on their way to beef barbecue restaurants. Rooker's destination was in a side street, down three steps from sidewalk level and behind an unmarked door.

Half a dozen people looked up from their drinks when he came in and a couple of them nodded to him. He stood at the bar and the big barmaid poured him three fingers of whisky without asking what he wanted.

'*Hola,*' she muttered as she slid the tumbler across the bar. She had stopped hoping that Rooker might pay her some attention.

He drank his whisky in silence. There was nothing decorative or homely about the place, only wooden stools and bare floorboards. It was dry and fairly warm and the drink was cheap, and no one who came here was looking for more than that. It was a bar for itinerant workers, fishermen, sailors and foreign kitchen hands, a dingy place in a frontier town at the furthermost end of the world. Or almost the furthermost end.

Rooker was finishing his drink and wondering about another when the fight started. It erupted without warning, for no discernible reason, as fights often did in this place. Suddenly a table was

4

overturned and playing cards fluttered over the floor. Two men growled and wrestled each other like drunken bears. One of them took the other by the throat and shook him, the other crooked his arm and his fist connected with his assailant's jaw with a sharp crack. They staggered, locked together, and fell over another table. Glasses fell and smashed, and black spatters of drink marked the floor. The other drinkers stood up or shouted and the barmaid wearily reached for the telephone behind the bar.

He sidestepped away from the fracas, his face expressionless. Rooker had seen too many bar fights; this one was monotonously the same as all the others. He reached the door and walked out into the darkness without looking back. He reckoned that he might as well go home, without thinking of the place in this context as *home*. It was ten minutes away, back up the hill, but in the opposite direction from the new hotel. He moved unhurriedly, his hands in the pockets of his storm coat, not noticing the cold or that it had started snowing again.

The house was a two-storey building, older than most of its neighbours, with protruding eaves and a little loggia at the front. For the few precious weeks of summer there would be flowers in the blue-painted oil drums that stood under wrought-metal lanterns on either side of the front door, but for now there were only crusts of snow, clinging to dead twigs, and a scatter of cigarette butts. Officially Marta didn't allow smoking in the house.

Rooker let himself in. In the hallway there was a smell of frying meat, an ornate carved-wood coat-stand and about a hundred framed pictures. Marta loved bric-a-brac. He had had to do battle, when he first rented his room, to get her to remove half the stuff that cluttered it up.

As he put his foot on the first stair, Marta stuck her head out of the door that led to her domain at the back of the house.

'*Qué tal*, Rook?'

Marta was enormously fat, but she had a lovely face, with smooth pale skin and sad dark eyes. Her husband had left her and she was on the lookout for a replacement. Rooker greeted her without checking his progress up the stairs.

He rented the upper back half of the house. The windows faced straight out on to a steep rocky slope so there wasn't much light, but in wintertime there wasn't much light anywhere so this hardly mattered. He didn't know where he would be when the summer finally did come, but it was unlikely to be here.

He hung up his coat and unlaced his boots. There was an armchair beside a small wood-burning stove, a bookcase, a table and a couple of chairs, and an alcove with a sink and a basic kitchen. In another alcove was a bed and a cupboard. The bathroom was out on the landing and Rooker shared it with the chef from one of the tourist restaurants, who rented the upstairs front.

'It's fine,' he told Marta when she showed the place to him. And it was fine, once he had made her cart away all the religious pictures and lace tablecloths and wool-work cushions that filled it up. He wasn't fussy about where he lived, so long as it didn't take up too much of his attention.

He began to make a meal. There was the remainder of a bean and beef casserole that Marta

6

had pressed on him, so he put the pan on an electric ring to heat it up. There was bread, and a block of strong cheese, and some smoked sausage. Rooker was just putting a plate on the table when he heard the unusual sound of someone ringing the downstairs bell. It would be a friend of Guillermo the chef's, he thought. Guillermo did have the occasional night off work. Or maybe Marta had found a new boyfriend.

There were voices in the hallway, Marta's and another. The caller was a woman.

Marta came puffing up the stairs and rapped on his door.

'Rook? You got visitor,' she called.

He looked around his room, instinctively checking for anything that might give away something of himself. But the place was almost bare, apart from clothes and food, and a few books on the shelves.

'Rook?' Marta repeated. Through the thin wood panels of the door he could hear her breathing, but no sound from the other woman, whoever she might be.

He opened the door. Marta's bulk almost blocked the aperture.

'Come up, honey,' she called over her shoulder in her heavily accented American English. His caller wasn't local, then.

Light, quick footsteps came up the stairs. Marta squeezed herself to one side and he saw that it was Edith.

'Ede? Christ. What're you doing here?'

She brought the smell of cold in with her. There was snow on her shoulders and her hair glittered with moisture. She tipped her head and her

7

eyebrows lifted. 'What kind of a welcome is that?'

'What kind of arrival is this?'

Edith didn't let her smile fade. He remembered how white her teeth always looked against her tawny skin. 'A surprise.'

'Damn right it is.'

She was carrying a bag. She let it drop now with a thump. Marta looked inquisitively from Rooker to Edith and back again.

Rooker sighed. 'Okay. Come on in. *Gracias*, Marta.'

'*De nada.*' She was offended not to be introduced and further included in the unusual event of her back lodger having a visitor.

Edith hoisted her bag, skipped past her and nudged the door shut with her shoulder. She looked around the room, not missing a detail. 'So this is home? It's not all that homely, is it?'

'It's not home. It's just where I live.'

After only two minutes Edith knew they had already got off on the wrong footing. Rooker felt her checking herself and trying a different approach.

'It's good to see you, Rook.'

She stroked her hair and settled it so it lay back over one shoulder. He took note, as she intended him to do, of how pretty she was and how small and fragile-seeming. Her feet and hands were as tiny as a child's.

'What are you doing in Ushuaia?'

She was still smiling at him. Her eyes danced. 'You know what I'm doing here. And now that I am here, aren't you going to offer me a drink?'

He was trapped. He looked at the door and at his pan of stew on the electric ring. It was smoking, so he lifted it off. 'All right, Edith. There's whisky. Will that do?'

'Sure.' She unbuttoned her coat and hung it over the back of a chair, and kicked off her snowboots. She stood in front of the stove, rubbing her hands, then took the tumbler of scotch he handed to her. He poured himself a measure and that was the end of the bottle.

'Here's to you and me,' she said softly and drank. He ignored the toast.

'How did you get here?'

'From Buenos Aires, how else? On this evening's flight.' The one he had seen coming in to land.

'Edith, I don't know why you're here. I don't know how you found me . . .'

'Frankie told me.'

'She had no right to do that.' Frankie was an old friend of Rooker's. She was younger than he was and although he had known her for fifteen years they had never slept together. He liked that, it made her different. Sometimes he e-mailed her from the *locutorio* off the main street. Frances was married to a chiropractor she had met at a Jerry Garcia memorial concert, and now lived in New York State with him and their three children. It still surprised Rooker to think of Frances with children, but all the evidence was that she had put her wild days behind her and settled down to being a wife and mother. He liked getting her e-mails about what the kids were up to and the latest funny thing the baby had said. Ross, her husband, was dull but decent.

'Well, she did.'

He kept his anger in check. Frankie had always liked Edith, out of all Rooker's girlfriends. And

9

Frankie had his postal address, because she had sent him a book on his birthday. It was *The Worst Journey in the World* by Apsley Cherry-Garrard. It stood on the shelf behind him now. He had read some of it.

'Rook?' Edith breathed. She put her glass on the table and came to him, holding out her hands. When he didn't take them she grasped the front of his shirt and lifted herself on tiptoe so she could kiss him on the mouth. She tasted of whisky.

'Don't do that,' he ordered. He disentangled himself from her grasp and turned away. The room was too small, there was nowhere to get away from this.

'I love you,' Edith said, in a new jagged voice that was raw with accusation.

'No, you don't. You've just forgotten.'

*   *   *

He hadn't forgotten. The last time he saw her was in Dallas. He had arrived in Dallas as a pilot for an air charter company but that job had stopped working even before it had started, so he was filling in on yet another building site. Edith had found work as a dancer. They had been living together, an arrangement that only lasted a few weeks this time, and they had gone out drinking one night.

Edith always set out to attract attention, particularly from men in bars, and that night was no exception. She was wearing a tiny skirt that showed her toffee-coloured thighs and a stretchy top that exposed most of her breasts. Before they left the apartment she was shimmying around in front of him, laughing too much and darting hard little glances at him from under her eyelashes. Rooker knew that even if he had loved her, even if he smothered her with enough admiration and affection to suffocate them both, it wouldn't be enough to satisfy Edith. She was born to be dissatisfied and doomed always to want more than she could get. If she had him, she wanted other men as well, for reassurance. If she didn't have him she wouldn't stop wheedling and threatening and seducing until he gave way to her. They had already split up twice before the night in Dallas. But Edith always knew which buttons to press.

That night she had been wild, fuelled by her anger with him and her contempt for the rest of the world. She had barely tasted her first drink before she had her tongue in some guy's mouth. The man's hands went straight down inside the little stretchy top and Rooker had hauled him backwards and pinned him against the bar. Even as he did it he was wondering why. He didn't care who Edith rubbed herself up against. He didn't want to be here with her, but he couldn't think of anywhere else that he wanted to be.

'Don't do that,' Rooker had said quietly to Edith's new friend.

The man tried to smile. 'Hey, I'm real sorry. I just thought . . .' There were beads of sweat in the bristles above his top lip.

Rooker felt as though he was standing beside himself, watching his own actions in boredom and disgust. His hands dropped back to his sides.

'Come on,' he said to Edith.

Outside, she moved up against him. She was lithe and taut, like a cat. 'Hey,' she breathed in his ear. As always, his aggression excited her.

11

The evening that had begun badly grew steadily more evil. There were more bars, much more drinking. They found themselves in a place where there was lap dancing and the next thing that happened was that Edith was dancing too, out of her mind and out of her stretchy top and tiny skirt. There was a man whose thick red arms were matted with coarse gingery hair, and Rook saw one of these arms slide between Edith's thighs. With a weight of sadness on him Rook grabbed her by the back of the neck, just as if she really were a cat, and pushed her out of reach. Then he squared up to the red man, seeing out of the corner of his eye the bar's security staff heading towards them.

'Fag,' the red man sneered.

'Outside,' Rook answered.

The night was thick and hot. At first Rook could hardly move against the pressure of ennui and disgust, but when the man's fist smashed almost casually into the corner of his eye the pain lit a phosphor-white blaze in his head. He hit out, and hit again. The man went down instantly and when Rook looked at him he saw that his face was split wide open. There were teeth and bone in a mess of blood, and Rook was certain that he had killed him. Sick horror and a wash of memories rose up in him and he staggered backwards, hands up in a vain effort to shut out the sight.

He left the man lying on the ground. He left Edith still inside the bar somewhere and he made his way home in painful and blurred slow motion. On the floor of the bathroom were the prints of Edith's feet outlined in talcum powder. He rubbed them out with the side of his fist as the floor seemed to tilt sideways and the man's smashed face stared out at him from the mirror on the wall.

When Rooker woke up again he was lying fully dressed on the bed with Edith asleep beside him. He squinted at her, because he could only open one eye. There were black pools of mascara darkening her eye sockets and her breath bubbled through her slack lips. The light in the room was dirty grey and the air was hot to breathe. He sat up very slowly, wincing with pain. There was dried blood on the pillow where his head had rested. Sour-tasting saliva flooded his mouth.

I have to get away from here, from this, he thought.

Before he could move again, Edith stirred. She blinked at him and briefly focused. 'Dear Jesus,' she muttered.

Rooker stood up and slowly turned his head to the mirror on her dresser. His left eye was puffed up, the skin crimson and shiny. His eyelashes were crusted black spikes embedded in the bruised tissue. A ragged cut with oozing margins ran from the centre point of his cheekbone to the corner of his eye. The man must have been wearing a heavy ring. He put his fingers up to touch the place, memories of the night before coming back to him in small unwelcome fragments. Edith lay motionless.

'What happened?' he mumbled. He meant what had happened to the man he had killed.

'You ran off and left me in some shitty bar with a bunch of creeps, that's what happened.'

'The guy, Edith. Is he dead?'

She coughed and then groaned. 'Dead? No. But he needed some help getting home. So did I, but you'd gone.'

Rooker gathered his thoughts.

Of course the man wasn't dead. Of course not. Immediately he felt reprieved. He had a chance after all, provided he grabbed it immediately. Leave now. The words pulsed in his head, taking on neon-bright colours that hurt the insides of his eyes. Just *leave*, get out of here and away from this.

He went to the closet and took out his old canvas holdall. He began stuffing clothes and books into it.

Edith raised herself on one elbow. 'What are you doing?'

'You can see what I'm doing.'

'Where are we going?'

It came into his mind how much he hated *we*. All the bars and street corners, all the beds and apartments in different cities that were contained in that small word, all the arguments and reconciliations and half-hearted bargains struck and reneged upon, not just with Edith but with other women, and to what end?

'*We* aren't going anywhere. I am.' He flung the last handful of his belongings into his bag and zipped it up.

'Fuck you, Rook.'

'Whatever you say.' His wallet was missing, he realised. Somewhere between the bar and his bed last night he had lost it, or more likely someone had stolen it. It didn't matter. Edith sat up. Tears started in her eyes and spilled out, running down through the black patches of yesterday's make-up. Even when she was looking ugly Edith was beautiful.

' 'Bye,' he said, hoisting his bag.

'Wait,' she shouted, but he was already at the

14

door. 'I hate you,' Edith screamed at his back. '*I hate you.*'

Rooker had gone first to Miami, where a friend of his from back in Christchurch had a small airfreight business. He was doing well. Rook stayed with him as his eye turned from red to black and then faded through purple as the cut healed, although raggedly, because he hadn't bothered to have it stitched. He had the idea that Ken might also give him some work, but instead he pointed out quite accurately that Rook hadn't logged any flying hours in three years and he would need some refresher training before any outfit could take him on.

'Back to pilot school?' Rook frowned. 'I'm forty-six years old.'

'Listen, mate. We both know you can fly. But this business is one hundred per cent above board and without current certification you don't step inside one of my planes. Get it?'

'Thanks.' Rook shrugged.

'Don't mention it. And you might consider throttling back on the booze as well.'

From Miami Rooker went to Rio, mostly because he had never been there before. After Rio he went to Buenos Aires, but restlessness gnawed at him and he found himself moving further and further south, as if he was being driven away from the populous centre of the world and out to the margins, where he belonged. He didn't try to swim against the current. He passed through Rio Gallegos and then, because there was still somewhere further to go, yet more remote, he drifted on down to Ushuaia. The southernmost town in South America clings on to the world between the tailbone of the Andes and the mountainous seas of the Drake Passage.

Now Edith had found him.

*   *   *

'Would I have come all this way if I didn't care about you?' she murmured. She touched the tight red scar that linked his eye to his cheekbone. 'Rook?'

'I don't want this.'

Her fingers were unpicking the tongue of his belt from the heavy buckle.

'Not even for old times' sake?' Her lips and eyelids looked a little swollen and he remembered they always used to thicken this way when they made love. It was an unwelcome recollection, but it still excited him.

Edith's fingers travelled downwards. 'But you do, don't you?' she whispered. 'See?'

Well, then, since you're here, we might as well, Rook thought. If this is what you've come all this way for.

He propelled her backwards and hoisted her on to his bed. Immediately she twisted her legs round his waist to hold him. Her head tipped back and her black hair fanned out on his pillow. Before he closed his eyes he saw that there was a triumphant glint in her smile.

Afterwards she nestled up against him, as light as a bird.

'We'll find a better place than this, Rook. I'll start looking tomorrow. Maybe one of those neat little tin-roof houses, painted bright blue or red, like I saw on the way up in the taxi? Then, once

16

I've got it fixed up, I'll look for some work. Perhaps in one of the hotels, or in the tourist office? I'll have a blue suit, maybe, and a name badge. That would be funny, wouldn't it? I'll say to the tourists, "Welcome to Ushuaia. You have a nice day." Then I'll come on home and cook us some dinner. We'll have a bottle of wine, watch some TV, then go to bed. Don't you think?'

Rook thought this scenario was about as realistic as Edith deciding that she was going to be elected president and planning what to do about the White House drapes.

The room was quiet and the silence outside was unbroken. Rook sat and listened to nothing. It was only on paydays that there was much noise around these streets at night.

Edith fell asleep, curled up around her small fists. He moved softly, putting on his coat and picking up his boots from beside the stove. At the doorway he hesitated, looked back at her and wondered if he was going to feel a flicker of affection or tenderness. Nothing came. He might have been looking at a stranger asleep on a bench at a train station, or at a picture of a woman in a magazine.

He was usually impervious to the cold, but as he let himself out of the front door and walked out into the street Rooker was shivering.

In a bar, a different place from the one he had visited earlier but the same in almost every respect, he met a man he knew.

Dave was a big, shaggy blond New Zealander who did odd jobs to fund his sailing and mountaineering habits. 'They're hiring down south, you know,' he told Rooker.

The only place south of Ushuaia was the Antarctic continent.

Rook took another mouthful of his drink. 'Yeah? McMurdo?'

McMurdo was the American polar research station down on the Ross Ice Shelf. Rooker had worked there for a brief summer season when he was in his early twenties. It had been a dull interlude. He had spent most of his time driving a shuttle bus between the gritty main street of the base and the airfield a couple of miles away. His few other memories mostly involved off-duty hours spent in a windowless bar. But it was watching the helo and fixed-wing pilots swooping away, lifting off the airfield and into the limitless white, that made him realise that he wanted to be a flyer himself.

Dave shook his head. 'Nope. It's a new station, some rich guy's bought a redundant base off the Brits and he's tooling it up to be run for, whatchacallit, in Europe? The EU?'

Rooker laughed. 'Needs something to spend his money on, does he?'

'I guess. Sullavan, that's his name. I came across the site on the net when I was surfin' this morning. Sounded kinda interesting, in a crazy way.'

It did, Rooker thought. Keep going, that was the idea. Keep going, while some place even further away still beckons.

He remembered how remote McMurdo had seemed, ringed by the ice and overlooked by the cone of Mount Erebus. In comparison, Ushuaia felt like a shimmering metropolis at the very epicentre of the world.

Dave was saying that if he hadn't fancied

18

heading away to Byron Bay for a summer's surfing and sailing, he might have given it a try.

'Is that right?'

Rooker bought him another beer and a whisky for himself. He had a long night to while away.

In the end he stayed up until the last bar closed. Dave had said goodnight and gone home hours earlier, but Rooker banged on his door until he got up and let him in to doze in an armchair. When the morning finally came he didn't show up for work. At 10 a.m., unshaven but sourly sober, he was waiting for the *locutorio* to open. Ahead of him in the line was a tourist couple holding a map open against the wind, the first arrivals of the summer's migration.

Paula, the *locutorio* manager, came up the concrete steps and unlocked the door. She flashed him a smile and gave him the best terminal in exchange for three pesos. Rooker logged on and began the search for Lewis Sullavan's polar website.

CHAPTER TWO

It was a warm, still day. There were pools of deep shadow under the great trees and the river reflected the light like a sheet of crumpled tinfoil. Drawn by the day's brilliance, Alice Peel had left her desk on an impulse and walked out into the University Parks. She moved slowly, letting the sun beat on the top of her head and the back of her neck. Once she stretched her arms out in front of her, absently noting the pallor of her skin. It was a weekday and it felt odd but distinctly pleasant to be wandering around in the middle of the afternoon. There were only a few other strolling or lounging figures dotted against the wide swath of grass. There was almost another month to go before the students returned and the academic year slipped into gear once more.

The scent of mown grass mingled with dust from the path. It had been a dry summer and the margins of the leaves were nibbled with brown. When she glanced up into the blue sky she saw a contrail sketched by the pinpoint of an aircraft. She wondered briefly where the plane was headed, with its cargo of passengers and their expectations. The speculation faded gently in her mind, like the vapour itself dissolving against the sky.

When the path reached the river she turned left to follow the curve of the bank. Ahead of her a footbridge and its reflection merged to make an O, the lower half blurred like a winking eye. She listened to the slow beat of her own footfalls and then to the tinny scratching of distant music. The scratching grew steadily louder and a punt rounded a bend in the river. Framed in the bridge's O, it turned watery furrows of pewter and olive-green as it surged closer. A girl was vigorously poling. When she lifted the pole between thrusts, droplets ran down her arm and beaded the smooth wood, then struck silvery chips out of the water's surface. The punt's four or five passengers lolled on the cushions, laughing up at her. Their voices cut across the music.

The girl's T-shirt rode up to reveal a tattoo on her belly. The punt was close enough for Alice to see that the design was a butterfly before she realised that the man sitting on the flat prow with his back to her was Peter. The thick hair was his, and the skull's distinctive architecture beneath it, and the faded shirt was the one she had washed yesterday and hung out to dry on the line in the back garden. He was leaning back, supporting his weight on his splayed hands. The unexpected sight of him made her heart jump.

The punt drew level. The voices and the laughter were loud, raised over the blare of music. The girl with the pole didn't glance at her. The long craft slid by, stirring the smell of mud and weeds mingled with boat varnish.

Peter's head idly tilted, then he caught sight of Alice, already receding on the riverbank. He sat upright. 'Al! Hello, Al!'

He scrambled to his feet, windmilling his arms at her. The punt rocked wildly and he danced barefoot on the slippery wood. She caught a brief glimpse of surprise like a flaw in the ready glitter of his smile.

'Aaaaa-al,' he shouted again. He was already into a jump, knees drawn up to his chest, the smile still seeming to hang in the air as his limbs hit the water. A plume of glittering spray shot into the air to the accompaniment of shrieks from the punt's passengers. The girl didn't shout. She stood looking back over her shoulder, her weight resting on one hip so that her body made a graceful curve against the willow trees on the opposite bank. The pole trailed in her hand.

Peter's head broke the water and he struck out towards Alice. A minute later he hauled himself on to the bank. Grinning and dripping, he shook himself like a huge dog. Dark droplets of water spattered the dust.

'Hi,' he gasped to Alice. ' 'Bye!' he called after the punt as it slid away.

Disregarding his sopping clothes, Peter swept her into his arms. A watery kiss landed on her cheek.

'Pete,' she said. She wasn't surprised. The shouting, the impetuous leap into the water, they were all typical of him. But she felt disquiet wrinkling her usual smooth tolerance of his extravagant behaviour. The declining sun shone straight into her eyes, causing her to frown. 'Who were they?'

He waved the arm that wasn't attached to her, spinning out more drops to pockmark the dust. 'Students.'

'I thought you were teaching today.'

Peter was an artist. He built big cuboid sculptures of tubes and wire and twisted metal that also incorporated found objects like pram frames and tailors' dummies. He didn't sell a lot of his work and he taught an art summer school for extra money.

'We were playing hookey. And I thought you were working. Hey. Since we're both not working, let's go and have tea somewhere.'

'But you're wet.'

'You're dry enough for both of us.' He kissed her again, on the tip of her nose. 'Lovely and dry and warm. Are you hungry? Come on. Scones and cream. You know you want to.'

She smiled at him. There was a café near the gates of the Parks. They walked there together, Peter comically wincing whenever his bare feet encountered a sharp stone.

On the way they met a sculptor who rented the studio next to Peter's. Pete introduced him to Alice and they lingered to talk.

'I was in a punt, Alice was on the bank, so what could I do but jump in and swim to her?' Peter laughed as he explained.

'Er, pole in to the bank and just step ashore?' Mark was literal-minded.

'You have no soul,' Peter rebuked him.

They ended up heading for the café together.

Alice walked beside Mark and Peter shuffled backwards ahead of the two of them so he could see and talk at the same time. As they passed a builder's skip outside the park gates he noticed a typist's chair with the padded seat and back support missing. He hoisted it by the metal claw foot and carried it away with him, spinning the shaft as he talked.

There was a table free in the little row on the pavement outside the café and they crowded round it. Peter took off his shirt and draped it over his salvaged chair skeleton. His arms and shoulders were well developed from lugging heavy materials and oxyacetylene welding gear. Steam rose gently from his damp trousers.

When it arrived, Alice poured the tea. The others were talking about art.

She half listened to a heated conversation she seemed to have been overhearing ever since she had known Peter. In her experience art always appeared to involve arguments. It was messily subjective. To Pete, one piece of work might be magnificent, enormously impressive, and another might be timid, derivative shit or mere fusty doodling (to employ his vocabulary), but Alice could never work out which was going to be which, or if there was any empirical evidence on which to base these opinions. She found it difficult to predict what Pete was going to admire and what he would dismiss, and whenever she thought she had mastered one critical vocabulary so they might at least discuss the matter, the entire language was prone to change.

In the end it came down to a matter of taste, she believed, and there was no measuring or calibrating taste.

Science was different. As a scientist herself and the child of scientists, Alice had reason and logic in her blood. Knowledge meant measurement, demonstration, proof. Theories could be postulated, but it was necessary to back them up with solid data. Evidence was searched for and analysed, and knowledge slowly but steadily built up, tiny accretions of it accumulating in layers to make solid bulwarks of unassailable fact. There was debate and there were opposing theories, of course, and there was international and personal competition, but the main thrust was mutually constructive and collaborative. Unlike art.

'What's funny?' Mark asked her. Alice hadn't realised that she was smiling.

'Nothing, really. I'm just listening.'

'But what do you *think*?'

Sunlight lay across the table. The tea in her cup reflected a glittering bronze disc. Pete sprawled back in his chair, lanky and at ease, grinning at her. Their life together was made up of a series of small encounters like this one. They met friends, had tea or dinner or went to the pub together. They went to parties and gave their own—were giving one the very next evening, in fact. Peter was gregarious and liked nothing better than to gather a crowd of people around him. It meant that she didn't see a lot of him on his own, but she didn't mind that. She had what she wanted in life.

She smiled more broadly now. 'I think I'd like another scone before Pete devours the lot.'

She didn't want to be drawn into the endless discussions about art. Peter never listened to anyone else anyway. He stopped with half a scone almost into his mouth and returned it to his plate. Scooping some extra jam on top, he transferred it to Alice's plate.

'*Thank* you.'

'What do you do? Are you an artist?' Mark persisted.

'A scientist. A sedimentary geologist.'

'My God,' he said.

'He's one theory. Not many geologists subscribe to it, though.'

They all laughed. Alice bit into the jam-laden scone, enjoying her appetite and the lazy bickering of the two men, and the prospect of going home with Peter to their house and the quiet late-summer twilight in their tiny garden.

When the scones had been eaten and the teapot refilled and emptied twice, they stood up. As they said goodbye, Peter invited Mark to tomorrow's party. Finally Peter shouldered his chair-remnant, and he and Alice headed for home. The route was so familiar to both of them that they could have walked it blindfolded. They crossed St Giles and walked down Beaumont Street. The end-of-the-day traffic was heavy, but when they turned into Jericho everything was quiet again. The little red-brick houses with their Gothic touches had been built in the nineteenth century for clerks and the more senior college servants, but lately they had become sought after and very expensive.

Alice couldn't have afforded to buy one, not on an academic's salary, and of course Peter wasn't able to contribute anything, but her mother had helped her with the down payment.

This sequence of recollections didn't quite play itself out in full as she opened the low gate, but it coloured the fabric of her thoughts. Sometimes it seemed to Alice that her mother's life was always the vivid, engrossing, three-dimensional backdrop against which her own activities were executed on a much dimmer and smaller scale.

Peter hoisted the wrecked chair straight over the wall, snapping one of the rose branches that she was training over a rope swag. It landed foot uppermost, the wheeled claw sluggishly rotating.

'Will it be safe there?' she asked as he followed her up the short tiled path to the front door.

He took her question entirely at face value. 'Should be. I'll take it over to the studio first thing.'

It was cool inside the house. From where she stood in the hallway, as Pete's mouth brushed against the nape of her neck, Alice could see straight through the kitchen doors into the garden. There was a blue-painted bench and a little rustic table, and a crab-apple tree for shade.

Pete's hands slid up and cupped her breasts. 'Mmm?' he said. 'Come on. Let's go to bed.'

Their bedroom would be cool too, behind white blinds.

With clasped hands they trod up the stairs.

A minute later they were stretched out on the

white-covered bed. Alice tipped her head back, her eyes closed, and Pete's hand secured her wrists above her head so she couldn't break free. On the bedside table the phone cheeped. Pete swore, but neither of them made a move towards it. After a dozen rings, the answering machine picked up.

'Alice, are you there?'

There was a pause and then an audible tut-tutting of annoyance. 'Well, wherever can you be, at this time of day? I need to speak to you. Give me a ring straight back, won't you?' The voice was brisk, busy as always.

'Yes, *ma'am*,' Pete murmured. He gathered Alice up and rolled adroitly so that she ended up on top. He never voiced any criticism of Alice's mother, the formidable Margaret Mather, but there was not much love lost. Alice didn't pursue this line of thought either. Now was not the time to be thinking about Margaret. Now was not the time to be thinking of anything but *this*.

Afterwards they lay with their legs interlocked, listening to the small sounds of the street through the open window. Pete hummed a little, an unborn sequence of notes reverberating deep in his chest. Alice smiled, her cheek against his shoulder sticky with their mingled sweat.

She would call in and see her parents in the morning.

*   *   *

Margaret Mather sat at the gate-legged table in the large bay window of the house on Boar's Hill. Books and papers and correspondence leaned in haphazard piles on either side of her computer monitor and keyboard. She had never been tidy, or even faintly house-proud, and the table was littered with half-full teacups and dirty plates as well as her sheaves of work. The rest of the room was cluttered and dusty, and the Persian rugs were matted with cat hair. The cat itself, a fat white creature with a penetrating smell, lay on the sofa and licked its rear parts.

Margaret's husband Trevor worked or read in his small upstairs study with a view of the sloping garden. His room was bare by comparison and together with Alice's old bedroom it represented the only ordered area in the entire house. Although Alice had long ago left home, her room remained exactly as it had always been. Her teenage books filled the shelves and there were framed school and netball team photographs on the walls. It wasn't that Margaret had preserved it as any kind of shrine to her daughter's childhood, rather that she had never got around to doing anything else with it. In the same way, a hopbine gathered on a country holiday twelve years earlier was still rakishly pinned to the beam in the kitchen, and was now a dust-and-grease fossil of its former self.

Margaret was listening to music and working through the morning's e-mails. She peered at the screen through her bifocals, reading interesting titbits aloud to herself and muttering the responses as she prodded them out of her keyboard. She was in her seventies, but she took to new technology with enthusiasm. E-mail made her complicated correspondences with friends and with fellow scientists all over the world much easier. She loved to explain to anyone who would listen that, for example, she could now chat on a daily basis with

28

her old friend Harvey Golding who was based in San Diego and whom she hadn't seen in the flesh for more than twelve years.

'And I can keep abreast. See what the others are up to. It's all there on the net, you know. Much easier nowadays.'

By 'the others' she meant scientists working in her field, marine mammal biology.

In the 1960s Margaret had made a series of television films about whales and seals in the seas surrounding Antarctica. She spent many months of the year living down on the ice, even doing most of her own underwater camerawork. She wrote the films' drily lyrical commentaries too, and narrated them in her strong Yorkshire accent. The series made her and her voice famous.

She was never short of energy. Even after she had become a celebrity she continued her research and maintained her reputation as a serious scientist. Her meticulous work on the breeding patterns of Weddell seals pioneered a subsequent generation of Antarctic studies.

This morning, Margaret was replying to a personal message from Lewis Sullavan.

There had been a succession of increasingly insistent communications from his staff and now there was one from the great man himself. She sat for a moment with her fingers resting beside the keyboard. She looked out into the garden without seeing the heavy trees that leaned over into the lane, then shook herself and began.

'My dear friend, I really cannot accept your kind invitation,' she recited as she picked out the words. 'Much as I would like to. The fact is that I am now 77 years of age and I have severe arthritis.

However, there remains the alternative proposal.'

The cat yawned and stood up to claw the sofa cushions. Margaret heard Trevor's footsteps crossing the upstairs landing from the bathroom to his study. The floorboards creaked as they always did.

'My daughter is very interested in the idea,' Margaret typed and whistled through her teeth as she sat back to review what she had written.

'We'll see, eh?' she said, addressing the last remark to the cat.

She heard a car and quickly looked up. Alice's car rounded the overgrown circular flowerbed that blocked the space between the house and the gate to the road, and drew up outside the front door.

'Soon enough,' Margaret added. She saved her unfinished message to Lewis Sullavan and was hobbling away from a blank screen by the time Alice came in.

'Ah, there you are at last,' Margaret said briskly.

CHAPTER THREE

Alice had brought a bunch of bright orange lilies with chocolate-speckled throats, her mother's favourite flowers. She wrapped her arms round Margaret, hugging her close. She saw that the room looked as it always did; it was her mother who seemed smaller, as if the disorder might finally be on the point of overwhelming her.

'Hello, Mum. Here I am.'

After a brief embrace Margaret leaned away, apparently for a better view of her daughter.

30

Alice's hair was thick and slightly wavy, the same texture and silvery blonde colour as Margaret's had also once been. Margaret's was white now, and she wore it bluntly chopped round her face They were both slightly built, but Alice seemed to grow taller as Margaret's painful stoop increased. Margaret said that her daughter was much more contemplative and serious-minded than she had ever been, but Trevor insisted that she was so like her mother at the same age that they could have passed for twins. Neither woman believed him.

'Mum, the music's very loud. Can I turn it down a bit?'

'Is it? All right.'

Margaret motioned to the CD player and watched with a touch of envy as Alice swung with an unthinking fluid movement and muted the sound.

'How do you feel?' Alice asked.

'I'm grand,' she answered, although the pain was bad today. 'And we're away on holiday in three days, even though we don't do so much here that needs taking a holiday *from*.'

'Come on, you're just going to stay in a nice hotel in Madeira and enjoy being waited on for once. Why don't you sit down?'

Margaret gave an impatient shrug but she let Alice guide her gently to the sofa. They sat down once Alice had pushed the cat aside.

'Where's Dad?'

'He'll be down as soon as he realises you're here. I want a word first.'

'Is something wrong? Have you seen Dr Davey?'

'Don't fuss, Alice. I'm perfectly fine.' Margaret's feet in elastic-sided shoes were placed flat on the floor, exactly together, toes pointing forward. She sat upright, hands folded.

Her mother wanted to be invulnerable, to remain as all-capable and all-knowing as she had always managed to be. Alice understood that perfectly. She knew that she despised her own increasing physical frailty, as if it were some moral weakness. In fact, there was nothing weak about Margaret and there never had been. She had been one of the first women scientists to penetrate the male domain of Antarctic research; she had filmed her seals beneath the ice of the polar sea and she had never shrunk from anything just because she was a woman, or a wife, or a mother. Her great energy and single-mindedness tended rather to make everyone around her feel weak by comparison. Recognition of this was one of the strongest of the many bonds between Alice and her father.

'No, this is about you,' Margaret announced.

Alice tried not to sigh. 'Go on. I'm listening,' she said.

'Would you like some coffee?' Margaret glanced over the top of her bifocals towards the kitchen, as if this were some hitherto-unexplored wilderness region. It wasn't that it daunted her, more that it didn't offer interesting opportunities. Her lack of culinary ability was legendary.

'Later. I'll make it.'

'All right. Now. Where were we? Yes. Listen to me. I've got a tip-top invitation for you.'

Margaret clapped her hands, then paused for dramatic effect while Alice wondered what awards dinner or institution's prize-giving her mother had been asked to preside over, and at which she would be offered as a disappointing last-minute substitute. Being Margaret Mather's daughter didn't mean that she could make an audience eat out of her hand the way her mother did.

'You have been invited to go to Kandahar Station,' she announced grandly.

Alice had never heard of it, so couldn't express either enthusiasm or reluctance. 'What?'

'Lewis Sullavan has *personally* asked you.'

'Lewis Sullavan doesn't know me from a hole in the fence.'

But Alice knew who he was. His media empire had been founded in the 1960s with a stake in one of the early commercial television companies. It had grown, hydra-headed, since then and now included newspapers and magazines in the UK and Europe, a Hollywood film company and interests in television companies across the world.

'And if he doesn't know me, why would he invite me out of the blue to go to some station I've never heard of?'

Margaret didn't even blink. Age had rimmed her eyes with red and faded her dark eyelashes to the colour of dry sand, but her gaze was as sharp as it had ever been.

Alice quietly answered the question for herself. 'Because of you.' For as long as she could remember she had been notable because of her mother's achievements rather than her own.

It made her feel mean and small to be resentful of this, and as an adult she was learning to accept what she couldn't change, but she used to wish that she could be just Alice Peel, making her own way via her own mistakes and minor triumphs. Instead, she was always living in the half-light of reflected glory. The house she lived in had been purchased with her mother's financial assistance and she even had a suspicion, lying just the other side of rationality, that her lectureship at the University was hers as much because of who she was as what she could do.

Even her choice of subject had been influenced by her mother. Alice might have wished to become a biologist herself, but there was no question that she could, or would, ever compete with what Margaret had done. Instead, she had chosen geology, her father's speciality. In her teens they had taken camping trips alone together, looking at rocks. These times, when she had had the undivided attention of one of her parents, were amongst the happiest of Alice's life.

Now, sitting beside her mother on the cat-scented sofa, she took Margaret's dry hands between hers, noting the tiny flicker of resistance that came before submission. Margaret had never been physically demonstrative. In her view excessive hugging and kissing were for film actors, not real people.

'Go on. Tell me. How do you know this media mogul and what is Kandahar Station?'

'I met him many years ago when I was making my first series for the television.' It was always *the* television, in Margaret's old-fashioned way.

'I didn't know that.'

Margaret's brief nod seemed to acknowledge that there were many episodes in her life that the passage of years and the accumulation of success had left half submerged. 'It's a very long time ago.'

She sounded *tired*, Alice realised with a stab of anxiety. It was a good thing that Trevor had been able to persuade her to take a ten-day break in Madeira.

Margaret withdrew her hands and smoothed her trousers over her knees. The jersey fabric was baggy and whiskered with cat hair. When she was younger, Alice remembered, her mother had had an ambivalent attitude to clothes. She had loved style and making a statement, but had been hampered by the suspicion that this didn't go with serious science. So she had adopted a look that was all her own, in which plain suits and conservative dresses were enlivened with wicked shoes, or ethnic necklaces, or a wide-brimmed hat looped with scarves. These days, however, she dressed mostly for comfort.

'Kandahar Station is Lewis's current toy,' she continued and her briskness came back again. 'It's a new research base. Largely funded at present by Sullavan himself, but with some EU support. As you know, he's passionately pro-Europe. The intention is that Kandahar will ultimately offer facilities for European scientists and joint European research initiatives across all the relevant disciplines.'

This sounded like a speech. And if Margaret had rehearsed it, then what she was going to say must be important.

'And where is it?' Alice asked, although she knew the answer to this question too.

'Antarctica.'

Of course.

Alice had grown up with the waterfall sound of the word. The pictures of it were as familiar as the view from this window. Some of them still adorned the walls and mantel here in Margaret's room. In the most famous one of all, the younger Margaret crouched beside a hole in the ice shelf, dressed in the corpulent rubber folds of a diver's drysuit. She had pulled off her rubber hood and the wind blew her hair away from her head like a silvery halo. A seal's head poked up out of the ice hole and it looked as if they were amiably chatting together.

In another a stiffly posed group of bearded men stood in the snow outside a low-built wooden hut. Margaret's figure at the end of the line looked tiny, like an afterthought, but her head was held erect and her chin jutted firmly forward.

Margaret was in her forties before her only child was born and most of her polar adventures were already behind her, but to the small Alice, hearing the stories, her mother's doings and those of Scott and Shackleton and the others had run together into a continuous and present mythology of snow and terrible cold and heroic bravery. She curled up under her warm blankets and shivered, full of admiration and awe, as well as pride that her own mother somehow belonged to this bearded company. At the same time she made a childish resolution that she would never venture to such a place herself and her decision seemed to be endorsed by the fact that her father had never been there either.

More than twenty-five years later, Alice saw no reason to change her mind. 'No,' she said now, smiling as she did so but without letting a tremor of uncertainty colour her voice.

'Alice, it's an honour. Sir Lewis wants to name the laboratory block Margaret Mather House. What do you think of that?'

'It is an honour,' Alice gently agreed. 'Do you

36

think it would be too much for you to go yourself? To see the ice again?'

Margaret's face flooded with longing but she shook her head. 'I would go if . . . if I didn't have damned arthritis and if I wasn't going to be a nuisance and a liability.'

Anyone planning to travel south would have to undergo medical and fitness examinations. Margaret knew she wouldn't pass any tests. And it would be Margaret's idea of misery, of course, to feel that she might be a burden.

'So. I want you to go instead. In my place. Lewis has asked for you.'

The imperiousness of her demand grated on Alice. 'I don't think I can do that,' she answered as calmly as she could. Antarctica was her mother's love, not hers. The idea of the southern continent lay in her mind like a vast, cold dead end at the bottom of the world. She didn't want its icy walls to close around her.

Margaret lifted one hand. 'Hear me out. It's not just a PR excursion, Alice. You are being offered a place on the base for the entire summer season. Just think. For a geologist to be given the chance to go to Antarctica? You can pursue your own research project. Write your own ticket. You will have funding, you can use Sullavan's infrastructure. It's a great chance, a career opportunity you shouldn't turn your back on. You've even got the time this year to do it.'

That much was true. After five years of teaching undergraduates, Alice had a six-month break coming up in which to pursue her own research. She planned to do some field work in western Turkey, making a broad analysis of sedimentary rock structures in a system of active faults. Travel to Turkey was easy enough to allow her to come back to Oxford, and Peter, as often as possible.

The familiar waves of Margaret's enthusiasm and determination pounded against Alice. She felt as if she were some eroding shoreline that had been withstanding this onslaught for a lifetime. She scrabbled against the undertow, trying to keep her balance and hold firm against the current. 'I'm flattered. And I can see that it would be a nice media hook for Sullavan.'

That was what it was about, of course. Some television footage, newspaper and magazine articles about the scientist daughter following in the scientist mother's footsteps, pictures of the base, a good excuse to bring out all the archive photographs from Margaret's heyday. It would be another publicity angle by which to promote a very rich man's latest way of diverting himself. Alice didn't admire what she had heard about Lewis Sullavan.

'But I have made my plans for the next six months, you know.'

There was the sound of creaking floorboards again.

'And now here's your father,' Margaret announced superfluously.

Trevor Peel was a small, pink-faced, egg-shaped man. He eased himself round the door, aiming to create the minimum of disturbance by his entrance. A fringe of feathery white hair clung to his otherwise perfectly bald head. From behind the shield of his gold-rimmed glasses he was trying to second-guess the temperature between his wife and daughter. 'Mm, aha. I've been putting some things in a suitcase. Better now than at the last minute. So what do you think?' he said to Alice. He knew about Margaret's invitation and also Alice's likely response to the idea of travelling in her place.

Alice loved her father dearly. His mildness was deceptive. He had a sharp mind, but it was coupled with a tolerant disposition. He had lacked the ambition rather than the intellect to reach the front rank himself as a scientist and he had always been aware of this deficiency. He had devoted himself to encouraging his formidable wife instead and in this they had been an ideal match. All through Alice's childhood, Margaret had often been away but Trevor was invariably there. They had formed a sympathetic company of two, moving quietly in Margaret's wake. Trevor had been retired for ten years now. He occupied himself with reading, crosswords, gardening and Margaret's needs.

Alice's eyes met his. There was no need to speak. Over the years they had developed a silent language of their own. Today's communication was *keep your head down.*

'I don't understand her,' Margaret announced. 'I would have thought she would jump at an offer like this.'

'Ah,' Trevor said.

Everyone understood that Margaret had known that Alice wouldn't do anything of the kind, but had assumed that she would be able to override her opposition.

'You've got a few days to think it over, Alice. I'll let Lewis know you're considering it very seriously. No one could expect you to make a decision on the spot. Although *I* would have done. We can discuss it properly when we come back from this holiday.'

39

She spoke the word as if it were *Gulag* or *torture chamber*.

The glance that passed between Trevor and Alice said *better try and nip this in the bud*.

Alice drew in a breath. 'Mummy, I don't want to go to Antarctica. I'm sorry to spoil a nice story and turn my back on history at the same time, but I'm not going. It doesn't fit in with my plans.'

This didn't come out right. She intended to be cheerfully firm but she ended up sounding feeble as well as petulant, as she too often did when she was forced into open conflict with her mother.

'Just give me your reasons why not,' Margaret said. So she could then set out to demolish them.

Alice reflected that there were many reasons, but they could all be placed under the same heading. 'Because I am happy where I am,' she said gently.

She thought about sitting in the sun yesterday afternoon, eating scones and listening to Peter and Mark. She remembered the cool bedroom light and the heat of Peter's mouth on her skin. Tonight their house would be full of friends and music. She knew where she would be and what she would be doing, next week and the week after that. Order and certainty were important to her. She didn't like question without answer, thesis without proof. She liked her work, even loved it, but she didn't want to make it her entire reason for living. Antarctica was an unknown and Alice preferred the known world.

Margaret's eyebrows drew together. She put her head on one side, in the way she did when she was considering a problem. 'I don't see what happiness has to do with anything,' she said at length.

No, Alice thought.

Her mother understood achievement, as in doing your best and then improving on that. She had no fear and no self-doubt. She didn't care much about her own comforts and not at all when she had a goal in mind. Happiness would come a long way down her list of considerations. This was what Alice believed, although she realised with a small jolt that the two of them had never talked about it.

'I'm sorry,' she repeated.

Trevor patted his tweed pockets, searching for his cigarettes. He only smoked outside the house, by Margaret's decree, and this was his unconscious signalling that he wanted to get out of the room.

'I'll make some coffee.'

'Is it too early for a sherry?'

Trevor and Alice spoke brightly, simultaneously. With difficulty Margaret stood up and walked slowly back to her table. She sat upright at her keyboard, hitching her loose cardigan round her.

I have disappointed her, Alice thought. It was not a new realisation. She went quickly and stood behind the chair, cupping her mother's shoulders in her warm hands.

'I will have a cup of coffee, thank you,' Margaret said.

Later, Alice walked in the garden with Trevor.

They descended a set of mossy steps and reached the fence that separated their land from the neighbour's plot. There was a sycamore tree in the angle of the fence, casting too much shade so nothing would grow beneath it. The bare earth was dry and scented with cat. They leaned against the tree's rough bark to smoke, looking up the garden at the cream-washed stucco of the house. It was too

41

big for two elderly people and it had acquired a neglected aspect. Paint was peeling off the window frames and there was a long streak of damp in the render beneath a broken gutter.

Trevor drew a line in the dust with the toe of his shoe. 'Are you sure?' he asked tentatively.

Alice had been remembering how big this garden used to seem when she had conquered the shrubbery and built dens in the hedges. As big as a whole country, and the swampy pond with its frog population had been a wide sea.

'Sure?' she repeated.

'About not going south.'

'Yes, I am. Realistically, what would my study be?'

It was much easier to talk to Trevor like this, not just because he was interested in the scope of her sedimentological rock investigations but because he listened to what she said, whether it was related to science or not.

'You won't need to apply for funding, as I understand it. You just go, look at something that interests you and Sullavan picks up the tab. That doesn't happen every day, does it?'

Almost all research projects involved time spent in the field, studying rock formations and collecting samples for lab analysis. Expeditions to remote places were expensive to set up and needed complex support. Proposals had to be carefully directed and worded to attract approval and sufficient financial support from the funding bodies, and this was often the hardest part of the process. Alice was still waiting to hear whether she would be awarded a grant for her next six months' research.

'What *is* the deal?'

She hadn't given Margaret the opportunity to explain even this much herself, so her mother wasn't the only one guilty of not listening. Sometimes, she thought, we bring out the worst in each other. We work against one another's grain, setting up ridges and splinters.

Trevor threw his cigarette end into the hedge. 'It's a maverick set-up, as you would expect with anything connected to Sullavan. Kandahar is down at the base of the Antarctic peninsula. It was built in the 1950s for the British Antarctic Survey, who closed it down in the late 1990s as surplus to requirements. The bay gets iced up in winter and it's difficult to supply as a year-round station. They were on the point of dismantling the buildings and clearing the site when Sullavan stepped in and offered to buy it as the base for his pet project: United Europe in Antarctica. It was much cheaper for BAS to sell the place standing than pay for clearance, so Sullavan got quite a bargain. Now he's got to get some decent science underway; it probably doesn't matter too much exactly what so long as it has popular appeal and preferably a few familiar names connected with it. Which is where Margaret comes in.'

And by extension her daughter, neither of them went on to add.

'I see.'

'Not tempted?'

A lawnmower was whining monotonously somewhere in the middle distance. The gardener was probably Roger Armstrong, a mathematician whose garden on the other side of the lane was tended with millimetric precision, in striking contrast to the Peels'. Trevor liked to wander between his hedges and stand rocking on the balls of his feet while he peered into his tangled flowerbeds. He believed that a garden should be a place to stroll or sit and think, a sanctuary, not a job of work. Today, as if to prove him right, it looked beautiful in its dishevelment. Clumps of goldenrod glowed in the sun and even the mildew on the asters took on a silvery glamour. Thanks to Roger Armstrong's efforts the air was full of the lush scent of late-season grass.

'Not in the least.' Alice smiled. It was easy to sound entirely certain.

Her father put an arm round her and hugged her. His smell, as always, was a compound of cigarettes and wool and something of himself, perfectly clean but also animal like a horse or a dog. She rubbed her cheek against his shoulder.

'Well, then. I'm glad you're so contented,' Trevor said easily.

As she lifted her head Alice heard a sigh and then a *click*, as if there had been a second's interruption of time. She looked along the path towards the goldenrod, seeing it as if she had never looked at it before, all broken up into waves of different depths of colour, and hearing the lawnmower's buzz separated into a series of vibrating notes that sprayed through the air like drops of molten metal.

Is this what happiness means? she wondered. Just this?

The thought sounded a single hollow note within her head.

Then the world remembered its path and moved forward again. There were just ragged yellow

44

flowers that were not much more than weeds and the sound of a neighbour working in his garden on a sunny Saturday morning.

'What about Mum?' Alice asked. 'Will you get her to have a rest on this holiday?'

Trevor hunched his shoulders, spread his hands slightly. They had been exchanging this gesture for many years, the two of them. They left the shade of the sycamore tree and walked back up the slope of grass to the kitchen door. Dandelion clocks released small seed parachutes as their feet brushed past. Margaret had turned the music up again. The orange lilies had been put in a green enamel jug and placed beside her computer.

The two old people tried to persuade Alice to stay for lunch. Margaret even said she thought there was some cold ham somewhere, by way of an extra inducement.

'No, I've *really* got to go because we're having all these people round this evening, and I've still got to make the food and buy wine,' Alice said.

'Can't Peter do something?'

It wasn't that Trevor and Margaret disliked Peter, more that they didn't understand how he lived a life with no particular plans, not even a proper routine. They thought that his habits and the hours he kept were incompatible with a productive existence. The few pieces of his work that they had seen left even Margaret with nothing to say. They believed that art lived on gallery or drawing-room walls and didn't incorporate the contents of builders' skips.

For his part Peter was always polite to them, but the politeness had a resistance to it that was almost ruder than if he had dispensed with it and just been himself.

'It's easier if I do it. He'll be in charge of the barbecuing. Are you sure you wouldn't like me to drive you to the airport on Tuesday?'

'Your father's arranged a car to pick us up.'

'Is there anything else I can do? Shopping? Packing?'

'I've travelled to a few places in my life, Alice. I can manage a ten-day package trip to Madeira.'

'I know you have, I know you can. So. Have a lovely time. Just sit in the sun. I'll call you before you go.'

Alice hugged her mother as she left. In her arms, Margaret felt as light and dry as a leaf. Alice had been aware of the change for the past year or two, but it was still uncomfortable to recognise that the woman who had been such an embodiment of strength for her whole life was growing weaker.

'Think about Kandahar,' Margaret called after her, as a parting challenge. She believed in having the last word.

Trevor came out to the car to say goodbye. 'I'd go, you know, if I were in your shoes,' he said, startling her so that she paused, halfway into the driver's seat.

'But you never did go.'

'Oh, *I* couldn't. Maybe I should have done, but that sort of thing was Margaret's role. She was the adventurer, so I was the stay-at-home. I loved her far too much to risk offering any competition, and then you were born and I didn't want to miss a single day of your life. But if I were you, now, today, that would be quite different.'

Not for the first time, Alice reflected on her father's unselfishness. He possessed enough for

46

two. For three, if she counted herself into the equation. She had no children, no husband, yet, no evident ties—except for Pete, although he was enough to keep her firmly anchored. At least I've come far enough to recognise that I *am* selfish, she thought. Trevor was beaming at her. The breeze fluffed up the white feathers of his hair.

'Then you wouldn't have been you. You wouldn't be you now. I don't want you to be any different from the way you are,' Alice told him.

He nodded. 'I don't think you need have any anxiety on that score. No new tricks for an old dog, you know.'

'Good.' She kissed his cheek. As always, Trevor convinced her that the world was a secure place.

'Have a lovely holiday. Look after Mum.'

'You know I'll do that.'

He stood back to watch her go, his hands in the pockets of his shapeless trousers and his hair like thistledown in the sunlight.

* * *

It was 5.30 and Alice was lying in a hot bath when Peter appeared in the bathroom doorway. She saw his reflection first in the steamy mirror, then turned her head to smile at him. He was carrying a bottle of champagne and two glasses.

'I think I'll join you.' He grinned.

Pete unbuttoned his shirt, unbuckled his belt and pulled off his jeans. He had olive skin and a flat stomach. Alice watched him, noticing the play of muscles in his arms and back. He looked clean, even his hands and fingernails were clean, unlike the way they usually were when he came back from a day in the studio.

'Were you working?'

He was naked now, but not in the least vulnerable. He stepped into the water, so that Alice had to sit up to make room for him. Heavily scented water slopped over the edge of the bath as he sank backwards.

'Yeah.'

She didn't say anything and after a beat of silence he added, 'I had a mass of paperwork. Invoices, bills, all kinds of shit. I hate doing all that.'

'I know you do. Pete?'

She was going to say, I had a moment this afternoon when I thought *is this all*? She had intended to ask him if he was happy, if what they had between them was good. If it was *enough*. But this, she knew, was what Pete would dismiss as a quintessential woman's question.

'Yeah?' He locked his legs round her. Bubbles of foam popped close to their ears. Pete gave her a misted glass of champagne, clinked his own against it and drank. He licked a silver rim of froth off his top lip.

'I've been asked to spend a season in Antarctica.'

'And?'

And what? she wondered. What if I said, 'I'm going, and I won't be back for six months?' Instead she murmured, 'Well, I said no, of course.'

Pete nodded. That was what he would expect. He was used to her, to her precise ways, to the regularity of their life together that provided a framework for his erratic behaviour. When they were first together he used to steal pages of her

48

work and frown over the stratigraphical analyses of rock structures. He would turn the equations that represented deformations upside down, playing up his bafflement. Alice used to try to explain to him that these equations were like pictures, abstract illustrations of dynamic relationships that to her were far more vivid than words or photographs. They were the same to her as his sculptures were to him: a shorthand expression of a solid state and at the same time an airy thumbnail sketch of sublime reality. They rendered down the universe, or they tried to.

Alice suddenly smiled. She was thinking in artists' language.

Pete sat up, sending another wave slopping over the side of the bath. He took her face in his hands and drew her closer so their mouths touched. Her champagne glass tipped sideways and she spilled some in the water.

'You know, Al. You're incredibly beautiful when you smile like that.'

She closed her eyes as he kissed her. But not before she had seen a twist at the corner of his mouth and a flash in his black eyes that she couldn't read.

Pete was the one who ended the kiss. He drank the rest of his champagne at a gulp and stood up, brandishing his glass. Water and bubbles slicked the black hairs on his legs into sleek lines.

'We're going to have a *great* party,' he said. He didn't ask any more about Antarctica. Alice had said that of course she wasn't going, so there was no need to pursue it.

*   *   *

49

It was a good party.

Pete flipped sausages and chicken pieces on and off the barbecue in the back garden. There were candles in little coloured glass vases hanging in the branches of the tree and the night air was so still that the flames burned without a tremor. People brought their paper plates of food and glasses of wine outside to sit in the moth-filled darkness, and music drifted out of the windows over their heads. In between last-minute preparations Alice had found ten minutes to pull on a black frock that showed her cleavage and new stiletto-heeled sandals that made her feel tall but also slightly at risk of toppling forward over her own toes.

'Nice dress,' Mark the sculptor said, with his eyes on her front. Alice laughed and put her arm through his to steer him into the middle of the next group. The house and garden overflowed with different people, painters and writers and lecturers and scientists as well as the old friends Alice had grown up with. Oxford had been her home for most of her life and she loved this bringing together and shaking up of different elements from within it. She moved through the crowd, laughing and talking, catching Pete's eye once in a while, checking that he thought it was going well too. They were good at this, making a celebration together. Recognising that the party was now moving under its own impetus, she gave herself up to the pleasure of it.

Alice's oldest friend Jo was there and her husband Harry. They had brought their three-month-old twins and put them in their car-seat cradles to sleep in Alice and Pete's bedroom.

'Al, I am so knackered,' Jo muttered. She had

black rings under her eyes and her flat hair clung to her cheeks. 'They never sleep at the same time. I never get more than an hour. What am I going to *do*?'

'They'll start sleeping better soon.' Alice took her friend's hands and rubbed them between her own.

'*When*?' Jo wailed. 'I want my life back. I want to be myself again.'

'You will be yourself. It's only time.'

Becky arrived late. Her current man was a psychologist, an unnervingly handsome Indian who didn't say very much. As always, Becky talked enough for both of them.

'I'm sorry, Al, have we missed everything? The traffic from London, you wouldn't believe, Vijay said we should just move to Oxford. Shall I come back, wouldn't that be a gas? Jo! Come here, baby-mother, give me a hug. Mmm, look at you. God, your boobs are so fabulous.'

Alice and Becky and Jo had been friends since the fourth form. Jo had once said, 'I'm the good girl, Alice is the clever girl and Becky is the star in the firmament.'

Now Jo said, 'I've just got to go up and check on them again. I don't know where Harry is.' She looked as if she was going to cry.

Becky and Alice glanced at each other.

'Harry's in the garden with Pete. I'll go up and make sure they're still fast asleep, *you* sit here and talk to Beck,' Alice told her.

She gave them both a glass of wine and went quietly up the stairs. The dancing had started and loud music came up through the floorboards but it didn't seem to bother Jo's babies. They slept in

51

their padded plastic cradles. One of them held his fist against his cheek, the thumb not quite connecting with his mouth. Alice stooped down to look closer and found that she wanted to touch the tip of her finger to his rosy skin. She stopped herself in case he woke up, but she crouched there for a long minute, watching and listening. Downstairs, someone turned the music up even further. The party was changing up a gear.

She stood up again, almost reluctantly, and walked to the door. It was ajar and from the semi-darkness of the bedroom she could see down to the half-landing where a pretty arched window looked over the garden. Pete was standing in the angle of the stairs, just out of sight of anyone who might be in the hallway. His hand slid slowly down the back of a girl who was pressed up against him, came to rest on her bottom. She was wearing a cropped pink top that exposed a broad expanse of skin above low-slung trousers.

Alice stood completely still. He bent his head and kissed her, then whispered something in her ear. She angled herself closer still, the movement eloquent of intimacy and familiarity. The two of them knew one another's bodies.

A second later the girl ducked away from him. She used her thumbs to flick her long hair back behind her ears and smiled at him from beneath her eyelashes before she skipped down the stairs. Pete leaned against the wall for a second, staring down into the garden. If he had looked the other way, up the stairs, he would have met Alice's eyes. But he didn't. He rose up on to the balls of his feet, as if balancing on the brink of something delightful, then followed the girl.

It was just a kiss at a party.

She told herself that it meant nothing, it was what parties were for. She would go downstairs herself and kiss Mark, or preferably Vijay.

But everything about the tiny encounter told her that it wasn't nothing; it was much more than just a kiss at a party.

Becky and Jo both stared at her as she came back.

'Hey,' Becky said softly.

'Are they all right?' Jo was already heaving herself to her feet.

'They're fine. I just saw Pete kissing some girl on the stairs.'

Now it was Becky and Jo who looked at each other.

'Which girl?'

Alice glanced around the crowded room. Faces nodded and mouthed through the smoke and music. A tide of dirty plates and ashtrays lapped against the walls.

'That one.' She was standing by the mantelpiece. Midway between the prominent crest of her hip bone and her neat bellybutton there was a butterfly tattoo.

'Never seen her before,' Becky said.

'She's one of Pete's students.'

'And where is he?' Jo asked in a let-me-at-him way.

Alice forced a smile. 'He'd better keep out of my sight for an hour.'

She drank some more wine and tried to reconnect to her earlier enjoyment. She kept talking and laughing, then she danced with Mark and with Harry. She saw Pete moving through the skeins of people, even caught his eye as she had done at the start of the evening, but it was only a brief connection. She wanted to dance with him, but they were never in the right place together.

At one a.m. Jo and Harry went home, carrying a baby seat apiece down the stairs. Becky and Vijay left at two.

'I'll call you tomorrow,' Becky said, concern showing in her eyes.

'Don't worry, I'm fine.'

The hard-core guests stayed until it was light. She would have liked to be drunk herself, but all she felt was cold. Pete had spent the last hour playing his guitar and singing with the remaining handful of people. Now he was sitting on the sofa, picking out chords and humming with his head down. There was a glass of whisky at his feet.

Alice stood in front of him and he raised his head to look at her. His eyes weren't quite focusing. The room seemed to press in around the two of them, full of the weight of their combined belongings and the evening's events.

Pete strummed a chord and sang, 'Just the two of us, just you and . . . *me.*'

'Pete, come to bed.'

The bedroom was disorientatingly light. Alice took off the black dress and hung it up in her cupboard, Pete stripped off his clothes and left them in a heap. They lay down and Pete gave a long sigh, then turned and lay against her, one arm heavy over her hips.

'Who was she?' Alice asked.

'Who was who?'

'The girl with the tattoo.'

'Tattoo? I dunno. All girls have tattoos. 'Cept

you.' He laughed into her hair and she shivered with the first wave of longing for intimacy that was already gone.

'She was with you yesterday. In the punt.'

'Punt? Oh, yeah, her. Georgia.'

Alice lay on her back, watching the ceiling. If he says anything else, she thought, it will be all right. If I have to ask him what he was doing with her it won't be. The seconds passed. Out of the furthest corner of her eye she was aware of the digital clock on the bedside table. The green numerals changed, 23, 24. Then she realised from Pete's slow breathing that he had fallen asleep.

CHAPTER FOUR

'Your mother's not very well,' Trevor said.

Alice was sitting at her desk in the Department of Geology. She had been trying to concentrate on her work but her eyes kept sliding to the square of sky visible from her window. Now as she pressed the phone to her ear the maps she had been studying lost their definition and ran together in a grey blur. 'What? What's wrong?'

'She's picked up a chest infection. The hotel doctor's a bit worried about her.'

'Can I talk to her?'

'She's asleep at the moment.'

'How long has she been ill?'

'A couple of days.'

'Why didn't you tell me?'

Trevor sighed. 'You know what she's like.'

Small, fierce, unfaltering, impatient with

weakness. As stubborn as a rock formation. Yes, Alice knew what her mother was like.

'Are you going to bring her home? Shall I come out there?'

'There's no need for that. Rest and antibiotics is what she needs.'

'Are you sure? I'll call you later and see how she is. Give her a kiss from me when she wakes up.'

After Trevor had rung off Alice tried to turn back to her work, but anxiety nudged at her and in the end she gave up. It was almost lunchtime. Jo's house was nearby and Jo would have constructive advice to offer. But it was Pete she wanted to talk to. She would call in at his studio and tell him about Margaret. They could have a sandwich and a cup of coffee together. Alice left her desk at once and rode her bicycle through the traffic.

The studio was in an old warehouse at the end of a cul-de-sac. Mark's side was closed up, but the heavy door to Pete's hung narrowly ajar, sagging slightly on its hinges. Alice padlocked her bike to a street sign advising that there was no parking. A smart new Mini was parked right alongside.

She edged round the door and slipped into the studio. It was dim inside after the bright daylight. Pete wasn't working, then. The blinds at the big windows were all drawn. The concrete-floored space smelled of dust and resin, and something familiar scraped at her subconscious in the split second before she identified it and the association. It was music, the same song that had been playing in the punt on the afternoon when Pete jumped into the water.

His latest work in progress loomed above Alice's head. It was a bird's nest of twisted metal and within the lattice cage some of his found objects were suspended on thin wires—a buckled bicycle wheel, a polystyrene wig block like a blanched head that revolved very slowly as the studio air stirred. The hair at the nape of Alice's neck prickled as she looked around for the source of the music. Peter's welding torch lay on the ground, with the black welding mask that made him look like Darth Vader discarded beside it. She took three quick steps to the inner door, past more accumu lated debris.

The door led into a boxed-off cubicle with a metalworker's bench at which Pete did his smaller-scale work. There was a grey filing cabinet, a kettle and a clutch of mugs stained with rings of tannin. The CD player was balanced on the broken typist's chair from the skip outside the Parks. A girl's handbag, an expensive-looking fringed suede affair, spilled its contents on the floor. The girl herself was perched on the edge of the cluttered bench, steadying herself with her hands. Her denim legs stretched out on either side of Pete's head.

Pete hadn't heard Alice come in. Just above and to the side of his right ear Alice could see the butterfly tattoo.

The girl looked straight into Alice's eyes as the song finished.

'Oh, shit,' the girl said.

Alice didn't move. There was a scramble of movements from the other two as Peter leaped to his feet and the girl pulled up and zipped her jeans. She bent down sideways and picked up her bag, briefly holding it in front of her chest as if it were a piece of body armour.

Peter shook his head and ran his hands through his hair. For the moment he was silenced.

It was the girl who spoke first. 'Look, what can I say?'

She had one of those low, drawling voices. Alice knew that it must be her car parked outside, probably a twenty-first present from Daddy. Pete liked girls who weren't going to rely on him for support. She belonged in that category herself. The thought struck a shiver of bewildered amusement through her and when he glimpsed it in her face Pete winced and said in a thick voice, 'Al, you know, it isn't . . .'

'It isn't what I think? Is that what you're going to say?'

He held up his hand. 'Georgia, you'd better go.'

With a part of her mind Alice was noticing how pretty she was and how young she looked. In contrast to this glowing girl she felt old and dull. She was also surprised by Georgia's self-possession. She had hitched her bag over her shoulder and now she was looking coolly around the little room to see if she had dropped anything else. She leaned across and pressed a button to eject the disc from the player. When she had tucked it inside her bag she stood facing Pete with her back to Alice. Alice gazed at the graceful lines of her neck and narrow shoulders.

'When will I see you again?'

He had the grace to look uncomfortable. 'I don't know. Perhaps not for a bit.'

'I see. Well, then, I'll call you.' She turned away and glanced at Alice. 'I'm sorry, I really am. It wasn't intended to be like this. But all's fair, as the saying goes.'

Then she left.

What does one say now? Alice wondered. Pete

was waiting, ready to take his cue from her. He looked like a schoolboy anticipating a scolding, half truculent and half defiant. She wanted to tell him that he was an adult, a grown man. He couldn't get away with being a naughty boy for ever.

'I came over because my mother's not well. I'm worried about her. I was thinking we could have lunch. Just a sandwich or something.'

Her words fell into the space between them. Pete's expression changed to one of relief, reprieve.

'Of course we can. Come on. Where would you like to go?'

'What? No. I don't want to go anywhere. That was before I saw . . . what I just saw.'

He rushed in: 'Al, believe me, it's one of those dumb things, it doesn't mean anything.'

'It's just a dick thing?'

His face flushed. 'No. Well, if you want to call it that, yes. I suppose.'

'How many?'

'How many times? For God's sake. She's just a student.'

'I meant how many other women.'

'Alice, please. What do you think I am? I'm with you, I love *you*.'

She stared at him. She wanted to have him put his arms round her and hear him saying that this was all a mistake—not in the guilty, formulaic way that he was saying it now, but in a way that meant she could believe him. And at the same time she knew that this was utterly unrealistic because she would never be able to believe what he told her, never again, no matter what he said. He had lied to her and he was lying to her now.

When he had finished protesting she listened

59

carefully. She thought she could hear a tiny, feathery whisper. It was the sound of her illusions, softly collapsing.

'I don't think so,' she said.

He thumped his clenched fist on the bench. It was a theatrical gesture. 'Listen, I'm sorry. I won't do it again. It was a mistake and I was regretting it even before you walked in. But it happens.' The way an avalanche happens, or a thunder storm, presumably. A natural cataclysm that was beyond his control.

Alice said carefully, 'You didn't look as though you were regretting it. I'm going back to work now. We'll have to talk about what's going to happen, about how to . . .' She was going to say put an end to everything, but she couldn't find a word that fitted. 'But I don't want to do it today. If you can't find a place to stay tonight, I'll go to Jo's.'

She was dry-eyed and her voice sounded level, but she didn't feel in control. Her stomach churned with nausea and the palms of her hands were wet. Then she turned round and walked out through the studio. The polystyrene head was still gently turning on its thread of wire. She had never understood Peter's art, she thought. She had longed to, had dragged her mind and her senses to contemplation of it over and over again, but she had never been able to make sense of it. She was like Trevor and Margaret, really: just a literal-minded scientist.

Unable to think clearly, she cycled back to her office, combed her hair and drank a glass of water. Then she sat through a long discussion with five of her colleagues about grant allocations for the coming year. She took the minutes, concentrating

60

on noting everyone's different points with meticulous accuracy. Once or twice, though, when someone spoke to her, she found herself staring at them and struggling to inject meaning into the babble of their words.

'Are you all right, Alice?' Professor Devine asked as the meeting broke up. David Devine was the head of her department and an old friend of both of her parents.

She smiled straight at him. 'Yes, thanks, I'm fine.' In fact, she felt sick.

From her office, she called Jo. 'Are you in? Can I drop in after work?'

'Of course I'm in. I'm always in. The babies are having a bit of a crap day, though.'

'I'll give you a hand.'

Jo and Harry lived in Headington. Alice cycled slowly up the hill, buffeted by the tailwind from passing buses, her legs feeling like bags of wet sand. She rang Jo's doorbell and leaned against the wall of the porch while she waited for her to come to the door. How many times had she stood here?

Jo opened the door with one of the babies held against her shoulder. She cupped the back of his head with one hand and kept him in place with her chin and forearm. There was a bottle of formula in her free hand. Alice kissed her, smelling baby sick and talcum powder.

'Come through,' Jo said. She edged past the double baby-carrier that blocked the hall and led the way to the kitchen. The second twin was in a Moses basket on the table. He was awake, his black-eyed stare fixed on the shadows moving on the ceiling above him. 'Cup of tea? Wine?'

'I'd love some tea, please,' Alice said. She didn't

61

think she could keep a glass of wine down although she would have welcomed the bluntening effect of alcohol. 'Can I hold him?'

Jo handed the baby over at once. He frowned and squinted up at Alice, who knew that she handled him with that stiff, alarmed concentration of the utterly unpractised. He responded by going stiff himself and puckering his face up, ready to start crying.

'Here, plug this in,' Jo said, handing over the bottle of formula. Alice poked the rubber teat into the baby's mouth and he began to suck. She eased herself into one of the chairs at the kitchen table, the Moses basket and a packet of Pampers and a pile of baby clothes at her elbow. Through the open doors into the garden she could see leaves and the ragged, dirty-pink globes of mophead hydrangeas. Getting into his stride, the baby snuffled and sucked more vigorously.

'How are you?' Alice asked and Jo half turned from the sink. She looked, as she so often did nowadays, on the verge of tears.

'I've had to start bottle-feeding in the last couple of days. I just can't go on feeding them both myself. This way, they sleep a bit longer between feeds and I can sometimes get as much as two hours myself.'

'That's much better, isn't it?'

Jo nodded, but without seeming convinced. She wanted to be a good mother, as well as a good girl, and that meant breastfeeding. Alice knew this without Jo having to say as much.

'Look at me, Ali,' Jo said quietly.

'I am looking.'

She was wearing a shapeless shirt under which her breasts swam like porpoises. Her skirt hem hung unevenly and revealed pale calves and unshaven shins, and her pretty face was drawn. Alice thought she looked older but there was also a new solemnity about her, an extra elemental dimension that added greatly to her appeal. Even in her weariness she was sexier than she had ever been before her pregnancy.

'Sometimes I think that no one ever looks at me now, even Harry. I'm an invisible appendage. I have no function except as a machine for feeding and wiping and tending Leo and Charlie. I'm just a mother. I want to be myself, but I can't even remember what I was like before this happened.'

'You are yourself. Only more so. This time will pass.'

Alice wanted to put an arm round her friend, but she was pinned down by the baby she was nursing. And this was only one of them, for a few minutes. When she looked out into the garden again she saw how narrow the view really was. Jo had told her how long it took to get both babies ready to leave the house, even for a walk to the shops. What must it be like, to think that the world had shrunk from its infinite breadth to the four walls of a house and a square of suburban garden?

'It's only twelve weeks since they were born. They'll grow up and start running around.' With the present helpless morsel of humanity in her arms, Alice realised how very far in the future this must seem.

Jo sighed. 'I know, of course they will. It is getting better, too. Remember at the beginning when some days I didn't even find time to get dressed? I'm sorry, Al. I don't mean to complain. I'm just sounding off because I've been here on my

63

own all day. I wanted them so much and I do love them. I didn't even know what loving meant before I had them.'

She put a teapot and two mugs on the table.

'Which one is this?' Alice asked sheepishly.

Jo laughed. 'Leo.'

'I'm sorry. I'll learn to tell them apart.'

'Don't worry. Even Harry gets it wrong half the time. D'you want some toast or a biscuit or something? 'Fraid I haven't made a Victoria sponge.'

Alice shook her head quickly.

Jo eyed her, then sat down next to her at the table. 'What's up?'

'It's Pete.'

'Go on.'

Alice told her. While she was talking Leo's eyelids fluttered and then closed. His gums loosened on the bottle teat and a shiny whitish bubble swelled at the corner of his mouth.

'I'm sorry,' Jo said at the end. 'And I'm sorry for going on and on about my problems without giving you a chance.'

'You didn't. You never do that.'

There was a moment of quiet in the kitchen. Both babies were asleep, and the oasis of calm silence was more notable and the more precious because it would last only a few minutes. Jo's face went smooth and luminous as she stared peacefully into the garden. Alice's sympathy for her twitched into sudden envy and she bit her lip at the realisation.

She said, 'The thing is, I'm not sure that Georgia is the only one. Now I've seen this much, all kinds of other details seem to be falling into place. Pete's so evasive and maybe I've been convincing myself that it's just because he's an artist, needs space, can't be tied down. When he doesn't come home in the evenings, when he goes off to Falmouth or London or Dieppe for days at a time, I just get on with my work and feel pleased about how . . . how separately productive and mutually in accord we are. In fact, he's probably got half a dozen women on the go, hasn't he?'

She started on a laugh to distance herself from this possibility and then a flicker in Jo's eyes made the laughter stick in her throat.

'What do you know? Jo, please tell me.'

Jo hesitated. 'Harry saw him one night. In a pub near Bicester.'

'Everyone goes to the pub, Jo. Quite a lot of Pete's working life seems to take place in them, in fact. What does he call it? Necessary inspiration?'

But when Jo said nothing Alice felt the last of her defences crumbling. *Was* I happy? she wondered. Or was I just determined to be? 'Go on,' she said miserably.

'Pete didn't see him, because he had his tongue down some woman's throat at the time. That's how Harry put it. He said they didn't look as if they were going to get as far as the car park before they . . . well. I'm sorry, Al. I'm so tactless. I've forgotten how to talk to real people, haven't I?'

'Was it Georgia?'

'It didn't sound like her.'

'No. I see.'

In the Moses basket Charlie stirred and gave an experimental whimper. Jo said, 'It's coming up to his lively time. He'll be awake now until about ten. I thought you sort of knew about Pete and that was the way you chose to handle it. Knowing and not knowing.'

'Perhaps,' Alice murmured. Humiliation made her want to bend double, as if she had a stomach-ache.

'You deserve better,' Jo observed, lifting Charlie out of his basket as full-scale crying got under way. She rocked him gently, shushing him softly.

'Perhaps,' Alice said again.

'Do you love him?'

Yes, she loved him. Or was it actually the idea of him that she loved, the *concept* of Pete? Not just the illusory domesticity that they had enjoyed, but the very way his disarray and lack of precision had made an anarchic foil for her own self-imposed orderliness?

Perhaps that was it. His work, his pieces of sculpture, were only just on the right side of giant rubbish heaps. (Of course they are, he would say. It is all a metaphor for our world. Arbitrary arrangements scraped together in a disintegrating society, drowning in its own discarded refuse. Or something like that. She never had quite mastered the language.) Whereas she had grown up with Trevor, sitting on a sun-warmed stone and watching her father frowning and scribbling stratigraphic measurements in his notebook. She had loved the names of the rocks. Gabbro and dolerite and basalt. The earth's apparent solidity and her father's dependability had somehow fused into a reassuring constant. It was only much later, as a geology student herself, that she began to appreciate the immense scale of the earth's restlessness. And now, in her mid-thirties, as the balance of power between them shifted and her

66

parents grew frailer, and as Pete's shape shifted, her notions of what was solid and dependable were all being overturned.

'I don't know,' she told Jo now. The realisation that she truly didn't know shocked her.

'What will you do? Tell him to behave or else?'

'It's a bit late for that. I was going to ask if I could stay here until he's moved out?'

They were both holding a baby. The sun had moved off the garden and the light was fading.

Jo said immediately, 'Of course you can.'

Alice made pasta for dinner while Jo bathed the babies and fed them again. Harry came home, his face creased from the day, and they juggled the wakeful twins between the three of them while they ate. Pete rang Alice's mobile every half-hour, but she didn't take the calls. He rang Jo and Harry's number too, and Harry did pick up the phone.

'Yeah, she's here. But I'd leave it for a while, mate, if I were you.'

The calls stopped after that. Before she went to bed Alice spoke to her father in the hotel in Madeira. 'Is she feeling any better?'

'The doctor called in again. He's been very good. We think she might be better off at home, you know, so we're going to take a flight tomorrow. All being well, that is.'

'Can you put her on?'

Alice put the flat of her hand against the wall of Jo's spare bedroom, wanting to feel its solidity.

'It's very annoying,' Margaret said into the phone. The words were hers but her voice was almost unrecognisable, falling between a whisper and a sigh.

'You'll be fine. Once you're home. A couple of

67

days and you'll be yourself again.'

'Will I?' She asked the question as though she were a child.

'Yes,' Alice said with a tremor in her voice.

*   *   *

In their bedroom, Jo and Harry undressed for bed. One baby was asleep, the other cried every time Jo put him down. They would alternate this routine throughout the night. If he had to work the next day Harry usually slept in the spare room, but tonight Alice was in it. Jo walked up and down, rhythmically rocking the baby against her, willing him to fall asleep.

'She's very precise. Not detached, or unsentimental, not exactly. But she doesn't waver, or change her mind. If she's decided it's all over with Pete then it's over.'

Harry took off his socks, balled them up and aimed them towards the laundry basket. 'Yes? Probably for the best, then.'

'Maybe. I don't know, though. She seemed happy with Pete. He countered that precision in her. Made her more spontaneous.'

Harry lay down and closed his eyes. 'Are you going to get into bed?'

Jo smiled, sat down on the edge of the bed and swivelled so that her back rested against the headboard, trying at the same time not to interrupt the rocking. She wanted to talk to Harry now, piecing together the day's events and impressions. Just for ten minutes, before she entered the hushed tunnel of another night when every living thing seemed to sleep except for herself and one or both

68

of the babies.

'Al's my best friend. But sometimes I think I don't know her at all. I mean, I've never even glimpsed it, but beneath all that cool logic there might be a wild heart beating. Don't you think?'

There was no answer. When she looked at him she saw that Harry had plunged into sleep.

*　　　*　　　*

Alice went home for a change of clothes. Pete had been there, she could tell from the crumbs on the counter and a single plate and knife in the sink, but there was no other sign. There was no note and she thought that most of his belongings were still in their accustomed places. She registered this much, then dismissed the thought. The latest telephone conversation with Trevor had left a hard knot of anxiety in her chest. Margaret had had a bad night and was suffering breathing difficulties. There was some doubt about whether she would be able to fly home at all, although she was still insisting that this was what she wanted. Alice said to her father that she would meet them at the airport but Trevor told her that he had arranged a private ambulance. Margaret would be driven straight from the airport to hospital.

'We're probably being overcautious. But there's no harm in that, is there?' he said.

'No. Of course not. I'm sure,' Alice answered. They had somehow entered a conspiracy of matter-of-factness, in which they both pretended that this was a routine way of ending a holiday.

The flight left, with Margaret and Trevor on board. It was too early yet for Alice to think of going to the hospital to meet them. She washed Pete's plate and knife and put them away, then walked through the house. It felt slightly unfamiliar, as if she had been away from it for much longer than one night. The arrangements of crockery in cupboards and books on shelves seemed irrelevant, as if already viewed through the distancing membrane of history.

After an hour she couldn't bear the house's silence any longer. She locked the front door and went to the Department. A few minutes after she arrived Professor Devine put his head into her office with a question about the minutes of the budgeting meeting. She told him about Margaret and he took off his glasses and replaced them again, a sign of dismay that she knew was habitual without ever having been aware of it before. Everything around her had a lurid clarity that balanced on the edge of nausea.

'If there is anything Helen and I can do, anything at all,' the Professor mumbled.

She isn't *dead*, Alice thought, while she was gravely accepting his statements of concern. She isn't going to *die*.

Eventually, after a long time, Trevor called again. They were in the ambulance. Margaret had taken a turn for the worse on the flight. He didn't any longer try to suggest that there was nothing to worry about. Their conspiracy now was about getting Margaret to hospital with all speed.

'I'll see you there,' Alice said. She left her office and drove to the hospital, and found a seat in the A&E waiting area. People flurried past her or sat and gazed into space. An ambulance with its blue light lazily flashing arrived under the canopy. The

70

steps at the rear were unfolded but it was a young woman carrying a baby who was helped down and hurried through the doors. Another half-hour dragged by before a long white car with blacked-out windows drew up. A stretcher was rolled out of the back and lifted on to a trolley. Alice glimpsed her mother's white hair on a blue pillow. She left her seat and ran in pursuit.

Margaret's eyes seemed twice their normal size. Her face was a parchment triangle that looked too small to contain them and there were purple marks like fresh bruises showing through the skin. She was breathing in fast, shallow gasps. Her hand moved just perceptibly under the red blanket that covered her, and Alice slid her own underneath and took hold of her cold fingers.

'It's all right,' she said gently and the memory came back to her of Trevor using exactly the same intonation when she woke up from some childish nightmare. 'It's all right now.'

Margaret's eyes remained fixed imploringly on hers.

Medical staff crowded into the cubicle. Alice and Trevor retreated together to a short row of chairs. They could see feet and ankles and rubber wheels and metal protruberances beneath the curtain hems of the cubicles facing them. Trevor's cardigan was buttoned up wrongly, with one button spare at the chest vee and another unmatched over the small swell of his stomach. His white hair stood out round his head and Alice wanted to smooth the wrinkles of freckled skin where it suddenly seemed too loose for his skull.

'The flight,' he murmured. 'I thought . . .' His eyes travelled to where Margaret was lying. He had

71

thought that she was going to die. Having seen her mother, the fear didn't seem irrational to Alice.

'The doctor will tell us everything.' It was important to get information and to act on it. She took his hand and found that it was trembling.

She sat still, holding her father's dry hand and waiting. The hospital setting was completely unfamiliar to her. She had hardly ever been inside one before today. None of them was ever ill. A sheltered life, she thought, aware of it sliding into the past tense. She pressed the soles of her shoes to the mottled grey floor, wondering how it remained motionless when everything was shifting.

At last a doctor came to find them.

'Mrs Peel almost certainly has a form of pneumonia,' she said. 'We are X-raying her now and we'll do some blood tests.'

Under her married name Margaret sounded like a stranger, Alice thought. She was always Margaret Mather, yes, *the* Margaret Mather . . .

'Can I go to her?' Trevor asked. There was suddenly a pleading note in his voice. Anxiety scraped away his reserve. It occurred to Alice that she had never been properly aware before of how deeply he loved Margaret. She felt like an eavesdropper outside the walls of her parents' marriage.

'We'll stabilise her first. It's a matter of making her comfortable.'

They went back to the row of seats and waited. Alice let her father sit quietly. A teenaged girl with her leg propped in front of her was pushed past in a wheelchair. She was wearing school uniform, the navy-blue and cerise of Alice's old school.

Once, Alice remembered, when she was eleven or twelve, Margaret had come to talk to the school to show one of her celebrated films. She stood up on the stage in the hall beside the rectangle of white screen unrolled in readiness by Mr Gregory, the biology teacher. Her neat navy-blue suit was unremarkable, but she wore it with a pair of stiletto-heeled shoes. The sunlight flooding in from the big window behind her made her hair glint like silver mesh.

'I am going to take you all on a journey,' she said. 'To one of the most remarkable places in the world.'

The blinds were drawn and the lights dimmed.

The film's images were already familiar to Alice. There were the rookeries of Adélie penguins on rocky headlands of the Antarctic peninsula. Thousands of birds seethed on a narrow rock margin between mirror-silver sea and steep walls of ice and snow. The intense chirring sound made by the birds swelled and filled the hall.

Margaret and her assistant moved through the dense colony, counting the eggs and the chicks. The chicks were newly hatched and the schoolgirl audience gave a collective *aaah* at the first close-up of a beaky ball of silver-grey down. Margaret stopped the film and continued her crisp commentary.

'The Adélie breeding season is short. Females lay two eggs apiece but only about sixty per cent of *Pygoscelis adeliae* chicks reach the crèche stage at the age of three weeks.'

The film started up again and the blunt arc of a

73

brown Antarctic skua swept out of the whitish sky and dived on a chick at the edge of the colony. The morsel of fluff was swallowed whole, head first. For a fraction of a second the tiny feet were visible in the slit of the skua's bill. The sentimental tendency of the audience dissipated after that.

There were shots of penguins flipping out of the sea between the ribbed flanks of icebergs, like dozens of tiny missiles, intercut with footage of the birds cruising underwater through the spinning maze of krill. Alice knew that Margaret hadn't used an underwater cameraman; she had dived down into the ice-bound sea to film all this herself. She wanted to nudge her neighbour and tell her so.

'Adult birds fish for krill, *Euphausia crystallorophias* in the main, in the rich waters around the continental edge.'

Margaret paid her audience the compliment of never talking down to them and she also had the knack of making them feel that she was sharing the complete experience. Her film included personal footage that was never shown on television. In one sequence she was cooking on a small stove outside her little orange pyramid tent. Her red protective suit and the tent made a dab of colour in an immense blank sweep of white and cobalt blue. In one close-up she looked over her shoulder and laughed straight up at the cameraman. Strands of her pale hair blew across her cheek and stuck there, seeded with ice. Alice drew her knees up against her chest and shivered, as if she were out in the ice herself.

The applause at the end was loud. Mr Gregory came back up on to the stage and thanked Dr Mather for coming to talk to the school. Margaret

74

stood beside him, even in her heels barely reaching up to his shoulder. She looked straight out into the audience and she appeared to be made of different materials and coloured more brightly than the biology teacher or the headmistress who was beaming on her other side. Alice realised now that that was the moment when she understood how sexy her mother was. Margaret was then in her fifties.

Margaret had another lecture to give after her talk to the school and she drove herself away straight afterwards in her green Alfa Romeo with the dented rear wing. Alice was surrounded by a group of girls.

'Your mum's rather amazing,' Becky Gifford said. Becky's own mother was a television actress, and Becky was the most sophisticated and confident girl in Alice's year. She had never noticed Alice before.

'She is a scientist,' Alice answered, wanting to make clear that that was what was most important.

'So are you going to be one as well?'

'Yes,' Alice told her.

*   *   *

It was probably true, Alice thought, that she owed her friendship with Becky to Margaret and that day.

A nurse came and stood in front of their chairs. 'You can come and sit with her now,' she told them. 'Could you pop these on first? They do up at the back.' She handed them a blue paper gown apiece. In silence, Alice and Trevor helped each other into the crackling shrouds and did up the ribbon ties at

75

the nape of the neck.

Margaret had been moved to a different cubicle, a glassed-in alcove to the side of the department. Beyond the glass partition three other trolley beds had also been drawn up. She was propped up on pillows with a clear plastic mask held to her face by an elastic loop. The mask looked too big for her, as if it might envelop the bones of her jaw and cheek. An intravenous tube was taped to her arm. Her eyes, wide with alarm, fixed on them as they approached.

'Here we are,' Trevor said. They moved one to either side of her. The bed immediately beyond the glass was occupied by a young Asian man, lying flat on his back with his eyes closed. 'Here we are now,' Trevor repeated.

Alice glanced around and saw a chair across the corridor. She carried it over and placed it for Trevor to sit down. He folded abruptly into it as if his legs were about to give way. He leaned to put his hand on Margaret's arm and she turned her head to see him better.

After a while she drifted into sleep.

The time passed, minutes divided from minutes by the slow sweep of the second hand of the wall clock directly in Alice's sightline. She brought her father a bottle of water from a vending machine, but he wouldn't leave his place for long enough to eat anything.

A nurse came every half-hour to check Margaret's pulse and temperature. The close-quarters bustle and clattering of the emergency department seemed to reach them through thick layers of close air. The young Asian man was wheeled away by a porter in green overalls and his place was immediately taken by an older man who looked around him in mournful bewilderment. The evening seeped away. Alice thought of the chains of car headlights outside on the bypass and of busy people on their way to somewhere familiar, at the end of an ordinary day.

A different nurse performed the observations, which meant that the night staff had now come on. Alice was just deciding she would insist that Trevor ate some food when Margaret opened her eyes. They focused, in an instant of confusion, then flooded with mute terror. Her free hand came up and clawed at the mask. She dragged it off her face and hoarsely whispered, 'I'll suffocate.' Her Yorkshire vowels were exaggerated: *soooffocaaate*.

Alice jerked to her feet. 'No, no, you won't. It's helping you to breathe,' she soothed.

'Mag? Maggie, darling, you're all right,' Trevor murmured.

Her silvery-haloed head rolled on the pillow.

'Are you there?' Margaret demanded.

'Yes,' they said. Her head turned to Trevor and then the other way, until her eyes connected with Alice's. Alice had never seen her mother afraid before, but her face was livid with it now. There were beads of sweat on her forehead. She breathed noisily with her mouth open and Alice tried to put the mask back, but Margaret impatiently knocked it away.

'I want you to do something for me.' She said it to Alice. Even now she managed a degree of imperiousness but it sounded a cracked note, the tremulous insistence of a frightened child.

'Of course I will.'

'I want . . .' Margaret took a breath. 'I want you

77

to go south. To Lewis Sullavan's station.'

'I can't go anywhere, not when you are ill.'

Margaret's hand twitched on the covers. 'This isn't it. Not by a long chalk it isn't. I'll be getting over this. But I want you to go, while you can, while you've got the chance. For . . . me. Do it for me.'

Alice understood what she meant, with the clear precision born in the most intense moment of an intense drama. She knew that she would remember this instant and her exact comprehension of her mother's wishes. There would be no denying or forgetting what was intended.

Margaret was looking at the spectre of her own mortality. She wouldn't die here, not yet, her will was too strong for that. But she knew, finally and empirically, that her strength was not infinite. And her intention was that her life would be carried forward for her, out on the ice where she had lived it most intensely, by her only child.

Somewhere beyond their glass box a telephone was insistently ringing. Footsteps passed, metal harshly scraped—the sounds they had been hearing for hours. Alice looked at Trevor and saw the mute imprecation in his face. Trevor had never, throughout her life, demanded a single thing of her. All he had done was to love the two of them, his two women. The telephone stopped ringing, then started up again.

'Of course I'll go,' Alice said softly.

The fear in Margaret's eyes faded, replaced for a moment by a clear sapphire glimmer of triumph. It was Trevor who smudged away tears with the back of his hand.

'You'll find details. E-mail, in my e-mail in-box,' Margaret said.

'Don't worry about that now.'

Gently Trevor lifted the plastic mask and fitted it over his wife's mouth. She nodded her acquiescence and her eyes closed again.

At 10 p.m., when Trevor began to doze with his head on the covers next to Margaret's hand, a different doctor came to explain regretfully that there would be no place available on the ward before the morning. Margaret herself was now asleep, so Alice drove her father home to Boar's Hill. She heated up some soup and once they had eaten and she was sure that he had gone to bed, she made up a bed for herself in her old room. She lay on her side with her knees drawn up, as she had done as a child, and looked across at the old books on the white-painted shelves. There was Shackleton's *South*, and Fuchs and Hillary's *The Crossing of Antarctica*, both of them presents, on different birthdays, from Margaret. She had written Alice's name and the date on the flyleaf of each. It was as if Alice could see straight through the stiff board covers now, into an Antarctic landscape where the reality of Margaret's films and the explorers' stories overlapped with a fantastical realm of ice turrets and rippled snow deserts and blue-lipped crevasses. Tattered veils of snow were chased by the wind and the howling of it rose inside her head, reaching a crescendo in an unearthly shriek that drowned out her mother's voice and the chirring of the penguins.

And now Antarctica lay in wait for her, with its frozen jaws gaping wide open.

*   *   *

79

Alice sat upright. Sleep was out of the question. She pulled on her clothes again, shivering in the unheated bedroom, and went downstairs. Margaret's chair at the gate-legged table in the bay window overlooked a dark void where the garden lay. Alice made herself a mug of tea and sat down at her mother's computer screen.

Do it, she exhorted herself. You made a promise. Do this much at least, before tomorrow throws any complications in the way.

Alice clicked *new message* and began to type.

If it was appropriate, and if her understanding of the present situation was correct, following her mother's serious illness she would be honoured to be considered in her place for membership of the forthcoming European joint expedition to Antarctica.

She attached a list of her scientific qualifications. At the end, against Previous Antarctic Experience, she typed *none*.

The tea had gone cold but she took a gulp of it anyway. She reread her short message and changed a couple of words, then checked that the address in the box was correct. She typed her own correspondence address and quickly pressed *send*. The out-box was briefly highlighted before the communication went to an unknown recipient named Beverley Winston, assistant to Lewis Sullavan.

There was nothing else to be done tonight. Alice poured her unfinished tea down the kitchen sink and went back to bed. She lay still under the familiar weight of the covers. She thought of her own bed in the house in Jericho and wondered where Pete was tonight. Only a little time ago they

80

had woken up in the same bed with nothing more than a kiss glimpsed at a party to separate them.

Now there was the prospect of half a world.

The acceleration of change seemed to open a pit beneath her. Opening her eyes again to counter another bout of nausea, Alice examined the contours of her room. She had lived a remarkably sheltered life. As she saw it now, she had made an almost stately progression from childhood to today. In Margaret's shadow and under her father's benign protection she had done what was expected of her and what she expected of herself. No more, nothing more than just what was expected.

And now, without Pete and with her mother's shadow shortened, there was *this*.

Suddenly, beneath her ribcage, Alice Peel felt a sharp stab of anticipation that shocked her with its ecstatic greed.

CHAPTER FIVE

With the steady approach of summer the pack ice in the scoop of bay was slowly, grudgingly, breaking up. This morning the ice was a dirty ivory colour, glinting here and there like polished bone. The expanding streaks of water were black and pewter grey under a matching sky, and a thin veil of ice fog hung over the cliffs that formed the opposite wall of the bay. Idle flakes of snow spun in the still air, floating upwards as well as down.

Rooker replaced the engine casing of the skidoo and twisted the ignition key. The machine obligingly coughed and roared, and Valentin

Petkov, the glaciologist, glanced back from where he was placing bamboo wands and marker flags out on the ice and gave a thumbs-up. The field assistant, Philip Idwal Jones, was nearby, coiling a rope. He finished it with a loop, slung it over his shoulder and trudged back through the snow.

'Hey. Rook.' The shout carried clearly in the silence. 'Time for a brew?'

Rooker pulled back the cuff of his glove to check his watch. It was midday and they had been out since 8 a.m. Petkov was keen to set up his markers and take the first set of readings. This part of his study, as Rooker understood it, was to do with comparing the speed of travel of the margins of the ice with the centre. If you could call it speed, he reflected, at the rate of millimetres per year.

Philip reached the skidoo, dropped his rope and took off his fleece cap to scratch at his spikes of black hair. He had a patchy black beard to match. Phil was only twenty-six but he had been travelling and climbing since he was seventeen. This was his third Antarctic season. As a mountain guide it was his job to assist the scientists in their fieldwork and at the same time to make sure they didn't fall down a crevasse or off a cliff.

'Piece of cake, I don't think,' he had confided to Rooker. 'That French bird thinks she knows it all, du'n't she?'

Rooker liked him.

'Ta,' Phil said now when Rooker passed him a thermos of coffee. 'Phew. Warm, innit?'

It was, compared with a week ago, when they had first arrived. Daytime temperatures then had hovered around −23°C, with a heavy wind chill. Today it was a mild and summery −5°C.

'D'you think Valerie's going to take a break?' Phil wondered, looking over at Petkov who was still zigzagging across the glacier. Phil maintained that Valentin wasn't a name at all, just a card you sent to your girlfriend if you remembered and could be bothered, and insisted instead on Val, which he then back-formed to Valerie. No one could be less effeminate than Valentin. He had a rich bass voice and a barrel chest, and a fondness for whisky and jokes whose punchlines didn't always survive the shift from Bulgarian into English. There were six different first languages at Kandahar Station, but English was the common tongue.

'Dead common,' Phil had inevitably quipped in his thick Welsh accent.

He beckoned to Valentin by waving a mug in a wide arc. It was hard to judge distances across the bland, grey-white face of the glacier. Only over to their left, where it suddenly tipped downhill and spilled towards the ice and the sea, splitting into a chaotic mass of seracs and twisted crevasses on the way, did its scale become more legible.

Phil sighed when the scientist cheerily waved back, either not understanding or not wanting to stop work.

'Daft Bulgar. I'll have to take it over there. Give us one of those butties, mate.' He took the thermos and a wrapped sandwich, and headed off across the snow again.

The skidoo had been tending to stall on the way out from the base. Rooker had found and cleared a blockage in the fuel line. He sat on the machine now, leaning back against the handlebars with his feet up on the seat. When he had looked into the radio room this morning, Niki had told him that the warm and windless weather heralded a storm. Nikolai Pocius was the radio operator, a gaunt Lithuanian communications genius who had spent ten years in the Russian army. Niki was probably right, but it was hard to believe it in this moment of perfect stillness. When he closed his eyes, apart from the faint breath of cold on his face, Rooker thought he could be in a vacuum. The depth of silence was crystalline and absolute, without the smallest possibility—a certainty anywhere else in the world—that it would be shattered in the next second by a jet passing overhead or a burst of distorted music or the whine of traffic.

Apart from the nine people currently occupying the two huts on a small bluff that made up Kandahar Station, the nearest human habitation was at Santa Ana, a Chilean base that lay 120 miles further up the peninsula. The Chileans maintained a snow ski-way for fixed-wing aircraft, and the Kandahar personnel had flown in there and then been transferred by helicopter to Kandahar. In partnership with the Chileans, Lewis Sullavan had leased for the summer season a pair of New Zealand-owned Squirrel helicopters with two Kiwi pilots and a mechanic. The machines and their crews would be based up at Santa Ana, but they would be available to transport Kandahar scientists out to field locations too remote to be reached by skidoo and sledge. Rooker envied the pilots. He would have liked to fly over the wilderness of glaciers, watching and trying to second-guess the extreme weather, but there was no chance of that. His fixed-wing licence was out of date and he had only flown a helicopter a handful of times.

The silence expanded and thickened around

him. He could feel it almost as a physical mass pressing inwards against his eardrums. In the ten days since they had arrived here, the peace had soothed him. He escaped outside as often as he could.

The hut was crowded. He found it difficult to live at such close quarters with the disparate group that Shoesmith had assembled here. Dr Richard Shoesmith was the expedition leader. Rooker had taken an instinctive and immediate dislike to him, but the rest of them were mostly all right. It was the mass function that he recoiled from. People were always talking, trying to make themselves heard above the hum of the other voices. They wanted to make their mark, all of them. Even the jokes were often about scoring points off someone else, or about forming miniature alliances. Sometimes the spectacle touched him, at other times he laughed with everyone else, but he found it impossible to join in properly. The layers that protected him had thickened to the point of impermeability.

Since he had left Edith behind he had grown accustomed to being alone. Before that even, a long time before that, he had stopped looking for company, except for sex or for someone to drink with. He drank on base, of course, although Shoesmith didn't allow private supplies of alcohol. There was always drinking company, as there was everywhere else in the world. Neither Phil nor Valentin took any notice of the prohibition either. But Rooker didn't want to know about their lives outside Kandahar, or to know what they dreamed of or hoped for. They didn't ask him about his life and that suited him perfectly.

Outside, alone, he felt comfortable. The play of

light constantly amazed him. The quality of it could change ten times in an hour, going from milky translucence to blade-sharp clarity to a thick yellow glow. He would sit on a rock with his hands hanging loose between his knees, almost oblivious to the cold, just watching.

McMurdo, the American base on the edge of the Ross Ice Shelf, had been nothing like this. In the summer season McMurdo could house over a thousand people. It had bars and buses and a constant round of parties, and he looked back on it now as just a more boring and much harsher version of Ushuaia. It had been too populous and insulated for him to feel the powerful presence of the ice, and because he had been working as a shuttle-bus driver he had had few reasons ever to go beyond the base and the airfield. Unless it was over to drink with the Kiwis on Scott Base a couple of miles away. But it was lucky that he had worked that meaningless long-ago season, because it was the magic phrase 'previous experience' that had secured him this job. He had been taken on by Sullavan and Richard Shoesmith to manage transport, and to act as base mechanic and maintenance man.

That was easy enough. Rooker was good with machinery. He had almost five months ahead of him now, and all he had to do was drive the Zodiac, fix skidoos, and keep the water and the generators running. He felt, at long last, that he had travelled far enough. No one would try to reach him or come pushing up against him here, nudging him for reasons or responses. At McMurdo, planes were constantly landing or taking off. There was always the lure of other destinations. But here, unless a helicopter came in from Santa Ana or a ship arrived in the bay, no one could arrive or leave. Including himself.

He could keep a certain distance from the eight other people. He had a corner that he could curtain off in one of the men's four-bunk pit rooms, and outside there was always the mercurial light and the silence that was only ever shattered by the wind.

No, he suddenly remembered, it would soon be nine, not eight.

Nine people, because there was another scientist arriving today.

Shoesmith had made one of his ponderous announcements over breakfast: 'As most of you already know, Dr Alice Peel, from Oxford, will be arriving later today. Please do everything you can to make her welcome.'

Jochen van Meer, the station's medical doctor, had raised his thick blond eyebrows and grinned across the table at the other men. 'It will be a pleasure.'

Eight, nine, Rooker thought. It made no difference.

A shadow flicked over his closed eyelids and he sat up to see what it was. A big brown skua gull had landed a yard away, and now it cocked its head and gazed at him. The skuas ringed the rocks outside the door of the base, scavenging for scraps of food, and they quickly learned to follow the sledges further afield. He rummaged in the zipped pocket of his parka, found a lint-coated square of chocolate and threw it to the bird. There was a snap and the fragment disappeared into the hooked beak.

The radio crackled in his inner pocket. Shoesmith's voice broke out of the buzz of static. 'Base, this is Kandahar Base, Base to Rooker. Over.'

'Copy you,' Rooker replied.

Everything about Shoesmith, including his radio manner, was irritating.

As soon as they met, at the hotel in Punta Arenas before the flight south, Rooker knew that Shoesmith had the English public schoolboy's conviction that what he did was right because it was always done that way. He had confidence, it seemed to Rooker, but it wasn't rooted in competence or insight.

The trouble was that his voice, his manner, even his pink, handsome face, reminded Rooker of Henry Jerrold of Northumberland, England, whom he wanted to forget for ever.

Rooker listened to the leader's instructions. While the glaciology team was working, Richard wanted him to come back to base with the skidoo and ferry the French biologist to one of her penguin colonies. After that, the supply ship was due. Rooker was to take the Zodiac out through the loose ice to meet the new arrival and bring her ashore.

'Roger,' he said.

He fired up the skidoo and the skua launched itself away in a long, confident glide. Rook nosed his way back along their outward ski tracks until he reached the point closest to the others, then dismounted and plodded across to tell them where he was going. His boots sank almost to the ankles in the soft snow cloaking the ice.

'You are not leaving us out here the whole night

88

with no more than one sandwich?' Valentin laughed.

'Don't you fret, Val, we can walk home, no problem. It's Rook who'll have to worry when we do get in,' Phil threatened.

He left them to their flagging, uncoupled the sledge and raced the skidoo back to base. The outward journey had been slow because he and Phil had stopped to test the snow ahead with a long probe wherever there was a shadow or a dip. Too many dogs and sledges and even men had vanished from history into the bowels of the ice for it to be worth taking any risks. But now he drove at full speed, bouncing along with the cold stinging his cheeks and the front skis skimming in the safe tramlines of their exploratory journey. The trail stretched ahead, a thin smudge winding into the blank distance. Exhilaration curved his mouth into a wide grin.

The base was six miles away. As he came over the last rise Rooker saw it lying ahead of him in a sheltered bay, two tiny carmine-red dots against a sweep of snow with the pack ice and a tongue of inky water as a backdrop. Escarpments of exposed rock rose on either side, and behind the base the sloping snowfield was crowned with a towering rock outcrop that marked the margin of the glacier. At the closed end of the bay another tongue of the glacier tumbled in vicious blocks and gashes down to sea level.

He made a wide circuit round the jumbled mass of rock and roared down the slope towards the huts. He could see a little red-jacketed figure crossing the isthmus of snow between the living quarters and the lab hut.

Rooker swept the skidoo in a circle and left it under a makeshift shelter at the rear of the huts. One of his extra assignments was to build a proper housing, using the wooden frame materials left by the supply ship at the beginning of the season. The sky had darkened to solid slate-grey and he noticed that the wind was rising now. Tiny eddies of snow chased around his feet.

'Ah, there you are,' Shoesmith said superfluously. He was sitting at the oilcloth-covered table in the middle of the living area with a mass of papers spread out in front of him. The only other work area at Kandahar was at the narrow benches in the chilly lab and most people preferred to do their less demanding work in the warmth of the communal area.

At the far end of the room, where a pair of windows looked out on the snow hill, the base manager, Russell Amory, and Niki were crowded in the kitchen. Niki was peeling potatoes in a metal bowl and Russ was making bread. Rooker thought that one of the best features of life at Kandahar was Russ Amory's bread.

The two men looked like one another's opposites. Niki was immensely tall and cadaverously thin. He had long, unkempt hair and a wispy beard that didn't hide his hollow cheeks, and when he laughed his honking laugh the tight skin and thin lips pulled away from bad teeth that looked as if one more headshake would jerk them loose from the gums. Russell was short and suntanned and completely bald except for a band of fuzz above his ears. Today a white apron was stretched round his middle, emphasising his broad belly.

Russ and Nikolai didn't pause in their peeling and kneading. Niki twitched his wrist and sent a long coil of potato peel spiralling down into the bowl.

'Where is Laure? Is she ready?' Rooker asked from the doorway. He didn't want to spend time getting out of his boots and outer clothes if he was going straight outside again, and Russ never appreciated people trampling snow and grit over the linoleum floors.

As if to answer him the Frenchwoman, Laure Heber, emerged from the door of the women's pit room. She had a full backpack in one hand and a pair of insulated boots in the other. The other three men all looked up.

'*Merci, Jeem,*' she smiled. '*Tout prêt.*'

Laure's shiny dark hair was cut in a tidy bob. She wore pearl studs in her ears and even her fleece tops were flatteringly shaped to show off her long neck. Compared with the eight men on the base she was a miracle of personal grooming. She didn't talk very much, but her tendency to raise one eyebrow whenever anyone else was speaking gave her an air of detachment and scepticism. There was a rota for everyone to take a day's responsibility for cooking meals and cleaning the living areas, and on Laure's day she had served *boeuf bourguignonne* garnished with chopped herbs and a *tarte tatin*. The men had wolfed it all down. Jochen van Meer had kissed his fingertips at her. The big Dutchman had also made a point of helping her with the washing-up afterwards while the others drew up their chairs to watch a DVD of *The Matrix*.

Now she took her windpants and red parka off the hook by the door tagged 'Heber' and began

91

pulling them on. She said to Rooker, 'Jochen is coming to the rookery as well. He will help with netting the birds. You can take two of us?'

'Sure,' Rooker answered. Laure was tiny. It would mean squeezing up a bit, but he didn't think Jochen would mind that.

On cue, van Meer popped out of the opposite bunk-room door. The living area at Kandahar was very small. Someone was always crossing purposefully from bunk room to bathroom or from kitchen to front door. It was like one of those stage farces, Rook thought, but without the comedy.

Beside the front door was a whiteboard, with a list of surnames and a box beside each name. A tick in the box indicated that you were safely on the base. If you were going beyond the immediate environs you wrote down your destination and estimated time of return. It was Phil's job, and also Rook's as deputy safety officer, to monitor the status of the board. He ran his eye over it now, thumbed out the line that declared he was assisting on the Spaatz Glacier, scribbled 'transport SW rookery' instead and added his initials. He would be back, he estimated, within the hour.

At the bottom of the list there was a new name: 'Peel'.

Laure and Jochen followed suit. Jochen picked up a radio from the shelf next to the whiteboard. 'TBC' on the board indicated that they would need return transport, time to be confirmed by radio link.

'You'll be back, Rooker, to make the pick-up from the ship?' Richard reminded him. The two scientists, heavy with packs and boots and outer clothes, were clumping out of the door.

92

'Barring accidents,' Rook said flatly and followed them.

Niki whistled softly as he tipped potatoes into a pan.

Thick black clouds had massed right across the sky. The snow was now the same luminous pearl as Laure's ear studs, and it looked almost as smooth. Ridges and hollows were robbed of their contours and the wind was whipping an opaque shroud off the soft surface, making Rook frown through his goggles and lean forward in concentration as he brought the skidoo round. Ducking their heads against the stinging air, Laure and Jochen piled their rucksacks into the rear pannier and Laure climbed on behind Rook. He felt her slither along the seat, and the light pressure of her hips and thighs closing against his as Jochen swung on the back. The skidoo settled under their weight. Rook checked over his shoulder. He twisted the throttle grip so they surged forward, and he felt Laure pressing closer still as her arms fastened round his waist. She dipped her head behind the shelter of his back to keep the wind out of her face, resting her cheek against his spine.

'Hold tight, won't you?' The touch of warning sarcasm was wasted as the wind tore the words out of his mouth and hurled them away.

They had made the fifteen-minute journey to the Adélie penguin rookery several times before. Rook accelerated, with tiny snowflakes driving pinpricks into the narrow band of skin left exposed between his goggles and hood.

The Adélie colony consisted of more than a thousand breeding pairs. The males had come ashore first, hopping and sliding on their long journey from the outer margins of the ice where they had spent the winter, all of them heading for the exposed rocks where a nest of stones could be built. The females had followed them for the brief mating season, and their pairs of eggs would soon be deposited amongst the stones. Rook stopped the skidoo a hundred yards short of the rocks, and first Jochen and then Laure dismounted. Jochen shouldered his bag but Rook hoisted Laure's and carried it for her. It was extremely heavy, he noted. She gave him a quick smile of gratitude from under the peak of her parka hood.

As they crested the rise, the noise of the rookery burst on them. It was a solid and constant chorus of guttural chirring. The rocks seethed with a black-and-white tide as late arrivals searched for last year's mates or for new partners, and new nest builders tried to thieve stones from established pairs. There was a flurry of flippers and beaks everywhere, covering every inch of rock. The smell was as powerful as the noise. It was a piquant mixture of fish and oil and guano, and it permeated the clothes and hair and even the skin of anyone who ventured near. One night at the base, after a day's work at the rookery, Laure had buried her face in her gloves and exclaimed 'Parfum de pingouin' with as much delight as if it were Chanel No. 5. She loved everything about penguins and Rook liked her for that. He could hardly distinguish what the other scientists specialised in. Especially Shoesmith. Shoesmith was the most bloodless man he had ever met. He sat over his papers as impassively as if he were carved out of wax.

Rook carried Laure's pack to the point a few

yards from the colony's edge where a hump in the snow made a small vantage point. He was happy to help her, but he also liked seeing the penguins. There was a whole miniature universe of greed and ambition and devotion and determination crowded on this expanse of rock at the bottom of the world.

As he watched, one bird turned its back on its perfunctory nest, and instantly two rivals filched a stone apiece and dropped them into their adjacent nests. The original owner turned back and made a threatening flurry in each direction, beak wide with outrage. As Rook stood there, three apparently unmated birds marched across the snow to investigate him. They came fearlessly up to the toes of his boots, then stood with their flippers slightly akimbo. They turned their heads to gaze at him, their white-ringed eyes unblinking. After a minute one of them sank down on to its front as if exhausted by the effort of curiosity.

Laure and Jochen unpacked the equipment. At this stage the task was to map the nest sites and ring-mark some of the birds. Later in the season, once the chicks were hatched and established, Laure would take feather and blood samples from her ringed birds for DNA analysis back in Paris. One of her studies, Rook had learned, related to the amount of heavy metals and toxic elements accumulated in the birds' feathers. The annual accumulation of pollutants could be measured and so provide a precise bio-indicator of new pollution levels on the subcontinent.

This was the gist of what she had told him one night at dinner, in her perfect English. In spite of himself he was interested. To emphasise something about penguin behaviour that particularly intrigued her she would rest her hand lightly on his arm.

It had become accepted that everyone sat in the same places every night, so now Laure was always on his right and Phil on his left. Shoesmith presided at the table's head, of course.

Laure had her net. She made a quiet circuit past the nests of birds she had already marked, then deftly swooped on a bird quietly sitting with its back to her. Once it was netted, she slipped a hood over its head. The extinguishing of daylight fooled it into lying still, she had explained to Rook, and she could either ring its leg or fire a microchip into a flipper. Jochen followed behind her, an eager assistant, and they moved deeper into the penguin universe.

Rooker would have liked to stay longer out here, watching the birds, but there was the ship and the new arrival. Of course, Russ or Shoesmith himself could have taken the Zodiac out, but whereas Shoesmith was flexible with the other members of the expedition he seemed to expect Rooker to do everything that fell within his area of responsibility, without assistance from anyone else. So he checked the radio link with Jochen and then left them to their work.

As he came over the headland, Rooker saw the supply ship already gliding towards the mouth of the bay. It was only a small cargo vessel with an ugly high prow and a squat bridge tower, but it looked huge against the black water and the white-draped cliffs. The cabin and mast lights made a glittering garland in so much emptiness.

The sea was getting choppy in the wind, with ice rattling and churning in the swell. It wouldn't be an easy journey in the inflatable. It would have been much better if the ship could have come closer in to shore, but the bay was too shallow. It was one of the reasons why the British had withdrawn from Kandahar. There was no deep-water landing in the summer season, and in winter the sea froze and the base became inaccessible by ship.

Either he made the pick-up right now, Rook thought, or the new arrival would have to stay on the ship until after the storm.

As he passed the radio room at one end of the lab hut he heard Niki's voice.

'MV *Polar Star*, MV *Polar Star*, this is Kandahar Station. Do you read me? Over.'

The laconic voice of the ship's radio op crackled back. Rook waited until Niki pushed his headset aside and gave him the thumbs up.

'The lady waits for you.'

Rook tramped to the main hut and exchanged his parka for a huge orange float suit. To fall into these ice-bound waters without protection would mean death within minutes. As he zipped himself in he saw that the table was laid for tea with Russell's fresh loaf, jam and a plate of chocolate cupcakes. Shoesmith was hovering nearby while Russ and Arturo, the precise little Spanish climatologist, pulled on chest-high waders.

'We'll give you a hand, mate,' Russ said.

Rooker took a spare life-vest. The three of them scrambled down the rocks to the shingle beach and ran over the jumble of ice and snow to the floating jetty where the Zodiac was tethered. It strained against the moorings as waves smashed around it. With Rook aboard, Russ and Arturo waited for a lull, then rushed the black inflatable out into waist-deep water. Rook lowered the outboard and to his relief it fired at the first pull. He was already broadside to the waves racing into the bay. A big one rushed at him and almost tipped the Zodiac over. He brought the boat round into the wind and opened the throttle. The inflatable roared forward, the prow lifting as high as his head as it breasted the waves, and ice and scudding water punched the rubber floor as he headed for the bay mouth.

The air was thick with spray and sea mist and gouts of snow. He turned on the powerful lamp he had brought with him and scanned the mass of heaving water for the ship. He caught sight of the masts pitching in the distance and drove steadily towards the lights.

CHAPTER SIX

Alice stood at the ship's rail with her kitbags at her feet. She had spotted the station in the distance—it was nothing more than a pair of reddish specks marooned against a vast expanse of hostile emptiness. Then the clouds of snow and fog closed in again to obliterate even that much.

The breadth of the land's desolation made her feel afraid, even though she had been longing for this moment ever since the ship had left Chile. She had been abjectly seasick for three days. The only glimpse she had caught of the Antarctic coast, when it finally appeared out of seas as high as mountains, had been through her cabin porthole. Yet now the moment had come to leave the little ship and the friendly Spanish crew, she was full of misgivings. She clamped her hands on the icy rail.

The base looked so tiny and she knew just how remote it was. More than three days' sailing to reach the southernmost tip of a distant continent again, then twenty-four hours of flying to reach home.

Two sailors lowered the flight of metal steps at the ship's side. As the ship rolled, the platform at the bottom plunged under several feet of glassy water, then it rocked up again with spray cascading off it. One of the sailors drew a finger across his throat and winked at her. Weakly, Alice smiled back.

Over the drumming of the ship's engines, she caught the higher-pitched note of another engine. At the same moment a nimbus of light formed in the white murk. The sailors ran down the heaving steps as confidently as if they had been a set of stairs in Benidorm. On the platform they unhitched ropes and waited. A black dinghy, pitched at a threatening angle, materialised behind the smear of light. A big man in orange waterproofs swept the tiller in an arc, the boat crested a wave and landed neatly at the foot of the steps.

One sailor made it fast to the steps, so that ship and Zodiac rolled in unison. Waves swept over the dinghy and the platform, and ice-clogged water cascaded everywhere. The other sailor ran nimbly up the steps again, grabbed Alice's luggage and yelled *'Vamos!'* at her. She let go of the railings.

The metal treads were steep and slippery. With Spanish instructions and the boatman's terse commands both unintelligible through the din of engines and surf, she half scrambled and half slithered down to the platform. Water immediately submerged it. The man's orange arm grabbed her and hoisted as the dinghy flew upwards like a fairground ride. On the downwards plunge Alice launched herself with a sob of panic on to the dinghy's floor. Her bags tumbled in after her and some nets of more-or-less-fresh vegetables.

The ropes snaked away and the Zodiac roared free from the ship's flank.

With his eyes on the white wave caps, the boatman kicked a red life-vest towards where Alice was cowering amongst the bags of onions and peppers. The water's cold sucked all the breath out of her. 'Put that on,' he shouted without taking his eyes off the sea.

She struggled to get her arms through the holes and fasten the clasps across her chest. A rogue wave broke amidships and icy spray stung her face. Even though she was wearing weatherproofs she felt she was soaked to the skin. Her teeth chattered uncontrollably.

Behind her there were two long blasts on the ship's hooter. Up on the bridge the captain and the mate were wishing the English scientist *bon voyage*.

The dinghy man loomed above her with his feet braced, one hand on the tiller, the other clasping a radio. He shouted again and Alice thought she caught the words *five minutes*. She huddled on the floor of the dinghy and prayed that they would either be ashore or dead within that time. She didn't even care which, so long as it was fast.

The Zodiac and the waves raced each other to the shore. She had never been so far from home or felt the effects of distance so acutely. Nor had she ever been so apprehensive of what lay ahead of her.

*　　　*　　　*

It had happened with bewildering speed. It was barely a month since she had arrived at Lewis Sullavan's London headquarters to be interviewed by Dr Richard Shoesmith.

The walls of the Sullavanco foyer were hung with representations of Sullavan newspaper front pages cast in bronze and television screens showed Sullavan TV programmes from around the world. There were three receptionists with identical smiles behind a long curved reception desk made of polished wood.

'The Polar Office? You'll find it on the fifth floor, if you'll take the lift behind you.'

The lift was one of the kind that slides up a glass tube mounted on the outside of the building and which always tended to give her vertigo. The carpet of the fifth-floor corridor seemed to rise up to meet her as she stepped out and she steadied herself with one hand against the inner wall.

The Polar Office receptionist sat behind another sleek expanse of curved wood. There was an arrangement of hot-orange flowers at one end of it that made Alice think of Margaret.

'Dr Shoesmith shouldn't keep you too long,' the receptionist said.

A secretary brought Alice a cup of coffee while she waited. This was all so mutedly but distinctly high-rent that it made her smile. It couldn't have been further from the dowdy clutter of the Department of Geology, or any other academic institution she had ever known. If the Polar Office was anything to go by, Kandahar Station would have an indoor swimming pool and a resident

101

manicurist.

Dr Richard Shoesmith did keep her waiting—a full twenty minutes. When he finally emerged from his inner office Alice saw a compact man perhaps ten years older than herself. He was noticeably good-looking, but there were pale vertical furrows etched between his eyebrows that stood out against his weather-beaten skin. When they shook, his hand enveloped hers. He looked fit and slightly out of place in the plush Sullavan offices.

'I'm sorry, Dr Peel. I was talking to the French. They maintain a full research programme of their own down south, as you know. There are Antarctic politics, as there are politics everywhere else in the world.'

'Yes.' Alice smiled.

They sat down, Shoesmith behind his desk, and Alice to one side and in a slightly lower chair.

'You have no previous Antarctic experience,' he began.

'None,' she said steadily.

He looked through a neat sheaf of documents. She could see that there were offprints of some her published research papers, a copy of the full academic CV she had submitted at the request of Beverley Winston, Lewis Sullavan's assistant. There was also an excellent reference provided by Professor Devine.

'Hmm. Doctoral studies, carbonate sedimentary rocks, western Turkey. Lecturer in sedimentology, University of Oxford . . . proposed area of study . . . mapping, stratigraphic survey and dating of sedimentary rock formations in the vicinity of . . . Yes.' Richard looked up abruptly and his eyes held Alice's. His gaze was unblinking. 'Lewis is very eager to have you join the expedition.'

Cautiously, Alice nodded.

'Perhaps you could give me your own reasons.'

She looked straight back at him. She would have to be honest. 'The enthusiast was originally my mother. She was, is . . .'

'Yes, I know who your mother is.'

Of course he did.

There was a small silence. Shoesmith was still waiting. Alice added softly, 'I have thought about it a great deal since the suggestion was first made.'

The truth was that an entirely unexpected desire had taken hold of her.

It wasn't to do with geological research, although her academic appetite for the new realm of Antarctic rock was beginning to grow. It wasn't even for Margaret's sake, although of course that was a part of it. It was much more that she wanted to push out from the secure corner of her own life, the place that her crumbled illusions about Peter had left dusty and unpopulated, and to turn disappointment into discovery.

All her knowledge of the south was second-hand, straitjacketed by book covers or seen through the tunnel of a camera lens. There was none of her own history in it, although its history surrounded her. She had been keeping her mind closed to it for years, until Margaret and Lewis Sullavan together had opened a door. And now the very remoteness and the blank page that it would offer had begun to draw her, as forcibly as they had once repelled.

She began to dream of Antarctica, vivid dreams painted in ice colours and scoured with blizzards. She woke up from these dreams relieved to find herself in her own bed and yet impatient with the confines of ordinary life.

Beyond the shaded windows of the Polar Office lay the olive-green river, threaded by tourist boats and police launches, and the dome of St Paul's and the busy bridges, the complicated and familiar web of London. Alice thought of the roads leading away from the centre, skeins of motorways passing the airports, the route that would take her back to Oxford, to the quiet house in Jericho where Pete no longer lived, and all the other avenues and niches of a populated world. Was going to Antarctica just running away from the overfamiliar, from the present disappointment of reality?

No one who went to the ice ever came back unchanged: Alice had heard that often enough, even from Margaret, the arch-unsentimentalist. Probably everyone who found themselves drawn south was on the run from someone, or something, and that included Richard Shoesmith. But she was running towards it too, faster and faster every day. The sound of her own footsteps pounded a drumbeat rhythm in her head.

She was ready to be changed.

Richard Shoesmith was waiting for her answer.

Alice felt her legs shaking and the palms of her hands grew damp. She crossed her ankles in the opposite direction and let her hands lie composedly in her lap, but even so she was sure he read the unscientific glitter in her eyes. She didn't think Shoesmith missed much. 'I want to see it for myself,' she said.

'Go on, please.'

Knowing that this was not the time to mention dreams of ice, or of running anywhere, she talked about European scientific co-operation, Antarctic geopolitics and the unrivalled opportunity to undertake valuable research. The words were measured, but eagerness coloured them and her voice shivered just audibly with absolute longing.

Richard Shoesmith took all of this in. His expression didn't change as he listened to her, but some of the rigidity seemed to melt out of him.

'It is a chance that any geologist would jump at, Dr Peel. A complete field season, automatic full funding, the opportunity to make your mark as part of a team at a brand-new station.'

'Yes. I do appreciate that.'

He picked up a smooth ovoid rock from his desktop and meditatively turned it in his fingers. Embedded in the dark siltstone Alice could see the pale, distinct bullet shape of a Jurassic belemnite. 'Because of the nature of our present funding, in the selection of personnel for this expedition there is an inevitable element of, how shall I put it, who you are and whom you know?'

He was looking down at the fossil, not at her.

Alice smiled before she said delicately, 'I think we both understand that.'

Because she knew about Richard Shoesmith, just as he knew about her and her mother's reputation.

Shoesmith was a famous name, but not by reason of Richard's own achievements. He was a palaeontologist. He had completed his PhD at Cardiff, had done post-doctoral work at the University of Texas, held a research post at Warwick and was currently Reader in Palaeontology there. She had pulled out some of his papers and read them attentively. He had done some new work on evolution and extinction of certain cephalopods and gastropods at the end of the Cretaceous, but he didn't have a big reputation in his field.

His grandfather, however, was Gregory Shoesmith.

As a twenty-two-year-old alpinist, poet and gentleman botanist, Gregory had been one of the youngest members of Scott's Terra Nova expedition. As an explorer he had acquitted himself with quiet bravery and dignity, and Mount Shoesmith, the majestic peak overlooking the Beardmore Glacier, was named after him. But it was for his poem, 'Remember This, When I Am Best Forgotten', that he was famous. For every schoolchild of the last century it was the epitaph for the heroic age of polar exploration.

Gregory came home from the ice with what was left of Scott's expedition and had almost immediately enlisted. He survived the entire war and was awarded the VC. He was widowed while he was still a young man, then married again in his forties. His second wife had three children and the youngest of these, a career soldier, was Richard Shoesmith's father. As the child of a services family Richard had seen his father's postings all over the world, but mostly he had grown up in English boarding schools.

This much Alice knew as fact. She also knew by intuition that she and Richard Shoesmith suffered in common the sun and shadow effect of their family reputations. For Lewis Sullavan it made perfect sense to have Gregory Shoesmith's grandson leading his first expedition, just as it would to have Margaret Mather's daughter amongst the scientists. Who you are, as Richard put it, provided them both with enviable opportunities. And the two of them had always to live without the certainty that what they did achieve was on their own merits.

Richard put down the belemnite stone but his fingers still rested on it, as if for reassurance. He considered for a moment, then seemed to reach a decision. 'Are you free to travel south at this short notice? Most of the members will be at Kandahar by the middle of October.'

A little more than two weeks' time.

Alice thought quickly. 'My mother has been very ill recently, but she's recovering. She would be there herself if it were possible and because it isn't she very much wants me to go in her place. Apart from my parents, I don't have any other ties. I could be at Kandahar in a month's time, if that would be acceptable.'

A silence fell. With his head turned to the city view of towers and cranes, and his fingers minutely caressing the stone, Richard was thinking. On the wall behind him was a framed aerial photograph of a slice of Antarctic coastline. It was a black-and-white image in which the sea was inky black and the mainland mountain peaks stood out in stark whiteness, ribbed with shadows almost as black and deep as the waters. In the fretted indentations of U-shaped bays, ice showed up in milky swirls as diaphanous as torn muslin. At such a distance the treacherous glaciers looked as innocuous as wrinkled skin on some great cooling and congealing milk pudding. Somewhere, on that peninsular margin between black water and white ice, lay Kandahar Station.

'As I told you, Lewis is strongly in favour of your joining us. And I would be happy to accede to that.'

She thought that this cool assurance was the last word, but then he surprised her.

'I love Antarctica with all my heart. I've always loved it, first the idea and then the reality. It's the only place, the only thing I have ever known that is always more beautiful than its admirers can convey, more seductive and more dangerous than its reputation allows. You can never forget it, and it never releases its hold on you. I hope that it will come to be just as important to you.'

'I hope so too,' Alice said. And then she smiled. It was her wide, infrequent and startlingly brilliant smile. 'Thank you.'

Richard coughed and turned his attention to a separate set of papers on his tidy desk. 'However, there are a number of things you will need to do before you can definitely join us. Medical and dental check-ups, and so forth. Beverley Winston will arrange for you to be kitted out with polar gear. Everything is supplied, with the Sullavan Company logo as well as the EU flag. You will also have to do some basic survival training. The British Antarctic Survey people have kindly agreed to provide that for our UK members, in the spirit of European unity and co-operation.' He smiled drily.

'At such short notice you may not have the opportunity to meet the other members of the expedition together, or even individually, before we all reach Kandahar. We're a far-flung group, geographically speaking. Which is part of the idea, of course—not to gather a little coterie of chums who were all at Cambridge together.'

Richard Shoesmith didn't belong to any such coterie, Alice understood. Nor did Lewis Sullavan.

'We shall be a full-season core of just ten people

in all. Six scientists, including yourself, and four support staff.'

She read the list of names that he passed across the desk to her.

Eight people she didn't yet know, with whom she would spend five months in a hut perched on the white margin at the distant end of the earth. Outside, in London, toy boats were plying their way up and down the river, and taxis were being hailed to take businessmen to lunch.

'Six nationalities,' Richard said. 'Seven, if you count Welsh. This is not a huge Antarctic research station like McMurdo or even Rothera. We shall be pioneers on an old base and we'll set out with no rules except safety regulations. We are there to help one another and to co-operate in everything from science to international understanding to cleaning the base kitchen. If there is a job that needs to be done, any job whatsoever, you will be expected to help out with it.'

A slow flush darkened Richard's already ruddy cheeks. He was moved by the thought of this, of their tightly knit and multinational group working together outside the common conventions, and Alice found that she was touched in response.

'You know your polar history? Of course you do. You know that Amundsen's bid for the Pole was for Norway's sake. It was a matter of national ambition and pride. Whereas Scott wanted the Pole, of course, but the real reason for his expeditions, the ideal that he and his team all fought and risked their lives for, was scientific exploration and discovery. We shall also be there for science's sake.'

She understood that Richard Shoesmith was a scientist through and through. He would be a meticulous, painstaking investigator but he almost certainly wouldn't write poetry passionate enough to inspire two generations, as his gentleman-botanist grandfather had done. Alice's sympathy and liking for him grew.

'Yes,' she said.

The meeting was drawing to a close. They talked for a few more minutes about the practicalities of preparation and travel, then Alice stood up and Richard walked with her to the door. They were shaking hands when he said, 'Are you free for lunch?'

It was twenty minutes past twelve and she had arranged to meet Becky at one o'clock in a bar in Clerkenwell. 'I'm sorry. I'm on my way to see a friend.'

He didn't have to ask her to lunch, it wasn't a part of the vetting process. He was asking because he wanted to. They recognised each other. She smiled at him again.

'Of course. Well, then, good luck with your medicals and so forth. We'll speak.'

'Yes. Thank you for asking me to join the expedition. I'm looking forward to it.'

As their eyes met for the last time they acknowledged this for a comical understatement.

Alice sailed down in the bubble lift, crossed the grandiose foyer and walked out into the cloudy morning. There was the smell of river and the dampness of autumn in the air. The faces of people walking towards her had acquired extra definition, she could read the words on the sides of buses crawling over Blackfriars Bridge. All her senses were heightened and sharpened with the intensity of anticipation. She had been insulated by her own circumspection, but now she was going into the unknown.

*　　　*　　　*

Becky was waiting. Her legs were hooked round a bar stool made of tortured metal, there was a drink on the table beside her and her head was bent over the *Evening Standard*. Wings of smooth hair swung forward to curtain her face and then she looked up and saw Alice. 'How did it go? No, I can see. You're the polar queen. You're really going? My God, Al, you *are*. C'mon, let's drink to it.'

Alice laughed. She couldn't quite catch her breath. 'I'm going,' she said faintly. 'I hardly know how it's happened, but I am.'

'How long?'

'Five months. The summer field season. I'll be leaving at the end of October and I'll be back in March.'

A drink materialised beside her. A long glass, ice, jaunty coloured straw. She took a long suck and almost choked with the intensity of the taste. Alcohol immediately fumed in her head.

Becky was wearing a khaki combat top with pockets and buttons and epaulettes, but the fabric was contradictory slippery satin. The way the light fell on it and reflected different sumptuous colours caught Alice's eye. Pete used to talk about colour, she remembered, as if it were food or sex.

Look at this carmine, look at this crocus-yellow. Don't you want to eat it? Don't you want to *lick* it?

'Alice? Are you okay?'

'Yes. I'm fine. I'm just getting used to the idea.'

'So let's talk about it. Tell me all.' Becky's

111

appetite for other people's lives was as keen as for her own.

Alice told her about Richard Shoesmith, and the list of names, and the sharing of work, and the tasks she would have to accomplish before she could leave. All the time she was reminding herself that she was cutting loose from everything she knew and heading for a place on which she had always, from her earliest memories, deliberately turned her back.

Is this how it happens, she wondered, in other people's lives? The moving on and the changing and the randomness that never seemed to affect her, only the people she knew? And then a series of events and coincidences link together and what was impossible at one moment becomes inevitable in the next?

'What about the house?' Becky was asking.

'Oh, I'll let it for this academic year,' Alice improvised. 'Maybe I'll travel for a couple of months on the way back. It would be a shame not to, wouldn't it? I've never been to South America.'

Becky was looking at her. 'What about Pete?'

'There's nothing much to tell. He moved out.'

'Is that it?'

*   *   *

While Margaret was still dangerously ill, Alice stayed at the house on Boar's Hill. Pete telephoned again and again, and when she wouldn't speak to him he turned up unannounced at her office one afternoon. She looked up from her desk to see him in the doorway—or a more than usually unshaven, crumpled, wild-haired version of him. He was carrying a bunch of florists' roses, dark red.

'Pete, don't do this.'

'What am I supposed to do?' he demanded. 'You won't see me, you won't talk to me. You won't let me explain what happened.'

'I don't think what I saw needs any explaining, does it?'

He looked around, then thrust the flowers in the jug she used for watering her pot plants. He slumped down on the only spare chair and put his head in his hands. His hair stuck up in spikes, as if he had been running his fingers through it in steady desperation. Of course Pete would turn rejection in love into a piece of performance art. He wouldn't be shaving, on principle, or eating or sleeping.

'I can't sleep. I've lost my appetite. Alice, it isn't *funny*. Why are you so fucking empirical about everything? I love you and I miss you, that's all that matters. I want you to come home.'

'Pete. I came to your studio and found you engaged in oral sex with one of your students. The same one I saw you on the river with, and the one you were kissing at our party. On the other hand Harry saw you in a pub in Bicester, kissing someone entirely different . . .'

'What? I don't think I've been anywhere near bloody Bicester in ten years.'

'. . . I am empirical, if you mean that I base my reaction to you on the results of observation. How else am I supposed to respond to the evidence? "Oh, look, there's Peter with Georgia. What he's doing actually proves how much he loves me."'

'I can't bear it when you're sarcastic. It doesn't suit you.'

'It doesn't really matter any more what you can

113

and can't bear about me.'

'Alice *please*.' He got up again and came to her. He put his arms round her and tried to draw her against him. He cupped the back of her head in his hand and rubbed her hair. It would have been very easy, knowing and missing the warmth and the smell of him as she did, to give way and bury her face in his shoulder and pretend that she believed him. But a pretence was what it would have been, and Alice preferred meagre facts to the most colourful and persuasive elaborations on the truth.

'I want you to move out. I am going to stay at my parents' house until you do. You've got time to find somewhere else, but that's what I want you to do.'

His face changed.

Under the veneer of his remorse there had been confidence, because he had assumed that he would be able to win her round. Realising this made her feel still more dismal. If he thought that, it was obvious that Pete had never really known her properly. They had shared a bed and made a home and a life together, and still she might as well have been a stranger, or Georgia, or the woman in the pub. It made her want to cry, but she couldn't bear to give way to that impulse either. She looked steadily back at him, dry-eyed.

'I see,' he said at last.

To do him credit, he didn't argue any more then. And he packed his belongings and moved out of the house within two days. He left a note for her on the kitchen table, weighted at one corner by the teapot still half-full of cold tea. The note said that he loved her even if he had a strange way of showing it and that as far as he was concerned this wasn't the end of things between them. Alice

114

crumpled the single sheet of paper into a ball and threw it into the kitchen bin.

*   *   *

'Yes, that's it,' she told Becky.

'I'm sorry, darling. He made you happy, you know. You were happy all this year. You laughed all the time and you didn't take your responsibilities as seriously as you usually do. Pete made you just a little bit frivolous.'

'I do know that.'

They had ordered some food and now it was put in front of them. Thinking she was ravenous, Alice had ordered seared tuna and glass noodles. Now she noticed that there were sesame seeds in the dressing and they looked like tiny myriapods. If she examined them more closely she imagined that she would see the filaments of their legs. Very deliberately she sliced a corner of fish, wound it in a web of noodle and placed it in her mouth. The food had a strange metallic taste.

'Alice, are you sure you're all right?'

'Yes, of course I am.' She smiled at Becky. 'I've learned to be frivolous. I've got it completely sorted. I don't need Pete and his antics. I'm just dropping everything and swanning off to Antarctica for months, aren't I?'

'That doesn't sound particularly carefree and impetuous to me. It sounds very uncomfortable and rather dangerous.'

'But I get to look at 400-million-year-old sedimentary rocks that hardly anyone's ever seen before. I'll wear a butch survival suit and learn how to drive a skidoo and how to rescue myself from a

115

crevasse, and on really good days I'll get a turn at cleaning the base kitchen. Dr Shoesmith promised me that.' Her gaiety was convincing to herself, at least.

'Oh, God.' Becky grimaced.

Through the open fronts of her Christian Louboutin sandals, her toenails were clearly visible. They were painted a softly luminous shell-pink and each nail was delicately rimmed in white. Her legs were smooth and tanned, and her fingernails were manicured too. There were small diamond studs in her ears and everything about her said *clean*. They looked at each other and laughed.

Alice realised that she had finished her drink and had even drunk most of the melted ice.

'Shall we have another couple of these?'

'I've got to work this afternoon, unfortunately. But what the hell. I'll have a glass of wine,' Becky said. 'You will come *back* safely from down there, won't you?'

'I will,' Alice promised.

No one ever comes back unchanged, she remembered.

'How does Jo seem?' Becky asked.

They drank their wine and Becky finished her food. They talked about Jo and the babies and whether Vijay was exactly or only approximately the man Becky was looking for. None of this was any different from the dozen lunches that Becky and she had shared this year alone, but Alice felt as if she had moved a little distance apart. There was a voice in her ear, a waterfall of syllables. *Antarctica*.

*   *   *

116

From the upright chair beside her bed, Margaret saw Alice walk down the ward towards her. She didn't want Alice to know how anxiously she had been looking out for her so she allowed herself only the quickest glance before composedly folding the newspaper in her lap. But she could see even in a second that there was more colour about her, her face had opened like a flower in the sun. The news must be good.

A flood of memories rose up and washed away the stuffy ward. Almost exactly forty years ago she had felt like Alice looked now: poised on the brink of the central years of her life with the whole breadth of Antarctica waiting for her. Even now, with pain twisting her joints so cruelly that she could hardly stand, she could remember what it was like to lie in a field tent with the wind banging and raging at the walls, or to stare down into the greedy blue throat of a crevasse where a snow bridge threatened to collapse in the late-season sun. Antarctica was a painful, perfect place. There was the astringent flavour of envy in Margaret's mouth and she reminded herself that it was absurd to feel envy at her age. Alice would go back there instead of her. Through Alice she would live in Antarctica one more time.

'There you are. What an age you've been, when I'm dying to hear all about it. Sit down. No, wait. Could you get that girl to bring us a cup of tea, d'you think?'

Alice kissed the top of Margaret's head where the shiny pink of her scalp showed through the strands of thinning hair. 'Do you want tea, before I tell you?'

117

'Don't be so damned annoying. Put me out of my misery.'

'Yes. I'm going. All right?'

Margaret's face sagged briefly with relief and the cross-hatching of tiny lines deepened beneath her eyes. 'Good,' she said firmly and took possession of her face once more.

Alice sat down and Margaret listened intently as she described her hour with Richard Shoesmith.

'I met his grandfather, you know,' Margaret said.

Gregory Shoesmith had been an old man, sitting with a plaid rug over his knees and a stick leaning against his chair—*just like me, now. Where do time and strength slip away to?*—but he had taken her hand between his two and leaned forward so their faces almost touched. He said, 'We have been privileged, you and I. We have seen places that we will never forget.' He had known war and too many deaths, and he had lived a long life, but it was the ice that filled his mind. Even in old age he was a powerful man.

Alice didn't look surprised. 'You met everyone.'

Margaret was listening, her head nodded at every point that Alice made, but she was caught up in the teeming mass of her memories. They swirled around her, thicker and faster, like a blizzard. Alice would inherit the memories. They would be different in their precise content but they would be made of the same material. It was like handing on your own genes, mother to daughter. Antarctica was what made me, Margaret thought. It will be the making of my child too, and she needs that. Alice has always been reticent, and now she will come into bloom.

Margaret had no fears for her, any more than

118

she had ever had for herself.

It had started to rain, and thick runnels slid down the windows. It was making her eyes swim. To clear her vision she looked down at her hands, resting on the blue cellular blanket that covered her knees. It always surprised her to realise that these veined and knotted appendages, with their swollen knuckles and brown blotches, were her own hands that had once been so strong and dexterous. The pain in her joints and in her chest sometimes seemed to belong to someone else too, to some old person who was leaning on her and whose weight she could thrust aside and step lightly away from.

Alice was talking about medical assessment.

'Don't worry about that,' Margaret said. Alice was so young, she moved so unthinkingly and confidently. 'You're just like me. As I used to be. Strong as a horse.'

'And less skittish.' Alice smiled. 'Than a horse, I mean.'

Margaret was tired now. She wanted to lie down and close her eyes, and think about what she had done and what Alice would do.

Alice saw it and she stood up, pretending to look at her watch. 'I'll come in tomorrow.'

'Do that. There's a lot you'll need to know.'

They kissed each other quickly.

'I'm glad, Mum. I'm glad to be going.'

'That's good,' Margaret answered. She was thinking, I may be old but I'm not daft. I know what it takes to do well down there and you have it, my Alice. You're more like me than you want to admit.

Three hectic weeks had followed. Alice fitted in all the things she had to do, but only just. She went to see Dr Davey, who had been the family doctor ever since she was born.

'You've never had a day's illness in your life, my dear. I don't need to run a battery of expensive tests to know you are in perfect health.'

He ticked a long list of questions, scribbled a paragraph at the end and signed the medical declaration. Alice countersigned it and sent it off to Beverley Winston.

She visited her dentist and had all her fillings checked. She went up to London and at a Sullavan-owned warehouse near the North Circular Road she was issued with her polar kit by a man with a heavy cold, who told her that he had spent six winter seasons down on the ice. There was a bewildering pile of fleece and Gore-tex inner and outer garments, all marked with the EU flag and Sullavanco logo, just as Richard had described. The massive red outer jacket, with matching windpants, had a big white rectangle on the back with the words '1st EU Antarctic Expedition' stitched on it. On the front there was a Velcro sticker that read simply 'Peel'. There was a pair of boots with insulated liners. And there was a balaclava helmet that covered her head except for a narrow eye slit. It was hot in the warehouse, and just trying all these items on made sweat run down and pool in the small of her back.

'Good lug,' the man with the cold said as she tottered away with her new wardrobe.

She went up to Cambridge for a three-day

induction course run by the British Antarctic Survey for their own departing personnel, where she was the object of curiosity and envy.

'I hear you people have got unlimited funding,' a sandy-haired climatologist remarked enviously. 'While we have to sign for every specimen bag and camp meal.'

A man wearing a jacket and tie laughed over his pint of beer. 'Sullavan will need to spend a few of his millions putting Kandahar straight. How long is it since we pulled out of there?'

'He wouldn't even notice it, whatever it costs him. There'll be en suite bathrooms and waiter service. Bit different from what we can expect, eh, Jack?'

The BAS men roared with laughter and Alice smiled politely.

They all went to lectures about the dangers of frostbite, and glacier travel, and ecological disposal of waste matter. There were practical sessions about mountaineering and survival. Trevor had taught Alice the basics of rock climbing on their Alpine holidays together. The instructor didn't patronise her quite so much when he realised that she knew how to put on a climbing harness and could tie a figure of eight knot in a rope.

The preparations absorbed her attention on one level; on another she observed her own dashings around as if she had become a stranger. Even her body felt slightly unfamiliar. She had lost her appetite, and if she sat down to collect her thoughts between work and meetings and lists she found herself on the brink of falling asleep. This she put down to being too busy, to delayed anxiety about Margaret and perhaps a reaction to Peter's absence. He often slipped into her thoughts, but she wouldn't see him and she didn't even know where he was living.

The last week came. The plane tickets for her complicated journey south were sent down from the Polar Office and she propped the folder on the small mantelpiece in her bedroom. She packed and repacked her books and clothes in the big orange kitbags supplied for the purpose. The house was tidy and empty—everything she didn't need for Antarctica had been put into store, and the tenants would move in the day after her departure. It was odd to look from the bare rooms to the October sky beyond the windows, and to think of being away for a whole winter. When she came back the trees would be putting out new leaves. She watched the dazed new students flooding the streets and reflected that they would be confident old hands by the time she returned.

*   *   *

Two days before she left, Jo and Becky gave a goodbye party for her at Jo's house.

'Are you sure you can manage it?' Alice asked her in concern.

'It's getting much better. Charlie only woke up once and Leo twice last night. There were two whole hours when all three of us were asleep.'

It was a good party, but different.

Alice wore the long johns and balaclava and huge insulated boots, until she got too hot in the crush and discarded them behind Jo's sofa. She was pulling a fleece vest over her head and briefly revealing her black lace best bra, which had shrunk

122

in the wash and exposed an unusual depth of cleavage, when she looked up and saw Pete. His eyes travelled over her. He had shaved and, apart from a mournful expression, looked just as he always did.

'Did Jo . . . ?' Alice began, thinking that she would have preferred to know that he was coming.

He shook his head. 'Nope. I wasn't invited, but I came anyway and Harry didn't turn me away from the door. You look wonderful. You must be excited.'

'Oh, Pete.'

He held out his arms and she hesitated, then let them enclose her.

'Dance?' he asked.

She nodded and they swung across Harry's sanded and sealed floorboards. They had always moved well together, she thought.

At the end of the evening, when most of the guests had hugged Alice and said goodbye and told her that she must take care to come home safely, Pete was still there. He hadn't drunk very much, he had talked to everyone and bursts of laughter continually erupted around him. When he wanted to he could always make himself the centre of a gathering. Even though she hadn't intended it, Alice kept track of where he was in the room and listened for his voice through the hubbub of music. The past had been swallowed up, the future was unreadable, and the present was nothing but this instant's narrowest margin between sense and desire. She had the feeling that her good sense, always her strongest asset, was inexplicably deserting her.

It was time to go home. Alice had an armful of

good-luck presents, several of which were toy polar bears even though the nearest real polar bears to Antarctica lived in the Arctic.

Becky kissed her, cupping her face briefly in both hands. 'Come back soon, Ice Queen, d'you hear?'

Now that the moment was here, it seemed like for ever in prospect. Alice smiled as confidently as she could. 'It's six months or seven months at the very most. I'll be back before you've even noticed I've gone away.'

Jo and Harry stood in the hallway with light spilling out into the darkness beyond the porch. Their house was full of the warmth and laughter of the evening. Alice felt that she was moving out of the web of friendship and familiarity.

Jo kissed her too.

'Have a wonderful, thrilling time.' She was envious, Alice could hear it. Jo would like to be going but she was tied to this house by her babies and Harry. Would I change places? she wondered. Yes, she thought, with the sad picture in her head of her own house empty but for the last boxes stacked in the hallway, and yet with Pete at her shoulder as if nothing had ever gone wrong.

And then, *No*, I would not.

'Good luck, Al.' Jo and Becky and Harry and Vijay gathered in the doorway to wave goodbye. Alice looked back at the tableau they made and framed it in her mind.

'I'll see you home,' Pete murmured.

'Pete's going to see me home,' she called and they all nodded, waving and understanding perfectly.

They went in Alice's car, with Alice driving, but

124

he did jump out at the other end to open the car door for her. He followed her up the familiar path, took her key out of her hand and unlocked the front door as well. They half turned to each other, hesitating, then Pete tipped her face up to his. 'I wish you'd let me say I'm sorry.'

'You can say it.' Her voice was raw in her throat.

'I wish you'd let me show you I'm sorry.'

Alice lifted her hand. It started as a warding-off gesture but her fingers seemed to melt. They rippled over the vee of her top which felt too tight, as if it only just contained her breasts, and fluttered over her belly. Her skin seemed to have developed a million new nerve endings.

Why not? she thought.

Why not just once more, after so many other times?

'To say goodbye?' she murmured.

There was a flash of triumph in his eyes, quickly extinguished. But you are wrong, the triumph's really mine, she thought.

'If that's what you truly want to say,' he answered.

He followed her into the house and closed the door behind them.

The shelves in the bedroom, the top of the chest of drawers, the bedside tables were all bare. Alice's kitbags with the flag and logo stood packed against one wall.

Pete slid his hands over her, cupping her breasts, drawing her hips against him. 'You're different. You're lovelier,' he breathed.

Am I? I am not sure that I even recognise myself, she thought.

But her body remembered the familiar rhythms

125

well enough and improved on them. Their lovemaking had always been affectionate, well-practised, almost invariably satisfactory, but tonight it went much further than that. In the absence of intimacy and trust, they were naked and greedy.

Afterwards, Pete lay with his head against her heart, listening to its beat. Her hand lightly cupped the curve of his skull. She could feel his limbs growing heavy as he drifted towards sleep.

I have just taken what I wanted, she thought, without weighing up whether it would hurt him or not.

The notion of revenge had never crossed her mind and this didn't feel like it, but there was a symmetry here.

Alice closed her eyes and thought of the long journey ahead and the ice waiting for her at the end of it.

In the morning Pete sat at the kitchen table drinking tea and watching her as she made toast from the end of a loaf. She emptied the crumbs out of the bread bin and wiped the inside with a wadded paper towel. She would spend tonight, her last in Oxford, at Boar's Hill with Margaret and Trevor.

'Have you finished with your plate?'

He looked at her and she steadily returned his gaze.

'Are you going so far away because of me?' he asked.

She smiled. 'No, Pete. I'm going because of me. And partly because of Margaret.'

Peter sighed. He stood up and looked around the kitchen. 'I made a good job of those shelves.'

They had come in a flat pack from Ikea. He had

assembled them and fixed them to the wall.

Alice suddenly laughed. She felt the upward swing of happiness. Everything was going to be all right. 'You did,' she said softly.

'I'd better get to the studio, I suppose. I'm still working on *Desiderata*, you know.'

The sculpture with the polystyrene head.

'How's it going?'

'There's something mutinous about it.'

'I see.'

It was Pete's turn to laugh. His eyes crinkled and the inside of his mouth was red. 'My lovely Alice. What you see is figures and graphs.'

'So I haven't changed all that much.'

He turned serious again. 'I think maybe you have. *Desiderata* will be finished by the time you come home. I'd like to show it to you. We can talk about it.'

'If I can find the right language.'

He nodded, not really understanding her reservation. She saw him to the front door and he kissed her goodbye, gently, on the mouth.

'We're still friends, Alice, aren't we?'

'Yes, we are,' she reassured him.

*   *   *

Margaret had spent a lot of her time in bed since coming home from hospital, but tonight she was up and dressed in a trouser suit with a flowing emerald-green scarf tied round her hair. Working together, she and Trevor had even assembled a meal of boiled ham and beetroot. Trevor lit the candles in the seldom-used dining room and Alice carried through a tray of food laid out on the best china. It was a celebration evening.

Trevor raised his glass of wine to propose a toast. The candlelight made his bald head glisten. 'Here's to my two Antarctic heroines. I am so proud of you both.'

Margaret clapped her hands. Looking as excited as a child, she made Alice tell her all the details of her final preparations. She listened eagerly, nodding approval about notebooks and labels, and the difficult choices of books and CDs. She ate very little, but she was more animated than they had seen her for weeks.

'What do you know? You are not a polar hand like Alice and me,' she teased Trevor when he chipped in.

'Thank God for that. We can't all go off to the bottom of the world, can we? I will just be glad to see Alice home again. As I always was when you came back to me, my darling.'

Memories glimmered in Margaret's eyes. She was thinking about those reunions, and what had preceded them. Watching her, Alice had a renewed sense of how difficult it must have been for her father, all those years ago. He hadn't tried to follow his wife south, or to stop her doing what she was good at because it didn't include him or reflect on him. He had simply stepped back and given her the space. How did the old saying go? If you want to keep someone, first you have to set them free? She wondered briefly if that was what she was doing with Pete and laughed inwardly. What she was doing with him was setting him free, full stop. Antarctica had come in his place.

Tomorrow she would set off. The unimaginable vastness and the glamour of the ice left her breathless and thrilled with anticipation. She wondered if this was how her mother had felt too and when she looked through the candlelight into Margaret's face she knew for certain that it was.

There was a silver and cobalt-blue streak of mystery in Margaret, forged from what she had seen and done. Now, maybe, she would be able to know her better.

Trevor sat quietly between the two of them, eating his food and drinking his wine.

It was only when the meal was finished and Alice had cleared the table that they saw how tired Margaret was. Trevor blew out the candles and Alice helped Margaret slowly up the stairs. She sat her on the bed and took off her shoes and rolled down her socks for her. Her bare feet were cold and Alice rubbed them to bring back the circulation.

'We used to do that in the field. Warm each other's feet,' Margaret remembered.

'Who will warm mine? Richard Shoesmith?'

Margaret giggled and Alice eased off her trousers and top for her. Her skin was so thin it was almost translucent, like tissue paper.

'Where's your nightie?'

'Under the pillow. Darling, you're not going south just because of your . . . because of Peter, are you?'

Alice had played it down. She told Trevor and Margaret that she and Pete had just decided to go their separate ways.

'No. I'm going because it seems like a good idea.' They had an unspoken agreement up until now, the two of them, that they would treat Alice's departure lightly. 'It's only five months. Whatever happens, it's not very long and then I'll be home again. Back to the Department and field studies in Turkey and Iceland.'

Margaret held up her arms and as Alice slipped her nightdress over her head she said, almost to herself, 'It's not a matter of time. Antarctica makes a different dimension altogether. You'll understand me, when you get there, and you'll know there is no wiping it out. Always, for ever, you see everything in your life through its prism. Through a veil of diamond dust.'

'What's that?'

'Clear air ice precipitation. Below $-40°$ ice crystals form by spontaneous nucleation and are deposited usually in short bursts. Storms of glittering points of ice, falling out of a blue sky. It's beautiful.'

Margaret lay back against the pillows. Alice sat beside her and they held each other's hands.

'I will think of you, with diamond dust falling,' Margaret added, with the deepest satisfaction in her voice. She didn't warn her daughter to be careful or insist that she must come home safely. Alice knew that her mother was offering her what had been the best and biggest experience of her own life. It was a gesture that was at once expansive and profoundly selfish, and thus perfectly expressive of Margaret herself.

She bent forward and kissed her mother on the forehead. Margaret's eyes were already closed.

'Thank you,' Alice whispered. 'I will think of you too, with diamond dust falling.'

*   *   *

130

Trevor drove her to the airport for the evening flight to São Paolo, where she would connect with a flight to Santiago and thence to Punta Arenas at the tip of Chile. At Punta Arenas she would embark on a Spanish supply ship for a three-day voyage across the huge seas of the Drake Passage, to the Antarctic peninsula and Kandahar Station. Richard and the other expedition members had preceded her two weeks earlier. As a late recruit, this awkward journey was the best that the Polar Office had been able to arrange for her.

In the car they didn't talk much until the signs for Heathrow were flashing towards them. Trevor had always been an alarmingly fast driver.

'How do you feel?' he asked.

'I feel like an impostor. I'm not Mum, I'm not a pioneer or even an innovator. I'm scared that I'm going to turn up down there and someone will tap me on the shoulder and say, "Excuse me, we were expecting Margaret Mather." I'm afraid of letting her down.' And myself, she could have added, although that never seemed to loom as large in the ranks of anxieties.

Trevor took his hand off the wheel and patted her knee. He was overtaking a truck at the same time and Alice shrank in the passenger seat.

'Never feel that,' he ordered. 'You can never be an impostor.'

She smiled and he took hold of the wheel and righted the car again.

'We'll see,' she temporised. She was leaving many things behind but she carried his love with her, a thread as fine and as strong as a spider's silk.

They checked in her baggage and drank airport coffee at one of the depressing Terminal Three bars. Trevor bought her a sheaf of newspapers and magazines, and the handles of the plastic bag dug into her fingers as they walked around, killing time. She thought she had never loved him as much as she did now.

'What was it like, seeing her off all those years ago?'

'I wanted to plead with her not to go. So I was glad when she disappeared, that I hadn't given way to begging. Then I just waited for her to come back.'

If you want to keep someone, you have to set them free.

At the departure point, Trevor stood behind the barrier and watched while she queued up to have her passport checked. She turned back before slipping past the screen that would hide her from him.

She blew a kiss and her father held up his hand.

Then she walked forward, out of his sight, towards the luggage screening machines and the distant south.

*   *   *

The huts of Kandahar loomed closer through the mist and spray.

When Alice looked again there was a line of surf and black rocks. A jetty broke out of the fog and so did two more orange-suited men, standing up to their chests in water. One of them, extraordinarily, was grinning widely. The other was whistling, as if this scene happened every day.

The engine was cut. The two men seized the rope that ran along the pontoons and hauled the

Zodiac through the surf to its mooring. Alice hoisted herself from her ignominious position in the bottom of the boat. The Zodiac driver had his back to her, busy with shipping the outboard. His hood and goggles masked his face, and she had no idea which of the team members he might be. The two men in the water held out their arms, she sat up on the pontoon and they lifted her effortlessly over the surf and swung her down on to the icy beach. She staggered, unused to solid ground, and they grabbed her to set her upright again.

'Welcome to Antarctica,' the smaller one said.

CHAPTER SEVEN

Up on the rocky bluff a door opened and a shaft of yellow light shone through the icy murk. A moment later Alice was stumbling into Kandahar Station.

The two men had led the way, swinging her baggage between them as if it weighed nothing.

Inside the doorway she reached for her sodden hat and pulled it off. Wet hair fell around her cheeks, and sea water dripped off her and puddled on the floor. She glimpsed a big table, laid with an oilcloth, mugs and plates. There were shelves with a clutter of books, CDs and video tapes. The wooden walls were decorated with pictures and maps, all related to Antarctica, and with dozens of photographs of penguins and sunsets.

'Hello, Alice,' Richard Shoesmith said. 'Welcome to Kandahar.'

She blinked and tried to compose herself. Her eyes stung and her nose ran. 'I'm very pleased to be here,' she managed to gasp.

'Would you like a cup of tea?' Richard asked.

Laughter at the absurdity of this exchange, as well as relief, welled up inside her. Kandahar might be remote, but with Richard it was just as if she had arrived by the four-fifteen train for a particularly well-organised country-house weekend.

'I'd love a cup of tea.'

The bigger of the two men who had helped her out of the dinghy peeled off his waterproofs and squeezed her fingers in a powerful handshake. He was broad and solid, almost as bald as Trevor, and his fleece top stretched across his stomach.

'Russ Amory. Base manager.'

The other one was young, slim and black-haired, with a gold stud in his left ear. He shook her hand too, much more gently.

'Arturo Marenas. Climatologist.'

'Hello, Russ, Arturo. I'm Alice Peel.'

Russell roared with laughter. 'We guessed as much.'

She looked around the room again.

There was an L-shaped desk with radio equipment and a computer under one window, and next to the door a row of cupboards and hooks marked with individuals' names. At the opposite end was a metal-topped table, a sink and a big cooker, shelves with saucepans and dishes, a tall, humming refrigerator. The effect was cosy and crowded, but the homeliness still didn't disguise the splintering wood of the walls and the chipped and curling lino tiles on the floor. Kandahar hut had been neglected and hastily brought back into service. There was none of the opulence that Alice remembered from the Sullavanco offices in

London.

The indoor warmth was in sharp contrast with what she saw when she glanced through the window, which seemed to be cold nothing. The shoreline and the sea ought to have been visible, just a few yards away at the foot of the bluff on which the hut stood, but instead there was a faintly luminous, thick white wall.

'Yes, it's snowing a bit,' Richard said at her shoulder. 'Forecast's not so good for the next couple of days. Won't you sit down here?'

Russell sliced a loaf of bread and grinned at her. An immensely tall, cadaverous man came forward and was introduced as Nikolai Pocius.

'Radio operator, me,' he said in a heavy Russian-sounding accent.

Arturo was already at the table. 'It is important to take one's place early on the days when my friend Russ has made new bread. It would be a tragedy of the first degree to have not one's fair share,' he explained.

'I see.' She smiled.

She sat down next to Richard, who was at the head of the table. As he passed the jam and butter she realised that she was ravenous after days of seasickness. She bit luxuriously into a thick wedge of bread. It was as good as Arturo had suggested.

Russell poured tea and gave her a mug.

Richard explained, 'We've got two teams out working in the field this afternoon. Valentin with Phil on the glacier and Laure with Jochen at the rookery. But Rook's gone to pick them up before the weather comes in. I don't know when we'll be able to get outside again, if the forecast's correct.'

Alice was fitting faces to names. She had read

the expedition list over and over again, so it wasn't difficult. There were four people here and two pairs still out at work. So the boatman, the ninth, must be James Rooker.

'What happens while the weather's bad?' Alice asked.

'We wait. Do what lab work we can. Write notes. Do housework. Painting and decorating, if we have a mind to it.'

'And then wait also some more.' Arturo shrugged. He took a Marlboro out of a fresh pack and clicked his lighter to it. 'Welcome to Antarctica.'

She glanced again at the dense whiteness beyond the window. The contrast between their precarious pinpoint of warmth and comfort and the hostile infinity that lay outside grew stronger.

Richard Shoesmith saw her face and lightly patted her shoulder. 'Don't worry. It's early season yet. There's plenty of time to get out there and get the work done. We'll be at Wheeler's Bluff in two or three weeks' time.'

Richard had written to her that Wheeler's Bluff would be their first joint objective. It was a long reef of exposed rock that reared up out of the snow 200 miles inland from Kandahar. From their deep field camp at the Bluff, Alice would carry out a survey of the sedimentary layers and collect rocks for analysis and dating, while Richard searched for fossils. His examination and identification of whatever fossilised flora and fauna were present would in turn enable her to date her rock samples with precision.

'That's good,' Alice murmured.

She wasn't worried about the work itself. She

136

was sure that she could do it when the time came and she was looking forward to losing herself in a new chapter of geological history. As she traced the sedimentary layers of ancient lakes or river estuaries she often felt as if she were reading the earth's own book. It was just that in spite of the homeliness of new bread and raspberry jam, this place was as utterly unfamiliar as if she had landed on another planet. She also felt a prickle of apprehension at the prospect of snowbound isolation in a group of strangers. There was a long time in this place stretching ahead of her and only two months ago, before any of this was dreamed of, she had been walking across the sunlit Parks to where a punt was coming round a bend in the river.

'Would you like to see where you'll be sleeping?' Richard asked kindly.

'Yes, please.'

Arturo and Nikolai were still downing bread and jam.

'Cake! There's chocolate cake here,' Russ cried.

'I'll come back for it.'

'Don't take the risk, with these two skuas around.'

'I will be saving cake for you, Alice, don't worry,' Nikolai assured her seriously. Food was evidently a matter of importance at Kandahar.

The women's room contained two sets of bunk beds, at right angles to each other, two sets of lockers and hanging cupboards, and a window looking towards where the sea should have been visible. One of the lower bunks was taken, and there were books on the nearest locker and photographs pinned to the wall. A part-curtain for the bunk itself had been made from a towel draped over elasticated wire. These would be Laure Heber's belongings. Alice sat down on the other lower bunk and Richard put her kitbags on the floor beside it.

'Welcome to Kandahar,' he said again.

'Thank you.'

He hesitated, then added, 'After a few days you'll feel as if you've been down south for ever. You've struck a bit unlucky to have heavy weather to begin with, before you get your bearings. There are difficulties sometimes; when you're cooped up, everyone gets on top of each other. It's only to be expected.'

He shot her a sideways glance, tentative, half apologetic. He was giving her an oblique warning.

Yes, Alice thought. There was an edge, a certain wariness, in the atmosphere here. She had felt it already, out in the communal area. And Richard was right, of course. In an isolated, confined environment like this, small events would take on major significance. She remembered Margaret admitting as much, even if only to brush it aside. 'You learn to live with people,' she had said. In Margaret's day people had meant men. There were no other women.

On the shelf under the window there was a tube of handcream, a roll-on deodorant and a black quilted zipper bag with a Chanel logo that probably contained make-up. A lacy thong was drying on the wire next to the towel. The dainty femininity of all this was slightly surprising and also heartening. Alice wondered what her room-mate would be like and was glad to think that she might have an ally. It would be much harder to contemplate isolation like Margaret's.

'It will be fine. I'll be fine.' Her eyes met Richard's.

'Yes. I'm sure you are your mother's daughter.'

And you, Gregory Shoesmith's grandson.

'I'll, ah, leave you to unpack, then.'

Alice went on sitting on the edge of her bed. The white veil beyond the window thinned suddenly and lifted to allow a glimpse of ice cliffs on the other side of the bay, but it lasted only an instant. When the fog and snow closed in again the curtain seemed even thicker.

After a few minutes she heard the sound of different voices, and doors opening and closing. More people had come in. There was a burst of laughter and a blare of music that was quickly turned down. She shivered a little, more from loneliness than cold. Thinking that she didn't want Laure Heber to walk in and find her at a loss, she unzipped her kitbag and busied herself with unpacking. After all the boots and fleeces and balaclavas and long johns were disgorged, her personal possessions made only a tiny pile. She put everything away, hoping that she wasn't overflowing into Laure's space. Finally, she stuck three photographs to the wall above her pillow. There was the famous one of Margaret sitting on the ice, face to face with a Weddell seal, one of Trevor on a summer climb in the Mischabel, high above Zermatt, and one of herself with Becky and Jo. It had been taken by Harry on a beach in Cornwall, two years ago, before Jo's twins had been thought of. The three of them were suntanned, with salt in their hair, sprawling in the sand with their legs twined together. They looked young, and silly and happy.

Almost an hour had gone by. It was 8 p.m., and the light beyond the window was still luminous and utterly opaque, even though she pressed her face against the cold glass and stared until her eyes stung. There was nothing to see except the thickness of snow and mist.

The outer door slammed again and she heard yet another set of voices. One of these was a woman's. Immediately, as if she was about to be caught trespassing, Alice jumped up from her bed. She stood uncertainly, waiting, until the bunk-room door opened.

A young woman came in. She had bright, slanting eyes and a bell of dark hair, tousled now from her hat. Her cheeks were reddened by the wind. She held out her hand at once, not smiling. Alice shook it.

'You are settled in,' Laure observed.

'Yes. I . . . I hope I haven't taken up too much room.'

'Pff.' The other woman shrugged. 'We are only two. My God, you know, it's a blizzard out there. I think we only made it back thanks to Rook. You are welcome to Kandahar Station, Alice.' She pronounced it, of course, Aleece.

There was a loud noise of metal banging against metal. It was time for dinner and Russ was beating a spoon on a tin plate.

The room was unnervingly full now. Alice hesitated in Laure's wake. Richard was ladling soup into bowls from a big pan on the table in front of him. There was one empty seat left, next to Richard again, and she slipped into it. She could feel the heat from the saucepan on her cheek. A hand descended on her arm and she turned her head to meet her neighbour. She saw a full, curly grey-black beard split by a wide smile, a pair of shoulders like a bull's, a chest that seemed on the point of bursting the zipper of a pair of ancient red salopettes. He looked like Father Christmas's much younger and more dissolute brother.

'You know, these are crazy people,' the man said.

Alice guessed who this must be.

'How do you do, Dr Petkov?' she said.

He bellowed with laughter. 'I love you British. You are always "How do you do? Would you like a nice cup of tea?"'

He was right, Alice thought. Richard and she, that was how they were. Valentin swept an arm round her and kissed her enthusiastically on the mouth. She kissed him right back. It would be good to have a friend like Valentin.

There had been a babble of loud conversation, but now it died away. She blushed under the sudden general scrutiny, but Valentin Petkov only laughed harder and slapped her on the back.

'Soup, Alice?' Richard asked.

Across the table was a big blond man with thick features and painful-looking cracked lips. 'Hi,' he said. 'Jochen van Meer. Base medic. The soup's really good, have some.'

From the other side of Arturo, Nikolai Pocius, the radio operator, poked his skull-head forward. 'He is right. Russ is making it, even though it's my duty day. It is a flavour known as not-Lithuanian soup.' Someone else gave an ironic cheer and Alice saw a dark-skinned impish-faced boy on the other side of Nikolai. Philip Idwal Jones, the Welsh mountain guide. He winked at her.

Richard had ladled soup into her bowl. Alice lifted a spoonful and tasted it. Jochen and Nikolai were right, it was very good. She was hungry, ravenous again. She could have eaten the entire contents of the big saucepan, straight down. Then, as she was trying not to devour her plateful too quickly, she noticed something else. It would have struck her at once, if she had not been distracted by Valentin.

A force field of antagonism divided the two ends of the table. In a moment's silence that was broken only by the clinking of cutlery, the separation seemed as obvious as a brick wall.

On one side, Richard Shoesmith's side, were Jochen the doctor, Arturo and herself, with Valentin somewhere on the borderline. On the other were Russell and Nikolai and Phil and, somewhat suprisingly, Laure. Laure was sitting with her head and shoulder inclined towards her neighbour and the swan curve of her long white neck drew Alice's eyes to the man at the far end of the table.

Her glance almost travelled over him and on to Philip, because there was nothing outwardly remarkable. The man was eating with quick economical movements, his head bent, looking at no one. She saw that his hair was shaved close to his skull and that it might have been white or grey or silver. There was a dark mole on his forehead, just at the point where his hairline came forward in a vee, and his skin was weather-beaten.

At that moment, with her eyes on him, Rooker lifted his head. She expected that he would meet her glance, but he did not. Alice had never seen such a withdrawn expression. James Rooker looked

142

at nothing and nobody, in spite of Laure's seductive posture. All he would see, she guessed, were the images that played behind his own eyes.

Her soup spoon drooped in her empty plate and she quickly put it down.

She folded her hands out of sight, under the table, in case they were trembling.

She told herself that she had imagined the force field. Antarctica must already be affecting her. There was no brick wall and no opposing ranks, only ten tired people having dinner in a remote place, and a ripple of dislike between two of them. There was antagonism between Shoesmith and Rooker, and Richard had even hinted as much, but anything else was mere fancy. It was the sensation of being trapped, closed in this room with the blizzard driving against the windows, that was heating her imagination.

Richard touched her elbow.

'Are you all right?'

'Of course.'

'It's a lot to take in. Have you worked out who everyone is?'

'Yes.'

'I'll just make a brief introduction.'

He tinkled his spoon against his water glass. There was no alcohol in sight. The low hum of talk stopped.

'Not all of you have had a chance to meet her yet, so I want to introduce Dr Alice Peel who has just joined us from Oxford. Welcome to the Joint EU Antarctic Expedition, Alice, and to Kandahar Station.'

The others made a polite murmur and now Rooker's abstract gaze briefly settled on her face. It made her feel uncomfortable. Alice nervously cleared her throat. She made a little speech about how happy she was to be here and how much she was looking forward to working as part of the team. There was a small patter of applause, not ironic, she thought.

'Bravo, Alice,' Valentin shouted. He put his arm round her and hugged her again, and she found this comforting.

There was a boiled ham and mashed potatoes to follow the soup, then tinned fruit salad. Alice had overestimated her appetite after all and couldn't finish hers, but Valentin obligingly exchanged plates with her.

After the meal she tried to help with the clearing up, but Russell told her that it was Niki's duty day and she would have plenty to do when her own turn came. Rooker and Phil had disappeared, and Nikolai went over to the radio room once the washing-up was done. As soon as the door opened a long arm of wind-driven snow and icy cold snaked into the hut and tried to snatch at them.

Everyone else was reading, writing notes or listening to music on headphones. Alice went to bed. She lay in the dark security of her bunk, feeling loneliness stretched out beside her. The wind sometimes fell to a low growl, at other times it rose to a high-pitched scream that battered at the roof and the walls.

She thought about the nine other people at the dinner table. Each of them had their stories behind them, all the people and places lined up in the recesses of their past, and she tried to imagine what they might be. Then she turned on to her back and lay with her eyes open, her fingers laced over her belly.

Quite soon, sleep came and claimed her.

*   *   *

The blizzard lasted for three days. It was impossible to leave the base—even crossing the few yards to the other hut was a serious excursion.

On the first day Alice thought she would go and talk about their joint geology projects to Richard, who was working in the lab. She put on her parka and a pair of snow boots, and told Russell where she was headed.

As soon as she stepped out of the door the wind slammed it shut behind her. She took an unthinking step forward as driving snow filled her eyes and mouth. She choked and lifted her arms to shield her face. The sudden movement and an extra-vicious gust of wind made her stagger, and she overbalanced and fell into thigh-deep snow. Coughing and gasping, she floundered on all fours trying to get her bearings. It was like huddling inside a tin of icy whitewash that was being violently shaken. Snow stung her eyes and half blinded her, and when she did shield them with a numb hand she couldn't see beyond her own fingers.

She had no idea which way to turn. The edge of the bluff was a couple of yards away in one direction, the main hut could only be the same distance away in the other. But she could see nothing. There was just the blizzard, a whirling wall of snow and sea fog, and the wind tearing as if it wanted to strip and flay her. She stood up again and glimpsed the blurred outline of her fall and the fumbling step that led to it, in a completely different direction from the one she would have guessed.

She retraced the step and the red-painted wall of the hut loomed ahead. With a sharp gasp of relief she felt her way along it to the door. Against the gale, it took all her strength to heave it open. When it yielded she fell inside in a slanting column of snow. Papers blew off the table and saucepans rattled. She forced the door shut and bent over, panting for breath.

It was like stepping from one universe into another. The noise of the wind was muted to a sonorous organ note. It was almost impossible to believe that the calm, domestic interior existed on the same planet as the wilderness outside, let alone that they were separated by only a few inches of insulated wall.

She had been out for one or two minutes. Russ was still sitting in exactly the same position at the table, reading a two-week-old newspaper. Arturo was beyond him, tapping at his laptop. They both looked up.

Alice's eyes were watering. She didn't know if they were tears of cold or shock.

Russ got up, went to the coffee pot and poured some into a mug. He put the mug on the table and guided Alice to a chair in front of it.

'Rough weather,' he said kindly. 'You're not adjusted yet. Best to stay put until it quietens down.'

'I had no idea,' she whispered when she could speak.

It was true. Every slow hour that passed seemed to underline the fact that she knew nothing about this place she had come to.

Since her arrival there had been no chance to explore outside the hut even for half an hour. All she knew so far was this tiny space, enclosed by four walls against the fury of the weather. Although she had tried to prepare for it, a world of such absolute hostility was completely new to her.

She kept reminding herself that compared with what the polar explorers of her childhood bedtime stories had endured they were living a life of ease at Kandahar. She was warm, dry, well-fed and quite safe. She didn't have to man-haul a loaded sledge across massive unseen crevasses, or shiver for days and nights on end in a precarious tent with only a sleeping bag made of soaking animal furs for protection. She wouldn't have to walk for days with no food, or eat the remains of the sledge dogs and consider it a luxury. But even so, the brief confrontation with the real Antarctica hit her hard. She was fearful, afraid that her first instinct, to stay away from this harsh place at the end of the world, had been the correct one.

As the second and third blizzard days of idleness crept by, Alice found it hard to occupy herself. Everyone else seemed quite happy. Russell ran the base, overseeing everything from food preparation to the sorting of waste. Laure had her Adélie penguin samples to work on and spent most of her time sitting at her microscope in the lab. Arturo and Valentin worked on their data too, or collated their notes, or read scientific papers. Richard was always busy. An air of abstraction clung about him, except at mealtimes when he made an effort to preside sociably at the table. Jochen van Meer, the stolid Dutchman, was content to read paperback thrillers and watch DVDs. His own scientific study, to do with respiration, nutrition and body weight at extreme temperatures, involved nothing more at present than taking everyone's blood pressure once in a while and enquiring about their appetite.

Whatever the weather, Niki had to spend most of his hours in the radio room. He had a series of schedules to keep with the Chileans and other bases, and with the ships in the vicinity. Alice found it comforting to know that even though while the blizzard lasted they were actually as far out of reach than as if they were on the moon, there were other people alive and well in this white inferno.

When she tried to think about home and her parents, or Pete, or Jo and Becky, they seemed too far away to conjure up. Each expedition member was allotted thirty minutes' on-line time every day for personal e-mails, but when she sat down to write, Alice couldn't describe her feelings of isolation and claustrophobia.

It's snowing, she wrote lamely. But I expect we'll be able to get outside soon.

In their replies their voices sounded unfamiliar.

Margaret was tired. It does snow, she wrote, without the brisk advice to get used to it that Alice might have expected. Becky's comment was how exciting, is it deep? She was plainly imagining somewhere not unlike Verbier.

Philip Idwal Jones and the boatman, as Alice still thought of him, Rooker, were less in evidence than the rest of the team. The four male scientists occupied one of the bunk rooms and the support staff the other. Philip and Rooker seemed to spend most of their days behind the closed door of their room, with Niki whenever he was off duty.

148

Sometimes Valentin joined them. Raised voices and laughter were occasionally audible. When the door did briefly open a breath of thick smoky air escaped.

Everyone slept a good deal, Alice supposed. Certainly Laure did, whenever she wasn't working. She slept very neatly and quietly, her spine curled against the room, threads of her dark hair spread on the pillow. Alice lay on her back, staring at the wooden base of the overhead bunk and listening to the wind.

Margaret had once spent fifteen consecutive days in a tent, waiting for the weather to break so she could get back to the base. Her food supplies had run so low that by the end she was on quarter rations. 'I just waited,' was all she said about it. 'It's not very long, out of a lifetime, is it? To get what you want?'

But Margaret had only worked on the coast or at the margins of the ice shelf, because that was where the animals she was studying were to be found. She never went inland, towards the white heart, where Alice would have to go to find her rocks. Sooner or later the blizzard would be over and the preparations would be complete, and she and Richard would head out into the field. They would spend a week alone together, collecting rocks, in contact with base only via a daily radio link. It was an intimidating prospect, but with the walls of the hut pressing closer and closer around her she was also longing to get outside, anywhere, to do anything at all that wasn't hanging around waiting and trying not to be conspicuous.

At mealtimes she covertly studied Richard Shoesmith's profile, wondering how they would work together out on the ice.

On the third day of confinement Alice was rostered for hut duties. It was a relief to have something concrete to do. She cleaned the bathroom, scrubbed the floor of the living area and baked scones for tea, as well as serving up lunch and dinner. As soon as she banged the plate and spoon, everyone flocked to the table. With so few other diversions, they were all inquisitive about whether the new arrival could cook. After her day in the kitchen Alice was relieved and flattered when her Spanish omelette and spiced beef casserole were both wolfed down.

'Bravo, Alice.' Valentin beamed again. 'You turn out to be a true gift.'

Over dinner there was a noticeably more cheerful atmosphere. Richard rested his elbows on the table, and laughed when Jochen asked whether he was going to invite any more geologists to join them who were good cooks *and* better-looking than Russ.

'Isn't Alice enough?'

Laure had her dark head turned towards Rooker and appeared not to be listening. 'And Laure, of course?' Richard added.

'I count only two girls. And there are eight of us,' Jochen complained.

'We're scientists. We're here to work, remember,' Richard said calmly. It was a reprimand but he did it gently, so that his words floated over the rest of the talk. Jochen only grinned.

Niki said that the weather forecast for the next forty-eight hours was looking much better. As a climatologist, Arturo usually regarded day-to-day meteorological predictions as beneath him but now he nodded in agreement. 'It will be weather for sunbathing.'

'Or for field training.' Phil winked at Alice. Before she could set off inland with Richard, Alice would have to practise safety and survival techniques, and it was Philip's job to instruct her. She leaned back in her seat and smiled at him. The cheerful little Welshman seemed even more jovial than usual tonight.

'I'm looking forward to it,' she said.

The room and the faces around the table were becoming familiar. This evening, the hands of the wall clock were actually jumping instead of creeping. She began to think that she might after all fit in here and even make a useful contribution. Outside, the wind blew with less fury. Tomorrow, Alice thought, with just a bit of luck, she would be able to step all the way outside the door.

After she had cleared away the dinner dishes and put the coffee pot on the table, Phil went to his room and reappeared with a guitar. He tipped back in his chair, strummed a couple of chords and then began to sing. He had a big, strong baritone voice, trained in a Welsh choir, that filled the hut and rode over the nagging wind. Within a minute everyone was singing with him.

Rooker had a good voice too. Looking nowhere, with his black eyebrows drawn together, he sang 'Brown-Eyed Girl', then 'Yesterday' as a duet with Laure. Everyone clapped that one and Laure laughed, forgetting to be poised for once and turning pink with pleasure. She let her head fall, just for a second, against Rooker's shoulder. Phil and Rooker went on singing, louder, absorbed in

151

the music.

'*Laure, s'il vous plaît?*' Jochen said. He stood up, beckoning her to dance. She looked as if she would much rather stay put but she didn't refuse. Valentin and Russ pushed aside some chairs to make room for them. Laure danced as if she were on MTV, Jochen waved his arms and hopped from foot to foot.

Richard took Alice's hand. 'Would you like to?' he asked.

'Yes, please.'

He was stiff at first, but then he loosened up. His hand shifted tentatively over her ribcage before settling in the small of her back. As they swung round, Alice saw him glance around the room, covertly gauging the mood. Understanding and a sudden affection sprang up in her.

Richard was shy and he was also anxious because the success of Lewis Sullavan's venture depended mainly on him. It was no wonder that he sometimes seemed ill at ease. But now his face had softened. He was pleased with the warmth that had sparked around the table tonight, and with the singing and dancing. They would settle down together, all of them, in this ice world.

'It's all right, isn't it?' Alice said, with her mouth to his ear as they moved closer.

'I'm not much of a dancer,' he protested, misunderstanding her.

A whisky bottle materialised on the table behind him. Valentin was busy filling glasses. Alice had guessed that Rooker and Phil and the others were drinking in their bunk room to pass the time, and it was obvious that they were several drinks ahead tonight. A sudden burst of laughter and the sight of

Niki draping a spindly arm round Valentin's shoulders confirmed it.

Richard had seen the bottle too. Now he would have to choose whether to make a heavy-handed objection, or to let tonight be an exception to his rule. It crossed her mind, with the music and the dancing, that she would quite like a drink herself. As if he read her mind, Valentin picked up a glass and waved it at her.

Richard hesitated, missing a beat and looking down into her face as if for reassurance. Then his mouth lifted at one corner and he gave a small, self-mocking, acquiescent shrug. It was such a tiny movement that Alice, in his arms, felt it rather than seeing it. They found themselves laughing, the warm laughter of people who have begun to appreciate one another.

Phil played a final loud chord and put his guitar aside to take a gulp of whisky. Richard bowed and led Alice back to her seat. Rooker was lounging at the other end of the table, his expression as unreadable as always.

Richard leaned across and picked up an empty glass, nodded to the whisky bottle. 'May I?' he asked pleasantly.

'Sure thing.' Jochen poured him a measure. Alice accepted the glass that Valentin passed to her across the oilcloth and saw that Laure had one in front of her too.

Richard lifted his drink. He considered for a moment and the table waited. 'Here's to the complete team, and to Kandahar, and to co-operation.'

'And to less bullshit,' Rook drawled.

Laure bit her lip.

The wind had dropped completely. After the days and nights of clamour, the silence was thick enough to touch.

Richard flushed, but otherwise it was as if he hadn't heard.

Alice had begun to distinguish undercurrents of tension between several of the expedition members. Valentin often made a mocking little pout at the sight of Arturo's earring or co-ordinated clothes, and Arturo retaliated by delicately pressing one finger to his ear when Valentin spoke, as if his voice was just too loud. Laure lifted a scornful eyebrow whenever Jochen leaned too close to her or dropped his big hand on her knee, although Jochen never seemed to notice this. But the discord between Richard and Rooker was like a big boulder just under the surface of a fast-flowing stream. For now the water cloaked it with a glassy skin but the smallest alteration would expose the jagged edge.

Valentin spoke first: 'The team.' He stood up and drained his glass, everyone else raised theirs and drank. Richard sat back, two red patches still showing on his cheekbones. Russ turned away and slotted a CD into the player, and the moment passed.

Somehow, against the odds, the evening was turning into a party. The music was a Latin-American compilation and Alice danced the tango with Valentin until she was breathless. He was an excellent dancer. Russell and Niki and Arturo snapped their fingers and stamped their feet in accompaniment. Alice noticed that Rook was watching. The nape of her neck prickled under his cool scrutiny.

Valentin moved on to partner Laure, and they performed an exhibition samba while everyone whistled and clapped. There came a moment, later on, when everyone was dancing—even Rook. No one bothered with partners. Pent-up energy from the days of confinement burned off in swaying and singing and waving of whisky glasses. When she looked at the clock again, Alice was amazed to see that it was almost midnight.

She had been aware of the door opening and closing, and stabs of cold air slicing through the warm fug in the room, and now Valentin took her by the elbow. 'You will come to look?'

She followed him, pulling on the parka he handed to her as they stepped outside the hut.

'See?' Valentin said. He made a theatrical and totally unnecessary sweep of his arm.

The air was magically still, although the lead-coloured overhead clouds were ragged from the storm. Over the bay the cloud had thinned away to long streamers of apricot and pale violet, tinged on the underside with jade. The snowfields and glaciers were washed with delicate shades of lavender and faded rose-pink, and the sea rippled with a long streak of molten gold. Alice drew in a breath. The sun just rested on the horizon. It was a perfect orb of brilliant flame-orange, except for the faintest flattening at its lowest margin. She glanced down at her watch. It was midnight exactly. From now, the beginning of November, until February there would be no darkness.

'Not bad?' Valentin chuckled. He was only wearing a T-shirt. The midnight sun turned the grizzled hairs on his arms to threads of gold.

'Not . . . bad,' Alice murmured. She wanted to

155

have this moment to herself. The unearthly beauty of it struck a shaft straight into her heart.

He nodded and heaved a sigh. After a moment he patted her on the shoulder and stumped away.

Alice clambered down the rocks to the beach. The chunks of ice lapped by waves looked as if they were made of pure silver. Wet shingle crunched under her boots and the smell of salt and sea water stung within the chambers of her head. After the three days of the blizzard and all the small anxie ties and human abrasions of the hut, it felt like walking out of a dark cellar and stepping into paradise.

She was so entranced that she walked all along the shoreline until she reached the tongue of rocks that marked the boundary of Kandahar Bay. The convoluted layers of rough sandstone were lightly whiskered with snow and she paused for a moment, out of long-ingrained habit, to follow the sedimentary contours by eye. But the murmur of the dying surf and the clinking of ice distracted her. There were fleece gloves in the pocket of her parka and she gratefully put them on before climbing the rocky outcrop. She reached the flat top with its icing of snow and looked down. On the other side lay a perfect crescent of shingle beach, with a dozen penguins standing like sentries on the shelves of rock.

She climbed down, enjoying the stretching of muscles and the precise search for toeholds with the tip of her boot. She exchanged a solemn stare with the nearest penguin as she passed by. Over the next rocky outcrop she found yet another crescent, smaller and more intimately enfolded by rock. The sound of waves breaking was caught and amplified

156

here, filling her head with music. She stood looking out to sea. Her mind was empty, all the questions and doubts that nagged her soothed away by the wonder of the scenery and by sunshine at midnight. The sun steadily lifted clear of the horizon and turned to a flat disc of blazing gold.

Alice turned slowly round, with coppery-green pennies of light dancing on her retinas. She looked up at the folded and crimped bands of rock, at the centre point of the beach's arc, and through the fading rain of sun spots she saw a flight of pale stone steps. They led straight from the shingle up to the overhang of snow at the clifftop, as precise as if a stonemason had just chipped them free.

It was a common geological formation, known as a dyke.

A column of hot magma had intruded into a crack in the existing layers of sand- and mudstone. The igneous rock showed as a shaft of a completely different colour and texture from the surrounding folds, and differential weathering had sliced it into horizontal and vertical planes, just like the treads of a staircase.

Alice knew all this as well as she knew her own name, but she didn't think of it. She saw the pristine steps leading from water to white skyline, perfect in their own mysterious logic, and she knew for certain that this was a remarkable place. She felt its holiness, just as if a hand had been laid on her head in blessing.

She sat down on a flat-topped stone to look at the steps and to let the atmosphere seep into her. This place was a temple, she thought, with the endless waves for music and with nature's flawless architecture to contain its spirit.

A breath of premonition stirred, coming from nowhere like a cold wind fanning her cheek.

Superstitiously, she tilted her head to look up at the summit of the steps, but they led to nothing more than a curling overhang of unmarked snow.

It wasn't that the temple disturbed her, just that its crystalline calm had opened up a new channel. Somewhere within her there was a buried fear, but she couldn't grasp what it was. It lay deep, but as she groped around its outlines she felt sure that when the time came, when she needed to, she would be able to face it and then reach beyond it.

It was very cold. The temperature was dropping as the skies cleared. Alice jumped up, flapping her arms and stamping her feet to restore the circulation. She was surprised by the direction her thoughts had just led her. She didn't believe in signs or warnings and she wasn't religious, but this place was the holiest she had ever known and she couldn't explain what she had just experienced as anything other than a premonition. She shivered.

'I'm a scientist,' she said aloud, trying a firm, cheery voice modelled on Roger Armstrong's, her parents' neighbour. But it came out thin and flat, hardly a voice at all, and was swallowed up by the immensity around her. Why am I thinking about *Roger*, of all people? she wondered. Was Antarctica unbalancing her, between a blizzard and a sky painted with more colours than she had ever dreamed of?

The circulation was coming back to her feet, but her nose and ears and fingertips were nipped with cold. Alice turned deliberately away from the temple steps and scrambled up and over the first rock tongue. She passed the penguins and scaled

158

the second outcrop. From the top she saw the warm lights of the base and the broad sweep of the water, now as flat as mercury. Then she stopped short. There was a man sitting below her, looking out to sea, directly in her path to the beach.

She looked left and right for another route that would lead her safely down. She didn't want to disturb him. Even though his back was to her, every line of his body indicated disconnection, distance, abstraction. His hands hung loosely between his knees and his head and shoulders drooped.

Alice hesitated but there was no other way to descend. She began to down-climb, moving deliberately but noisily to announce herself. At last, when she was almost on top of him, the man looked round. It was Rooker.

'Be careful,' he said in a low voice. He moved aside a little and she was about to step past when he indicated a rock seat beside him. In silent surprise she sat down.

'Are you warm enough?' he asked.

Alice thought these were the first remarks he had addressed to her, except for ordering her to put on the life jacket in the Zodiac. Without waiting for an answer he took the whisky bottle out of the pocket of his parka, wiped the flat of his hand over the neck and passed it to her.

Alice took a long gulp. The spirit's heat flashed through her. Rooker took the bottle back and absently tilted it to his mouth.

'I didn't mean to disturb you,' she said.

He said nothing and the silence erased even the echo of her words. There was a force field around Rooker. It made her skin burn under the heavy fabric of her parka. She wanted to get up and move

159

away, but she was rooted to the flat rock. She watched the sun sliding up the sky and the burnished track that it laid over the water, and her awkwardness slowly dissolved. Rooker sat so still, it made her wonder what he was thinking about that absorbed him so totally.

When he did finally speak, it made her jump. 'You are quiet. I mean, you don't talk all the time. You didn't disturb me.'

'Do you know the steps? Back there?'

He glanced at her. 'Yes. It's a good place.'

She wondered again what it was that turned his face opaque and gave his eyes the look of always staring inwards.

'It's a dyke. The rock formation. I've seen thousands. But . . .' She shrugged. She wouldn't try to put into words what she had felt there.

He only nodded and lifted the bottle to his mouth again. If he was drunk he was intentionally, almost doggedly so. 'Look.'

Alice followed his pointing finger. A supple dark shape was gliding through the waves close to the water's edge. A big head broke out, and powerful shoulders, then the body heaved itself through the line of surf to reach the shingle. It was a leopard seal. The cruel wide mouth showed as it turned its head to check the lie of the land, and the narrow hips undulated as it propelled itself up the beach. It flopped down to rest, its head pointing out to sea.

'Leopard,' Rook said.

'My mother studied them. She made films for television.'

Why am I telling him this? Alice wondered. I am proud of her, yes. But it's as if I'm offering what Margaret did because I don't want to give anything

160

of myself away. He's right, I am quiet. Not just now, but always.

Another thought followed this one. She didn't argue about art because she didn't want to commit herself, or reveal too much. It wasn't a matter of language so much as inclination. She had bundled up her feelings about Pete and hurried south with them, relieved not to have to reveal how much he had hurt her. But she was beginning to realise that down here it wouldn't be so easy to be noncommittal. For strangers living in a cramped space with a wilderness outside, reality lay close to the surface. There was nowhere to hide, no place for smokescreens.

It was partly anticipation of what this might mean that had touched her in the temple.

She said quickly, to get it out of the way, 'Perhaps you saw her films? Her name's Margaret Mather.'

'There's a plaque with that name, waiting to be put up on the lab block.'

'Yes.'

'I wasn't watching much television around the time when your mother was probably making her films.'

He had never heard of her. Alice was pleased to realise it because it made her feel less circumscribed.

'Where did you grow up?' she asked. His accent was an odd mixture that she couldn't quite place.

'All over,' Rooker said shortly. He was getting tired of her questions.

The seal rolled on its back and folded its flippers against its spotted belly. It looked as though it was asleep.

Alice stood up. 'I'm heading back to base. I'll leave you in peace.'

The idea must have amused him, because he gave a snort of laughter. But he stood up too and she found herself dismayed at the prospect of having to walk back with him. Would they try to talk, or scramble in awkward silence?

He was much taller than her. As she turned to go he put a finger on her shoulder and then touched the Velcro label on the breast of her parka. He lifted one black eyebrow and the sun caught the side of his face. The cropped hair above his ear glittered.

'Is that an order? Or an invitation?'

She was suddenly aware of a raw sexual challenge that was so direct, and so at odds with his usual inscrutability, that it took her breath away. She stared at him as shock subsided and anger fluttered in her throat, making it harder to speak. 'Neither. It's my name.'

Rooker grinned. He raised the whisky bottle in a salute and abruptly sat down again on his rock. 'Don't go too close to the seal.'

It was not unknown for leopard seals to make aggressive lunges at solitary intruders. 'I know that, thank you. My . . .'

'Your mother told you not to.'

A furious retort rose in her—along the lines of *don't patronise me, you pisshead*—but she swallowed it. She turned her back instead and carefully climbed down the rocks to the beach. She made an exaggeratedly wide circuit round the sleeping seal and walked on up to the base. She didn't look round, but she was sure that Rooker had resumed his motionless contemplation of the

162

water.

The hut was quiet. Philip was sitting in a corner, plucking at his guitar and softly humming. Niki sprawled in another chair, his long arms dangling to the floor, the picture of melancholy.

'Scotch always gives Nik the blues,' Philip murmured. Alice stroked the Lithuanian's shoulder as she passed him and he grabbed her hand and held it briefly to his cheek.

'We are all lonely people.' He sighed. 'Islands, just tiny islands in a cold sea.' There was a tear on his cheek.

Richard was working on his notes at the end of the table. He glanced up and said, 'Go to bed, Niki.'

Niki ignored him and Philip went on humming.

'It's beautiful outside,' Alice said. The hut's warmth made her cheeks burn.

'Wait until you see the rocks, out at Wheeler's Bluff,' Richard said.

If everything went according to plan they would be out in the field in eight days' time.

In the women's room, surprisingly, Laure was still awake. She was brushing her hair in front of the tiny wall mirror. She tilted her head one way and then the other, arching her white neck. Alice squeezed past her to reach her bunk and began taking off her layers of clothes.

'Did you go for a walk?' Laure asked.

'Yes. Not very far. I haven't got my bearings yet.'

'No,' Laure agreed thoughtfully. And after a pause, 'You like him, don't you?'

Alice was startled. As far as she knew Laure didn't go in for personal observations. 'Who?'

'Richard.'

'Of course I like him. He's the expedition leader. I think he's very good.'

Laure smiled. 'I meant, you *like* him.'

'Laure, I haven't thought about him in that way. It wouldn't be advisable or professional, would it?'

The other woman put her hairbrush away and climbed under the tidy covers of her bunk. 'You English. Why are you so afraid of what you might feel?'

Alice turned the question around in her head. A month ago, or even a week ago, she would have said that she was afraid of disease, of incompetence, even failure, but never of her own feelings. Now she wasn't so sure. Antarctica had already peeled away a layer of her defences. There was raw skin underneath.

By the time she had worked out a deflecting answer she saw that Laure had already curled on her side, back to the room, and retreated into the appearance of sleep.

Alice lay down too. She heard some of the men using the bathroom, a door opening and closing and a loud burst of music that was quickly muted after someone had turned the knob on the CD player the wrong way. Usually the hut settled quickly but tonight there was unrest. She thought about Richard's attempts to control his team members. Alcohol was only a detail, really. He would think that it was important to establish command over the group from the outset and then to maintain it at all costs. With his background, Richard would think it was essential.

There was quiet at last. As she lay and waited for sleep, Alice thanked heaven for the absence of the wind.

A week went by and the weather improved enough for Alice almost to forget the force of the blizzard. The sun shone out of a fierce blue sky and the scientists worked long hours out of doors. Alice embarked on several days of safety training with Phil Idwal Jones.

The slope was steep, and slick with ice where the sun's heat had melted it the day before and it had refrozen overnight. Alice slid downhill, head first. She had fallen on her back and a kaleidoscope of sun and sky flashed in her eyes, faster and faster as she gathered momentum. Her grip tightened on the ice axe held across her chest, then she gathered all her strength and rolled over on top of it. The pick bit into the ice and she clung on, feet slithering down the hill as her headlong descent abruptly stopped.

A black figure outlined with a halo of fuzzy gold light appeared on the skyline above her. It stood with hands on hips, gazing down to where she lay hunched over the axe.

'Not bad, girl,' Philip shouted.

Alice spread her arms and legs like a starfish pinned on the sheet ice and laughed delightedly at the sky. She was warm with scrambling up and down the steep hill, and the sun was so bright that it was hard to believe that the temperature was fifteen degrees below zero. She was happy with the long morning's training that Phil had put her through and she was very hungry.

'Phil? What about something to eat?' she shouted.

'Food? You've got to earn your dinner. I'm sorry to tell you that half a dozen ice-axe arrests and a bit of glacier travel's not nearly good enough.'

She scrambled to her feet and plodded up the slope yet again.

'If you do trip and fall, at least you stand a chance now of stopping yourself before you get to the cliff edge,' Phil judged.

'Thanks. What's next?'

'I'm glad you asked me that. We're going down a crevasse.'

They spent an hour gripped in the blue jaws of a shallow specimen while Phil showed her how to use a loop of cord to drag herself painstakingly up a rope, in the event that she might find herself dangling at the end of one. It was hard work.

At last she half rolled and half scrambled over the icy lip and lay prone in the snow. 'Will that do?' she begged.

'I'm marking you down on powers of endurance,' Phil threatened.

'What? My will to survive is indomitable, given that we've been out here for hours on end and I know quite well there are two box lunches in the pannier of that skidoo.'

'All right, then,' the Welshman said. 'You can have your dinner now.'

They sat in the lee of the skidoo, passing a flask of coffee between them and rooting through the contents of the boxes Russell had handed them.

'You're not bad, really. I'm quite impressed,' Phil told her.

Alice's face lit up. 'Truly?'

'For a geologist, that is. You've been in the hills before.'

166

'My dad used to take me to the Alps when I was a kid. He used to go climbing and mountaineering quite a lot.'

'Did he? You were dead lucky, weren't you? I grew up in Pwllheli. Hitched out to Chamonix when I was sixteen, that was my first trip abroad.'

'We're a long way from Pwllheli,' Alice said softly.

They sat looking at the view. In the bright light of the middle of the day the landscape was reduced to its basic components of black rock, water like a silver mirror and oblique snow slopes puckered and cratered with depths of cold blue and grey shadow.

'Yeah. Good, innit?'

'So you like it down here, then?'

Phil shook his head, grinning disbelievingly at his own good fortune. 'It's a bloody paradise. Look at all that. And there's nothing crap, is there? No rusting trucks down the bottom of the valleys. No litter bins with half-eaten Big Macs and fag ends and cans of Special Brew. No people, 'cept for us lot. You like it too, I can tell. You've brightened up no end since we got out here. I thought you might be a bit of a sad case, like, when you got here. But you haven't stopped laughing and smiling since we started. It's good, that, and I'm not such a bighead that I think it's because I'm a top teacher.'

'But you are, Phil.'

It was true, Alice thought. She enjoyed his company and learning from him. These exhausting, invigorating days of practising survival techniques had been some of the most enjoyable she had ever spent. But there was much more to it than that. They didn't often stop to admire the scenery, but however absorbed she was she saw how the light

167

and the texture of the whiteness changed with every hour of the endless day. There was nothing static or frozen about this place. It continually shifted and re-formed itself, molecules of water and ice and the forces of wind and cold fretting against each other, dissolving and crystallising, creeping in the glacier bottom or flying before the blizzard. She tried to look harder, to bring her senses to bear more intently, so that she would miss nothing.

She had almost forgotten her initial insomnia. As soon as she lay down now, sleep rolled over her like a warm snowdrift. She never woke until her alarm clock pinged under her pillow, and then she sat up immediately to look out of the window at the colour of another day.

Phil finished his food. They collected up the scraps of crumbs and wrapping, and stowed them carefully back in the lidded boxes, then shared the last of the coffee.

'What are we doing next?' Alice asked.

Phil nodded at the skidoo, its bright-red fairing and rakish windshield incongruous but reassuring against the sweep of glacier. 'You've got to learn to handle this.'

'*Yess.*' Alice pounded her mittened fists in delight.

'Not just roaring around, mind. Basic mechanics, how to fix a simple problem in the field, recognise a problem that you can't fix. Most of that we can do back on base, but you can have a bit of a turn now. Don't think you're going to get to drive everywhere, though, or you'll put Rook and me out of a job.'

Rooker. If he remembered asking her whether

168

'Peel' was an invitation or a command, he hadn't shown it. Sometimes she found herself watching him, but he gave no sign of noticing her scrutiny.

Alice perched astride the big machine while Phil patiently showed her the controls.

'Brake, throttle. Keep her level, head that way off the glacier where there's no crevasses, don't go careering away into nowhere or I'll be jumping off and leaving you to it. Remember to steer.'

At first she could only inch along with the motor racing, then she accelerated too hard and they shot forward so fast that Phil yelled and snatched at her waist to stop himself falling off. They ran up a snow bank and the skis tilted at such an alarming angle that Alice was sure they would overturn and be crushed. She yanked at the handlebars and they zigzagged in the other direction. Phil clung on while she fought for control.

It took a few circuits before she got the hang of it. But then she found that she could do it. It was as easy as riding a bicycle and five times as much fun. She raced the machine over the frozen waves of snow, bouncing over crests that shone like beaten egg white. She could turn tight circles and forge uphill. The cold stung her face and her thumbs ached from gripping the controls but her face was split in a wide grin of delight.

Phil said laconically, 'You're just about okay at the fun part. Let's go back and you can change the plugs and clean the fuel filter. Tomorrow we'll do the snow cave. If you're good you get to spend the night in it. With me.'

'Can I drive us back now?'

'And put me out of a job?'

But he did let her. As they swept down the hill

towards the base, Alice saw the little cluster of utilitarian buildings, the brave red standing out against the ice.

It looked like home, she thought.

CHAPTER EIGHT

They heard the gnat's buzz of the helicopter engines before the black speck appeared, emerging out of a sky curdled with soft cloud. Rooker and Phil had prepared a landing square in the snow and erected marker flags to provide some definition for the pilot. Everyone else who was on the base looked up from what they were doing and went outside to watch the arrival.

The red and white Squirrel hovered briefly over the landing area, then settled like a roosting bird within the flagged square. The down-draught from the rotors whisked loose snow into a miniature blizzard before the engines were cut. A moment later the pilot and his number two had taken off their headsets, climbed down and unloaded a couple of bags. They were the first visitors Alice had seen on the base.

She had been ready to leave since breakfast time. But there had been a series of delays while Santa Ana considered whether the local weather was good enough for the helicopter to set out, and monitored the conditions at Kandahar and what it was likely to meet at Wheeler's Bluff. The flight to take her and Richard out to the field had been off and on again twice already, and it was now early afternoon.

As the morning dragged by and Niki reported yet another change of plan, Russell had explained that it was always like this.

'Waiting for flights. Waiting for weather. Don't expect to go anywhere in Antarctica until you've actually left. And don't expect to arrive until your boots hit the snow. There's always the chance of a mid-flight turnaround.'

She sighed and slumped in her chair at the mess table. Richard was impatient to be off too. He stood at the window and fiddled with his watch strap, then asked Russell yet again to go through the list of responsibilities that he would take on as Richard's deputy.

'No worries,' Russ said.

But now, at last, the transport was here.

The pilot handed over the cargo bags. There were fresh vegetables from the supply ship that had just reached Santa Ana from Punta Arenas at the tip of Chile, and there was mail. Alice hadn't been away long enough for much mail to reach her, but there was an airmail package from Pete.

The crew came in and lounged at the table, lanky in their red flight overalls, drinking coffee and exchanging gossip with Russ and Niki. One was called Andy, the other Mick.

Andy grinned at some question of Russ's. 'Too right. Sandy Wilmot? Christ. Last I saw of him was in Neil's bar in Christchurch. Man, that was a night.'

There was a din of people talking over each other, the new arrivals making the small space seem even more crowded. It was strange to see unfamiliar faces in the accustomed places around the table. The pilots brought a draught of the

171

outside world with them, a place beyond the carmine walls of Kandahar that had seemed too remote to bother about.

Alice found a corner and opened her package from Peter. The letter was short. He told her that he missed her and that he was sorry. 'I acted like a total prick' were his actual words. She unfolded a couple of sheets of thick paper enclosed with the note and saw two charcoal sketches of herself. In one of them she was sitting with her head bent and a hank of hair falling across her face, and in the other she was looking straight into Peter's eyes. She remembered the night he had done them, not long after they had first met, and how impressed she had been by the way the quick strokes captured more of her than seemed possible in just a few black lines. Pete drew well, and she had wondered why he didn't do more work like this instead of concentrating on welding spars of metal into cages for discarded shop dummies and broken fan heaters.

A Polaroid photograph fell from between the two drawings. It was a picture of Pete, standing beside the construction that had been preoccupying him before she left. He was pounding a clenched fist into the palm of the other hand and smiling in triumph. The metal ribs and spars with their festoons of found objects reared above him. She noticed that he had incorporated the dismembered typist's chair.

'*PS. Finished it!*' he wrote. She stared at his familiar features and tried to remember exactly how she had felt about him. And she wondered who had taken the picture.

A hand touched her shoulder. 'Are you ready?'

Richard glanced from the photograph to Alice's face. She saw that the crewmen had stood up and everyone was streaming outside. She folded the letter and sketches round the photograph and stowed them inside her parka. Then she hoisted her kitbag and followed them.

Rooker had stripped down the second of the base's two skidoos, and he and Phil slung it beneath the helicopter's fuselage. He conferred with the pilot now about the security of this and the rest of the weighed camp baggage as it was loaded inside the machine. Richard and Alice handed over their personal kit for stowage. Russell patted her shoulder and told her that when she came back she would be an old hand.

'I don't know about that. But I'll be glad not to be such a no-no.'

No-no was Phil's catch-all word for her, meaning know-nothing. It was politer than fingy, which translated as fucking new guy.

Valentin hugged her against his barrel chest. Niki saluted before turning back to the radio room. Jochen and Laure and Arturo were all out at work.

'Come back to us soon,' Valentin shouted as the pilot waved her into the helicopter. She blew him a kiss as she took one of the three rear seats next to Richard. To her surprise Rooker swung in after them.

'You're coming with us?'

'You're going to refit the skidoo yourself?'

The doors were shut. Alice took the headset that Andy passed to her over his shoulder and put it on. The rotors started turning, the helicopter trembled on its skis and as she watched the hut roof sank out of sight. The machine briefly hovered, the pilots'

173

voices crackled in her headset and she looked down past Richard at the furious eddies of snow driven upwards in their ascent.

'Kandahar, Kandahar, this is NZ20. Airborne.'

'Roger NZ20. You are clear,' Niki answered.

The helicopter rose higher and swung in an arc. Alice saw the sheet of bay water tilting beneath her, the scumble of rock and glacier, then the base was way below and behind them as they headed south-east, into the field. She felt her stomach turn over, partly with vertigo and partly with excitement. She was longing to see what lay beyond the horizons of Kandahar, and she was looking forward to the demands of an isolated field camp with a mixture of fascination and apprehension.

The flight took forty minutes. Rooker leaned away from her, his close-cropped head turned silently to the view beneath. On her other side Richard exchanged matter-of-fact comments with the pilots. Alice stared straight ahead through the curve of windshield. A white and blue and grey-stippled immensity of space unrolled, crumpled by the chaos of vast glaciers edging to the sea. Near the brink of the peninsula the whiteness was gashed with rock crests that appeared as black as ebony, and further inland there were the peaks of nunataks. These were the tips of huge mountains, protruding through the great mantle of polar ice. Alice realised that her mouth was open and her eyes were stinging from gazing so hard. A draught of pure adrenalin surged through her, pulling her upright in her seat straps. She swallowed and became aware of Rooker looking round at her.

He smiled, an unpractised version, but the warmth did light up his black eyes. 'Yeah,' he said.

He didn't have his headset on so she couldn't hear the word, but she saw the way that his lips formed it, felt the click of a connection between them. Her cheeks were suddenly hot.

After a while the pilot said, 'See ahead there? One o'clock?'

She craned forward against the chest straps of her seatbelt. In the distance there was a long black-and-white ridge of rock, rising out of the tumbled ice and snow like the fin of a great sea creature from the ocean. Some time during the age of the dinosaurs a huge eruption of jet-black doleritic rock had burst upwards from the earth's molten core, squeezing through and buckling the layers of sedimentary siltstone. Even at this distance Alice could see how the igneous dolerite lay like a heavy black chocolate topping on the paler sponge-cake layers of the lower cliffs. This was their destination, Wheeler's Bluff.

The helicopter put down on a flat expanse of bare blue ice about half a mile from the cliff. The wind had scoured the snow off the surface here, so the pilot could see exactly what he was settling on. When the engines stopped the machine almost bucked in the wind. Even before the doors opened Alice could feel why the ice was bare.

The full force of it hit her as she ducked beneath the resting rotors. It tore at the hood of her parka as she tried to pull it up over her head and made her think of the first time she had stepped out of the hut. There was no turning back to shelter here, though.

The men set about the unloading. Rooker and Andy unleashed the skidoo chassis from its sling underneath the body of the helicopter and towed the haul bag containing the detachable parts alongside it. Mick tossed bags of kit and boxes of rations out to Richard who stacked them on the ice. Alice pulled her weatherproofs round her and ran to help. The pilots wanted to get back in the air and on their way to Kandahar before the weather deteriorated any further. There was a sledge that would be towed behind the skidoo, and Alice took the unwieldy packages from Richard's stack and loaded them on to it. The work was strenuous and after a few minutes she forgot the cold and the wind.

It took Rooker half an hour to reassemble the skidoo. Well before he had finished, the crew were in their seats in the Squirrel, exchanging weather information with Niki back on the base. Rooker refilled the fuel tank that had been drained for the flight. Covertly, Alice watched him working. He gave the job all his attention, and his movements were quick and precise. Now he jumped astride the machine and turned the ignition key. The engine caught at once and he drove the skidoo in a tight circle, revving it hard.

The pilot leaned out of the Squirrel and urgently waved his arm. Rooker held up two fingers. Meaning two more minutes, perhaps. He dismounted, lifted the casing off the engine and checked it over again. Then he gave the thumbs-up.

Richard and Alice stood back. Rooker glanced once at Alice and she thought she read speculation in the look. 'Anything else?' he asked Richard.

Richard ran his eyes over the mounded sledge. 'That's it,' he said.

Rooker was already sprinting to the helicopter.

'Have a good week,' he yelled over his shoulder. 'See you.'

A minute later the Squirrel lifted off the ice. Alice saw Andy's face framed in its headset and a hand lifted in a wave before a whirl of driven snow made her crouch down and shield her eyes. A minute after that the helicopter was just a red dot busily homing on Kandahar.

She looked around her. For hundreds of miles there was nothing but ice, wind, rock and Richard Shoesmith.

He was busily coupling the sledge to the skidoo. 'All set?' he shouted.

The plan was to drive closer to the Bluff, where the rocks would afford some shelter from the wind, and set up camp there. Alice raised her arm to show that she was ready; trying to make herself heard over the wind already felt like wasted effort. She climbed into the sledge and found the brake. It was a lever toothed with metal, and if a crevasse opened in front of the skidoo she would jump on the sledge brake as hard as she could and pray that the teeth would bite into the ice and hold them both.

Richard nosed carefully forward and the tow rope tightened. Slowly, they began to move over the blue ice.

*   *   *

It was 9 p.m. before they had camp set up.

By the time it was done Alice was sweating with exertion inside her windproofs, but she was pleased with the way she and Richard worked together. The skidoo and unloaded sledge were parked right

177

in the lee of the rocks and the skidoo was protected by a nylon cover, pegged down and weighted with rocks. The two yellow pyramid tents were up, openings facing away from the wind, the food boxes and cooking gear stowed inside one and the geological and climbing equipment inside the other. Two inflatable mattresses had been blown up, one for each tent, placed on karrimats and topped off with sheepskin underblankets, sleeping bags and waterproof bivvybags. There was even the blue flag with its circle of gold stars, stretched taut by the wind from a telescopic metal flagpole.

The sun was low and long steel-grey shadows flooded out from the Bluff. Snow rolled towards them in hazy drifts off the ice sheet. When she stopped work and stood still to ease her aching muscles, beneath the wind's constant refrain she could hear the absolute silence.

Richard was putting up masts for the VHF radio antennae. She crunched across the snow to help him.

'Time for some food?' she asked.

'I'd say so.'

In her tent—the one in which the kitchen had been established—Alice lit the Primus. She filled a pan with snow and sat back on her heels. The tent's interior glowed a soft yellow and the Primus's roar and its kerosene scent took her back to holidays in the mountains with Trevor.

'Hello, Dad,' she said softly. 'Here I am.'

Richard and she would take turns at being cook for the day. Most of their meals, two-man portions packed in a box for each day, were freeze-dried but for tonight Russ had sent out chicken portions and prepared vegetables in Ziplock bags.

When the snow-water came to the boil, Alice made mugs of tea, then threw handfuls of rice into the remainder. Tonight there would be fried chicken and vegetable rice.

At 10 p.m. Richard finished the prearranged radio schedule with Niki and presented himself at Alice's tent door.

'Dinner is served.' She grinned up at him.

They talked about the rock sections they would make and measure tomorrow. Richard reclined against her mattress. His aquiline, handsome face was masked by a thickening beard and the yellow light of the tent blotted out the anxiety lines etched between his eyebrows. Alice was sharply aware of the tiny compass of their camp and the hostile miles that cut them off from Kandahar. Richard and she might have been the only people in the world. The training that she had done at Cambridge and with Phil seemed suddenly inadequate to equip her for survival in this harsh, isolated place. *Kandahar* now represents civilisation and safety, she thought, with a tremor of amusement.

'Can I ask you something?' she said, as Richard licked his tin plate clean and peered into the saucepan to see if there might be a spoonful of leftovers. There were apples and chocolate for pudding, and Alice passed his share across to him. He polished his apple on his fleece leggings as he waited for her question.

She hesitated, wanting to admit to some of her anxiety without sounding too vulnerable. 'Why haven't we got a field assistant out here with us? Phil, or Rooker? Isn't that more usual? I suppose I'm worried that I won't be able to do everything

I'm expected to, because it's my first time.'

She added this in case he might think that she was being critical.

Richard weighed his apple in his hand. 'It's a fair question,' he said after a moment. She broke her chocolate into squares, lined them up and put the first one into her mouth. Thick sweetness melted on her tongue.

'It's easier to provision a two-man camp. There's less kit and food to transport. It also means we're not taking out a man who would be just as useful, probably more useful, back on the base. But you are right.' He sighed, then flicked her a glance as if he was wondering whether or not to level with her. 'Those aren't the real reasons. The truth is that I prefer it like this. Without extraneous people. You and I know what needs to be done and we can do it. It's simpler. It's peaceful. Isn't it?'

And it was. Out here, even the wind seemed less an aggressor and more a fourth dimension of the landscape itself.

Alice saw, suddenly, how much Richard longed for peace.

The demands of being expedition leader and the expectations of Lewis Sullavan were weighing more heavily on him than she had guessed. What Richard really wanted was to immerse himself in science, to be left alone with his fossils, and yet some contrary impulse had driven him to take over the leadership role. A sense of obligation to family expectations and history, she thought. *Just like me.*

Richard wasn't good at defusing the prickles of tension back at Kandahar. He was awkward about giving orders. He couldn't deal with Rooker's overt aggression or unspoken scorn, and all his speeches about community and teamwork left his little group separately bemused rather than united. Alice knew all this, because she felt a version of it herself. Science was seductive because of its orderliness, its silent pathways through the maze along which you followed the patient thread of conjecture. You didn't have to go out and sell yourself in order to sell other things, as Becky did, or even blunder through the minefield of motherhood, as Jo was learning to do. You collected rocks or fossils and took them back to the laboratory for analysis, and your web of data thickened into knowledge and thence understanding of the world's dynamic process.

The light in the tent was fading, and the wind banged and rattled at its thin skin. Another pot of snow was melting on the Primus for hot drinks.

'I understand,' Alice said quietly.

He nodded, leaning back against her bedding with his chin sunk on his chest. Suddenly, she was reminded of a photograph she had seen reproduced in half a dozen books of polar history. It showed the interior of Scott's hut at Cape Evans with Scott himself presiding at the head of the mess table. It was Christmas on the ice and halfway down the row of bearded faces was Gregory Shoesmith's. Richard bore a marked physical resemblance, tonight, to his famous grandfather. And Alice could sense how deeply, for the whole of his life, Richard had wanted to be like him as well as look like him.

'I'll be field assistant. I think I can just about remember what Phil taught me.'

Richard sat up, visibly struggling out of his melancholy. 'You're far too good a geologist for that. I need your expert sedimentologist's eye. But don't worry, we'll be quite safe, the two of us.'

Alice tried not to acknowledge even to her inner self that she was not reassured. She dismissed with equal speed the thought that if Phil or even Rooker had said the same thing it would have been quite different. Instead, she looked at Richard's attractive but closed-in English face. His cheeks above the margins of his beard were reddened by the wind and his lips were slightly chapped. She realised that she wanted to put her hand to his cheek. She didn't even know if he was married, she remembered.

She cleared her throat and he watched her as she leaned forward to burrow amongst the food boxes. 'Would you like coffee? Or herbal tea?'

When she had made the drinks, Richard thanked her gravely for a delicious dinner, just as if they were in Sussex or Gloucestershire. But then he added, 'And for your understanding. Goodnight, Alice.'

She curled up in her sleeping bag, drinking tea and thinking. They had a week's work to do out here, the two of them. That was the thing to focus on, not a momentary desire to touch someone because of the furrow between his eyebrows and the anxiety in his heart.

As soon as she put her empty cup aside and closed her eyes, Antarctic sleep came to claim her, as thick and soft and featureless as a blanket of fresh snow.

*   *   *

The days in field camp at Wheeler's Bluff quickly

fell into a rhythm.

They were very busy but they were also peaceful, as Richard had predicted.

The weather was good. The wind dropped to a gentle southerly breeze and the sun shone. The temperature rose above freezing in the middle of the day and it was surprisingly pleasant to be outside, moving about in the shelter of the rock ridge.

Alice was caught up in her close-quarters study of the rocks that were held in a matrix of finer-grained silts and muds. Veins of quartz flowed around her, and rivers of boulders and pebbles. Her head was full of her work and the hours flew as she measured and drew in her notebook. She loved the sense that she was deciphering a single page in the earth's history book. Wheeler's Bluff was interesting to them both because the rocks encompassed the transition between the Cretaceous and Tertiary periods, and the sedimentary layers were particularly rich in molluscan fossils. Richard had studied the extinction of mollusc species in other parts of the world, and he intended to establish the dates of extinction here and relate them to his earlier studies.

He worked with quiet absorption, moving up and down the rock band, tapping with his geological hammer to extract another promising specimen. The metallic ringing sound carried a long way in the silence. Whenever Alice looked up, to rest or just to enjoy the sun on her head and the breeze on her face, she would see him with his head down, intently scribbling in his notebook or blowing the rock dust off a sample with a sharp puff of breath. When he removed a specimen he took a GPS reading to establish its exact location and sealed it in a marked sample bag.

His industry spurred her on. She clambered over the outcrops, running her hands over the chunks and blocks of rock, chipping at shards with her hammer and picking with her fingertips at the remains of flora and fauna that had been embedded there for millions of years. She chose places where she could climb easily to make her painstaking measurements of the thick sections and she wedged herself into cracks and perched on ledges to draw detailed stratigraphical sections in her notebook. She collected thin sections from the crucial boundary margin, and labelled her samples with the index of the profile and an individual sample number. Back on the base she would analyse the rock fragments for mineral composition, then make a more precise analysis with all the facilities of her lab in Oxford.

When one or the other of them judged that the day was half over they would scramble down from where they had been working to the skidoo parked at the base of the rock band. They didn't usually travel more than ten or fifteen minutes from the camp, but their time and the fuel seemed too precious to waste in going back there in the middle of the day. They brought a rudimentary picnic instead, and the first one to down tools laid out the food on the seat of the skidoo and opened the flask of hot coffee. It was a good time to sit and look at the view.

On some days the ice sheet was a diamond-hard expanse of silver and blue, on others billows of snow swelled up in the wind and swept towards them, hiding the sun or dimming it to a disc of dull tin. They talked quietly about the location of the next section, the identification of Richard's molluscs, their intentions for the following day. Once they had devoured everything they went straight back to work for another four or five hours. The outline of the days was featureless, but they were crowded with incident.

One afternoon they scaled the rock face to reach the top of the Bluff. They put on climbing harnesses and roped up, and Richard led up a hundred feet of puckered and weathered rock. Alice followed, carefully placing her hands and feet, half intrigued by the rock's composition and half terrified by the height and her exposure. As she scrambled over the top, Richard gave her his hand and pulled her up.

She was elated, and breathing hard with relief.

'Well done.' He smiled, with his face close to hers. 'And just look.'

She turned and gasped. The puckered and pleated whiteness stretched away into infinity, textured with every shadow of blue and grey. Far in the distance, like mountains glimpsed in a dream, she thought she could see immense sharp silver peaks fretting the sky. It was the most beautiful sight she had ever seen and the most desolate. Every day Antarctica seemed to offer a fresh set of superlatives and a continual reminder of how far she had travelled from the ordinary world. Out here, on the ridged back of a mountain that was like a monster rising out of a frozen sea, it was as if she and Richard Shoesmith were the only two people in the universe.

That night, Richard heated up freeze-dried beef and dumplings while Alice made the nightly radio connection with Kandahar. She gave the weather report to Niki, temperature and wind speed and direction and cloud cover, and noted the forecast.

'And what's going on back there?' she asked at the end, and through the static heard his fat chuckle that always sounded at odds with his skeletal physique.

'So. You are missing civilisation, I think? Or missing me, maybe?'

'Of course I miss you, Nik. I miss everyone.'

Niki told her that Valentin had been out on the glacier with his drilling equipment, taking core samples of the ice, and Phil had been assisting him. Arturo was busy with his wind profiling and Laure, with Jochen's assistance, had netted and microchipped almost a hundred penguins.

'And Rook is building a beautiful hut for the skidoos. So you see, life on base is much as it always is.'

'Good. Roger, Niki. Same schedule tomorrow.'

'Goodnight, Wheeler's Bluff. Over and out.'

In fact, Alice thought, she wasn't missing life on base at all. She had never felt as alive and yet as peaceful as she did out here. Field life was just as simple and satisfying as Richard had predicted. There was work, there was food, there was sleep and there was human company. The two of them fitted together neatly and unquestioningly, linked by their work and the pared-down rituals of the day. She forgot that she had ever felt afraid of being out here.

From the other tent, where Richard was dishing up the evening meal, came the sound of a spoon banging a tin plate. Alice zipped up Richard's tent against the wind and scuttled the four steps to her own.

They had fallen into the habit, after they had eaten, of talking for an hour before bed. When the sun dipped behind the Bluff it grew dim in the tent, so Alice lit her tilley lamp and stood it on the pot box. She thought of how their tiny camp must look from across the great distances of the ice sheet: two fragile golden triangles glowing in the pearly emptiness.

She was talking about her father. He was often in her mind out here.

'I remember his work,' Richard said, although Trevor's field of structural geology had relatively little bearing on palaeontology. She was pleased with this, that it should be Trevor's achievements that were noted, for once, rather than Margaret's.

She told him, 'We used to go to Zermatt every summer, just the two of us. My mother would be on lecture tours, or making a film, or catching up on her students' work. Trevor would collect rocks and show me granite and dolerite and quartz and felspar. Once he scraped a rock chip on the metal shaft of his hammer and it made a chalky mark. "That shows us it is calcareous," he said. I can hear him saying it. He taught me to rock-climb too.' She laughed. 'Although you wouldn't think it.'

'You did well today,' he said and meant it.

'He loved the mountains. So do I.'

*   *   *

She remembered the sunsets. The sun sliding down the sky and the way the snow peaks flushed pink and apricot. The Matterhorn made a hooked dark cut-out of itself against the luminous light. The

187

sight of it always made her shiver, when everyone else exclaimed about its magnificence.

One evening Trevor had taken her on a walk, up zigzagging paths that led between the old stone and wood houses, to the church overlooking the old town. There were wildflowers, campion and cow-parsley and buttercups, in the long grass that brushed her bare legs as they climbed. The little white church had a squat tower, and a shingled roof and spire. There was a small graveyard surrounding it and as Trevor led her around she was surprised to see from the inscriptions how many of the dead were English.

'But they are *young*,' she had said. She was affronted by the idea that death might claim anyone but ancient people. Yet these were men and women who had died in the prime of their lives, in rock falls and avalanches and glacier accidents. These mountains, so ethereally lovely in the evening sun, were clearly dangerous.

Inside the church, by the slanting light from high windows, they read the stone tablets on the walls: 'Died in a fall on the Matterhorn, aged twenty-eight years, Member of the Alpine Club'; 'Aged twenty-two. Erected by his friends of the Cambridge University Mountaineering Club, in Affectionate Memory'.

A troubling thought stirred in Alice as she gazed at the memorials. 'You were at Cambridge University and you belong to the Alpine Club. I know that. I've seen the letters in your study.'

Trevor took her hand. In those days his fine hair was still sandy-blond and it covered most of his head. 'You are right.'

'*You* go climbing. I know you do. There are

photographs of you. But I don't want you to die.'

The cry came unthought, straight out of some dark place in her soul, and she was surprised and almost embarrassed to hear it.

'I won't die,' Trevor said mildly. He didn't let go of her hand as they walked out into the brightness again. 'I used to climb mountains when I was young, long, long before you were born. But after we had you, Alice, I stopped doing it because I thought it was important for me to be here. In case you need me.'

'I do need you. Every day, every minute.'

This was not a usual conversation for them to be having, but she knew it was important.

'And so here I am and I always will be. I don't need to climb mountains any more. I've got you and Margaret.'

This idea made Alice feel happy, as if there were a bird flying in her chest. Her father had given up something for her, something she sensed was important to him, because she herself was even more important.

From that moment in the graveyard at Zermatt a bond of trust grew.

Trevor loved her and had made a sacrifice for her. He considered his own safety and took steps to preserve it for her sake. He would always be here; she knew that because he had told her so. Margaret was unpredictable and often absent but Trevor was her rock. Geology and her father's dependability knitted together in her mind, twin solid pillars that had stayed with her all her life.

'But I'll tell you what,' Trevor had added. 'I think we should go out and do some climbing together. You and me. Then you'll understand that

189

if you are careful, and if you never forget that it is often harder to turn back than go forward, climbing isn't as dangerous as many other things in this world. Would you like that?'

'I don't know,' Alice said doubtfully.

The next day they went to a shop in the main street and a man with a seamed face and two fingers missing from his right hand fitted a small harness round Alice's chest and hips. She was surprised by how deft the remaining fingers were as he did up the buckles.

'Why was his hand like that?' she asked Trevor as they walked away with a rope, and Alice's harness and a small pair of climbing shoes.

'His hands got very cold and the fingers died and had to be removed. It's called frostbite,' Trevor said.

She looked up at the snows that cloaked the high mountains, even now, when it was so warm down here amongst the shops and cafés. 'Will we get it?'

'No,' Trevor said.

She watched her father climb a slab of rock. He moved so smoothly that he looked almost as if he were dancing.

When he reached a ledge he stopped and after a moment the rope drew tight between them. 'Now you,' he called from fifteen feet above her head. Reluctantly, she put her hands on the warm granite. The rope and the harness tightened still further and at once she understood that she might slip, but she could not fall. Trevor held her safe. She climbed up to the place beside him and watched as he clipped and knotted the rope to make her fast. It wasn't the rope and the slings she put her trust in but her father.

'He never did let me fall,' Alice told Richard. 'What was your father like?'

'He was a serving army officer.'

'Yes,' she said gently. 'Did you see much of him?'

'No. I went to boarding school; holidays were mostly with my mother's parents in Suffolk because my father and mother were always overseas.'

'That must have been hard.'

'What? No, not really. Most of us children at school were in the same boat. At least I had the name. People—boys—were impressed, as if it made me someone. I knew it didn't, though.'

She could imagine the housemaster reading aloud from *South* or *The Worst Journey*, and Richard in the row of small boys with upturned faces, worrying that he might never match up to his father, let alone his famous grandfather.

'And now here you are,' she said, letting her thoughts run on.

'Here we both are, in fact.'

Alice studied his wind-reddened face again. Richard's eyes met hers. 'Did you know your grandfather?'

'I don't have many memories of him. I was only eight when he died. There was his house near Cambridge, my father and mother took me there just a few times. I remember brown-panelled rooms and a clock ticking, and a certainty that I mustn't speak too loudly or knock anything over. My grandmother tiptoed and the rest of us followed suit. There were photographs everywhere: Grandfather receiving his polar medal from the

191

King, Grandfather with Scott's widow. There was one that terrified me. It stood on a table in front of the french windows, and when the light outside was bright enough the glass reflected and you couldn't see the picture itself. I was always glad of a sunny day at Grandfather's. The picture was taken by Ponting, who was the expedition's photographer—you know that, of course, I'm sorry—and it was of a killer whale. The creature's blunt head was rearing up out of a narrow crack between the ice floes and its mouth was wide open, a huge trap lined with terrible teeth. You could see the thing's tiny eyes, and if I closed mine to shut it out I was right in the water and the jaws were closing round me. It used to give me nightmares. I'd wake up screaming and I couldn't tell my mother why.' Richard collected himself. 'It's strange, the things that frighten children.'

'I don't think that's strange. It gives me a shiver just to hear you describe it.'

'Yet your mother went diving amongst them.'

'The thought of Antarctica scared me too. I liked the stories, I just never wanted to come here myself.'

'And yet?'

Alice didn't feel caught out, as she might have done before they had come to Wheeler's Bluff. Richard and she were confiding in each other now. 'My mother wanted me to come because she couldn't travel herself. I agreed because of her, but I feel differently now.'

Richard was smiling. 'Better, or worse?'

Alice lifted her hand and made a wide gesture that took in the tent's shelter, the height of the Bluff in one direction and the frozen desert in the

192

other. 'I imagined what it would be like, but this is beyond imagination. I wouldn't have missed it, this, here and now, for anything else in the world.'

She felt it passionately but the words' comparative poverty made her blush. She could feel the colour creeping up her face.

'I'm happy to hear that,' Richard said.

His voice and the look in his eyes told her: he's going to kiss me. He had leaned closer to her in the cramped space and their mouths were only inches apart.

Do I want him to? Alice asked herself. The answer was yes. The wind and the silence that always lay beneath it drummed in her ears.

But he didn't kiss her.

Their cheeks almost brushed. Richard picked up his tin mug and drained the last of his cold tea. Alice hooked her arms round her knees, feeling like the awkward girl at a party.

You are a scientist out in the field with a colleague, she reminded herself. And at the same time she thought of Becky, who wouldn't have waited for Richard or anyone else to take the initiative.

'What's funny?' Richard asked.

'Nothing, really. Um, do you have children yourself?'

'No. I was married but I've been divorced for two years. Helena was never happy with the amount of time I have to spend away from home. In the end she found herself a marketing consultant who comes back for dinner every night.'

'I'm sorry.' She could almost feel the layers of diffidence and loneliness in him, like her own sedimentary rocks, except that Richard's layers were the accretions of British upper-middle-class reserve, and stiff-upper-lipness and fear of showing your feelings.

'I've got the advantage over you. I know from your CV that you're single and childless.'

His words set up a shiver at the base of Alice's spine. She didn't know why and the lack of a reason was like the whirling blank spot at the centre of her field of vision that heralded a migraine. 'Yes.'

'Who was that in the photograph?'

For Richard, this was a seriously personal question. She had to think for a second. Of course, he had caught a glimpse of the Polaroid. 'That's Pete. My ex-boyfriend. He's an artist.'

Obviously Richard didn't know any artists. For an instant he looked as baffled as if she had said trapeze artist or fortune teller—but then, neither of these sounded as outlandish as fossil hunter.

'Is he a good one?'

Alice hesitated. 'I can't tell.'

'That's it exactly. I can never tell. One of the reasons why I'm a scientist, I suppose.'

'Not all that good. Probably. Does that sound disloyal?'

It was getting cold in the tent without the Primus burning. Alice was beginning to think of the warm layers of her sleeping bag. Tomorrow, if the weather held, they planned to move ten kilometres further east along the Bluff and set up a new campsite. It promised to be a long day.

'I don't think you would ever be disloyal, Alice.'

He touched her wrist then, with just the tip of his forefinger. In their profound isolation, where there would have been no one to see or care if they had cavorted naked and rampant in the snow, it

194

managed to be the most intimate gesture she had ever known.

'Do you miss him?' Richard asked.

'No,' Alice said. They didn't look at each other.

There didn't seem to be anything to add, for tonight.

Richard began to gather up his windproofs. His insulated boots lay beside the door and he pulled them on, careful not to turn round and accidentally trample on her belongings. Finally he unzipped the flap and thin flakes of snow gusted around him. She watched him crawl out backwards, like a rabbit disappearing the wrong way down a hole. They agreed, before he withdrew his head, on a 6 a.m. start.

Alice brushed her teeth with the last of the water and spat out in her tin mug. She undressed to the two layers of thermals that she slept in and crawled into her sleeping bag. Left alone, she did miss Pete. Or not Pete himself but the warmth and reassurance of another familiar body. She turned on to her side and tried to imagine the pressure of his chest against her spine, the way his knees fitted into the crook of hers, the moisture of his breath against the nape of her neck. Within seconds the body she was imagining was not Pete's but Richard Shoesmith's.

At once she turned over and lay flat on her back. The tilley lamp was still burning so she reached an arm out of her cocoon to extinguish it. Sleep had begun to flutter like moths' wings at the margins of her consciousness, but now in the tent's twilight it flew away out of her reach. Her eyes widened and her thoughts quickened.

She was cold, even in her layers of insulation,

and the chill reminded her of the shiver that had touched her earlier.

What had he said?

There was the nauseating blank spot again, in the middle of her mind's eye, while her thoughts spun faster and faster.

I know from your CV. Was that it? Yes. *You are single and childless.*

The spot contracted to a single blinding point of light. Alice felt a pain like hot wire in her elbows, across her shins, round her ribs. She stopped breathing and stared up at the yellow planes of the tent's inner skin. The wind's drumming seemed to grow louder until it took on the rhythm of her racing heart.

Very slowly she flexed her fingers. She lifted her hands from her sides and laid them over her stomach.

How long? Oh God, how long, and why had she only just thought about it?

She forced herself to reckon up. Not regular, no. She never had been. The Pill hadn't suited her and she had had a coil fitted after she met Pete. Dr Davey had done it for her.

Think.

So much else to fill her mind in the last weeks.

It was now—what?—the end of the third week in November. Her last period had been at the beginning of October, when Margaret was ill and there had been the flurry of decisions to make about Kandahar.

That was it. She remembered now, she had bled more heavily than usual and felt tired and cramped, but she had taken some painkillers and paid no more attention. Since then, nothing. Alice's scalp tightened. She had to remember to breathe. Nothing, that is, except the night of the farewell party at Jo's house. Going home with Pete, opening the door of the house they had shared. The bare shelves and empty drawers, the bulky shapes of her polar kitbags on the bedroom floor.

There had been a barefaced passion, where once there had been intimacy. She did remember that, quite clearly.

Her period was now more than three weeks late. Therefore, counting from the date of her last period (it was like insisting on a correct punctuation mark, this accuracy, in a torrent of feverish babble), she could be about seven weeks pregnant.

She writhed on the air mattress, twisting as if she were delirious.

This was not possible. She had taken responsible precautions. It was a mistake and the real reason for the absence of her period would become plain if only she could think clearly enough.

Instead, she remembered something else.

Becky and Jo had been waiting for her in a café. Jo had a half-drunk cup of coffee in front of her, Becky an untouched glass of water. They were all eighteen and it was a hot July day at the end of their last week at school.

Alice slid into the seat facing them. The red plastic covering was hot against her bare legs.

'Well?'

Becky slowly shook her head. 'The only really likely explanation for a missed period in a healthy, sexually active young woman is pregnancy.'

'Who told you that?'

'I rang a family planning clinic. Gave them your

197

name, actually.'

Even in a crisis Becky tried to joke. Then she held up a Boots bag. 'This is the test. I'm going to do it tomorrow.'

In the end Becky had had an abortion and had gone up to Cambridge that same autumn as if nothing had happened. Only Jo and Alice knew how much the ordeal had affected her. And the exact words she had muttered on that hot afternoon came back to Alice now.

The only likely explanation. She was young enough and certainly healthy, and she had been sexually active.

Wait, she thought. Don't jump to conclusions. There *could* be all sorts of reasons: cold, exertion, anxiety. But as she ran her hands over her body she knew, with a woman's certainty that she would have denied only an hour ago, that she *was* pregnant. Her breasts were fuller, and her thighs and hips had acquired a new solidity, as if under skin and dense layers of muscle the blood itself was richer and circulated with more purpose. Her fingers met over her abdomen. There was a dome where once there had been a hollow. Already? Was that possible?

A flood tide of dismay swept through her as she realised that she had no idea.

She lay on her back and tried to think rationally. But all that came was panicky non sequiturs, flutters of astonishment and spasms of terror that squeezed her heart. It was as if all her years of training as a scientist melted away in an hour. She had been a meticulous layer of plans, always prepared with facts and data, and now there was an inner chamber of herself that was susceptible to none of her scientific armoury and yet would change everything in her world.

The hours passed. She lifted her wrist once in a while to see the luminous dial of her watch. Sleep was unthinkable.

At ten minutes to six she heard Richard moving around in his tent. The wind had dropped during the night, but it had started to snow. She had listened absently and unreflectingly to the slithering kiss of it on the tent's panels. The nylon sagged slightly above her head with the accumulating weight.

At six o'clock, wearily shaking herself, Alice crawled out of her sleeping bag. She dressed in her layers of clothes, managing the zips and toggles even though her fingers trembled, and crawled outside to fill a pan with snow for tea. The world that met her eyes was drained of all colour and definition. The Bluff and the ice sheet were invisible behind veils of spiralling snow. Snow had drifted against the sides of the tents and over the skidoo. A reddish shape lumbered a few feet away from her. It was Richard in his windproofs, already dismantling the radio antennae in preparation for moving camp.

'A thick day,' he called. 'But I think we can travel.'

Alice licked her dry lips. 'Right.'

She melted snow, then stirred oats and dried milk powder into the hot water to make their breakfast porridge. While they were eating she listened to Richard outlining the day's objectives. She nodded and spooned up the food, thinking of it as fuel. Do what was expected of her, that was all she could hope for today. When there was time to think properly, when the shock had subsided, she would decide what to do.

They loaded the sledge with mounds of gear and the heavy boxes of rock samples. The final task was to take down the tents. Alice slid the telescopic poles out of hers first, leaving the fabric securely pegged until the last, when she was ready to bundle it up and stow it. Richard sealed up the bag of their frozen waste and hoisted the lidded barrel that contained it on to the back of the sledge. Everything, even this, was classified as 'retro'—to be flown back to Kandahar and, in the end, shipped out of Antarctica.

Richard took a compass bearing. The Bluff was intermittently visible through the white veil, but not reliably enough to navigate by. They started to move forwards. Alice drove the skidoo, Richard plodded a little ahead through the fresh snow with a long glacier probe in his hand. He stared into the blankness, trying to see a dip or hollow that might betray a big crevasse. The skidoo tracks rode up and down over the rigid waves of sastrugi. Alice concentrated as hard as she could, her eyes fixed on Richard, keeping the machine moving forward at the same slow pace.

After an hour they changed places and after another hour they changed back again.

It was the longest journey Alice had ever known. After four hours they stopped briefly to eat chocolate and drink from the Thermos.

'How much further?' Alice asked, trying to sound as if she were enquiring out of mere curiosity.

'I reckon we're halfway. Are you okay?'

'I'm fine.'

Cold and exhaustion gnawed at her when she drove the skidoo. When she trudged through the deepening snow her eyes ached and stung from staring at the white void and her leg muscles screamed with the effort of keeping going, but at least she was reasonably warm. At last, when she had begun to think that the walk would never end and life would for ever be a matter of putting one foot in front of the other or bumping over vicious ridges with cold racking her bones, Richard stopped. He stood with his back to the snow, extracted his GPS handset from an inner recess in his parka and took a reading. Then, to Alice's joy, he jerked her the thumbs-up signal.

It was windier here than at their first camp. The Bluff was lower at this point and wind howled over the top of it, scouring up loose snow and flinging it into their eyes and mouths. They tried to work quickly, unloading boxes and preparing to set up the tents. By this time Alice was blundering with tiredness. She unpacked her tent and spread it out on the snow, turning aside for a second to pick up the poles. A strong gust of wind licked over the invisible Bluff and roared over the ice. It snatched at one corner of her tent, then sucked it into the air with a flap like a giant bird's wing. She had forgotten Phil's First Rule. Never leave your tent unpegged, even for a second.

Her hand, holding the now useless peg hammer, fell to her side. The orange wing soared into the air beyond her reach and was whirled away into infinity.

She turned to Richard. 'I'm very sorry,' she said tonelessly.

'We'll share.' He pegged his all the way round

201

before sliding in the poles.

They went through all the morning's activities, in reverse.

At last they were crouching within the shelter of the remaining tent. Alice stirred a pan of chilli and beans while Richard made the scheduled radio contact with Niki.

'Kandahar, Kandahar, this is Wheeler's Bluff. How copy?'

'Hello, Wheeler's Bluff,' Niki's voice came back like a warm handshake. 'How are you this fine evening?'

Niki gave them the weather forecast. 'Put on your warm clothes out there.'

'Okay, Kandahar. Thanks for that.'

Alice squatted on her mattress. With both their sleep kits laid out there was no room to move around.

'Good job we travelled today. We may have to sit out a couple of stormy days,' Richard said cheerfully.

'And I let my tent blow away.'

She was wedged between two insolubles, the immediate one of tents and weather and isolation and the other, distant but so enormous that it overshadowed all the familiar scenery of her life. Her hand was shaking and the tin spoon rattled as she stirred the pot of food.

'Worse things could have happened,' Richard said. She wondered if he meant it or if he was repeating what his grandfather would have said, then felt ashamed at the thought.

They ate, sitting side by side with the stove still burning to keep the tent warm. Hours of cold and exertion meant that they were both hungry,

202

although Alice was surprised by her appetite. Keep going, for now. That was all she could do. Maybe I'm wrong, she kept thinking. But she knew she was not wrong.

The stove and the light of the tilley lamp and the food they were sharing made the tent an intimate place. But after they had eaten and wiped the plates and drunk some tea, there was no attempt to have their usual hour's talk. There would be no saying goodnight to close the conversation safely, because they would be lying here side by side.

Alice took off a couple of layers of clothes and squirmed into her sleeping bag. She closed her eyes, lying as still as she could and resisting the impulse to lace her fingers over her stomach. Richard moved around for a few minutes, then he lay down next to her and turned out the lamp.

In their little bubble of shelter against the snow, Alice wondered how it would be if she raised her voice over the wind and said, *I think I am pregnant.* But even the thought made her hot with dismay. It would be to admit that without any warning her life had slipped out of her control—here, of all places, where control was the only way to survive against the elements. No. She would have to work out her own strategy and act on it.

A foot away from her, Richard was thinking too. When the pressure of anxiety forced her eyes open, she saw that he was watching her in the yellow light. He lifted one hand and touched her hair. Then his fingers moved across her cheek and rested on her mouth.

Last night—only *last night*?—she would have welcomed the caress. But now, with her body still defensive with shock, she flinched. She didn't mean to, she should have caught his hand and held it, warmly, yet to stop him going any further. But it was too late.

He withdrew his hand as if she had bitten it and turned on to his back. 'I'm sorry. That was completely inappropriate.' He sounded as stiff as a Victorian uncle. As if Gregory Shoesmith had ventured too far with a fellow officer's sister at a tennis party.

'No, it's me. I mean . . .' Her voice trailed away, was swallowed by the wind. She couldn't tell him, it's not that I don't want you to, didn't want you to, only this is happening and I don't know anything any more . . .

'I understand. One has to be very careful. Out here. It's very easy to cross boundaries that then can't be, you know, put up again. If necessary.'

She did understand what he was saying, in his choked-off way. In this place raw feelings swelled much closer to the surface. She could read Richard's face and the pucker of emotions that rippled under the skin. He could see her, and so could Valentin and Laure and Russell and the others. There was nowhere to hide: the light was too bright and clear, and the days were too long.

She would have to be *very* careful.

'I know. Richard, I . . .' She was going to tell him that she liked him. Admired him, whatever it was. Fancied him, then. But it sounded too banal.

'Yes. Yes,' he said quickly, so as not to have to hear anything else.

He turned a little on one side and hunched his shoulder. Alice lay still, waiting for whatever would happen next. Almost at once she fell into an exhausted sleep.

In the morning she crawled out of the tent and found Richard already outside, testing the air. It was cold and completely still. And then, when she lifted her face she saw that the heavens were thick with sparkling motes. Tiny pinpoints of ice cascaded out of a clear sky and caught the sun as they spiralled downwards. It was celestial confetti and the beauty of it took her breath away.

Diamond dust, that was what Margaret had called it.

'I'll think of you, with diamond dust falling,' she had said when they parted.

To think of Margaret, and home, was to open channels that Alice wasn't ready to navigate yet. Instead, she stood with her face to the sky, soaking in the glamour of the day and the place. Her concerns shrank, she felt her whole being shrinking until she was no more than one of the points of ice, and the awareness of infinity comforted her.

The sound of Richard's voice made her jump. 'We'll get a day's work in. Bad weather's coming,' he called.

They ate porridge, pulled on their windproofs and began on the new section of the Bluff.

Alice remembered it, oddly, as a perfect day. She threw herself into her work, into the rock page of the history book. The reckoning of years by the hundred million soothed her and silenced her racing thoughts. In the middle of the afternoon, just as she was beginning to tire, Richard called her over. From a section of black mudstone, residue of the ocean that had once covered this spot, he had hammered out a fossilised mollusc, complete in every detail. He laid it in the cup made by her gloved hands.

205

'I don't know what this is. Look at the whorls, there. It's a species I don't recognise.'

His voice was hoarse with excitement. He looked like a small boy on his birthday.

His elation touched her, caught fire in her too. 'It's a good day.' She smiled.

That night the wind started again. It was a different wind, which came at them with a roar, then rose to a howl of fury.

CHAPTER NINE

As far as Rooker was concerned, sometimes the place was claustrophobic while at others it could be almost companionable, but being there mostly just meant that you quietly did your work, you slept or rested or drank a little, and you let the days slide by.

Everyone on the base responded differently to living at Kandahar.

Antarctic life suited the easy-going Phil and Valentin, whereas the more highly strung Arturo and Niki were often moody. Jochen's thick-skinned insistence got on other people's nerves as well as Laure's, and he was often the focus of criticism that he always ignored. Russell was too experienced an Antarctic hand to be anything but efficient and professional. Now, Rooker found, without Richard Shoesmith's constant interfering presence life was even more straightforward. Doing things his own way, he unloaded materials from a pallet that had been brought ashore by ship at the beginning of the season and began to build the A-frame skidoo shelter on a rock foundation behind the base.

It was heavy work, but it wasn't particularly difficult. Rooker went at it steadily. He called Phil or Russell over to help him when he needed a second pair of hands, but mostly he was alone. That was nothing new, but the empty brilliance of the air and the monochrome landscape provided fewer immediate distractions than he was used to. Or maybe the certainty that he would have to stay here meant that his mind wasn't always working around the question of the next destination, like a tongue around a jagged tooth. Whatever the reason, thoughts and memories that he was adept at suppressing seemed to rise closer to the surface.

It wasn't just that he thought about Henry Jerrold because Richard Shoesmith brought him to mind.

He even began to hear her voice in his head, as clearly as if she had crept up behind him.

Darling? Jimmy, darling, is that you?

Once he even whirled round, but all he found was Laure who had brought him an unnecessary mug of coffee.

Her smile glinted at him. 'Won't you have it before it goes cold?'

'No. Thanks,' he said. He turned back and swung the mallet to drive in icy wooden pegs.

At night he was tired enough to sleep.

One evening he was standing at the locker beside his bunk, folding clothes. He had flung them on the line in the generator hut and the shirts and trousers had stiffened into careless creases. His back was to the room and his head was full of voices that he was trying not to hear. Then someone put a hand on his shoulder.

He didn't think about it. He just spun on his heel and pinned the guy back against the wall, fingers and thumbs splayed against his throat.

Phil's alarmed eyes goggled at him. Russell had been lying on his bunk listening to his Walkman, but he levered himself upright now.

Rooker let his hands drop. 'Christ. I'm sorry.'

Phil coughed and massaged his neck. 'Remind me not to upset you. Did you think I was Shoesmith? How seriously is this place getting to you, boy?' With his concern his Welsh accent grew stronger.

'I didn't. It isn't. I was thinking about something else.'

Russell and Phil glanced at each other.

'It can affect you. Isolation, confinement,' Russell began.

'It was just an automatic reaction, all right?' Rooker snapped.

He put his half-folded clothes on the bunk and left the room. He closed the door as gently as he could, but a second later Phil followed him out into the main room. Niki and Valentin were in the radio room, talking to the Ukrainians on their base further up the peninsula. Everyone else appeared to have gone to bed.

'Why are you so fucking angry? All the time? I'm just asking, you know,' Phil said.

'I said I was sorry.'

'Yeah, you did. It doesn't matter. But if you want to explain anything about why a simple tap on the shoulder makes you go for a man's throat, you know, you can be my guest.'

Rooker would have liked a drink, but the bottles were where he and Phil usually stashed them, in the zipper bag under Phil's bunk. To reach one he would have to confront Russell again, but maybe Phil would go for it.

'Do you want a whisky?'

Phil hesitated, looking at Rooker as if he was trying to work something out. 'No. Thanks all the same,' he said quietly. 'I'm just going to go to bed.'

Rooker stood still, staring at the crumbs on the oilcloth table cover and the grey smeared eye of the computer monitor on the desk by the wall. The sky outside the uncurtained windows was luminous dark-blue. A feeling of pressure that he recognised as sadness squeezed at his heart.

He put on his parka and went outside. The wind that met him was restless, turning in circles and raising eddies of snow. Rooker balled his fists and stuck them deep in his pockets. For no particular reason he walked around the perimeter of the hut. There were crates and empty gas cylinders stored against the walls. A skua shifted on its rock, staring at him without rotating its head. As he passed the window looking into the living area, Rooker saw the door of the women's bunk room open, and Jochen came out. He looked red-faced and displeased. He had been making a try for Laure, Rook guessed, but he didn't look as if he had got quite far enough. But if it now meant that Laure would stop following him around, Rooker was happy with that. He had shaken Edith off and he had no intention of replacing her.

He walked along the shoreline, wishing that he had a whisky flask with him. He passed the place where he had sat with the woman geologist, Alice Peel, and climbed over the outcrop that separated it from the little bay with the natural rock steps. As

209

always, being in this tiny amphitheatre of rock and ice quietened his mind. He sat down halfway up the flight of steps and watched the brash ice undulating with the waves.

Memory was a curse. Whenever you stopped moving, it came up on you like a fog. That was why he preferred cold places, where the wind assailed you if you hesitated for too long. Places like this, where to keep moving was to keep warm. To stay alive.

*　　*　　*

Jimmy, darling, is that you?

He closed the door carefully, because slamming it always made her headache worse. He found her lying on the daybed in front of the television. Her hair was yellow, the colour of pale straw, but the roots showing at the parting were as dark as his own.

'How was school today?'

'Okay.'

'Give me a kiss, then.'

When he leaned over she smelled of bourbon and talcum powder and indoor sweat. It was a hot day, but she had the blinds drawn. She was watching a movie. Big faces filled the screen and then mouths kissing. The volume was turned right down, though. She didn't ever listen to the words, just looked at the images. Words made her heart ache, she used to say. Jimmy Rooker thought that everything in her life made some part of her ache.

'Do you want some tea?' she asked, but she didn't take her eyes off the kiss. It was a long one. He went through into the kitchenette and looked in the fridge. There was a carton of milk and some leftovers that had been sitting there for a couple of days. He put a finger into a dish of congealed gravy and tasted it, but it wasn't improving. He ate a bowl of cornflakes instead.

When he had finished he washed his bowl and spoon, and put them on the draining board; then he made a cup of Nescafé with sugar, just how she liked it, and carried it through to her. The kissing had finished, at least.

'You're a good boy.'

'Why don't we go out for a bit? It's a nice day. We could go for a walk.'

He imagined how it might be. They'd walk down the road and turn into Main Street, saying hello to people they met, then maybe they could cut down the side of Paulina's Hair Parlour and take the path to the river.

'I can't, not now. Lester's coming round.'

Jimmy didn't say anything, but he thought it. Bloody, bloody Lester. He was always around, these days. Lester wore a mulberry-red silk scarf knotted round his neck and a belt with a buckle in the shape of a pair of hands shaking. He would flutter around her, telling her that she was beautiful but she should make more of herself, maybe a brighter lipstick, maybe a new hairstyle. He would lift the strands of straw hair in his ringed fingers and fluff them out, and their two faces poised one above the other would make identical pouting expressions in the mirror.

Jimmy knew that she was beautiful, but not in the way that Lester meant.

'I'll go and see if Gabby's home then,' he said.

'Gabby? All right, darling. Don't be late, will

211

you?' Her voice was vague.

With Gabby Macfarlane he went down to the ponds. Gabby was a thin, watchful boy who had moved down with his family from the North Island somewhere. He was a year older than Jimmy, but he was in the same class. They sat on the bank of the big pond, watching the fish rise. They seemed just to kiss the surface and ripples spread in perfect circles to mark the spot. Neither he nor Gabby had a fishing rod, so they threw stones at the ripples instead; then further along the bank they found a pile of concrete fence posts waiting to be dug in to replace some splintered wooden ones.

It took the two of them to lift one post and totter to the water's edge with it, but when they swung it between them, then let go, it made a huge and satisfying splash. Soon, every post had sent up its oblong coronet of silver-khaki water. After that there was nothing much to do, so they wandered home again. Lester was sitting beside her on the sofa, drinking and giggling.

'You are nothing but a troublemaker, Rooker,' Brice, the headmaster, had told him. The farmer had been to the school, and Jimmy and Gabby had been hauled out of class.

Rooker nodded. It seemed easier, less of a battle all round, just to agree with him. 'Yeah,' he said.

*   *   *

It was too cold to sit any longer on the rock step. That was good. He jumped up and began walking, fast, because his nose and hands had gone numb. Keep moving, that was the idea.

In the morning, Phil came out to breakfast wearing a helmet and boxing gloves. He dodged and feinted around Rooker, who looked startled and then laughed. Rooker was glad that the little Welshman hadn't taken against him after all.

Laure looked up from the book she was reading. 'Is it one of your jokes, Philip?'

'Nah, matter of life and death,' Phil answered.

'English sense of humour.' Jochen sighed.

'Welsh, if you don't mind.'

Rooker blocked a punch. 'Did you bring those with you, just in case?'

Phil shook his head. 'Sullavan supplied them. Leisure activities. There's ping-pong in one of them crates, as well.'

'Is there now?'

Valentin stood at the window yawning and scratching himself. 'You boys will always be arsing around. Meanwhile we have snowfall.'

Niki monitored the weather reports, his long, melancholy face clamped between the twin protuberances of his headset. Today the helicopter had been scheduled to come from Santa Ana, then fly on to Wheeler's Bluff to pick up Richard and Alice. But the Chileans reported heavy snow and winds gusting up to fifty knots. There was no flying.

Out at the Bluff, Richard reported that he and Alice had been left tent-bound by the blizzard. Billows of snow were flying upwards, whirling like tornados. They had four days' supply of food left and were rationing themselves in case they should be marooned for longer. At Kandahar itself the wind was less vicious, but Valentin was right. Snow

213

had closed in again.

'I think maybe Richard will be quite comfortable.' Jochen grinned. 'Especially since he has lost one tent.'

Laure looked prim.

Rooker and Phil devised a game. They took the ping-pong bats and ball out to the skidoo shelter and played a version of squash. The ball ricocheted around in the confined space as the bats smashed at it. Rooker was handicapped because he had to stoop, whereas Phil could more or less stand upright, but Rooker's longer arms gave him a better reach. Shed squash caught on. Everyone joined in, even Laure and Arturo, and Valentin drew up a competition ladder. Without Richard, and with no outside work to be done, the industrious culture on the base rapidly broke up. People lounged around the mess table playing cards after dinner and there seemed little point in getting up early in the morning for another day of waiting. Into this relaxed atmosphere the e-mail from Sullavanco arrived like a reprimand.

Russell had been monitoring Richard's work messages for him and on the fourth day of bad weather he read a communication from Beverley Winston. It announced that Lewis Sullavan planned to make a personal visit to Kandahar in the week before Christmas. He would be accompanied by one of his assistants—'probably myself'—and a media crew. He would fly in to Santa Ana and be ferried down by helicopter. He planned to stay for two days, then travel on to New Zealand.

'All the above arrangements are, of course, weather permitting,' Beverley Winston concluded.

214

Russell flung himself back in his chair. 'Jesus H. Christ,' he groaned.

'Trouble at home?' Phil murmured.

'Fifty thousand times worse than that, mate. Trouble at Kandahar.'

'What?' Phil read over his shoulder. 'Oh, dearie me. Let's have a look at the dates.'

He consulted a Sullavanco calendar that was pinned to the wall beside the terminal. No one at Kandahar ever knew the date or even what day it was. Life was governed by quite different principles.

'It's less than two weeks.'

Russell buried his head in his hands.

When he heard the news, Jochen threw his big head back and roared with laughter. 'That'll bring old Rich back from dallying in his tent with a pretty geologist, eh?'

Niki passed on the news in that evening's radio schedule with the Bluff.

Richard's voice fairly crackled out of the receiver in response. Just as soon as the weather eased enough to allow the helo to take off, he would be back and preparations would be put in hand. In the meantime he would speak to Russell.

Russell came back from the radio room with a long list of instructions. 'You'd think it was Queen Liz herself coming to stay.' He sighed.

Valentin and Arturo were the finalists in the shed squash tournament. Rook's height had told against him in the end, and Phil had been beaten by Arturo's combination of cunning and agility. Everyone crowded round the shed during a lull in the wind, listening to the metallic *plang-kerplang* of the ball hitting the aluminium sheeting of the

215

interior, and taking it in turns to peer in through the crack in the door. Laure jumped up and down like a cheerleader, shouting their names in turn. Then a fierce rally ended in a meaty slap and a howl of agony from Arturo. A second later he lurched out of the shed door with his hands cupping his nose and blood dripping down his chin. He was yelling in Spanish.

Valentin burst out in his wake. 'He got his silly head in the way. Bat smack in face.'

Jochen took Arturo's wrists and dragged the hands from his face. Arturo shouted louder as snow and wind drove into the crushed-strawberry remains of his nose.

'Uh-oh,' Jochen muttered. He took him by the arm and propelled him inside.

Valentin and the others followed. Valentin shrugged his shoulders up to his ears and spread his shovel-sized hands. 'I didn't mean to hit him. Little *maricón*.'

Of course not, Phil and Rooker agreed. It could have happened to anyone.

'Shed squash. It's a man's game and a man must take risks,' Phil said solemnly.

In the hut, Jochen had Arturo in a chair with his head back. He shone a torch up each pulpy nostril and into Arturo's eyes while Laure laid out dressings and syringes.

'Could be broken,' Jochen said.

Arturo gave a thin howl.

'But I would have to X-ray to be certain and here I cannot, so I must do what I can for your pretty face and we will hope for the best, my friend.'

'Jesus, Maria,' Arturo moaned.

216

By the evening he had two swollen black eyes and his nose was obliterated by a huge swath of splints, bandage and sticking plaster.

'I dunno, Artie,' Phil said. 'I can see that it's different all right. But I'm not sure it's an improvement.'

Arturo held up his middle finger, then winced.

Valentin rapped the table for attention. 'I am asking the company present for one decision. I am champion, yes, since Arturo here retired hurt?'

There was a chorus of contradictions. Finally Phil and Rooker, as the game's inventors, were allowed to adjudicate.

'Rematch,' Rooker pronounced. 'Nose status permitting.'

The night's weather report indicated that conditions at Santa Ana were improving, with only moderate winds and precipitation. The pilots would assess the situation again in the morning. The news from the Bluff was that Richard and Alice were ending their fifth day in the tent, the fourth of their unscheduled extra stay. They were running low on food.

'Tomorrow is always another day in Antarctica,' Phil said.

*   *   *

Alice opened her eyes. The pyramid reach of the tent over her head, the smell of her sleeping bag and her own unwashed skin, the *hrggh* sound that Richard made when he cleared his throat and prepared to turn a page of his book, were all as familiar to her as if she had grown up with them. She would not have believed it possible to spend so

217

many hours confined in such a small space with a man she barely knew, but still she *had* done it.

It was only a few seconds ago that she had woken from a deep, populous sleep—during the blizzard she sometimes wasn't sure if she had been properly conscious for even one hour in twenty-four—but it was clear that there was something different happening outside. The tent walls bellied and then grew taut, but slowly. There was no roaring and banging, even when she shook her head to clear her dulled ears.

Richard was kneeling at the radio box. She studied the outline of his profile and the fuzzy promontory of his beard as intently as if he were beloved to her. As if he were her lover.

She did love him, in a way, after the six days that they had just endured together. They had sung songs, recited poems, played cards and talked until it seemed that they had no more memories to share. Alice had told him about her mother, and about how Margaret had already experienced and triumphantly survived even what they were doing right now. 'Sometimes I feel as if all my life already belongs to her. That was one of the reasons why I was reluctant to come down here. I can't do any of it any differently, any better, than she did. Is it the same for you?'

Richard said, 'I longed to come. I knew as soon as I was old enough to know anything that it was what I had to do.' His eyes burned with zeal.

We're not the same, Alice thought. Not quite the same.

When one of them feared that the wind would never stop blowing, the other joked and cajoled the sufferer back into optimism. They confessed to

218

each other when they felt the grip of homesickness, took it in turns to stumble out to the barrel dug into a shelter a few yards from the tent, made each other laugh and listened to each other's dream-ridden sleep. But they did not become lovers. That avenue had turned into a cul-de-sac.

Alice hadn't explained the reason why. Once or twice she felt the words forming, but this news was so momentous, so personal to her in the way that it was embedded in the tissues of her body, that she had never spoken of it.

She had done plenty of thinking instead. She had chased reasons and plans and possible courses of action all through the claustrophobic hours of the blizzard. There had been moments of pure panic, but these had been balanced by incredulity and joy.

She was pregnant. There would be a baby.

She counted up the weeks and calculated that it would be in early July. It seemed a long way off, yet, but the day would come. It must come, that at least was one thing she was certain of. Alice had been with Becky after her abortion and had listened to her weeping. Even now, more than fifteen years later, Becky still grieved for the child she had lost when she had been little more than a child herself. This unplanned baby, hers, was hardly more than an idea but there could be no destroying it. The thought alone made her draw in her shoulders and hunch her spine to make a protective cage round it.

But first there was her old life, the one she was used to living. That had to be given its due, too. Everything would change, but before it did there was this precious interval.

Alice considered the possibility of making her

announcement as soon as they got back to Kandahar. There would be surprise and concern—Richard, Jochen and Russ would say that a research base in Antarctica was no place for a pregnant woman. There would be a hasty helicopter ride, a flight onwards from Santa Ana to South America and the rest of the long journey home.

For what reason?

Her house was let for the academic year, her role in the Department was on hold, no one expected to see her before the early summer.

If I go straight home from here in March, she calculated, instead of travelling for another couple of months, I will still only be twenty-one or twenty-two weeks pregnant.

She had confidence in her body. It always did what she wanted it to, or had done until it sprang this surprise on her. It could look after itself for another two or three months, why not?

I can finish what I promised to do here, Alice thought. No one need know until I get back home.

She would not have to creep back early and tell Margaret, my coil failed, can you believe it? The device would stay inside her and be harmlessly expelled when the baby was born, she thought. She must have read that somewhere. *I'm going to have a baby.*

Trevor would be delighted. He would want her to go home right away, whatever the circumstances. But Trevor always did the safest thing. Margaret, on the other hand . . . Alice could see how her face would tighten at the news.

'Well, are you pleased? You must be,' she would say. 'But what a shame that it should happen right now. And what about Peter?'

What about Peter.

He had slipped into a corner of her mind, one that she didn't often visit. This was her baby, not his, not anyone else's. She would make her own decisions.

The last factor in her reckoning was Antarctica itself. Even as the blizzard sucked and bellowed around their speck of shelter, making even the briefest dash outside a blind odyssey through choking snow and wind, Alice knew that she didn't want to leave the ice. Not until it was properly time to go. Yesterday, with food and fuel running low, they had rationed themselves to one hot meal of a mug of porridge made with water, and divided the last of the chocolate and dried fruit between them for the rest of the day. They were hungry and the interior of the tent was a cold and squalid tangle, but Alice felt a bud of determination forming inside her, as strong and tenacious as the baby itself.

She would not easily give up this savage and beautiful place. She was learning to live with it, not against it.

Richard was searching for radio contact: 'Kandahar, Kandahar, do you read me? This is Wheeler's Bluff camp. Do you read me? Over.

'Where are they?' he muttered impatiently.

Niki's voice faded in and out through the static, then grew clear. 'Good morning, Wheeler's Bluff, Wheeler's Bluff, do you copy?'

'Yes of course we do, what are they playing at?' He frowned at Alice.

'Copy you, Kandahar. Sitrep, please. Over.'

'We have some news, Wheeler's Bluff.'

Alice sat up. A shower of ice crystals from the roof of the tent fell over her head and neck.

'Weather window now opening. Helo transport left Santa Ana at o-nine-thirty hours. ETA at Kandahar two-zero minutes from now, estimated departure time for Bluff eleven-thirty hours. Do you copy?'

Alice gave a little whoop of delight.

Richard had already taken the weather observations. He recited them to Niki.

'Roger, Wheeler's Bluff. Repeat contact in one hour.'

'Hooray,' Alice said.

'I think it'll be touch and go. But let's get on with it.'

They lifted their hands and clapped them together.

Outside, it was still blowing. There was a lot of work to do. Their camp had to be packed up and and every bundle weighed, ready for loading on the helicopter. The last job of all would be to take down the tent and dismantle the radio antennae. If in the end the helicopter was delayed, they would need shelter and radio contact.

The temperature was falling. Alice zipped up her one-piece padded suit over all her other layers of smelly clothing, wondering if it was only her imagination that made it seem much tighter than it had been a week ago.

She began to work, packing the Primus components in the correct box, then starting work on the kitchen equipment. As each box was closed, she helped Richard to weigh it on a hand balance and made a note of the result. The work occupied her mind.

En route from Kandahar to Wheeler's Bluff, Rooker listened to the pilots' laconic exchanges through his headset. The weather at Kandahar had been fairly calm, but out here over the glaciers and nunataks the visibility was steadily deteriorating. For the last five minutes it had been like flying through milk. The navigator peered forwards and downwards, his helmet rotating in Rooker's sightline as he strained to pick ground features out of the wall of white. There were blue ridges of bare ice beneath them, visible for a few seconds before they were swallowed up again by the billowing mist and snow. Andy and Mick were as calm as if they were on a training run out of their home airfield, but Rooker knew there was no cause for celebration. He sat still with his hands loose in his lap, waiting for what would happen.

The helicopter turned in a tight circle and a savage gust of wind made it buck and judder. The Bluff suddenly appeared below them, its black back jagged in the surrounding void. Then they caught sight of a tiny orange triangle out in the wasteland. Rooker stared down at it as they circled closer. The isolation of this place and the utter precariousness of the shelter struck him forcibly. People wouldn't survive for very long out here if their little props were swept away.

The pilot circled once again and Rooker saw two small figures next to the tent. A landing square, properly marked out with poles and flags, swam into view. The machine's hover churned up a whirling wall of snow. A moment later the skis settled on the square and they were down.

'Nice job,' Rooker murmured.

'Let's get loaded up and back to the coast before we start to party,' Andy answered.

Cold and wind assaulted them as they stepped out. Richard and Alice were already shovelling snow and hauling rocks off the flap of their tent, ready to stow it. Rooker headed straight for the skidoo pegged under its nylon cover. With barely a word exchanged, all five of them set to work in a methodical rush to get everything packed away before the weather deteriorated further and left them all stranded there.

When it was done, Rooker saw Alice look around her, just once, to where the marks of their campsite were already being rubbed away by blowing snow. Then she walked towards the helicopter.

She looked different, even though her face was masked by her hood and snow goggles. She held her back straighter and there was a different angle to her head. Something has happened to her, he thought.

When they were airborne again he leaned towards her. In the cramped rear seats their sleeves were rubbing together, but he couldn't feel her arm under the layers of insulation. 'Good trip?' he asked.

'Yes, thank you,' Alice answered. He noticed the warm flash of her smile.

Richard hadn't entrusted his new mollusc to the sample boxes stacked behind them. He had put the bag with the fossil sealed inside it into the inner pocket of his parka. Once or twice during the flight Alice saw his hand go to the pocket zipper, to

224

check that it was properly closed.

Over the coast there was a layer of clear sky sandwiched between snow and cloud. Its margins shimmered with silver and the undersides of the clouds were washed with a pale green as delicate as a bird's egg. The red walls at Kandahar looked shockingly bright as the helicopter darted home over the glacier.

The hut door opened and tiny people spilled out, ready to greet them. Valentin and Niki stood at the door of the lab hut, looking as they always did, like one another's antithesis. Russell stood with his hands shading his eyes and Laure bobbed beside him. The helicopter circled once, then dipped to the landing square.

They had been away in the field for thirteen days, but to Alice it seemed much longer. She was glad to see the huts and the jumble of antennae and stores, and she immediately noticed the new skidoo shelter with the light dully reflecting off its metal walls.

'Hey, look.' She pointed as the engines stopped.

Rook grinned. He took off his headset and hung it up. 'There's a story attached.'

Richard looked round immediately, but Rook didn't elaborate.

As Alice climbed to the ground a shaft of pure lemon-yellow sunlight shone through a slit in the clouds, reducing everything that it didn't touch to gunmetal-grey. She remembered as she heard them again that there were homely, man-made noises here—the clink of metal, the steady thrumming of the generator, people calling to each other, and it made the remote place they had just come from seem even more unreal.

We did it, Alice thought.

A wash of triumph and joy swept over her. She was proud of her survival and happier to be back at Kandahar than she would have believed possible when she first came.

She was sure, now, that she had made the right decision. She couldn't think of leaving the ice until it was time to go.

At the same time she noticed that Rooker was watching her. He inclined his head in a strange, small nod of collusion.

There were people all around them. She saw Niki's ruined smile, Valentin's arms held out wide as if she had just walked in from the Pole itself, Laure who came straight across and hugged her. It was momentarily confusing to see so many faces after the days of isolation.

'Don't come too close. I stink.' Alice laughed.

'There's hot water for a shower. I made sure,' Laure told her.

'There's coffee and fresh doughnuts as well. Come on in. The guys'll unload the helo,' Russell insisted.

'Hot water? Doughnuts? Have I died and gone to heaven?'

'You would have done if I'd been there when you forgot Phil's First Rule,' Phil said. 'Only without the heaven bit.'

It was like coming home to the warmth of friends. Richard and Alice were swept into the hut on a swelling, confusing tide of voices. Inside, there was almost too much to look at and smell and hear. Alice sat down at the table and sipped her coffee. The warm, fatty, sugary taste of the doughnut was so potent that she had to close her eyes as she licked the crumbs off her lips.

When she opened them again she saw someone who looked a little bit like Arturo, except that his eyes were almost invisible in circles of puffed-out crimson and purple bruises, and his nose was a shapeless plum-coloured mass twice its original size. 'Arturo, whatever happened?' she managed to ask.

At the same time she saw Richard's hands come down flat on the table. He stood up, leaning on his arms, and swung his head in Rook's direction. Obviously, much too obviously, he was assuming that Rook must be the culprit. But he can't be, she thought. He wouldn't do that to someone who is only half his size.

Rook said nothing. He stared flat-eyed back at Richard, one corner of his mouth lifted in a semi-smile.

'My fault entirely. But was an accident, you know. A stupid thing.' It was Valentin who broke the smouldering silence.

'Just a game,' Arturo muttered thickly.

Richard's face twisted. 'A *game*? It looks as though it half killed him. Can't I leave you, can't I trust you to behave like reasonable people when I am off the base?'

It was the wrong thing to say. A litle ripple of protest went round the table.

'It looks somewhat worse than it is. A few days, the swelling will be going down and the bruise fading,' Jochen interjected.

'Before Lewis Sullavan gets here?'

Jochen stared. 'Not completely, no.'

No one spoke for a few seconds.

Then Richard collected himself. 'Are you all

right, Arturo? One of you had better tell me exactly what happened.'

Out of sympathy for Richard's clumsiness Alice swallowed her doughnut and slipped away from the table to the bunk room. A minute later Laure came in after her. The two women looked at each other.

'He would be a better schoolteacher than expedition leader,' Laure murmured.

'I know. But he doesn't mean it. He just wants very much to do it right, so much so that he does it wrong sometimes.'

Laure regarded her, a shrewd and measuring look. 'I think you don't like him so much. After two weeks with him, perhaps you have decided that?'

Alice coloured. 'I do like him. I admire him. I just think he is like a lot of Englishmen, who feel and believe all the right things but find it hard to express them. Their inhibitions tangle their tongues.'

Peter was the opposite, though. His tongue worked very well, artistically silvering and shining the less palatable truth. She took the Polaroid he had sent her out of her pocket and put it away in the drawer of her locker.

Laure gave a graceful shrug. 'Then I am glad to be French. But this way of Richard's is not fair to other people. To Rooker, *par example*.'

'I think maybe quite a lot of things in life have not been fair to Rooker. I also think that he can look after himself.'

'Yes.' Laure nodded. 'You are right.'

Alice went and took a shower. It was the first time she had stripped since going out into the field. To be naked felt vulnerable and delicious. She shivered with pleasure as the hot water sluiced over

228

her itchy skin and when she soaped herself she saw with mild dismay that the suds as they swirled away were quite grey. Now, for the first time in two weeks, her hair and hands wouldn't smell of kerosene. When she was clean she stood for another luxurious minute and let the water cascade over her bent head. Water was precious and hot water was Antarctic gold, but one more minute after two long weeks surely wouldn't matter.

She pressed her scrubbed hands over her stomach, noticing how it protruded. It felt solid and full, with a purpose, nothing like it did when she had overeaten. Then she examined her hips and breasts. There was no doubt about it, her breasts felt tender to the touch and her hips and thighs were thickening, ready to carry a new burden.

Alice tilted her head back, letting water run into her mouth and eyes.

She had never felt so connected to and yet so in awe of her own body. It was doing what it was meant to do, almost without reference to the Alice who lived behind her eyes, inside her head.

She was strong. Everything would go well. There was nothing physical to be afraid of, only to rejoice in.

For lunch there were fresh tomatoes. A supply ship had called into Santa Ana and the helicopter had brought them down. The colour and the dewy bloom of the skin were more luscious than anything Alice had ever seen. She ate her portion as slowly as she could but it still disappeared too quickly, the sharp sweetness filling her mouth, a thin trail of juice overflowing and running down her chin. She mopped it up before anyone could see, but Rooker's eyes were on her again.

He said carelessly, 'Here, do you want mine? I don't like tomatoes.'

'Thank you,' she said, unable to help herself, and ate them too.

After the meal, Richard called for attention. Everyone was present. Richard himself was still wearing the clothes in which he had come in from the field.

'As you all know, Lewis Sullavan and a camera crew will be arriving in four days' time. I don't think I need to explain how important this visit is for Kandahar. Mr Sullavan is our principal funding agent at present, and we have an unexpected and enormously valuable opportunity to show him at first hand the research work we're doing. For each listed project, therefore, the scientists should be ready to demonstrate in breadth and in detail exactly what is involved in the work. We will take Mr Sullavan and his people out into the near field wherever it is safe and practicable, and I will go through the arrangements for this separately with Russell, Philip and Rooker. The support staff should also be ready to discuss their separate and joint contributions to the various scientific projects—for example, Niki, your monitoring and logging of weather patterns in the local area—as well as their more general role on the base.

'I know you will all do your utmost to make this VIP visit successful. Are there any questions?'

Russell leaned slowly forward. 'The party's going to consist of five people, right? Four men and one woman?'

'That's correct. Lewis Sullavan and his assistant, a two-man television crew and a journalist. There will be TV and press coverage of the entire visit.'

230

Richard couldn't hide his satisfaction at this prospect.

Alice thought, he's quite right to be happy about it. He works very hard; he hasn't even given himself time to shower and change. And being on television will mean that maybe a few people will know who he is, instead of always asking him if he's related to Gregory.

'So where are they all going to sleep?' Russell asked, ever practical.

'The assistant in the women's room, Mr Sullavan in the scientists' room and the other three men in the support staff's room.'

Looks were exchanged around the table. Phil chafed his beard.

'Four of us, therefore, will have to move out into tents for the duration. Arturo is injured. Niki should remain in the hut in case there is a communications emergency. Likewise Jochen for medical purposes,' Richard continued.

'In case the old boy has a heart attack, finding himself without an en suite bathroom or room service?' Phil murmured.

'Or if he decides to call up the helo and have himself flown straight out again,' Rooker added.

Everyone laughed, even Richard.

'Volunteers?' he asked. 'I'm happy to give my bunk to Mr Sullavan.'

To volunteer was the correct thing to do. In the old days, for his grandfather and the polar heroes, it was a matter of honour. A matter of course. Alice knew how much Richard wished that he could volunteer for a Winter Journey, for a selfless dash to save another man or to fuel a camp, instead of just to give up his warm bed for a media mogul.

'Looks like us three, doesn't it?' Phil stabbed his finger at Rook and Russell in turn.

'It's a kind of volunteering,' Russell laconically murmured.

Valentin flung up his arms. 'And I, I give up my place for my leader. I prefer. In tents we have some fun. Some cards, maybe a glass of my special *rakia*. Better than best behaviour inside, I think.'

'Well done, Valerie,' Philip cheered.

*   *   *

It was good to be back.

Alice spent the days that followed unpacking and examining the samples she had collected at Wheeler's Bluff, making preliminary microscopic analyses in the lab and writing up her notes. The time passed quickly.

She read her accumulated e-mails and wrote back about the field trip. The words came slowly at first as she tried to describe how intense the experience had been, then flooded out as soon as she stopped considering and lost herself in living it all over again.

Margaret replied, *Yes, I remember. That was just how it was. Thank you for bringing it back.*

The brief message from Jo was the one she hesitated longest over. *They've started to sleep much better. Four and sometimes five whole hours at night, can't tell you what a difference it makes. Days are still a bit tough. It's the never having a single hour to yourself that's so hard. When I think of all those hours, days, I SQUANDERED before they were born . . .*

Flashes of panic at the prospect of motherhood

232

made Alice's skin shiver, but her alarm alternated with a hungry fascination. She remembered the way the babies had felt in her arms, their milky smell and the fleeting frowns and smiles that had changed their tiny faces. How would it be when she held her own?

She wanted to bombard Jo with questions. It would have been the greatest luxury to have a friend to confide in. But she knew that if she was going to keep her pregnancy to herself for another three months it would have to be *entirely* to herself. No one else should have the responsibility for keeping her secret. Any information, any medical information she needed, she could look up in her daily half-hour on the Internet. She would have to keep her correspondence short, that's all.

Richard spent hours combing through the reference books in an attempt to classify his mollusc. It was a gastropod, a type of periwinkle with a shell in the form of a conical spiral, but in significant aspects it was unlike any of the species that had already been described. 'I think we have got an entirely new form,' he said. 'A late Cretaceous rapid evolutionary development, much earlier than I would have expected to see anything similar. Is this the centre of origin for the species? It could affect the developmental dating of Gastropoda from the period.' His face looked as if a bright light had been turned on under the skin.

Alice made a careful notation of the locale and the rock composition. Only a couple of weeks ago the discovery would have intrigued her. Now, the importance of even this major find seemed less immediate. It was disconcerting to realise that her engagement as a scientist was diminished by the insistent presence in her womb. She bent her head over her notes with extra determination. Even so, in the early afternoons she sometimes found herself nodding off.

Preparations for the visit went ahead. Everyone worked hard. The huts were cleaned and tidied from top to bottom. Russell drew up menus and Niki radioed for supplies to be sent down with the helicopter transport. The scientists chose the best places to show off their fieldwork, and Rooker and Phil plotted how to transport five inexperienced visitors to the various sites without pitching them down crevasses or into the sea.

There was a lot of joking and mock-complaining, but the prospect of critical strangers arriving in their midst made them work as a team in a way that none of Richard's speeches had done.

'If they've got to come down here and bother us, we want Kandahar to be the best effing base in effing Antarctica, right?' Phil said.

On the scheduled day a radio message from Santa Ana announced that the fixed-wing flight from Punta Arenas in Chile had just landed.

'Not even one hour's weather delay?' Russell said in disbelief. 'Sullavan must be more powerful even than we thought. He must have a direct line straight to God.'

'Nah. He *is* God,' Phil corrected him.

In the afternoon, under a fierce sun, they stood waiting. Rooker half expected Shoesmith to line them up like a military guard of honour. They heard the helicopter's buzz before it appeared against the breadth of blue sky.

As soon as it landed and the rotors stopped the doors flew open. Andy and Mick sprang out and

234

manoeuvred steps. A man clambered down and walked backwards across the snow with a camera on his shoulder. Another man followed with a recorder and a microphone, and a third emerged and stood beside him. The pilots grinned at the waiting line, but the other new arrivals formed a semicircle beside the helicopter with hardly a glance over their shoulders. There was a moment's pause, then a woman appeared. She was tall, and even in her padded parka she looked slender and elegant. Jochen gave a low whistle.

Beverley Winston had skin the colour of pale milk chocolate and the cheekbones of a goddess carved out of stone. Her lips were a set of perfectly symmetrical seductive curves. She was the most beautiful woman any of them had ever set eyes on.

This vision looked coolly around her, then lifted one hand in a signal as she stood aside. The cameraman began filming, the third man spoke urgently into the microphone held close to his mouth by the second. Lewis Sullavan appeared at the door of the Squirrel.

He stood still to allow his television crew to film his proprietorial gaze out over the ice. He stepped slowly and confidently on to the snow and they filmed that too. Then he smilingly held out his hand to Richard, who was hesitating in the middle of the waiting line. Richard hurried forward and they shook hands. Lewis Sullavan was shorter than he was, but he still managed to look bigger and broader, and more powerful in every way. He had a high gloss to him, as if he had been hand-buffed with rolled-up wads of money. The camera and mike homed in.

'Welcome to Kandahar,' Richard said, his voice

235

somehow catching in his throat and coming out cracked.

Lewis swept his arm in a broad gesture that took in the line of waiting scientists and staff, the homely red huts, a pair of watching penguins, and the glittering expanse of snow and blue bay water. 'This is a wonderful place,' he intoned. 'This is a place to treasure and to preserve. It is ours, for as long as we do valuable work here, but we must always remember that even though the flag of the European Union flies overhead, Antarctica truly belongs to the community of the world.'

It was an excellent performance, Alice thought. The humility of the words in no way masked Lewis Sullavan's proprietary manner. He acted just as if he owned the whole place.

And in effect, of course, he did. Without his money none of them would be here.

CHAPTER TEN

Richard and Alice stood close together, smiling to order, just next to the peeling red wall of the lab hut. A sweep of snow was satisfactorily visible behind Richard's left shoulder, but even Laure had not been able to persuade the penguins required by the director to wander into shot.

'We'll cut in some bird footage,' he said to the cameraman.

Alice shuffled her feet. Either God or Lewis Sullavan had arranged a day of scintillating sunshine, but it was cold standing in one place while the TV crew conferred.

Beverley Winston came out of the main hut. She was wearing wrap-round sun goggles and a gilet made of some long-haired silvery fur that fired off tiny rainbow darts as she walked. All the men, who were working to set up the shot or otherwise trying to look busy, stopped what they were doing to watch her. She was five inches taller than the harassed director.

'We'll be ready for him in just a couple of minutes, Beverley,' the man said.

Phil and Rooker finished screwing the plaque to the wall of the hut and Russell checked that it was level. All three of them were taking exaggerated care over the tiny job. No one else paid any attention, however. Wherever Beverley was, her beauty absorbed all the available regard. And then, when Lewis Sullavan was present, she reflected on him, so that he was bathed in the lustre of having such a creature for his handmaiden. Not that Lewis himself was physically unimpressive. For a medium-sized man with ordinary features he glowed with supernatural amounts of power and energy. When the two of them were in the room at the same time they seemed to take up all the available oxygen, leaving everyone else feeling dim and lifeless.

'What about the flag?' she asked the director now, having consulted her pocket organiser.

'Well, Beverley, we tried it draped over the plaque so that Lewis could unveil it.'

Valentin had stood in for Sullavan during this exercise. He had whisked the blue and yellow flag back and forth several times, winking and mugging for the camera.

'But it looked too cheesy, if you know what

237

I mean.'

'Cheesy?'

Beverley turned her stone goddess head slowly to look at him. Her expression was unreadable behind the black shades but they could all guess at it.

The cameraman waded in to the rescue. 'Too like the Queen opening a new leisure centre in Gateshead or somewhere?'

Cheesy might be perfectly all right for the Queen, but it certainly would not do for Mr Sullavan. Beverley nodded briskly. 'We thought that tracking away to it flying up there would be better.'

Eight flags, representing each of the nationals at Kandahar, flew from the poles above the window of the radio room. Phil had insisted that the Welsh dragon was included. Above them a much bigger EU flag fluttered in the stiff breeze, with the glinting silver filaments of radio antennae criss-crossing in front of it. A skua strutted on the hut roof.

'Good. We'll do that, then. Is everything else okay?'

Beverley checked that there was nothing untoward between the two huts for Lewis's gaze to fall upon, then went to see if he was ready for the camera.

Lewis wore the apparently identical red parka, complete with the EU and Sullavan logos, as all the Kandahar personnel, but his looked less stiff and unwieldy, and it was a subtly more attractive shade. 'Let's do it.' He beamed, as if he had been as involved as everyone else in the meticulous setting up.

The new plaque on the lab hut wall read simply:

Margaret Mather House

The sound recordist held up the mike as the director spoke his intro and the cameraman panned over the line of flags. Theatrically, the skua spread its wings, then settled again.

The camera came in on Lewis. He gave a little speech almost identical to the one he had made when he stepped out of the helicopter, but it sounded spontaneous as well as sincere. He said how proud he was that the operations at Kandahar were being headed up by two scientists whose names were already written in the history books. Alice wondered how Laure and the others would react to the suggestion that as a recent no-no she was capable of heading up anything polar.

When her turn came she delivered her rehearsed soundbite about Margaret's career as one of the first women to work this far south and added that times had changed. Antarctica now offered opportunities for all scientists, regardless of race or gender, and Kandahar was in the forefront of this revolution.

A shot of Laure and herself sharing a skidoo ride or even performing some science together might be cut in here, she thought. Unless the idea was rejected as too cheesy.

When Richard's turn came he spoke about his grandfather's legend and how proud he was, almost ninety years later, to have followed him south. He made a graceful tribute to Lewis for having the vision and determination to bring Kandahar Station back to life and give it a new incarnation.

There was a drumming of mittened applause, firmly led by Beverley.

Lewis came forward again. He tilted his head at a respectful angle. 'In honour of Dr Margaret Mather, biologist and inspiration to two generations of scientists, this laboratory block is named Margaret Mather House.'

The low sun made the plaque shine like a square of molten gold. Alice was always proud of her mother but sometimes the pride was diluted by exasperation. Today, however, it was as uncomplicated as the day long ago when Margaret came to talk to her school. She thought of how single-minded she was and how brave she could be, and she felt her mother's presence as strongly as if she were standing at her side. The cameraman closed in to film Alice studying the plaque.

She was glad she had kept her secret. If she had blurted it out as soon as she had got back from Wheeler's Bluff she would almost certainly be on her way home by now. She would have missed this, and with the liquid gold blinding her eyes, spiky cold air prickling her skin and the heat of family pride in her blood, she knew that it was one those memories that you should keep, and hold, and remember when you were tempted to ask yourself whether anything really mattered.

The filming of the small ceremony was over. Lewis strode back towards the main hut, pounding his hands together and talking to Richard, and calling instructions to the director. The expedition members turned away too, thinking about dinner. Russell had been cooking for most of the day and the centrepiece of the evening meal was to be a saddle of roast New Zealand lamb. Everyone on

240

the base had been looking forward to this treat for days.

Left to herself, Alice traced the line of her mother's name with the pyramid of her mittened fingers.

If the baby is a girl, she thought. If she is, I'll call her Margaret.

*   *   *

When they gathered later they found that Russell had transformed the mess table with a white cloth, wineglasses and candles.

The soft light flattered the dilapidated room by hiding the stained wood and peeling paintwork. It flattered the faces of the expedition members too by disguising the cracked lips and chapped skin, and the dirt that seemed to stay faintly ingrained in their skin no matter how diligently they scrubbed at it. In their best approximations of clean clothing most of the men looked like suntanned polar heroes from another age, burly and invincible behind their dark beards, yet with the paler circles left by goggles that made their eyes seem peeled and vulnerable. Arturo kept to the shadows, probably on Richard's orders, concealing his unsightly injuries as best he could.

Lewis automatically took Richard's place at the head of the table, overthrowing the established order and setting up an immediate alert for where Beverley would place herself. Without a second's hesitation she sat down next to Rooker, the only person who had already taken his usual seat. The five extra place settings meant that the chairs were crowded together and people's shoulders were touching. Jochen van Meer used his weight to push himself in on her other side. There was an almost audible sigh of disappointment from the other men.

Alice found herself between Philip and Valentin, which suited her fine. She glanced around the table and briefly caught Laure's eye. A smile flickered, their only mutual acknowledgement so far of how unkempt Beverley made them feel. In the women's room her soft, rich clothes were hanging next to their stained and stiff ones. Then there was her scent. Of the five senses, smell was the only one that was understimulated at Kandahar. There were few scents that were strong enough to survive the cold and the scouring wind, which was on balance a good thing, Alice reckoned. But the general absence of ambient smells made Beverley's perfume the more striking. It was warm and vibrant, a distillation of blossom and citrus absolutely remote from Antarctica. When Beverley walked or turned, the sweet drift of scent made Alice think of home and, more disturbingly, of sex.

Laure's gaze moved on. She was looking at Rooker, who was now talking to Beverley. Alice wasn't surprised, because Laure was always stealing surreptitious and then not so surreptitious glances at him. Rooker generally ignored her. Beverley poured red wine into his glass and her loose cuff fell back a little to reveal her bare wrist and its fragile knob of bone. Jochen looked as if he might fall on the inch of naked flesh and devour it.

In a room full of men who suddenly seemed unaccountably desirable, Alice also noticed how handsome Rooker was. The dark mole on his forehead, just at the hairline, drew her eyes. His

242

beard was trimmed closer than the other men's and it emphasised the shape of his mouth.

Is that an order, or an invitation?

He had been drunk, that night. But the memory of his finger pointing to her name label still made Alice shift in her seat.

Lewis and Richard were leading a general conversation about geopolitics. Russell and Niki brought the glossy lamb and dishes of fresh vegetables to the table.

Next to her, Philip was muttering something. 'Are they an item, then?'

'Who?'

'*Her*. And himself.' He jerked his chin, certain that no one was looking at them.

'*I* don't know. No. I shouldn't think so. Didn't he get married again a year or so ago?' She rummaged in her memory for the details of a magazine article she had read. There had been photographs of a luxuriantly pregnant bride in white lace Versace with Sullavan beaming beside her. Pregnancy, then marriage. Alice coughed and talked faster. 'That's right, he married an American film actress. Gabrielle somebody. She had a baby, so he's on his third family. He's been married twice before. He wouldn't bother having liaisons with the paid help, would he? No, I'm sure Beverley's role is to prove that he *can* have someone like her just to manage his diary and field his phone calls. She looks after his every need. She heightens his lustre.'

Philip sighed. 'Do you think she ever goes off duty? I'm as horny as one of my dad's old rams in a pen full of ewes.'

'Fancy your chances, do you?'

He groaned, loudly enough to make Arturo on

243

his other side look round. Arturo and Rooker were the only ones apparently unaffected by Beverley's presence.

'A man can dream, you know,' Phil said. 'A man can dream.'

Alice turned to Valentin. His round dark eyes were moist with longing. He forked lamb and carrots into his mouth as if he had never seen food before. 'I must feed one appetite, or die of the other,' he murmured.

This is just *one woman*, Alice thought. She was dismayed, as well as amused. The even balance of their life at Kandahar seemed suddenly precarious, that it should be rocked by the arrival in their midst of one desirable woman.

Sex had flown in and unbalanced them all. Even me, Alice thought. Here I am, a pregnant geologist who's never done one single thing in her life— except for coming to Antarctica—without weighing and calculating all the possible eventualities, and I feel as madly turned-on as a teenager. The thought made her smile. Rooker saw the smile and raised one sardonic eyebrow at her.

It was a convivial meal. The TV crew ate normally, without paying much attention. Lewis Sullavan politely sampled everything and complimented Russell on his skills. The Kandahar people devoured every glistening morsel they could get and wiped their plates clean. Beverley hardly touched hers. She murmured something in a low voice to Rooker, who shrugged indifference.

'I'll drink your wine, though.'

The wine had been brought in the helicopter. It was very good, Chile's best. In the end Jochen ate Beverley's leftovers, his cracked lips shiny with grease in the reddish mat of his beard.

Lewis Sullavan held court, leaning back in his chair and nodding at the bottle if anyone's glass happened to be empty. He turned the blaze of his attention on each of them in turn. He asked Alice if she would let him accompany her in the field tomorrow.

'Certainly.' Alice smiled. They would go up to an outcrop behind the base that she had already mapped. That was planned. Beverley had probably allotted it a space of x minutes in the diary.

'And what about you, James? What brings you to Antarctica?' Sullavan asked suddenly.

'Rooker,' Rooker said.

Richard's forehead twitched, so that the pale vertical furrows between his eyebrows were swallowed up. He disliked Rook but he was eager for each of them to acquit themselves properly in front of Sullavan, not just for his own sake but for the team and the good of the project.

Alice thought, he's too dutiful to be calculating. He can't manipulate any of us, let alone Lewis or Rook.

'Rooker,' Sullavan repeated smoothly.

Rook drained an inch of cognac and set his glass down. He said, 'Money. And it's a place to be. It's not quite the same but it's not all that much different from any other place.'

'I see from your CV that you are a pilot.'

'I was.'

There was a small silence, but he didn't elaborate.

Lewis laughed. He nudged the cognac bottle towards Rook and sank deeper in his seat, as if they were two guys in a bar settling down to an evening's drinking and boasting. 'You're a bit of a maverick, aren't you?'

Rooker didn't give him the satisfaction of an answer and Lewis only laughed more delightedly. At the same time he was studying Rooker's face.

'A loner, a chancer. I like that.' He chuckled. 'I recognise the breed.' The implication was that Lewis himself was of the same breed and that as a man he found Rooker more to his taste than, say, a meticulous scientist. Richard smiled tightly. Everyone round the table was listening now.

'Where are you heading next?'

'I have no idea,' Rooker said.

Beverley lowered her curved eyelids a fraction as she absorbed and stored the information.

Lewis rubbed the side of his mouth with the pad of his thumb. 'I see.'

Rooker's blank gaze held steady. I doubt it, his expression seemed to say.

Lewis hesitated, then his head swivelled. 'Valentin, my friend. I was in Sofia last week. Is it your home town?'

The corrugations across Richard's forehead eased. The conversation jerked and speeded up again. Rooker had let no one down, at least for now. Rooker himself only leaned across Beverley for the bottle and replenished his glass.

At midnight, Beverley politely excused herself and stood up. She headed for the women's room, drawing ripples of longing in her wake. After she had gone the media crew unbent and began laughing noisily with Phil and Russell. Melancholy had crept up on Niki again. He rested his bony chin in one cupped hand and stared at the place that Beverley had occupied, then unfolded his skeletal height from the table and drifted away to the radio room. Lewis and Richard were discussing investment in new infrastructure for the base.

At 1 a.m. exactly Lewis consulted his watch. 'I think we'd better call it a day. It's another busy one tomorrow.'

The party was over, without negotiation.

Alice wasn't ready for sleep. Her skin buzzed and prickled, and a cavalcade of images marched through her head. Remembering that Russell would be spending the night out in a tent she murmured to him that she would make a start on the washing-up.

The room emptied. Alice stacked plates, then stood at the sink and began to scrub pans. The lights in the sky above the sweep of snow and rock outside were violet and pearl and ochre. She could see the two tents pitched in a sheltered angle of rock. There was a light glowing in one of them. Rooker and Phil and Russell and Valentin would be playing a couple of hands of cards and finishing the second bottle of cognac. She guessed that Beverley Winston would be amongst the topics of conversation.

The mundane activity of scouring saucepans and the contrast with the light-bathed glacier occupied her attention. It was enough to find herself alone in the small hours, up to her wrists in greasy water and with the folds and caverns of blue ice to gaze at. She wasn't even thinking about the baby, or the future.

A pair of hands descended on her shoulders. Instead of whirling round she hunched herself forward, protecting her belly against the metal frame of the sink.

Richard whispered in her ear, 'I'm sorry. I didn't mean to startle you.'

Very slowly Alice turned to face him. Their faces were only an inch apart in the dimly lit room. She looked into his eyes. She could see the striations of colour in the irises, the minute dilations of the pupils. A second passed, then another. They could both hear the tiny popping sound of soap bubbles in the sink.

The dammed-up sexual tension of the evening threatened to discharge itself. Alice almost melted against him. She shivered with longing to be touched. It was a long time, weeks of being muffled under layers of protective clothes, and now she felt acutely the tiny thicknesses of fabric that separated Richard's hands from her naked skin. But the glinting light in his eyes and the heat of his breath on her cheek made it easy to resist. There was something wrong. She sensed in him a minute deviation from normality without being able to identify what it was.

'Thank you', he said, so softly that she read rather than heard the words, 'for being an ally.'

She knew what he was talking about: the antagonism between himself and Rooker that divided Kandahar.

Am I an ally?

Of course I am. Does that make me Rooker's opponent?

'You are quite right, of course,' Richard went on. He took a strand of her hair and twisted it between his fingers. She wished he wouldn't. She remembered how he had touched her wrist in the tent at Wheeler's Bluff. The climate and the landscape that surrounded them were so harsh, and their place in this remote world was so tenuous, that even in her wariness these small gestures of intimacy were more erotically charged than most of the sex she could remember.

'About what?' she managed to ask.

His eyes travelled over her face. 'That it's not a good idea to do this. Not while we are living in this place, while we are working together. But I wanted to kiss you just once. I've wanted to kiss you since the day you came in to the Polar Office.'

Her skin crawled now. The moment of awkward physical desire flipped into panic. 'No. I'm sorry . . .'

He seized her round the waist, trying to pull her against him. Fear trickled icily down the back of her neck. He would *feel* her thickened waist, the flesh on her hips, her protruding stomach. He had never touched her before—except for a finger on her wrist—so how could he know the shape she had once been, or the difference now? Even so, the trickle of dismay became a flood.

She took a step sideways, feeling the cold metal of the sink against her back. A shadow fell across his face. There was the crease between his eyes again and an expression indicating that he was used to disappointment. He expected to be disappointed even before anything had happened and this told her more about his history than all the information he had given her in the tent out at the Bluff. There had been too many of the wrong expectations placed on him. All his life he had been struggling to make himself fit a predetermined shape.

She forced herself to touch his arm and smile remorsefully. 'I'm sorry,' she repeated. 'You know, it's being here . . .'

'You're right. I've already told you that much.'

He added, 'You have a wonderful smile. Oh, Christ. That's enough. Why don't you leave the bloody washing-up until tomorrow?'

'I think I will.'

At the door of the women's room they wished each other goodnight in low voices.

'Don't worry,' Richard said. He was reassuring her that he wouldn't make demands on her or make public what had passed between them tonight.

'Thank you.'

'But when we get back to England?'

I'll have a *baby*.

The leap of imagination required to take her from Kandahar to motherhood was too much. Her future broke into a scatter of tiny images. Her later pregnant self, hand to back, leaning on her heels to balance the weight in front. A baby buggy and a set of miniature socks and vests. Jo in her kitchen in Oxford, torn between exhaustion and helpless love.

'Everything will be different, Richard.'

Her hand touched the doorknob. Kandahar was always alive with static electricity and now a shock jolted her so that she almost cried out. The door opened.

'I'll have to hope, then.'

'Goodnight,' she said and slipped inside.

In the bunk room Beverley's perfume was everywhere. Alice undressed and lay down. Laure was breathing heavily, a small snore catching with each breath in the back of her throat. From Beverley's bunk there was total silence.

*   *   *

The next day Rooker and Phil took Lewis and Alice on the skidoos up to the rock outcrop. Alice unloaded her pack and hoisted it on her back. They were only a mile from the base but she had a rope, emergency food and an insulated bag to crawl into for shelter in case the weather came in. The sky was unbroken blue but Alice knew enough about Antarctic weather systems by now not to place any store by this.

Lewis waved the safety officers away. 'Alice and I will be just fine. We have plenty to talk about.'

'I'm not going to want to listen in, am I?' Phil muttered. 'Have you got the radio?' he asked Alice for the second time.

She patted her pocket. 'And I've tested it.'

'Don't want anything to happen to either of you, do we?'

'Indeed not,' Lewis Sullavan said expansively.

'See you, then. Give us a call when you're ready for a pick-up.'

The motors revved and the machines shot away, bouncing over the crests of sastrugi. Rooker hadn't spoken at all.

Lewis turned to Alice. Even if she had had no idea who he was, she wouldn't have mistaken him for anything but a rich and powerful man. He was *shiny*. His protective clothing was all new and of the finest quality. His skin was lightly tanned, not cruelly weather-beaten, he was clean-shaven and his hair was expensively cut. He had beautiful teeth and manicured fingernails.

'Just show me what you normally do.' Lewis smiled.

'Don't step anywhere except where I lead, will you? I've mapped all this section of rock and I know where the crevasses are.'

'No ma'am,' he said.

Alice laid out her geological hammer and compass, and opened her notebook. She planned to make a detailed survey of a section that she had only glanced at in the mapping process. Narrow sedimentary bands had been forced upwards and doubled over into fantastical folds and pleats by magmatic eruption over a hundred million years ago. Chips and slabs of quartz and mica embedded in a finer matrix had been eroded so that the whole face of rock was patterned with serpentine swirling bands of different tones and textures to make an intricate mosaic. The outcrop was on too massive a scale to be properly compared with any human creation, but it looked like a piece of highly worked sculpture.

'The work isn't very interesting to watch, I'm afraid,' Alice apologised. She drew the parameters of the section in her notebook. 'This is a vertical section. It's actually on a slant just here, of course, because the molten rock burst up from the earth's core and pushed it into this series of striking folds. The older sedimentary rock now lies on top of the younger.'

She talked as she worked, fluent from countless undergraduate field courses. She was aware of Lewis standing just behind her shoulder, listening with apparent attention. She measured a sequence of layers and drew them in her notebook, then tapped out a series of samples, bagged them up and labelled them. It was comfortable in the shelter of the rocks and the sparkling air was absolutely still. She became absorbed in the work. There were traces of carbon film here that indicated fossilised

252

fragments of plant stems and roots. Richard would be interested. She wasn't sure how many minutes had passed before she looked round for Lewis. Out of the corner of her eye she caught the red flash of his parka, maybe twenty feet away.

Her sharp cry of warning squeezed out of her throat at the same time as his yell of alarm. As her head jerked fully round, he disappeared from view. A split second later she saw his head and upper body. His arms were akimbo, wedged against the snow. The rest of him had disappeared into a narrow veiled crevasse. His mouth was hanging open and he groaned as if he had been punched in the solar plexus.

Alice sank to her knees to bring her eyes level with his. 'Keep still. Don't thrash around.'

Keeping eye contact with him, she shuffled sideways on her knees to her pack and detached the ice axe from its loops. She ran through Phil's instructions in her head. The rope was in the pack. Oh, God. She had known the crevasse was there. She should have kept him on a rope. How could anyone keep *Lewis Sullavan* tied on the end of a rope?

Don't think about that now. Concentrate.

She uncoiled the rope, knotted a loop in the end, paid out a length and tied another knot. She passed the shaft of her ice axe through the second knot and drove the whole shaft deep into the soft snow until the pick bit into the rope knot and held it firm. She secured herself to the rope and took a self-locking carabiner off her harness loop.

'Lewis,' she said quietly. He was motionless, his face grey with shock.

She snapped the carabiner into the loop of rope

and moved carefully over the snow to kneel in front of him. She pressed the gate of the carabiner open to remind him how it worked.

'Lewis, I want you fasten this into the loop of your harness. Can you do that for me?'

Slowly he reached out his mittened hand and took it from her. The rope snaked over the innocent snow with its tell-tale pucker. His arm was trembling, but it moved obediently. His face screwed up in an agony of concentration, then he dared to glance down as he groped at the unfamiliar configuration of his safety harness. Alice edged forward to look too. The crevasse was narrow and Lewis was wedged into the vee shape. On either side of him blue ice dropped away into seeming infinity. There was a metallic snap. She peered down and saw that he had clipped the carabiner. She had him on the rope now.

'Well done.' Alice smiled to reassure him, although she could hardly breathe. She stepped back to where her axe was buried in the snow and put her boot firmly on the head. She gathered the rope in her mittened hands and braced herself.

'Now. I'm going to haul on this end. Can you pull on that end and try to scramble out?'

He bit his lips, then nodded and clamped his mittens on the rope.

Alice put her back into it. He wriggled, trying to kick his legs free. She pulled, but it was like dragging a dead weight. Lewis worked one elbow deep into the snow and hauled on the rope with the other hand. He rocked his hips and an inch of his chest emerged, then another. The rope bit into Alice's palms and she looped it round her wrists for extra traction. In a rush, Lewis's torso emerged

254

from the mouth of the crevasse. He got one knee up over the lip, scrabbled wildly, and the other followed. He fell forward on all fours, his head hanging, his breath coming in rough gasps.

Alice gave him a few seconds' respite, then put her hands under his arms to help him to his feet. 'Let's move away from the edge.'

She unhitched the rope from her ice axe and led him away to the safety of the rock outcrop. He sat down on a flat-topped stone and rested his head in his hands. Alice found the Thermos of hot coffee in her pack, poured a cup and gave it to him. Then she took the radio out of her pocket to call up Phil and Rooker. Her hands were shaking and the sweat of fear prickled under her arms and in her hair.

'Wait,' Lewis ordered. She sat obediently, watching him sipping his coffee and looking away from her down the slope of the glacier. The cobalt glint of the sea was visible in the distance.

'You did well,' he said after a moment.

'Not really. Phil would have said it was unorthodox. And I shouldn't have let you wander off in the first place.'

Amusement struck cold sparks of light in Lewis's eyes. He was recovering himself. 'Do you think you could have stopped me?'

It was an academic question, Alice thought. 'Are you hurt anywhere?'

'No. I'm not hurt.' He went on, 'It was my fault. I'm sorry. Thank you for keeping your head. I won't forget what you did, but I'd much prefer it now if we continue as if nothing has happened.'

Alice could perfectly well understand why. It was a matter of dignity. 'Of course. Would you like me to call up and say we're ready to head back to the base? Or shall we do some more geology?'

Lewis smiled. When he chose to use it, he had considerable charm. 'We could just sit here in the sun and talk for half an hour?'

'Of course,' Alice said again. She poured more coffee into his cup and put a pack of biscuits on the rock beside him. He seemed to have recovered with remarkable speed, but at some level he must still be shocked. It was hard to judge how old he was. Somewhere in the early sixties, she guessed. An unroped fall into a crevasse would scare anyone, whatever their age.

'Don't get cold,' she advised.

He pulled the flaps of his fleece hat down over his ears and leaned forward, resting his elbows on his knees and nursing the heat of the coffee. 'You are like your mother,' he said.

'Not very, unfortunately.'

'I don't know about that. You look like she did, in the old days. And seeing you working with that rope, every fibre of your being concentrated on it, made me think of her. Margaret is the most single-minded woman I have ever known.'

'Yes.'

'I loved her, you know,' he said.

There was no wind. Alice hadn't misheard. She stared at him as he lifted the tin cup to his mouth. The faint chink of metal against his teeth told her that his hand was still shaking.

'You didn't know.' It wasn't a question. Reaction was loosening his tongue. A fleeting glance into the face of death had opened a door in him.

'She was fifteen years older than me, but I had never met anyone like her.'

'Were you lovers?'

256

There was a pause. 'Yes,' he said.

It was Alice's turn to stare away down the glacier. 'Perhaps I don't want to hear this.'

'It only lasted one summer. There was no question that she didn't love your father and you. She was loyal, where it mattered, I always knew that. She was making her second television series. I was just a beginner in the business and Margaret was like an electric wire. She lit everything up and she had the gift of making everyone she came into contact with shine more brightly as well.'

Alice remembered her on the stage at school, how she had looked more vivid than the teachers. The moment when she realised that her mother was sexy. 'I see,' she said quietly, wondering whether she really did.

There was an explanation now for Trevor's reticence. Perhaps less of a one for his unbroken devotion.

'Were you the only one?' she asked, already knowing the answer.

'I have no idea. I only know that I have never forgotten her. And we have stayed friends over the years.'

Alice wasn't all that surprised, now that this little mineral nugget of the truth glinted at her. Maybe at some level of consciousness she had guessed long ago that her mother had had lovers. It was something to do with the tilt of her head, the way she crossed her ankles, the outlandish details of her clothes and shoes. Her long absences from home. She always looked for and accepted male attention as nothing less than her due. Perhaps, Alice thought suddenly, she hadn't particularly liked Peter because he didn't play the game of flirting with her.

'I see,' she said again. She didn't like to think of the pain that Trevor must have suffered. Sometimes their summer holidays in the mountains had a melancholy edge that she had been too young to understand. Yet Margaret had always come home to him in the end and there was no doubt that the two of them were happy now. They were as inextricably entwined as ancient tree roots.

There are many different ways to make a marriage work, Alice reflected. Almost as many as there are marriages.

Lewis had drunk his hot coffee and eaten two biscuits. Warmth and sugar worked to restore his equilibrium. He brushed a fine spray of ice crystals from the shoulder of his parka. 'It's a long time ago. I was a hungry young man in those days.'

'A bit of a maverick?' She said it without thinking but he nodded, not at all displeased. He was as vain as powerful men always are.

'Yes.' He chuckled. 'Like your friend Rooker.' He remembered the conversation of the night before. His memory was faultless; he would pride himself on that.

'My friend?' she repeated.

'What do you think of him?' It was an apparently casual question, but to Alice all the turns of this conversation were outlandish. It was strange enough just to find herself perched on a rock talking to a tycoon who had yesterday been no more than a name in the newspapers and a logo on her parka. Today she had put him at risk of his life and learned that the tycoon was her mother's long-ago lover. Antarctica had this effect. It distorted and diminished what was familiar, and at the same time it threw the unfamiliar into such close and enlarged focus that it obliterated everything you thought you knew.

Rooker, he was asking about Rooker.

What she actually thought was that there was something about him that required everyone else to take up a position. It was either *your friend Rooker*, or *thank you for being my ally*—and therefore by definite implication not Rooker's. And yet Rook himself was utterly absent from all these transactions. He gave no sign of even being aware of them.

She said precisely, 'I think he's dangerous.'

Lewis laughed. He was delighted with this. 'Most interesting men are dangerous. And every interesting woman, take my word for it.'

Alice was chilled. The sky was still bright, but they had been sitting and the sweat from her exertions with the rope was cold on her back. She tried to hide a shiver but Lewis noticed it.

'I think I shouldn't have blurted out about Margaret and me,' he said.

'I understand,' she told him. And now Margaret Mather House stood here on the windswept peninsula as a footnote to history. She took the radio out again and called up Phil.

'Be with you in five,' he chirped. She stood up, a little stiffly, and coiled and stowed the rope. She buckled the axe to her rucksack, and she and Lewis were standing watching as the two skidoos rounded the corner of the slope and raced up the glacier towards them.

At the last moment Lewis held out his hand. Alice gave him her left because she was holding her rucksack in the other and they shook awkwardly.

259

'Everything okay here?' Phil asked as he dismounted.

'Fine. Very interesting,' Lewis smoothly answered.

Alice climbed on behind Rooker. She sat well back, holding on to the seat strap for balance as they bounced away again.

The base was quiet. On a fine day with Lewis Sullavan in their midst, the scientists except for Richard were out in the field. The media crew were on the beach, filming three Weddell seals sunbathing on an ice floe.

'Now then, what's next?' Lewis asked.

Richard had scheduled a visit to one of Laure's penguin colonies further down the coast. Rooker was standing by with the Zodiac.

Lewis rubbed his hands together. 'What are we waiting for?'

Alice watched him go. She could see now that his shoulders were slightly bowed. He was tired and still feeling the grim mouth of the crevasse clamping round his hips. But he would keep going, because that was what you did. Tomorrow the helicopter would come and fly him on to the next set of decisions and another cohort of minions. She didn't envy him.

Inside the hut the harsh midsummer sunshine made the room look smeared and dusty, in spite of all Russell's efforts at cleaning it up. There were too many people for the cramped space. Flakes of paint shaken from the wooden walls speckled the floor like dandruff, and the visitors didn't take off their boots at the door so there was sand and melting snow everywhere. Russell himself emerged from the storeroom with a sack of flour in his arms.

There was another gargantuan meal to prepare.

'I'll give you a hand,' Alice said and he gratefully patted her on the shoulder.

*　　　*　　　*

Rooker drove the prow of the Zodiac hard at the shingled beach and Richard leaped out to make it fast. There were so many penguins here that the dinghy's arrival made almost no impression on the hordes of birds streaming up and down the beach. The new arrivals flipped out of the water and marched determinedly uphill to their nests. They were fat with fish and their white breasts were clean. Those coming in the opposite direction were leaner and their fronts were smeared with dirty pinkish guano. They looked like little old men after a heavy night on the town. They made miniature detours round the boots of the invaders, but they were so intent on the business of getting food that they paid no further attention. The chirring sound of 100,000 birds was loud enough to drown out the regular slap and scrape of waves breaking on the shingle.

The red blobs up amongst the rocks rising from the steep snow above the beach were Laure and Jochen, working. There were a dozen murky reddish ribbons connecting the rocks to the water, each of them dotted with bobbing black and white heads. These were penguin motorways, linking the nest sites to the sea and food.

As always, Rooker felt delight at the sight of so much intense and single-minded activity. He stepped into the water in his waders to moor the dinghy and a breaking wave erupted around his calves with hundreds more black torpedo bodies. They pitched forward on to the glittering shingle and instantly began the waddle uphill. At the nest, their hungry mates were sitting on a pair of eggs. Rook knew from Laure that soon, around the New Year, the chicks would hatch.

He saw that Richard was helping Lewis Sullavan ashore. The woman assistant, Beverley whatshername, was next. She was unused to boats and stood up too quickly, then almost fell over as a wave slopped against the dinghy. Rooker leaned in and steadied her, then put his arms under hers and lifted her on to the shore.

'Thanks,' she murmured. He could feel the way she was loose against him.

The media crew scrambled in their wake, passing the camera from hand to hand.

When everyone was safely on the beach Richard said over his shoulder, 'Wait here for us, Rook.'

It wasn't what Shoesmith said so much as the tone of his voice that made Rooker's fists clench.

It was like being eleven years old again.

*   *   *

Uncle Henry Jerrold on the stone steps of the house with blunt-faced stone lions guarding the door, soaked grey light and a ragged grey sky trailing rain. 'Wait here, James.'

So he did, with his coat dripping and his suitcase at his feet.

After she died, there was really nowhere for Jimmy to go except back to England.

There was an orphanage in Dunedin; he had spent the first three months there while his care worker sorted matters out 'with your folks back home', as he put it. Shane was all right, Jimmy thought, insofar as anyone or anything was all right in those blank, whirling days. But Shane's job was only to make short-term arrangements for children like Jimmy Rooker. It wasn't as though he could go and live with him or anything like that, or even be friends, really.

Uncle Henry Jerrold was his family now and the arrangements that were made were for Jimmy to travel back to England by ship, retracing the journey that he had made with her to New Zealand when he was a baby. He had been too small to remember anything about the first voyage, but on the way back the ship's rolling in the glassy sea swell and the regular beat of the engines had stirred the ghosts of memory in him.

He had heard plenty of stories about their journey, she told them over and over again, but those were about different things, not waves or the smell of salt water. The bandleader had played her choice of dance tunes every night, and during the day there had been deck games and fancy dress competitions. There had been a photograph, somewhere, of Jimmy as a little devil, with a tail and a fork and a pair of horns made from card and fastened to his head with a loop of elastic. She had dressed up as an angel, that time, with a sweep of white bedsheet and wire-framed wings fledged with a thousand white paper feathers. His father had made the wings. He was a mechanic and he was good with his hands. The photograph had disappeared when people came to clear up the house, after it all happened.

Jimmy travelled back to England on his own,

under the care of the nursing sister who ran the ship's infirmary. He had a little cabin near hers, low down in the ship where the engines thrummed and there were no porthole windows to look out on the waves. Uncle Henry was at Southampton to meet him. When the ship's sister handed over her charge, with plain relief, his uncle formally shook his hand. It was the only time Jimmy could remember touching him.

It was a long train journey up to Northumberland. Jimmy had never seen such rain. At home it rained too, but that was rain that drummed and bounced and roared out of the waterspouts. It was rain with a purpose that started and then stopped. But in England it fell helplessly out of a smeared grey sky and there was no end to it. He leaned his head against the train window and stared out at the tiny fields and rounded hills crowned with trees that looked like black scribbles against the clouds. Uncle Henry sat next to him, silently reading a newspaper and smelling of wet wool.

Henry was her older brother.

'A good old English snob and stuffed shirt,' she had told Jimmy once, laughing, her mouth wide and lipsticked. 'Not like us, eh?' He had only wondered vaguely what the shirt was stuffed *with*.

He didn't mind Uncle Henry's silence. He didn't want to talk to him either, so that suited them both. When he did speak, it was in a ridiculous voice, blaring and stifled at the same time. His lips didn't move.

'Wait here, James.' A big old door, a stone-slabbed hallway, a cold and silent house. Aunt Eleanor and Uncle Henry had no children.

She said to him, once, when she had her bottle of wine on the table between them and they were talking, or rather she was talking and he was listening, because that was what they did, 'One thing I've got that they haven't, Jimmy, eh? I've got my big boy. I don't need anything else in the world. Not your father, rot him, that's for sure. Not family, either, except for you and me. We're all we need. And a few bob in the bank, of course. That wouldn't go amiss at all.' She laughed and lit a cigarette, lipsticking the butt.

Life had a way of turning on you, he had discovered. They didn't have each other any more, because his mother was dead. Uncle Henry and Aunt Eleanor had him now, even though he was the last thing they wanted.

Rooker thought about all this as he watched the penguins going about their business.

It wasn't Richard Shoesmith's fault that he looked and sounded like Uncle Henry Jerrold, but just to be in the same room with him brought back memories of the five years he had spent in Northumberland. Five years of rain and routine misery, during which Rooker had taken to a life of rebellion as if he had been born to it. As Annette Rooker née Jerrold's son, he *had* been born to it. At first he was just mute and the Jerrolds had taken his silence as insolence. They were expecting gratitude for rescuing him from the orphanage in Dunedin, but none was forthcoming. In time, he had taken up real insolence, defiance, truancy and petty thieving. He had been expelled from two schools.

'You don't care, do you? You don't give a damn,' Henry had once said, in a rare attempt at

265

communication with the surly adolescent whose resentment curled through the house like smoke.

'No,' Jimmy said. It was the truth. What was there to care about?

On the day before his sixteenth birthday he finally walked out. He got a job packing boxes in a Tyneside factory and lodgings in a draughty house belonging to a thirty-year-old divorcée who liked to be kept warm at night. He never went back to the Jerrolds.

*   *   *

Rooker didn't like recalling the past and this tide of memories was particularly unwelcome. If it weren't for Richard Shoesmith's accent, and all the associations that went with it, Henry Jerrold would never have entered his head and he could just be watching the penguins. Maybe if he had had a chance to meet the expedition leader before they all flew in to Kandahar he would have changed his plans and just travelled on somewhere else. But perhaps he wouldn't, and maybe it didn't particularly matter because he liked Kandahar otherwise, and Antarctica was harsh enough and immense enough to make even Rooker's demons seem insignificant. He could ignore the man, most of the time. It was only when he had had a few drinks that the anger threatened to crack his reserve.

'Hi,' a voice said, breaking into his thoughts. Rooker turned to see Beverley Winston. 'They're cute, aren't they, these little guys?' she added. Penguins continued to bustle past their feet.

He didn't think it was necessary to agree with

the obvious. Beverley was standing close to him, their eyes almost on a level.

'You don't say much.' Her smile was very bright. She had taken her hat off and her hair was cropped close so that he could see the bones of her skull. The nape of her neck was a long groove. Against so much whiteness she was like an ebony carving.

'No.'

Beverley took a pack of cigarettes out of her pocket. Fumbling with her gloves, she took out two cigarettes and put one between Rooker's lips. Their heads came close together as their hands cupped round the flame of her lighter. She stood back and inhaled deeply. A long way off, high up amongst the rocks, Rooker could see Sullavan and the others.

'Quite a place,' Beverley said. She kept her voice low but he could hear her perfectly, not just what she said but what she was suggesting. He had been amused by her effect on the other men, but now that it was turned on him alone he felt the full force of her allure.

'What happens later?' she asked.

'What do you want to happen?'

She smiled at him. Her perfume was so intense it made his head swim. 'I'm sure we can think of something.'

She finished her cigarette and extinguished it in the snow. Tidily, she dropped the butt into an empty film canister and snapped the lid.

'Yes,' he agreed. 'Why not?' It would be a straightforward transaction and the prospect was enticing.

She shot him another smile and strolled away to the water's edge. Melting ice swished and rattled where the waves broke and the shingle was crusted with pitted slabs of it. Penguins surged in both directions.

*   *   *

Russell and Niki collaborated on a second big dinner. The hut interior was steamy with cooking fumes and condensation misted the windows. The guests had all taken showers in the narrow slit of communal bathroom, so there was no hot water left for washing-up. The gas cylinder that heated the water and powered the oven was now running low, ten days before schedule. There was one spare, but that would have to last until the next visit of the ship in January. The room was crammed with people and the cooks were sweating. The expedition members were ragged with the efforts of hospitality but the guests were clean and relaxed, looking forward to a good meal and the arrival of the helicopter the next day.

Lewis beamed. He was pleased with the operation of the base and with his brief tour of the science programme. In the morning he would look at Valentin's glacier project and Arturo's weather survey. Beverley had changed into jeans and a soft white sweater that showed the velvety scoops of her collarbone. She slid into her seat next to Rooker and put her hand on his arm when she asked him to pass her the salt. No one had said anything, but it was clear to everyone—except Lewis, who was too insulated to bother to take note—that it was a done deal.

'Fuck me,' Phil murmured. His jaw sagged with frank envy and awe.

'I don't think so.' Alice laughed. She felt vaguely discomfited but wasn't sure why.

The other men watched Beverley. Cutlery rattled and the atmosphere prickled with tension. Lewis talked about his ideas for the next science season. He planned to install a bigger dormitory block, better kitchen facilities, extra support personnel. Richard listened attentively, putting in answers where required. Rooker filled his glass whenever the bottle came within reach. It was a relief when the meal finally ended. Lewis tapped his glass for silence and made one of his speeches. He thanked everyone for their work and the warmth of their welcome, and proposed a toast: 'To next year. Antarctica.'

They echoed his words. Next year, Alice thought. Her once-loose fleece pants felt too tight round the middle. Not Antarctica, that's for sure.

*　　　*　　　*

The generator shed was Rooker's domain. He serviced and maintained the main generator and the back-up, and kept his tools racked along the wall. Washing lines criss-crossed the overhead space where the heat rose from the machinery. The only reason for any of the others to come in here was to collect or hang up laundry, and the lines were bare now except for a forlorn trio of unmatched socks.

Rooker leaned against the wall, listening to the steady diesel-powered chugging. After a few moments the door opened on to a slice of royal-blue sky. Beverley appeared, wrapped in her parka. They slid together without exchanging a word.

269

After the kiss ended Beverley put her hands on him. 'This place. It's so primitive. Makes you act primitive.'

He liked the way she was matter-of-fact about what she wanted; without dressing up her desires with wiles and pretences. He kissed her again, sliding his hands under the parka and her white sweater. Her skin was like satin. It was extraordinary after so much cold and rough work to feel smoothness and warmth that seemed ready to melt under his touch. Her hands tangled with his clothes, pulling them aside until greed swept through them both. Locked together, they stumbled back against the generator housing. The machine's vibrations drummed through them. Rooker looked around and saw an old chair against the shed wall. He sat down, and guided Beverley astride him. She stood up for a second, looking down at him with defiance that was almost a glare. She wriggled her jeans down round her hips. A second later they were connected. She dropped her head and he felt her lips and tongue against his neck, hot enough to burn his skin.

They rocked together, gently at first.

Rooker forgot everything.

He was arching his hips to push higher and harder when the door opened again, admitting the same section of sky. The outlined head and shoulders were unmistakable.

It was Uncle Henry, authoritarian intruder in a child's lonely bedroom.

It was Richard Shoesmith, checking up.

Beverley gave a long sigh. She stood up, not in any great haste, and in one fluid movement hoisted and buckled her jeans. Rooker bundled his clothes

270

approximately into place.

'What's this?' Richard demanded. He was flustered by what he had discovered and was covering his embarrassment with fury.

Rooker stepped up to him. 'What does it look like?'

Richard's head gave a wobble of outrage that was much too familiar.

Rooker swung his fist and hit him. Richard went down in an untidy heap and lay there.

Beverley looked coolly at the body sprawled at her feet. 'Oh dear,' she said softly.

Rooker bent over him. 'He'll live.'

'I think I'll leave you to deal with the aftermath,' she said unhurriedly. Her fingertips brushed the top of Rooker's head. Her legs looked very long in the jeans as she slipped away.

CHAPTER ELEVEN

They all stood in a circle beside the resting Squirrel. Lewis shook hands and murmured a word to each of them. He moved in a bubble of importance so insulated from the concerns of others that he was the only person on the base who didn't feel the after-effects of Beverley's play for Rooker and Rooker's assault on Richard. Everyone else was sharply aware of what had happened. There was no concealing drama on this scale in such a confined world.

To Alice, Lewis said, 'I won't forget. And give my best wishes to your mother.'

To Rooker, 'Get in touch when you're through

271

here. I may have something for you.'

And to Richard, 'You're doing a fine job, you and the team. Now I've seen how tough living conditions are on the base we'll be working on improving your budget.' He gripped Richard's hand in both of his, then stepped in for a statesmanlike embrace. At such close range he could hardly miss the damage to Richard's jaw and he did an exaggerated double take. 'Hey. What happened here?'

'I took a fall on the ice.'

Lewis swung round to look at Arturo, whose eyes and nose were now shaded in blotches of purple and yellow.

'You people are accident prone, aren't you? I wouldn't want to be in your shoes, Doc.'

Jochen smiled obligingly.

The TV crew stowed their metal equipment cases in the helicopter. Andy and Mick were in their seats, waiting for the visitors to be ready.

Beverley came out of the hut in her white sweater and silvery fur gilet. She strolled across to the group, her expression unreadable behind her wrap-round sunglasses, and held out her hand to Richard. 'Thank you,' she said warmly. 'Antarctica is a wonderful place.' Then her attention turned immediately to making sure that all Lewis's bags were safely aboard and that he was happy with the flight schedule.

Lewis rubbed his hands. 'Let's go. The dirty old world beckons. I'm sorry to be leaving and I envy you all for being able to stay right here.'

'Sure you do,' Phil murmured as Beverley followed Lewis up the step into the cabin. Everyone watched her rear as she ducked inside.

The rotors sliced the sky and spun into a blur. No one moved as the helicopter lifted off the snow square and buzzed away northwards. It disappeared quickly into a crystalline haze and only then was there a collective sigh of relief. Russell marched straight back to the hut. Laure announced to no one in particular that she was going for a walk.

Rooker had been looking at an iceberg out in the bay. The berg was the size of a church and the lower sides were an intense, sepulchral sapphire pocked and sculpted into twisted pillars and grottoes. The blue ice was the oldest, hundreds of years old, calved from the heart of the glacier.

Richard swung round to him. 'I want to speak to you.'

The others moved off. One of the difficulties of living at Kandahar was that there was nowhere for private conversation except outside.

With an effort, Rooker took his eyes off the berg. 'I owe you an apology. I shouldn't have decked you,' he muttered.

Richard sagged. The spontaneous admission took the wind out of his intended rebuke. He had prepared a sharp warning that any more disruptions would see Rooker on his way back to Ushuaia on the next supply.

'Does it hurt?' Rooker mildly asked.

Richard tried to regain control. 'I won't stand for any more from you. You're surly, you drink on the base, you're subversive. You can either get yourself into key with the rest of us or get out. Do you understand?'

Rooker stood and listened. It seemed that he had been hearing a version of this speech for as long as he had been able to understand the words. His response had been to shrug and ignore it until, sooner or later, it became easier to get out than to stay. This place, though, was different. He didn't want to leave, because of the silence and the light and the blue-ice cathedral majestically drifting in the bay, and also just because it was so far that there was nowhere else to go. If he ended up back in Ushuaia he could head northwards again, or he could go back to the hotel site and try to make the Mexicans work. He was momentarily struck by the oblique similarities between his role there and Richard Shoesmith's here. Making unwieldy compromises, making the best of poor materials under difficult conditions.

His mouth hooked in a smile. 'Yeah,' he said.

Richard's fists clenched. He had expected his anger to be met with anger but Rooker outmanoeuvred him. 'I should have hit you back.'

Rooker's short laugh clearly said *As if*.

Richard was watching the iceberg now, too. The wind was driving it aground in the shallow water at the head of the bay. It would remain captive for the rest of the season for them to admire, and for the wind and waves to sculpt into further fantasies. They stood with a yard of shingle separating them, the space prickling with antipathy.

At last Richard sighed. Almost to himself he admitted, 'I underestimated the force of it.'

'Of what?'

'Sex. It's the real power in a closed world like this, isn't it? There's no money, no hierarchy to speak of, no physical escape, no distraction apart from work. Then sex unfolds in a blank landscape and it's overwhelming.'

274

Rooker shrugged. He hadn't noticed that Richard was so smitten by Beverley Winston. Then he realised that he wasn't talking about Beverley at all.

It's the geologist, he understood. Dr Alice Peel, with her deceptive mildness and an occasional flash in her eyes that betrayed the opposite. Rooker disliked this thought and the surprise caused him to consider what Shoesmith had said.

Edith had wielded a certain kind of power, that was true, and so had some of the other women he had known over the years. But it was a short-lived, tawdry version of it. Even in this confined environment Beverley's appeal hadn't been overwhelming, not by any means. He had felt momentary lust and had casually taken the opportunity to gratify it. Only her perfume remained with him. He remembered how it had cloaked him in the generator hut when Shoesmith clumsily opened the door, then his own thwarted desire and the wave of anger that it had triggered.

But in the back of his mind Rooker knew that there was a force much more powerful than sex. He was fumbling to identify it while Shoesmith was still talking.

'At least my grandfather never had to take account of *that*.'

In the hut photographs of celebratory dinners, or in the stories of superhuman sledging feats, there had been no swooning perfume or little fur designer gilets, only beards and frozen mittens, and the absolute courage of men out of the sphere of women.

'Do you wish you were him?' Rook asked.

'I never could be. I only do what I can here, in

my own way.'

The intensity in the words was startling, but Rook only blinked. Indifference was a defence. He didn't want to hear Shoesmith's story, or risk its effects on him. He wanted to maintain his distance, because to be distant was to remain impervious.

It was Richard who turned and made Rooker face him. He held out his hand. 'Shall we declare a truce, then? I don't expect friendship, or even loyalty if that's really beyond you, but I do require absolute co-operation.'

Rooker recoiled from this.

Shake, like a gentleman. Your word is your bond.

It was Uncle Henry incarnate, every Victorian mock-heroic syllable of it. He stood still for a long, insulting minute while Richard's conciliatory smile slowly congealed. Then he lifted his hand and shook Richard's as if it were a dead snake.

'Good,' Richard said carefully. 'That's good.'

They walked back up to the hut, not exactly together—Rooker stepped deliberately three paces behind—but they arrived simultaneously. Russell was cooking again, the others were clearing up the mess left by too many people living without a daily routine. The smells of coffee and baking bread competed with cleaning fluids. The floor was no longer gritty underfoot. Valentin was rubbing the windows with one of the newspapers that Lewis had brought. There was an air of expectancy and some sidelong glances to see how the face-off had proceeded.

'There will be no more fights of any kind on this base,' Richard announced stiffly. No one spoke. 'We are here to co-operate and collaborate.'

Phil didn't actually say that he personally would have been happy to collaborate with Beverley at any time, given the chance, but everyone knew what he was thinking anyway.

Richard maintained just enough dignity to hold their silent attention, even with the split skin from Rooker's knuckles angry on his jaw. There was no joking or muttering.

'And now that our guests have gone, we can all get back to work. Rook?'

'Right,' Rooker agreed.

*   *   *

Looking around the table when they gathered for lunch, Alice noticed that the change that had begun before Lewis Sullavan's arrival appeared complete. The intrusion of people who didn't belong to the group or understand the subtle mechanics of it had forged a team spirit. Everyone was talking and smiling, united by their relief at the departure of the visitors.

Laure was herself again, joking with Jochen over the division of the food. Richard discussed the next month's work schedule that would keep the scientists and support staff fully occupied. No one mentioned Beverley but there was an unspoken collective expectation that in the end, in time, the havoc that her availability and her choice of Rooker had caused would become one of the jokes on the base. Alice watched him covertly, and she also saw that the men checked from time to time to see how he was reacting or what he might be thinking. The episode had improved his standing, but he gave no sign of being aware of this. He was impassive, as always.

It was nine days before Christmas.

*   *   *

That was the beginning of the best time at Kandahar.

The weather was extraordinary. 'There is no such thing as ordinary weather down here,' Arturo always said and the experienced Antarctic hands agreed with him, but even so the present spell was unusual. The skies were almost always clear, the sunshine only veiled from time to time by thin high cloud like a layer of tattered lace. Dozens of rainbows arched delicate filaments against the blue backdrop and rays of pale-green and apricot and rose-pink fanned upwards from the horizon, so that it looked as if immense stage footlights played on the sky from somewhere beyond the blocks and crumpled ice tenements of the glacier across the bay. Often, when the sun was high, beams of coloured light struck from each quarter like outstretched arms. At the end of each arm another sun was suspended in a nimbus of soft hazy colour and in turn more rays struck from each of the new suns, until it looked as if the firmament had been invaded and conquered by a new population of suns which obeyed none of the old laws of the mundane universe.

Alice knew that these suns were parahelia, sun dogs caused by ice crystals falling with their bases level to the horizon and bending the light through their tiny prisms, but knowing the physical explanation for the phenomenon did nothing to decrease her wonder at the sight of them.

278

At night, which was night by the clock although no darkness came, the sky to the south of them burned with richer colours, complex meshed layers of viridian and indigo and scarlet, while the sun hung like a copper ball at the centre of the skein and the glaciers and ice cliffs were splashed with orange and gold and saffron-yellow. Alice went regularly along the water's edge to the secluded bay where the flight of natural stone steps climbed to the clifftop. She sat on the top step with her parka hood pushed back, even though the cold was intense, so as not to miss even an eye's blink of the light show. She believed that the baby was somehow absorbing the light and colours as it unfurled within her.

She felt as well as she had ever done in her life and reasoned that, if she was well, the baby couldn't be otherwise. She ate heartily, and although the work she was doing was hard and often physical she didn't find it too much for her. She climbed rocks in the course of her mapping and sampling, and pulled sledges and spent long days out in the sunshine. Her face was deeply tanned, like all the others', with white blinkers over their eyes where the skin was shielded by glacier goggles.

The boxes of bagged and labelled rock samples slowly filled up. There were other valuable fossil discoveries, but nothing that intrigued Richard as much as the Wheeler's Bluff gastropod. While they worked in the lab hut together he talked about the paper he would write on it and how it would break major new ground in his field.

At night, Alice slept as she had never done before. It was like falling and flying into a huge cloud of feathers. She gave herself up eagerly to the soft oblivion, and woke every morning to the view from the bunk-room window of the giant berg stranded in the bay, and the silver and cobalt ripples of water fanning around it. Sometimes she dreamed—tiny, detailed vignettes from her childhood, or reassuring and mundane reworkings of the day that had just gone.

She began to be friends with Laure. One morning Laure brought her a mug of tea in bed and after that they took it in turns, so that the other could lie there a little longer and watch the kaleidoscopic water. Alice was relieved that she didn't feel sick—she hadn't felt even remotely ill since the ship's crossing, and before that in the hectic days of Margaret's time in hospital and her rushed preparation for the expedition—but she was grateful for a few extra minutes to emerge from the heavy oblivion of sleep. They talked a little, in the bunk room, when they were changing after work or getting ready to go out again.

'I think I was being stupid.' Laure sighed as she brushed her hair. Her neat bob was growing out in a series of frayed kinks round her neck.

'What about?'

'Ah, about Monsieur Rooker.'

'Why?'

'I was dreaming of love.'

'I don't think he's the right character to fit into that particular dream.'

'No. It's so easy to make these mistakes. I have been doing it since, ha, since I was a teenager. This boy, you know, everyone knows he is a bad sort but I can make the difference, I can make him be a good sort. Then—hm—he's doing whatever it is with some other girl, your good friend more than likely, and you are crying in your bedroom for one week.'

Alice laughed. Laure's eyes danced as she deprecated herself.

'I know. It's a pattern. Falling for the same but different Mr Wrong over and over again.'

'I am like this now, with my boyfriend in France. I think, one of these days I can make him put more value to me than his mother. But we have been together for four years and still *maman* is the first in his life. If she says come, Paul is running. So I am away for my Antarctic season, maybe then Paul will miss me. Not that I am not here for penguin work too, of course,' she added hastily. She sighed and put her hairbrush away in her Chanel bag. 'But I cannot see any great signs of how much I am missed.'

'Maybe it will be different when you get home,' Alice said, without too much conviction.

'And maybe I will look for someone else altogether. But he is very handsome, though, and so sexy, don't you think? A bit of a dish?'

Alice laughed again. 'Rook, you mean? Yes, he's a bit of a dish all right. But not one I want to eat off, thanks all the same.'

'You are right and again I am crying in my bedroom. I think maybe you are always right, Aleece. You are very sensible.'

'Not really,' she said.

Briefly, she thought how luxurious it would be to confide in Laure.

For one thing, it was becoming difficult to manoeuvre herself while dressing and undressing to hide the distinct bulge of her stomach. By her

281

calculations Alice reckoned that she must be not quite twelve weeks gone. She went through it in her mind, over and over again. There had been the heavy, abnormally heavy and cramping, bleeding around the first week of October when Margaret had been so ill and she had been too busy to pay any attention. After that, nothing. And then the last night with Pete before she left to travel south. That was right, it all made sense. Even in her relative ignorance Alice knew that you counted in weeks from the first day of your last period. She wouldn't have expected anything to show yet, but then everyone's body was different. She had been thin before and so perhaps the changes were more noticeable.

But telling Laure was out of the question. Alice didn't want to be banished from the present beauty of Antarctica, but the main reason she didn't say anything was that it would be unfair to ask another person to keep her secret. If something went wrong—it wouldn't, in her bones she knew it wouldn't—but if it did, she alone must be responsible. So she dreamily hugged the baby to herself, not quite believing in or even understanding the magnitude of what was unfolding.

For the first time in her life, she reflected, she was doing what she wanted to do. Not because she should, or because it was expected of her by her parents or her teachers or the University or her students or even Pete, but because of herself. She wanted to finish what she had come here to do, in this magical place, then she wanted to go home and plan for her child.

She could do it, she knew that. And she would

have to do it alone, as a parent, when the time came, so she might as well get used to being alone now.

With Laure she went on talking about their work and life at Kandahar, and making wry jokes about men and boyfriends. She tried not to say too much about her own intentions for the future, so that when the time came Laure wouldn't feel that she had been hoodwinked.

'You are good at listening,' Laure told her.

'I don't know about that,' Alice answered, feeling guilty.

Christmas came.

*   *   *

Work at Kandahar didn't follow the set pattern of weekdays and weekends. While the weather was good everyone went out and did as much as they could without taking a rest day, knowing that there might be a long stretch of enforced down time with the next spell of bad weather. The sunshine following Lewis Sullavan's departure meant that the whole team worked for nine days straight. When Richard announced that, whatever the weather, Christmas Day and Boxing Day would be official rest days, there was a cheer around the table.

Richard had another suggestion, too.

Everyone had brought presents and cards from home to open on Christmas morning, but Richard said there should be an exchange of gifts amongst the team members too. They should each put one present into a sack, and take out a different one.

Laure's forehead creased. 'But, what to give?'

'You can make something, from whatever you can find on or around the base. Or you can give one of your own possessions, maybe something you value or which has significance for you. You can choose, you can use your imagination. Of course, you don't know who is going to receive your present.'

Alice said, 'That's a very nice idea.'

'It's not original,' Richard answered, but he was deeply pleased by her approval.

*   *   *

On Christmas morning everyone slept for an extra hour. Alice and Laure opened their eyes on a silver and gunmetal sea, and saw that the berg had faded to pearly grey, like slippery satin. The spell of fine weather was ending. Someone was playing a loud recording of Christmas carols on the living area CD player.

The kitchen was low on bottled gas and cooking had been severely curtailed for the past week, but today there would be no restrictions. Russell had defrosted a turkey and Alice had improvised a stuffing for it using dried apricots, tinned chestnuts and dried herbs. Kandahar cooking now involved a lot of improvisation as supplies ran low before the New Year resupply, but Alice enjoyed the challenge of opening the store cupboard and trying to devise custard or pasta sauce or chocolate cake from its contents. For their Christmas dinner there was also plum pudding and rum butter that had come down with the original supplies, and Russell had made mince pies. Richard relaxed the no-alcohol rule for the day.

'*Bon Noël, Aleece,*' Laure said. They hugged each other.

The living area was decorated with tinsel and candles, and a big picture of a decorated Christmas tree was pinned to the bulletin board. The day's eating began with a convivial breakfast of scrambled eggs and fish, which Valentin and Niki had caught in the bay and smoked in a home-made smoke box. Russell produced two bottles of champagne and made Buck's Fizz with concentrated orange juice. Led by Richard they shook hands and wished each other Happy Christmas, then drank a toast to families and friends. Rooker drained his in one gulp, Alice noticed, but he didn't join in the chorus of the toast. He looked more withdrawn today than usual, if that was possible. His black eyes were hooded as he regarded the rest of them.

After breakfast there was the exchange of team presents. The only sack Russell had been able to find was a black bin bag, but Alice and Laure had cut out paper snowflakes and stuck them all over it. It made them laugh, to be manufacturing fake snowflakes when they were surrounded by an abundance of real ones.

After much thought, Alice had chosen to make someone a present of her treasured copy of *The Rime of the Ancient Mariner*, with reproductions of the Doré illustrations from 1875. In one of them a frozen ghost ship glides on black water between towering cliffs of ice. Overhead, a solar arc spans the sky, just as strange suns had disturbed the skies in the last nine days. The thin volume had been a school prize, and her name and the date and the words 'For Excellence in Mathematics' were

285

inscribed on a bookplate inside the front board. She had always loved the poem, and now that she had seen them for herself she thought more than ever that Coleridge's description of the realms of ice was the most chilling she had ever read.

The verses ran in her head as she wrapped the book.

When her turn came to draw a present Alice reached into the black mouth of the bag and took out the first item that her fingers touched. With everyone's eyes on her she unwrapped some crumpled paper and looked down at the gift in her hands.

It was a piece of driftwood, rubbed bone-smooth by the waves and curved in a shape that fitted in her two palms. The outlines already suggested the finish, but the wood had been carved with a few extra deep, deft lines that made it into a sleeping, swaddled baby. The piece was beautiful for its simplicity. Alice knew that Rook had done it. She had seen him carving before, his head bent in preoccupation over the wood and the blade of his penknife almost swallowed up in his big hands.

Blood rushed into her face as she looked up.

He must *know*. Who knew, who else?

Then her eyes met his hooded glare. Of course he didn't know. How could he have determined that she would pick this gift? It was a coincidence, no more than that. She took a breath to compose herself. 'Thank you. It's beautiful,' she said quietly. Some of the darkness melted out of his face.

Jochen was the recipient of her Coleridge. He looked puzzled by it. Valentin had put in a bottle of his special Bulgarian *rakia*, which was drawn by Phil.

'Ta, Valerie,' he said with evident pleasure.

Richard's present was a handsome old brass-bound compass, which went to Niki, but it was Arturo's contribution that drew the most admiration. He had collected a varied pile of beach stones, black basalt and ribby quartz and greenish olivine, rounded shapes that nestled smoothly in the hand, each one with a hole rubbed right through it by the agitation of the sea. He had taken a length of smooth white cord from the stores and had linked the stones with macramé knots beween each one to make a heavy chain, too massive for a necklace, like a stone snake.

Laure gave a surprised wince when she felt the weight of the package, then her face flowered into a smile when she tore off the paper. She arranged the stones and the cord coiled sweetly between them. 'Oh, it is a sculpture,' she cried. 'I love this.'

Arturo basked in the praise.

Afterwards, everyone went outside. The sky was purled with cloud now and they missed the sun that they had begun almost to take for granted. There was an assortment of old skis in the store, left behind by the British. Phil and Rooker got the skidoos out of the shelter and fixed tow ropes, and everyone took it in turns to be pulled up the longest slope behind the hut and to ski down again. Alice wondered if it was reckless of her, but she reckoned that if she could be pregnant and rock-climb then she could ski too, and anyway the exhilaration of swooping down from the lip of the glacier almost to the back of the hut was too pleasurable to miss.

Rooker didn't ski; he drove the skidoo uphill over and over again with whooping skiers hanging on to the back.

'I never learned,' he snapped when Alice asked him why. She realised now that it was always Phil who went off on the cross-country skis to teams in the field when both skidoos were in use.

'You have to try.' She laughed. 'Go on. I'll be your instructor. Bend ze knees, remember.'

He studied her face for a moment. 'All right,' he said.

He borrowed Phil's skis and boots, cramming his feet into the boots with a grimace. Alice walked a little way up the slope with him, took his hands and gently towed him as he ploughed downhill. They did it several times, ascending higher each time. For a man of his size he generally moved with economy and agility, and it was strange to see him looking awkward. At first he responded to her praise and encouragement with the usual shrug, then he gave a slight smile followed by a sharp glance to see if she really meant it. He learned quickly, with a kind of wolfish concentration.

After another half-hour she drove the skidoo to the top of the slope with Rook wobbling on the tow rope. 'Slowly.' She pointed to the shallowest angle of descent. 'I'll drive alongside.'

He launched himself away immediately. His shoulders were rigid with determination.

'Relax. Bend your knees. Keep your hands low,' she shouted after him. But he knew what to do. He would turn out to be a natural.

He was gathering speed and she accelerated after him. She told him to lean all his weight on one leg, then on the other. A series of lurching turns developed.

'Hey!' he yelled in unaccustomed delight.

Laure came swooping by in an elegant arc, a plume of snow feathering up from her ski tails. She was an excellent skier. Rooker lost his concentration and plunged forward, crossed his ski tips and somersaulted down the slope to end up in a heap.

Alice shot forward to reach him. 'Are you all right?'

He was lying in the snow, a tangle of long limbs and skis and poles. She felt a beat of concern and then she saw that he was laughing. He let his head fall back in a snowdrift and laughed up at the sky. She had never seen him look this way before, never even heard him laugh with all his heart. The blankness had all broken up and he was alive with momentary happiness.

'I can't get up,' he gasped.

She dismounted and flopped down on her knees beside him. She released his bindings, took off the skis and untwisted his legs and arms. To touch him in this unceremonious, affectionate way made her breathe faster and feel grateful for the shield of her goggles. They clasped hands like a pair of drunks and half lurched and half hauled themselves to their feet. There was powder snow glittering in the close fur of Rook's hair and in his black eyebrows. He shook his head like a dog, the lines of laughter still transfiguring him.

'Again!' he demanded.

Like a child, Alice thought, as if his childhood had been largely unexplored and he had just glimpsed a corner of it. They realised simultaneously that their hands were still linked and quickly let go.

They did it again, faster, and this time he didn't

fall.

She bounced up and down on the skidoo pedals and applauded him. Rook stared around as if he didn't quite recognise his surroundings. Everyone except Phil had gone back to the hut, in search of the *vin chaud* that Laure had promised to make.

Phil sat with his boots up on the other skidoo, smoking and grinning. 'Downhill champ, boy,' he called.

'Yeah,' Rook sneered, recollecting himself.

'You could be, you're really good,' Alice insisted.

He hesitated, then put his arm round her shoulders and hugged her. 'Thanks. I enjoyed that.'

He was very strong, she could tell from the absolute solidity of him under the folds of his parka. She didn't want him to let go, she realised, but he did.

A freshening wind was riffling the bay water and twisting little whirlwinds of snow around their feet. The idea of indoor warmth suddenly became inviting. Alice stood and waited while the two men drove the skidoos into the shelter, briefly thinking of home and the e-mails that would probably be waiting for her later, when her half-hour turn at the Internet came. Then the three of them climbed the rocks round to the hut door and went in together, laughing about the ski lesson.

The smells of cinnamon and roasting turkey wafted at them.

Phil hung his parka on the peg and rubbed his hands. 'I'm hungry enough to eat my own head,' he said.

'Alice just taught me to ski,' Rook announced across him. He didn't often volunteer a spontaneous remark. There was an instant

290

drumming of good-humoured applause and an ironic cheer from Jochen. From his place across the room, Richard looked at them. There was a beat of silence before the general talk and laughter started up again.

*   *   *

Alice opened her in-box. There were a dozen messages waiting for her. Becky's was first.

Christmas Eve, not a mouse stirring at my dear sis's place. Everyone gone to midnight mass, her kids asleep at last altho touch and go for an hour. Vijay and I too frazzled from drive up here, so babysitting. No idea how V is going to deal with family gathering, my dad insisting on Queen's speech, mum dropping heavy hints re weddings and babies, toddlers underfoot etc. etc. Love him for at least agreeing to come . . .

Am all Xmas partied out. Seven in a week, darling. Feet deformed from new Gina stilettos, skin mottled crepe w alcohol oozing from every pore, eyes two holes in a blanket. I need week at health farm to recover, not 3 days overeating in bosom of family. V suggests little holiday in Jan, somewhere warm. Well, why not?

Missing you. Can't imagine what it's really like down there, ice and polar heroes? Your messages not very informative!! Please expand. Are you sure okay?

Happy Christmas dearest xxB

No, they were not very informative, Alice could only concede. It was hard to know how much or how little to say, to admit to, when the changes inside her and around her were so significant and her day-to-day life was so far removed from Becky's and Jo's. She didn't want either of them to guess, and then have to worry about her or try to persuade her to do something different.

Hectic! Mum here for 5 days, helpful but also hindrance if you know what I mean.

Harry v busy week at work, surprise surprise. Twins now almost sitting up! Fall sideways on cushions and look startled, but definitely on the way.

Sleep still getting better, thank God. Dad and Naomi also coming for Xmas dinner with her son Dan, Mum a bit mournful but determined to be modern as she puts it. However it works out with me and H I NEVER EVER want to get a divorce. Couldn't deal with all extended bloody family ramifications. Envy you down there in the spartan south, bet not too much cooking and conciliating and smoothing feathers to do! Enjoy it—must be the strangest Christmas ever.

Can't wait for you to come home.
Love and xxxs Jo

And yes, it was the strangest Christmas. Half listening to the voices and bustle behind her, Alice thought what an unexpectedly happy one it was turning out to be.

Margaret wrote too:

292

Lewis's people sent me a jpeg picture of the hut naming. How marvellous! I feel quite a heroine. I am so pleased that you were there for me. Thank you. I must say, you look as though you've taken to polar life like a seal to the waves. What did I tell you?

There's very little news up here. Oxford is cold and everyone is full of complaints, but it only makes me think even more of a summer season down south. I read your description of the parahelia and stranded berg over and over again. It brings it all back.

Between the clipped lines Alice read her mother's love for the place and her nostalgia for the glory days. She was glad all over again that she had come, most particularly because Margaret had so much wanted her to.

She veered away from thinking about her mother and Lewis. It was a long time ago. And, as she was now beginning to understand, there were places that functioned outside the ordinary rules of time and experience. Maybe her mother's love affair had taken place in one of those.

Trevor's message was much shorter. He had never been an e-mail enthusiast.

Happy Christmas darling. I miss you and love you so much. Dad.

There was also one from Pete. Alice saw his name, but his message was at the bottom of the list so it was fine to leave it until last.

Alice, precious Alice, how far away you are.
Why don't you write to me? Remember last
Christmas, in the house, when everything
seemed right? How has it gone wrong? I'm in
London, wanted to get away from Oxford for a
while.

Borrowed a studio, sleeping on the floor.
Been pretty busy working on a new piece.
Chase & Castle (gallery) interested in giving
me a show. I might agree to go with them. I
wish, I wish all kinds of things, what chance of
any of them coming true?

All my love P

You know what went wrong, Alice mentally
retorted. The tone of the message was irritating,
yet so characteristic of him. She didn't think the
things he was wishing for were very likely to include
a surprise baby. Peter always wanted what he
couldn't have.

There would be difficulties ahead, but she would
deal with them when they arose and there was no
point in worrying about them until the time came.

Behind her shoulder, Laure was making small
fidgeting movements indicating that she was
waiting for her turn. Alice logged off and gave up
her seat. Oxford would be raw and damp, with a
mist over the river and the water meadows, and the
streets smoky and black with moisture. The big
trees in the Parks would offer up leafless branches
to the swollen sky and the windows of houses in
Jericho would be lit up and then tight-curtained
against the descent of mid-afternoon twilight. She
felt a powerful gust of homesickness, and a longing
for familiar places and for the company of friends.

In that moment she would have given up everything Antarctica meant to her for the chance to spend Christmas night with her parents and Jo and Becky. But it was the same for everyone at Kandahar, she reminded herself. They were all spending Christmas away from home. Except for Rook, maybe. He didn't claim his half-hour of Internet access.

Dinner was a success. Russell carved the turkey and the team fell on it. After the plum pudding there was an Antarctic quiz, set by Niki. Everyone enjoyed it and competition was intense. Arturo won, by one point from Russell, much to his satisfaction. Richard proposed charades and they played a couple of rounds, but Valentin and Arturo didn't see the sense, and Phil made it clear that he found it all a bit country-house for his taste.

'What next? Croquet?' he asked.

They fell back on singing. Phil brought out his guitar, and after they had done all the carols they could come up with from each nationality they sang rounds and Valentin's drinking songs, and old Beatles hits because Jochen knew all the words of these.

Then it was time for dancing. The room grew hot and the windows ran with condensation. After a while Alice sank down in a chair to get her breath back and found Rook next to her. He was watching with a full glass in his hand rather than dancing himself, but his face was animated, the characteristic blank expression that had slipped during the ski lesson still absent.

'I think this is one of the nicest Christmases I have ever had,' Alice told him.

'Is it?' He was surprised. He didn't have much

295

idea of what Christmas would be like for people who came from ordinary families, although he had a picture in his head that might have come from a Victorian story book.

When she was still alive there had been parties. Always a gathering of odd people who didn't want to go home, or didn't have homes to go to. One year there had been a man with two artificial legs whose party trick, once he was drunk enough, had been to unstrap the legs and twirl around on his thick arms. The stumps were naked and fascinating to a small boy, the way the flesh puckered and dimpled round the severed bones. In the later years when the drink had got the better of her, Jimmy used to pick her up and mop her face, then haul her to her bed while she muttered and clawed at him. The very last year there had been Lester.

At Uncle Henry's there was church, which smelled of fir boughs for the day, as well as damp and mice. Uncle Henry read one of the lessons; the joyful message of Christmas seemed to be for other people, for the rosy faces in the small congregation, not for the Jerrolds. His uncle and aunt gave Jimmy books, when he wanted toy weapons and television and his mother back. He realised that he must have been a difficult presence in their clock-ticking, sombre house.

Alice was saying something to him. Her face was a bright, still oval in the jigging room.

'What?' he asked abruptly.

Her expression changed, becoming uncertain. 'I was just asking if you have a family. I'm sorry, I didn't mean to sound intrusive.'

He remembered the skiing lesson and he wanted not to reject her friendliness now. He searched his mind for what to say. 'It's all right. I don't have a family. Some . . . friends, but no wife or children.' The words felt unused in his mouth, rusty. He should have been in touch with Frankie, he thought. He could have sent her and the kids an e-mail at least. Alice was still looking at him and he could feel the happiness in her like heat radiating from a fire. An answering smile seeded itself in him. He wanted to go on talking and it was an unusual sensation.

'I've never celebrated Christmas. My mother died when I was a kid in New Zealand and then I lived with relatives until I was old enough to move on. I don't mean I never did partying or seasonal excess.' Her mouth curved in response to this. There was a small indentation beneath her full upper lip, he noticed, like a tiny fingerprint. 'But no tree or sack of presents or family reunions.'

'This is a family tonight. Don't you think?'

Rooker shrugged. It sounded sentimental to him. Families were people who would make sacrifices for each other.

'And we had the sack of presents. I liked your carving very much.'

'How do you know it's my carving?'

She smiled. 'I put two and two together.'

'Ah, I see.'

'Shall we dance?' Alice asked suddenly.

Phil was picking at his guitar and crooning, with a tumbler of Valentin's *rakia* at his elbow. Jochen and Laure were turning smooth circles and Niki was hopping up and down with his elbows sticking out.

'Are you offering to teach me to dance as well?'

'I think you know how to do that,' she said.

They stood up and the others moved to make room for them.

He clasped her hand and bent his head over it. With his other hand at the small of her back he drew her close to him. She was small and light, and there was no waft of heavy perfume when she moved. He thought he caught just the faintest scent of her skin. She moved two or three steps in his arms, then seemed to collect herself and draw back to leave a hair's breadth of empty space between them. But still a kind of electricity danced in the air.

Looking over her head to the window, Rooker saw that it had started to snow. Thick flakes swirled out of blue-grey space and pelted against the glass. The snow and the room's convivial warmth together seemed to make an eccentric version of his Victorian Christmas picture.

At the end of the song Jochen came and claimed her.

Half an hour later Rooker noticed that she had slipped away to bed. He and Phil sat up until very late, playing cards and finishing the *rakia* with Niki and Valentin.

The next day was grey inside, with most people nursing hangovers and irritable tempers. Outside, the wind gusted and battered the hut walls, driving the blizzard so that no one could go out for exercise or to escape the atmosphere of ill humour. As she sat trying to read, Alice saw that Rooker claimed his half-hour of Internet time along with everyone else, although Arturo tried to insist that he had usurped his slot. Rooker's face was dark and closed-in again. He didn't look directly at her, or anyone else.

The blizzard lasted for another five days. After the prolonged spell of sunshine and long days spent outside, confinement affected everyone. There were spates of pointless arguments, between Arturo and Jochen, between Valentin and Niki. Even Phil was snappy and disagreeable. Then, on New Year's Eve, the wind lessened. The familiar landscape outside the hut was blunted with heavy layers of new snow and the berg had acquired a thick, dead-white topping, like meringue on a cake.

As soon as she could get out Alice walked through the deep drifts along the shoreline to the secluded bay and beat her way up the steps of the dyke. As always, the place soothed her spirit. She watched a family of crabeater seals surface in the choppy water, then haul themselves through the ice on to the shingle. There were two pups with them, fat sleek creatures who rolled against the flanks of the cows. The sun was just visible as a hard white disc through a veil of cloud. Only ten days after the Antarctic midsummer it already hung lower in the sky. Alice thought of the time when it would dip below the horizon into polar darkness and shivered. It was too cold to linger at the steps. She pulled her hood close and trudged back to the hut.

Throughout the early evening, as the midnight hour in the various countries of Europe came and went, the expedition members wished each other a happy new year while thinking of their absent families and friends. Russell and Richard tried hard to generate a more cheerful mood, but the melancholy persisted. Alice knew that Becky was giving a party, and she found herself longing for silly shoes and gossip.

This time next year, she thought, where will I be?

It was then, standing at the window and looking out at the shifting vista of ice and water, that she felt it.

It was a movement inside her, like being gently nudged by another person, a small featherlike stroke, only it came from within.

She knew immediately what it was, this intimate pressure.

The baby was moving.

She was amazed, flooded with awe at its wholeness, its presence as a new being, but it also made the hair stand up at the nape of her neck.

And she knew at the same time that her calculations were wrong. Fourteen-week foetuses moved, they twisted and swam in their sea of uterine fluid, but you couldn't feel it. This baby was older, bigger than that.

CHAPTER TWELVE

The supply ship was due to reach Kandahar on 5 January but it was delayed for two days.

At last the *Polar Star* glided past the ice cliff at the eastern end of the bay and drifted out in the deep water. It rode there like a toy, incongruous against the waste of snow. Rooker and Phil were ready in their orange float suits. The Zodiacs bobbed out from the jetty and zipped prow-high across the waves to the ship's side.

Alice stood watching from the hut door. The last week had been a torment of indecision. Even now, at this last minute, there was still time for her to say that she would have to leave with the ship. The sentences ran through her head as they had done almost hourly, ever since New Year's Eve: *I've got to leave, yes, go back to London. I'm pregnant. No, I'm not sure how many months, I don't know, I'm sorry . . .*

She didn't say anything. There was a flurry in the hut where Russell and Laure were preparing breakfast for the ship's captain, who would be coming across with the dinghies for a brief visit to the base. The two Zodiacs had reached the ship's side. She lifted Russell's binoculars to take a look at the chain of sailors forming up on the metal steps. Bags and boxes were speedily passed down to Phil and Rook who stowed them in the dinghies. There would be plenty of fresh food now, and bottles of gas for cooking and hot water.

'Are you okay, Aleece?' Laure called.

'Yes.'

She should help with the breakfast, but she couldn't take her eyes off the ship. It was a lifeline and a sentence of execution all in one. It could remove her from her present dilemma, but to allow it to do so would mean the end of her Antarctic life.

Stay, a siren voice whispered in her ear.

Through the binoculars she watched the ship's captain descend the metal steps with the first mate behind him. A minute later the dinghies, wallowing a little under the weight of their cargoes, circled away from the ship and ploughed back towards the shore. The link was easily made when the ship was here but once it was broken Kandahar would be wrapped in isolation again.

Richard and Russell and Arturo drank coffee and chatted in Spanish to the officers. The rest of them unloaded supplies and did a series of carries up the beach to the base stores. Alice stopped to catch her breath with a box of apples resting on the jut of her stomach.

'Heavy?' Phil asked as he came by with a tier of three boxes.

'Not at all. Can you manage those?'

'Pfff,' he retorted.

At the end of the visit everyone strolled back down to the jetty. Six new gas canisters stood above the waterline, wrapped in a shroud of tarpaulin. The empties were stacked in the bottom of one of the Zodiacs, to be shipped back to Punta Arenas with the rest of the retro. The captain stood with his hands in the pockets of his windproof, proudly surveying his waiting ship.

'Who's coming? All aboard for civilisation,' he joked in English as Rooker waded out to bring the dinghy close in to the jetty for him.

Alice's inner voice muttered, *Wait, I am, I'm coming with you.*

'No takers,' Richard responded.

She stood with her boots planted on the shingle, listening to the slap of waves and the rattle of brash ice. The packaged waste had already been hoisted into Phil's dinghy and Rook waited in thigh-deep water for the ship's officers to scramble aboard.

'*Buenas días,*' the first officer called. '*Muchas gracias.*'

Phil fired his outboard and headed again for the ship.

The captain beamingly shook everyone's hand. 'If you cannot be persuaded to leave now, we see you in March.'

Polar Star was scheduled to return on 15 March, before the bay iced for the winter, to take them all back to Chile.

Alice was rooted to the beach. There was a chorus of goodbyes as the ship's officers saluted, Rook opened the throttle and the outboard roared. The second Zodiac raced after the first and Alice swallowed hard against the mixture of emotions rising in her throat. Finally she got her breathing under control again.

There, it was done.

She hadn't burned her boats, exactly, but she had just waved goodbye to them. The certainty filled her with a kind of reckless glee. Staying here was the most irresponsible thing she had ever done, no question, but as she stood watching Rook in the dinghy she knew it was what she wanted.

Now she would be here until the end of the season, two months away.

If she was already as much as twenty weeks pregnant—how this had happened she had yet to work out—it would be a much closer-run thing than she had originally allowed for. But she would still be back home in good time.

Richard and Laure and the others walked back up to the hut but Alice stayed put, pulling the flaps of her hat down against the wind. She watched the officers going aboard and the boxes of waste being manhandled up the ladder. As soon as the Zodiacs turned away from her flank the ship began steaming out of the bay. She stood staring until her eyes watered, staring until the *Polar Star* had edged out of her sight.

Phil and Rooker shipped the outboards, hauled the dinghies up the beach and made them secure to the concrete mooring blocks. As they trudged past in their huge suits Phil called out, 'Homesick?'

'No. Not a bit. Fresh air, you know, it's nice out here.'

Her voice rang falsely in her ears. She turned her back on the empty sea and hurried after them. Phil diverted his steps towards the skidoo shelter and she found herself alongside Rooker.

'Rook?'

'Yeah.'

She was glad of this opportunity to catch him out of earshot of the others and she hadn't rehearsed her request. 'You don't always use your Internet time.'

His black eyebrows made a solid line and he gave her a glare as cold as a skua's. Clearly, he took her observation as an intrusion into his privacy.

'And I wondered . . . I've got some research . . . if, you know, I could trade some time? Do your kitchen duty, maybe, in return?'

His gaze didn't warm. Alice quailed, wishing she had never raised the subject. She was allowing herself to admit that she was interested in him, but he frightened her too. There was a rawness under the layers of his self-containment.

At the very last second, as they reached the hut door, he jerked his head. 'Have it. I don't need to trade anything with you.'

That was all. There was no sign of the intimacy that had sprung up between them at Christmas. Rooker had retreated within himself again.

'Thanks,' she murmured, but it was to empty air.

Extra time to check a couple of websites, that was all she needed. Some privacy would have been ideal too, but that was definitely not forthcoming. She dreaded one of the others looking suddenly over her shoulder and seeing a lurid pink web page headed 'Pregnancy and Baby'. Jochen had loomed the day before but she hunched forward to hide the screen.

He showed his gums when he smiled. 'Okay, Alice, relax. I do not spy on you. What is it, love letters? Or perhaps a naughty porno site?'

'Neither.'

He retreated, licking his lips. 'Oho, secrets. How exciting.'

She scribbled her name in the access diary immediately above Rook's. Now she had an hour. With any luck, that would give her fifty-five clear minutes before the next surfer started hovering behind her.

She typed and clicked, then read quickly as the pages came up.

From 14 weeks fluttering movements may be felt, but the first 'quickening' is typically experienced between 18–22 weeks . . .

The sensations she now regularly felt were hardly flutters, more like firm nudges.

At 15 weeks you will be beginning to show . . .

Beginning? Hardly. But then she was eating more heartily than she had ever done in her life, and she had had a small frame and a flat stomach. Once.

The measurement from pubic bone to fundus (the upper part of the uterus) will approximately equal the number of weeks you are pregnant. 20cm = 20 weeks.

That was much more helpful. A tape measure,

that was what she needed. Maybe Laure would have one.

Week 22. Sex may be very fulfilling at this stage, due to increased blood supply to the sexual organs . . .

She gave an involuntary cough of laughter at this. Chance would be a fine thing. Out of the corner of her eye she saw Jochen look up from his book and raise an eyebrow, so she straightened her face again and read more about the importance of a healthy diet that did not involve eating for two, fresh air and plenty of exercise, throughout a normal pregnancy.

That's all right, then, she thought. Couldn't be doing more of the right things, except for the being stranded in Antarctica bit.

When exactly fifty-five minutes were up she logged off smartly and left the screen blank. She went to the bunk room in search of Laure, who was tweezing her eyebrows with the help of a compact mirror wedged against the window. 'Laure, do you have such a thing as a tape measure?'

'What is that? Ah, I know. No. I am sorry. What is it for?'

'I, er, just want to measure something.'

'Maybe a ruler, then.'

In the end Alice stretched a piece of twine from her pubic bone, digging in with her fingers to find it, to the top of her bulge. Then she laid the length of twine against her geologist's steel measuring tape and read 18.5cm. It was maddeningly imprecise but in any case, now the ship had gone there was nothing to be gained from knowing the dates. She must trust to luck and her body, and in the meantime Antarctica held her in its tight grip. She watched the skies and the colours painted by the sun as it dipped closer to the horizon, and even when the winds howled down the glacier to the sea, or the shoreline was hidden by the caprice of blizzards, she counted her blessings in being there. The disparate group of people at Kandahar had finally become a team and she was part of it.

*   *   *

In Oxford it was a raw and damp January. Margaret sat at her table in the window, rubbing her aching knees and checking her in-box for Alice's bulletins. She read them eagerly, and in her mind's eye she clearly saw the iceberg in the bay, the pack ice driven by the wind and the balls of silvery-grey fluff that were new-hatched Adélie chicks.

Alice wrote about her work, the great explosions of the weather, her daily walks to the little bay and the rocks she called the temple, the other scientists and their work, the small routines of life on the base. Margaret remembered her own times vividly enough, but these descriptions of Alice's brought to the surface memories that had been silted over by the passage of time. In her dreams she was there again, pursuing seals between the pendulous grey stalactites that hung beneath the surface of the ice, or leaning into a wind that squeezed the air out of her lungs. When she woke up she was momentarily amazed to discover that she was old, hardly able to hobble across her own bedroom without wincing in pain. Alice's journey was making her feel young again, even if it was only for brief moments. Margaret smiled as she read her messages, nodding in recognition and approval.

307

'She seems happy enough down there, do you think?' Trevor commented, anxiously reading over her shoulder.

'I knew she would be. I told her it would suit her, didn't I?'

Margaret didn't notice that Alice wrote almost nothing personal. Her daughter was a scientist: it was the science that mattered and the extraordinariness of a continent of ice, and the practical matters that enabled one to be briefly tamed for the benefit of the other. In her own day Margaret had ignored the hostility of most of her male colleagues and faced down her own loneliness. She expected nothing less of Alice.

Trevor read the messages for himself, frowning as he did so. It was his private opinion that there was too little of Alice in them, as if she was keeping almost everything back except what was obvious and therefore safe to pass on.

More photographs of the hut-naming ceremony had arrived from the Sullavanco Polar Office. Margaret slotted them into Perspex frames and arranged them on the windowsill in front of her desk table. Now when she looked up from her screen it was not to stare into the dripping black garden. She could see the carmine-red walls of Margaret Mather House instead, the sun turning her name plaque to a tablet of molten gold and Alice smiling in her weatherproofs with the black ovals of her glacier goggles masking her eyes. Lewis was standing next to her.

*   *   *

That same day Lewis Sullavan was in the news.

He had added a small chain of resort hotels in Bali and Thailand to his empire, but this had been of interest to no one until a bomb exploded near the swimming pool of one hotel on Ko Samui. A young British honeymoon couple had been killed and half a dozen other people injured. The bombing was the work of a tiny protest organisation claiming to act on behalf of the very young Thai girls and boys who worked in the sex trade at the resort. One twelve-year-old boy, it was reported, had recently died of an overdose of heroin given to him during an assignation with a German sex tourist.

There was no direct connection to Lewis Sullavan, but his company did own the hotel. The fact went unreported in his own newspapers, but there were plenty of rival publications eager to print his picture next to photographs of the devastation around a tropical-paradise swimming pool. He responded by calling a press conference to express his grief and sympathy for the dead and injured and their families, and to say that he was now taking personal steps to dismiss all staff at his hotels who had ever had anything to do with providing prostitutes of any age for guests.

Margaret and Trevor sat watching the television news. Margaret was fidgeting with the thin gold circle of her wedding ring. Her finger joints were knobbed and swollen with arthritis, and she couldn't force the ring off over her knuckle. The skin where it rubbed was flaky and raw.

'Sordid business,' Trevor said.

*   *   *

At Kandahar, where no one wanted to use up too much of their Internet time on news sites, the details arrived late and in fragmentary form. Alice noticed that sports results always seemed to be with them almost instantly, world events took longer, and now it was clear that anything reflecting adversely on Sullavanco hardly filtered through at all. Then an e-mail memo to Richard arrived from Beverley Winston. In view of recent unfortunate events it would be most opportune if Mr Sullavan's beneficial work for the EU in Antarctica could in some way be given an extra highlight. Some of the film footage and photographs from the recent visit might be released early, before the season's end. And any major scientific discoveries would, of course, receive their proper wide coverage.

Richard rubbed his chapped face, his eyebrows knitting with anxiety.

Phil scowled over his mug of tea as they discussed it. He said, 'Sullavan can't come over all righteous and pretend not to have known what goes on in those resorts of his. I'm sorry for that poor couple on their honeymoon and for kids who have to sell themselves to tourists, but the fact is that half the people who go out to those Thai places are after a bit of underage legover. Him sacking a couple of managers and hall porters isn't going to make any difference. It's the way the world goes round, rich old tourists, hungry young kids, that's just a fact of life. And our Beverley can't come on all proper, either, because she wasn't averse to a bit on her Antarctic awayday, was she?' His Welsh accent thickened when he felt strongly about something.

Most of the others were nodding in agreement.

310

Niki grinned at the mention of Beverley, his long face brightening.

'Unless I'm mistaken, she wasn't under age,' Rooker drawled. 'And I'm certainly not.'

'That's enough,' Richard snapped.

As Alice had guessed it would, the Beverley Winston affair had turned into a joke amongst the other men.

'So we're going to have our mugshots in the papers to make Sullavan look good again,' Russell remarked.

But they were so far away, down here on the edge of the ice, that the teeming events of the warm world seemed hardly to touch them.

Only Richard was really concerned. His anxiety to make Kandahar a success that would improve Lewis Sullavan's reputation led him to step up the work rate on the station. He introduced new schedules that involved longer hours for them all and took to supervising the progress of the research more closely. His interference annoyed everyone, and from being harmonious and productive, the atmosphere on the base turned sour again.

Another ripple produced by the bomb explosion beside a far-off swimming pool was that Richard decided the gastropod discovery was so important that he must look for similar or related specimens in other sections of the fossil-bearing strata of Wheeler's Bluff. He told Alice that they would be making another big trip into the deep field, this one to last two weeks. He had already spoken to Niki about radioing the pilots at Santa Ana to schedule an airlift.

'Is something wrong?' he asked as she digested

311

this information. They were in the lab, where Richard had been working at the microscope. Laure was in the next seat, labelling phials of penguin blood ready for refrigeration.

'Nothing at all,' Alice said hastily.

What was wrong was that she was gripped by anxiety about the dangers of the deep field. The weather problems they had encountered on the last trip had been no more than routine, but still they had been seriously delayed out at the Bluff. And the memory of Lewis Sullavan buried in the crevasse kept coming back to her, so that she couldn't dismiss it. It had happened so quickly and it could so easily have been fatal, even on the doorstep of Kandahar. Pregnancy seemed to be loosening the tight strings of her body and sapping her courage as well. If anything happened to Richard when they were alone far out on the ice she doubted that she could deal with it properly. And if *she* were to be the victim, she wondered if Richard would be quick enough or decisive enough to take action. He might be too distracted by concerns outside Kandahar and the field, too determined to make a find at all costs that would satisfy Lewis's desire for positive publicity.

The unwelcome realisation that she didn't have proper confidence in him worked under her skin, chafing and scraping. 'I think we should take a field assistant with us this time,' she ventured.

She could read each successive thought in his eyes.

He knew she didn't trust him.

And they wouldn't be alone together.

And they couldn't take the safety officer away from the base for two weeks because the personnel remaining at Kandahar would need Phil's support.

So that only left Rooker.

'Why is that?' Richard demanded.

'With an assistant, we'll be able to work more efficiently. We'll have more time if we don't have to handle camp routine.'

It sounded convincing, in a way.

'Maybe,' Richard said stiffly. 'I'll speak to Rooker.'

Laure glanced up at Alice and looked quickly away again.

And so it happened. When Richard told her Rooker would be accompanying them back to the Bluff and that this time he would be staying, her heart made a startling leap into her throat.

*   *   *

The new camp was further along the Bluff to the south-east of the first ones. Richard determined the location, and Rooker obediently pitched two tents and reassembled the skidoo and sledge. When Andy and Mick and the Squirrel had lifted away again, Alice fumbled in her tent with the camp kitchen, trying to prepare a hot meal. The floor of the tent was covered with clods of melting ice, and the stove tipped and almost overbalanced when she put a pan of water on it. This site was even more exposed and inhospitable than the last one. The great crest of black rock was broken up by glaciers and winds roared down the chasms of ice, gathering speed under the pull of gravity to shriek and batter around the two tiny tents that lay in their path.

Whenever she left shelter Alice had to draw her

parka hood tight round her goggles to cover every square inch of her face. It was so cold here that any exposed skin would be frostbitten within minutes. She moved slowly, patiently, under the assault of the gale. She thought of the wind as a physical burden that she had to carry on her hunched back.

The work was the same as on the first field trip, but Richard was even more driven and dogged in his searching of the fossil-bearing layers. They trudged through the snow and climbed through the bands of rock, measuring and noting and chipping out samples. Sometimes they worked for hours without exchanging more than a few words and these were shouted above the roar of the wind. Rooker drove the skidoo and hauled the sledge. He was very strong, seeming almost unaffected by the wind and cold. He handled the ropes whenever there was a glacier crossing or some exposed climbing to do, always checking Alice's harness before she moved off. Once he saw that a narrow slice of her bare cheek was showing and he tightened the drawstring of her hood. The deftness of his big mittened paws surprised her and a flush of warmth mottled her hidden face.

In spite of the cold and ceaseless wind, Alice felt safe with Rook's dark bulk close at hand. She was less conscious of the vast hostile distance from camp to base than she had been on the last trip. The work itself was unceasing but it had become familiar. Field life was a monotonous alternation of geology, performed under harsher conditions than anywhere else but still a practised routine, and short tent hours where they cooked uncomfortable meals, tried to keep dry in spite of the showers of ice and to warm up their bones after a day outside.

Alice got used all over again to never taking off any clothing except the outer windproofs. She was glad of her baggy fleece layers because no one could have any idea of her shape underneath them, or any interest in speculating about it. The baby swam and turned somersaults inside her. Sometimes it prodded so hard that she had to cover up an exclamation of surprise. She shook out her fleecy camouflage like Margaret's cat puffing out its fur at the sight of Roger Armstrong's Labrador, then smiled at this tiny memory of home. The two bearded men gazed at her over their tin plates of food. They had been eating in silence, the clink of spoons rubbed out by the shriek of the wind. Rook grinned back, but Richard's glance flicked from one to the other as if he believed they were sharing a joke against him.

Their work might have been the same, but the atmosphere was not.

Richard and Rooker were working and living in close proximity, and sleeping in the same small tent. It was evident from every remark and every gesture that they loathed each other.

Richard's anxiety was making him impatient and autocratic. Every minute that wasn't spent out on the rocks was wasted for him, so he ordered early morning starts and called a halt later and later in the day. Rooker did what he was told, but in a silence that was more scathing than words. Alice tried to smooth over the hostility by being cheerful, but she was hampered by the knowledge that she was the cause of at least some of the trouble.

The intimacy that she had shared with Richard at the last camp was gone and when she thought back she couldn't even recapture the quality of it.

I was a fool, she thought. I shouldn't have let even that much happen.

She hadn't understood, then, that the longing for intimacy, for the touch of another's skin, was a reaction to the harshness of the ice. It affected them all, Laure and Valentin and Richard and Jochen and herself, and Beverley Winston too. It was the human instinct, in this overwhelming place, to draw close round the saving spark of sexual warmth, like hands cupping a match.

Rooker didn't seem to feel it. But then Alice often looked up and caught him watching her. Richard noticed it too and his frown deepened.

There was the twice-daily radio link with Niki at Kandahar. Richard crouched over the radio transceiver in his tent, exchanging details of the current weather conditions and noting the forecast. Then he asked searching questions about what everyone had done and whether they had kept to the work schedules. One evening Russell reported that Jochen had stomach pains and had spent the day resting in his bunk.

'Really? I hope he'll be fit tomorrow. His study's not progressing that quickly as it is. Over.'

'I've no idea about that,' Russ's voice crackled back. 'He's the doctor and I'm base manager, and between us we judged that he's not well enough to work. Over.'

'Of course. Yes. Well, give me another update in the morning.'

'He's losing it,' Rooker said later to Alice.

After they had eaten their evening meal, Richard had taken to getting straight into his sleeping bag to write notes or read by the light of his head torch. The noise of the wind was such that

316

a conversation a couple of metres away was as inaudible as if the distance were fifty miles. In the other tent Rooker was helping Alice to wipe plates and rinse cooking pots.

'Losing what?'

'Sense of proportion. Control. He's going to get worse before we get off the ice.'

Alice started to contradict him and then gave up the attempt. Richard's diligence was sliding into obsessiveness. He would announce an 8 a.m. start and then brusquely order them to hurry up if they weren't ready to leave camp at 7.45. He would begin a search of one section of rock, only to notice that another site a hundred metres away looked more promising and insist that they shifted to that. Alice did her best to be patient with his erratic decisions and to deflect his impatience by being ready earlier and quicker to do whatever he asked. But Rook grew increasingly mutinous.

'We only just got up here,' he snapped when Richard decided that he wanted to move on from one inaccessible rock outcrop to another even more difficult spot.

'Your job is field assistant. I decide where we work and you'll get us there,' Richard shouted back.

'Not if I judge that it's dangerous.'

'You advise, Rooker. You don't give the orders.'

'Ah, fuck you,' Rook muttered in exasperation. But he set up the abseil that lowered the three of them safely back down to the glacier. Richard never took his eyes off the undulations of the Bluff as they travelled on again, and he leaned forward into the searing wind as if by sheer willpower he could make them move faster and force the rocks

317

to yield up their fossilised secrets.

As he became less reasonable, Richard's physical resemblance to his grandfather increased. He was too impatient to eat properly because stopping for food meant that no work was being done. His cheeks were hollow under the rough spikes of his beard and his eyes sunk into their orbits. When she looked at him Alice kept seeing the pictures of Gregory Shoesmith.

'Don't judge him too harshly,' she said to Rook.

She piled two of their three cooking pots next to the stove and lit the flame under the third to boil water for tea. Rooker poured whisky from a flask and handed her the tin mug. She took a long gulp of the spirits. It was warm enough in her tent now with the gas burning and Rooker's body generating heat, but during the short clamorous hours of the night she felt too small and insignificant to fill the icy space. She was always on the edge of a shiver, and whenever she hunched up to conserve warmth inside her sleeping bag a fine powdering of ice crystals fell from the nylon tent inner and drifted over her. When she shone her torch she saw the faint twinkle, like dim stars at the edge of a chilly firmament. Her own personal diamond dust.

She thought back to the last field trip when she and Richard had been living and sleeping side by side. It seemed a long time ago. She was afraid now, not exactly of Richard himself but of what might happen to him, and as her anxiety had grown her reliance on Rooker steadily increased. Rooker's saving presence out here was like a rope leading out of a crevasse. The rope was within her reach. She could grasp it if she felt that she might fall.

He reclined opposite her, drinking whisky straight from the flask. Alice wore her fleece hood but he was bareheaded, as if minus twenty degrees was a mild summer's night. Away from the base his hair was growing in a thick thatch. His beard was darker.

'Why does he care about that jackass Sullavan or the European Union?' he mused. 'Do the job, yeah, if you must. But not like that.' His head jerked towards the other tent.

'It's partly because he wants to deliver what Lewis Sullavan expects of him and to make a significant scientific contribution that will justify the existence of Kandahar as an EU base—to enable all of us to contribute—but I think those are only relatively superficial reasons.' Alice tried to choose her words carefully but she guessed that to Rook she just sounded pompous. 'He is so driven because of who he is.'

Rook gave a derisive laugh. 'We all act the way we do because of who we are. That's no justification.'

This was the first even remotely personal remark she had ever heard him volunteer. She stared at him in surprise.

'I don't know about you. I do know that Richard wants more than anything to live up to his grandfather's name.' She felt disloyal, talking in this way about him.

Rook appeared to read her mind. 'Don't worry, I won't repeat our conversation. But we are out here, the three of us. We have a degree of responsibility for one another.'

'I know that.'

'Shoesmith won't live up to his grandfather's

319

name because he can't and his trouble is that he knows it.'

Alice stirred one of their teabags in the pan of boiling water, waited for the brew to turn dark brown, the way Rooker liked it, then tipped it into two tin mugs. Without asking her whether she wanted it or not he added a generous slug of whisky to each of them. In any case, Alice was glad of anything that helped to keep the ache of cold at bay even temporarily. Rook drank his and added, 'He isn't a hero. It's not his fault. He's a neat-minded, anxious man who's afraid to be ordinary just because his name isn't Jones or Brown.'

'You may be right,' Alice agreed.

'I am right. And in a place like this our ordinary leader's longing to be extraordinary makes him dangerous.'

A small icy fingertip, colder than the wind that worried at the tent, touched the nape of Alice's neck. 'He's not a fool,' she said sharply.

'Oh, no. It would be much simpler if he were. The trouble is that he knows exactly what he is and how far he's got to go to be anything else.'

She drank her tea, registering the strong whisky taste with deliberate attention. There didn't seem to be anything more to say.

Rooker was bored with Shoesmith as a topic of conversation. 'And what are *you* afraid of, Alice?'

He was taunting her, she thought. She considered the question seriously, because a straight answer wouldn't be what he was expecting. 'I used to be afraid of disappointing my mother. Rather similar to Richard, you see, which may be why I feel more forgiving of him than you do. I was so afraid that I deliberately withdrew from her and turned my back on what she valued so that there would be a lesser risk of exposure. But coming down here has changed that. For me and for her, it was the right thing to do.'

Her eyes met Rooker's now and she found that she was smiling. Her ears and neck were suddenly warm inside the fleece hood.

'I see,' he said.

'And you?' she countered.

He gave the same derisive laugh. 'Nothing. Nothing's important enough.'

She waited, but he didn't elaborate. 'Go on?'

His eyes moved over her face. The image of hands cupped round a match flame came back into Alice's mind. Even Rooker, out here in the wilderness where the winds tumbled down from the plateau, might feel the need for intimacy. But he only raised one eyebrow and yawned. The conversation was finished and the shutters came down over his face.

'What time tomorrow, did he say?'

'Half seven.'

'Well, then, time to sleep. Are you warm enough in here?'

What would you do about it if I said no? Alice smiled again. 'It's not too bad.'

'Sweet dreams,' Rook said.

In the morning's radio link Russell reported that Jochen was worse. The doctor's self-diagnosis was appendicitis.

Richard pinched the bridge of his nose. Alice and Rooker looked at each other and listened in silence.

'You'd better advise Santa Ana,' Richard responded.

'Niki called in this a.m. The helo is standing by but the forecast's for winds gusting up to fifty knots.'

'Thank you, Kandahar. Keep me posted.'

After he had signed off Richard turned on them. 'Come on. Let's get moving.' His mouth looked pinched.

It was a long, bleak day. A capricious wind stirred up twisters of snow that enveloped and momentarily blinded them. Alice worked doggedly in Richard's wake, examining and chipping at the sedimentary layers and logging the sections whenever the visibility improved enough to allow her to do so. The sight of Rook's bear-like bulk trudging ahead of her was the counterbalance to Richard's increasingly frenzied darting.

They reached camp again only just in time for the evening's radio link. 'Kandahar, do you read me? Over,' Richard shouted into the transceiver.

'Wheeler's Bluff, Wheeler's Bluff, this is Kandahar,' Niki's voice patiently responded.

The news was that the helicopter had managed a landing in a window of calmer weather at 4.30 p.m. and had immediately flown Jochen back up to Santa Ana where a fixed-wing flight would take him onwards to Punta Arenas, to hospital and a probable appendectomy.

'Right, Kandahar,' Richard answered. 'Thank you for that.'

'Now we have no doctor on the base,' he muttered once he had signed off.

'But Jochen will be all right,' Rooker observed.

Richard brushed the concern aside. 'Yes, yes. I'm sure. The problem I'm facing now is whether to bring down another medic for the last month of the season. It's a very costly option. I'll have to consult the Polar Office. I wonder if Niki can patch me through to London from out here?'

This turned out not to be possible. Richard had to decide between heading back early to Kandahar, where most of his team were caught without medical cover and with only one safety officer, or staying on at the Bluff to pursue his fossils.

'If we can only uncover one or two more Gastropoda. Just one specimen would do,' he kept repeating to Alice. Rooker silently prepared the food for the evening meal. Alice tried to persuade Richard that Russell could deal with the Polar Office in London.

'Maybe, but I should be at Kandahar to talk it over with them. I'm the only one who can make the decision.'

It was true that Richard didn't know how to delegate. Rooker was stooping over the frying pan with his back turned but Alice knew that his eyebrows would be drawn up into sarcastic peaks.

'What's the forecast?' Rook drawled.

Richard had written it down, but had been too preoccupied to take it in. He looked at the left-hand page of the camp log where the twice-daily forecasts were recorded—'2 February. Wheeler's Bluff: cloud cover variable, winds strengthening, twenty to thirty knots.'

It was not much of a variation on the preceding days, slightly better if anything.

Rook shrugged and tipped hot rice into the three tin plates. The rising steam was instantly damped by the tent's clammy cold air. They ate the food without interest, hunger and tiredness fighting their usual battle.

Alice suggested, 'Let's do another day's work, wait for Niki to give us the response from the Polar Office tomorrow evening, then decide. There's nothing to be done now, it's midnight in London.'

Richard nodded, repeating the plan as if he had come up with it himself. 'And that means a prompt start in the morning, please.' He spoke brusquely to Rooker, as if he had been late every morning of the trip.

'Aye aye, sir.' Rook lifted one hand to his temple in a lazy salute.

Richard frowned but he let it pass. Five minutes later, after repeating that another Gastropoda find was all that really mattered, he said goodnight and withdrew to the other tent.

'It's only an ancient bloody dead snail,' Rooker sighed.

Alice was tired. She wanted to complete the fieldwork, but the thought of a hot shower followed by a warm bed at Kandahar was deeply alluring. She was pricked by anxiety to think that there was no doctor on hand, even if that doctor was Jochen, but on the other hand the speed with which he had been evacuated was reassuring. 'No. To him, it's much more than that. But you're not a scientist.'

Rook only laughed. 'That's for sure.'

The next evening Niki passed on a message from Beverley Winston. Lewis was in Ecuador and could not immediately be contacted.

'Meanwhile we sit here on the ice and wait for a word,' Richard fumed.

'You wanted extra time to pick around the rocks,' Rooker pointed out.

It was, in any case, only another four days before they were scheduled to return.

The forecast was more or less unchanged but they woke up to a viciously howling wind and a blinding wall of blown snow. From the mouth of Alice's tent the other tent was barely visible and the snow igloo that sheltered the latrine barrel was completely obscured.

'No leaving camp today,' Rooker announced.

Richard put his dish of porridge aside, having barely touched it. 'We'll give it an hour, then see.'

'No,' Rook said.

They waited in Alice's tent. Rooker and Alice tried to read but Richard rocked up and down, opening the flaps to look outside and constantly checking his watch. After two hours he said, 'Right. It's clearing. Let's move.'

'It isn't doing anything of the kind. I'm safety officer here. No one leaves camp.'

'We're going to work. It's six hundred yards to the nearest section of the Bluff. We'll head there.'

'No.'

'Alice?'

After nine days of avoiding eye contact, Richard looked straight into her eyes. *Choose*, he silently challenged her.

She crawled to the tent door and stared out. It did seem that the wind was relenting. Through the whirl of driven snow she could just make out the outline of the igloo, ten yards away. Richard was asking for her loyalty. Rooker was stubborn. This confrontation was about their mutual detestation as much as it was about work or safety. Alice didn't want to be a pawn in their play. She would make her own decision.

She did think that the weather was improving and almost anything would be better than a whole day confined to the tents in this atmosphere of rancid dislike. She picked up her parka from her pile of damp, filthy belongings and began to pull it on.

Rooker's hand shot out and clamped round her wrist. His grip was like a steel band and it hurt when she tried to shake it off. 'Don't be a fucking idiot.'

'Let go, Rook. I'm going to work.'

He glared at her, then gave a sharp hiss of exasperation. 'I'm sorry. You've got less sense than I gave you credit for.'

He let go and turned away, and she was surprised by how uncomfortable it felt to have disappointed him.

'I'm not coming with you. I'll stay here with the radio.' He tossed a hand-held radio to each of them. 'Call in every thirty minutes without fail. If I don't hear from you twice in every hour I'll know you're dead, and I'll pack up and get back to base.'

'I will make a note in the log of your refusal to accompany us,' Richard said.

'For Chrissake, Shoesmith, this isn't 1913. Write whatever you like in your fucking logbook. I'd do it before heading out into that blizzard, though, because you might not get the chance to do it later.'

To Alice, as they were ready to leave, he murmured, 'You really don't have to go.'

'I know I don't have to. I'm making a choice.' She hastily pulled on her fleece hood as she spoke, and he untwisted it for her so that the face opening fitted snugly over her eyes and nose.

She crawled in Richard's wake out into the snow.

It was like her first day in Antarctica all over again. Snow worked its way behind her goggles and into her hood, and for a few seconds she was sure that the air was too thick with it and too cold to breathe, and she would suffocate. She half walked and half stumbled into the whiteness, her stinging eyes glued to Richard's back. Don't stop moving. Don't lose sight of him.

As soon as they were underway she knew that it had been a mistake to leave camp.

The skidoo seemed to be suspended in a dense white vacuum in which up and down were meaningless. She knew that they must be moving forward because the engine was engaged and the tracks were turning, but there was no way to tell. There was no view ahead, no landmark to steer by, only blankness. It was utterly disorientating. Richard was navigating by compass bearing. They were crossing the glacier towards the Bluff, moving parallel to the crevasses that had become familiar in the last few days, but ahead and to the side there was only the unbroken wall of blowing snow. She gave up the attempt to see what was coming and ducked her head instead. At any moment they might plunge sickeningly into a cleft in the ice. She had seen it happen to Lewis on a clear sunny day. She tried to hold herself in readiness for the jolt and then the terrible drop.

Instead, the skidoo engine stopped and the wind hit her full on again as Richard climbed off. Ahead, so close that the invisible crest threatened to topple on them, the black contours of the Bluff were just visible through the blizzard clouds. Without waiting to take stock, Richard was immediately plodding across to the rock. With his hood up and his head bent he looked like a robot. Alice battled grimly in his wake.

They attempted to work, although it was clear from the outset that there was almost no point. The wind was so strong that it tore the pages of their notebooks and threatened to snatch instruments out of their hands. It was impossible to talk, only to shriek above the gusts, and it was too cold to take off mittens or goggles for even a few seconds at a time. Richard pressed himself against the snow-plastered rocks and began sweeping them bare with his parka sleeve. As soon as a patch of fossil-bearing rock was exposed the snow obliterated it again, but he pressed closer still, trying to shelter the section with his body. He chipped at the rock with his hammer. There was no hope of labelling a sample bag, even of holding on to it for long enough to seal up the specimen. He dropped the chunks of rock loose into the pocket of his parka.

Alice watched in dismay, anxiety swelling in her chest.

After thirty minutes she was frozen. Her cheeks had lost all feeling and the skin of her lips was welded to the ice building up in the layers of fleece and Gore-tex covering her mouth. Her hands and feet were numb. With infinite difficulty she extracted the radio from her inner pocket and tried to huddle in on herself to call Rooker. Her lips tore painfully as she tried to speak.

'I read you. Over.' His voice was steady.

'We're trying to work. Visibility nil, conditions deteriorating. Over.'

'Are you coming in?'

'I'll try to make him.'

She tottered the few steps to Richard and thumped him on the back. He half turned, startled and then impatient. Alice waved her arms, signalling *enough* and *let's go back*. Sharply he shook his head, then held his splayed hands up at her to signal *ten more minutes*. She knew what he was thinking. Against all the odds, these might be the crucial minutes. This minute, or the next one, he might make the great find.

She hunkered in beside him, counting the time away. Once, she looked back over her shoulder. The skidoo was gone, or rather it had turned into a rough snowy hump indistinguishable from a dozen other lumps of rock.

He had had long enough now. She grabbed his shoulder, pulling him away from the rock face. Okay, he signalled. Wait. Alice knew that she was beginning to panic. She slowed her breathing and made herself watch as he took out the compass to get the reverse bearing for their journey back to the camp. His head bent and his shoulders hunched while the wind assaulted him. Then he dropped the compass.

In an eye-blink the instrument hit the ground beside his boot, hung for a second in the ruff of soft snow mounded around his tracks, then toppled again and began to slide. It gathered speed, skidding faster, out of sight down the small slope to the glacier. They were so cold that they hardly moved. There was no point in plunging after it. It was gone for good.

Two things, Alice thought, her numb brain slowly working. GPS reading, get their exact position. Then call Rooker. Rooker had the back-up compass.

The GPS unit was in her inner left pocket, on the opposite side from the radio, against her body where it would be warmest. Richard was close beside her. The red of his parka dully vibrated against the rest of the white world. He saw what she was doing and tried to take the unit out of her hand, but she gripped it hard and punched the buttons. There were seconds to wait while the system searched the skies for satellite signals from which to take the co-ordinates. She stared at the little screen through veils of snow.

Instead of the reassuring digits of a reading, a neon-green message flashed at her. *Weak signal*. It meant that the positions of the navigational satellites inexorably wheeling over the continent were not in their favour. The little unit could not currently get a fix accurate enough to pinpoint their position.

She stared upwards, as if she could see into the skies and will the satellites into place. But there was nothing except the wind, driving loose snow in ever-increasing gusts. Nothing to see. In zero visibility and without a compass the 600 yards back to camp might as well be 600 miles. She turned to Richard. She could hardly see his face, but his expression seemed oddly clear. There was resignation in it and there was also a kind of wild satisfaction. This was meant to be. This was destiny.

She could even hear his voice, as if the wind transmitted his thoughts straight into her head. *Here I am. I'm ready.*

Her own consciousness bawled an answer. *I don't have a death wish, even if you do. My destiny's different from yours. I am my mother's daughter. I will be a mother myself. Nothing will stop me.*

Richard's arm was pulling at her. She thought he wanted her to sink down in the snow with him. Violently, she shook herself free. If the GPS presently failed her it would function soon. In the meantime there was the radio.

'Rook? Rooker, do you copy? *Please*, do you copy?'

'Alice. Report please. Over.'

She blurted out what had happened.

'Listen to me. Don't move. Take what shelter you can against the rocks. Huddle together. Monitor the GPS. I'm coming to get you. Over.'

'Thanks.'

I'm coming to get you. The simplest words, Alice thought, but lovelier than the most beautiful poem ever written.

Richard had moved two steps away. He was leaning forward with his forehead against the Bluff wall, his arms spread out as if to gather it up. She hauled at him, pulling him down into an angle between rock and slope. There was a tiny diminution of the wind here. She drew him closer and he responded by putting his arms round her. They half lay and half crouched, in a parody of an embrace.

She didn't know how much time passed. Time and her heartbeat slowed together, but she could feel the baby kicking against her stomach wall. It was always wide awake at this time of day.

Then she became aware of a noise that wasn't the wind. It was whistling and the banging of metal on metal. It came and went with the gusts of wind and driven snow, but it was coming closer. She pushed Richard away and struggled to her feet.

331

'Here!' she yelled. 'Rook-er. Rook-er. Here!'

There was a red blur, just visible through a momentary lull in the blizzard. The whistling was a sharp high note and the banging oddly reminded her of Kandahar, with all the associations of safety that went with it. Alice ran forward to where she had just glimpsed the red parka, but there was nothing—only snow and wind, and now the whistling seemed to come from an entirely different direction. Disorientation made her dizzy.

Then the clanging was beside her, right at her shoulder. She whirled round and saw Rook. He had a whistle between his teeth and he was banging two metal saucepans together. The Kandahar meal signal. Alice remembered now that Captain Scott and Shoesmith and the others had gone out from Hut Point to search for one of their team-mates lost in a blizzard, and had used just the same means of making a loud noise. If Richard was also recalling this he gave no sign of it. Dazedly he pulled himself upright and looked around as if he didn't recognise his surroundings.

Rooker uncoiled a rope and secured the three of them. They shuffled forward in a line, like old men defeated by the fury of the weather. Ten steps brought them to a mound of snow and a few minutes' frenzied digging uncovered the skidoo.

Half an hour later Alice was crawling into her sleeping bag. Her teeth were chattering and she shivered as if her bones were going to crack. Rooker poured boiling water on to instant soup mix and handed her the steaming mug, then passed a second mug to Richard.

Richard had barely spoken and nor had Rooker, except to give terse instructions. But from being mute and apparently shocked Richard was regaining his composure. 'That was well done,' he told Rook now.

'I can't say the same for you.'

'I do my job, which is to lead this scientific expedition and to make the necessary decisions. Your job is to provide transport and safety back-up. Which you did very competently today. Thank you.'

Richard was trying hard to be generous in the face of his own discomfort, but Rooker wouldn't see it that way. He was no diplomatist. 'You went out in appalling conditions and then you dropped the bloody compass. You could have died out there, which is up to you, but you were risking the life of another team member as well as your own . . .' He spat out the words.

'I went of my own accord,' Alice interrupted.

Rooker glared at her. 'And you are a fool.'

She held his gaze. 'I know that. Thank you for coming to the rescue.'

'That's enough, Rooker,' Richard snapped. He drained his mug and put it aside. Food didn't stay hot for long in the iced-up tent. 'I'm going to radio Kandahar now for an up-to-date forecast and then make a plan of action for the next few days.'

After he had gone to the other tent Rooker scoffed, 'A plan? To cancel the blizzard and call in the helicopter to ferry us comfortably home? But not until he's found the crucial dead snail that'll win him the Nobel Prize, I suppose.'

Now Alice was shivering with delayed shock rather than cold. They were safe for the time being and she didn't have to go out into the blizzard again, that was all that mattered. She had no energy or appetite for bickering with Rook, or with

Richard either. She huddled up silently with her head on a pile of damp clothing. Rook glanced at her, then put his warm hand inside the mouth of her sleeping bag to feel the temperature of her neck. With his other hand he stroked back her hair. Then he pulled the bedding close around her and lifted her up so that he could put his own hat on her head.

'You'll warm up soon, then you can go to sleep. None of us is going anywhere for a couple of days, whatever Shoesmith's goddamn plan may be.'

Alice smiled vaguely. Drowsiness was already enveloping her.

*   *   *

The storm continued for two and a half days.

Alice slept for at least half the time, finished the biography of Samuel Pepys that she had brought from base, then devoured a thriller that Rooker lent her. Richard had become even more withdrawn. He spent most of the time in his own tent, reading or writing notes, so she and Rooker were thrown together. He lay opposite her, impassively studying the roof of the tent or propping himself on one elbow to listen while she talked. He was a good listener, Alice discovered. She told him about Oxford, and Trevor and Margaret. She described Pete and *Desiderata*, and Rooker laughed at the sound of the sculpture. She promised to show him the Polaroid picture of it when they got back to Kandahar.

'If we ever get back.' She sighed. The hated wind was so familiar that it had become part of her, like chronic pain.

'We'll get back,' he said easily.

'I can't go on doing all the talking,' she said suddenly. 'I don't know anything about you.'

There was a cold moment when she knew that he was going to snap at her and retreat behind the shutters. But instead he said awkwardly, 'What do you want to know?'

'Where did you grow up?' she asked, startled into banality.

He told her that when he was a small boy he had emigrated with his parents from England to New Zealand. His mother had come from a landowning family in Northumberland, and his father had been an actor and a singer. He had left his wife and son not long after they had settled, and neither of them had seen him again. His mother had died about seven years later, Rook added abruptly.

'Then what happened?'

He had been sent back to England, to live with his mother's brother and his wife. A childless couple, who didn't like children very much.

'That must have been hard.'

'It was.' His tone and his expression indicated that he didn't want any more questions.

Rooker lay on his back. The tent inner wheezed and strained under the assault of the wind. He laughed shortly. 'Do you know what? Everything that Richard Shoesmith says and does reminds me of Uncle Henry Jerrold.'

'I see,' Alice said. She didn't really, but it was at least a partial explanation for Rook's animosity.

*   *   *

On the evening of the third day the wind died away.

335

They crept out of the tents and saw the sky clearing of ragged pewter-grey clouds. A stillness descended on the snow-blown expanse of the glacier and over the black teeth of Wheeler's Bluff. Niki reported from Kandahar that the helicopter pilots hoped to reach them tomorrow.

Twenty-four hours later the Squirrel buzzed down towards the familiar contours of the bay. The landscape looked less familiar now because solid sea ice had formed in the deep U-shape of water that sheltered the base and the big berg was frozen in the centre of it. As she looked down through the Plexiglas bubble in the nose of the helicopter and saw the tiny carmine-red huts and the scribble of poles and antennae enclosing them, Alice felt almost drunk with relief and exhilaration. Luck was still with her. She had risked another expedition to the Bluff and survived with her secret intact.

As Kandahar came closer she thought that it looked more than ever like home.

CHAPTER THIRTEEN

By the end of February the bay was solid with ice, a full month earlier than the year before.

Down here there's no such thing as normal, Arturo had said. An average season is a meaningless concept in Antarctica, where unpredictability is the only constant. But even so, contradicting themselves, the old hands agreed that this was an unusual summer.

Blizzards alternated with days of eerie calm when not even a breeze stirred the EU flag on its

336

pole. The sun sank lower over the glaciers and the skies flared with lurid refractions of multiplying suns and rainbows. Every day these light shows were brutally extinguished by flooding darkness that grew longer and colder with each successive night. Cold stalked the Kandahar people whenever they left the fragile shelter of the huts. When a gale blew it scoured tears from their eyes, which then froze and glued their eyelids and lashes together. Winter was opening its jaws wider as the sun deserted them.

The bay had frozen almost overnight. The loose chunks and shreds of bergs welded together and thick ice mounted between them in solid wave forms. The stranded berg was now just a bigger ziggurat that tilted out of a plateau of similar spikes and shards, all trapped until the next spring's thaw would set them free again. For the Kandahar people it was a morning's scramble over the uneven meringue-white glinting ice to reach the berg and to be able to touch its cobalt-blue innards. Richard and Russell went out one morning with Phil and Rooker to assess the state of the bay and its accessibility to the relief ship. For something to do, Alice accompanied them.

The berg ice was fluted with dozens of vertical rills where bubbles of trapped air had escaped and in rising to the surface had precisely chiselled the ice to resemble cathedral pillars. She stood with her mitten resting against the grooves of one pillar as she gazed into the berg's hollow heart. The voices calling out around her sounded small and reedy, as if at any moment a great blanket of silence might descend and muffle them all for ever.

The men could only agree on what was already

337

obvious: there was no question that the bay wouldn't thaw again before next spring. The ship wouldn't be able to enter the bay when it returned in the middle of March; it would take an ice breaker to achieve that. They were faced with a choice of making their way out on foot, over the sea ice to open water, or of bringing in the helicopter to ferry them and their belongings to the ship's side.

There was no talking as they tracked slowly back to Kandahar. Richard led the way, staring straight ahead of him as he marched on. They each felt the blackness of Antarctic winter rushing up behind them, and the grip of the ice threatening to seize and hold them fast. Alice scrambled alongside Phil. Occasionally he put his hand out to help her up over some curled and particularly slippery lip of ice.

'Will we be able to get out?' she asked him. A slow pulse of anxiety was beginning to beat in her. She felt it like a cramp tightening her stomach wall, a premonition of the first contraction that would inevitably come. She had begun to think of pregnancy and the delivery as only a prelude to a much bigger event, whereas even at the last field camp it was the birth itself and the days leading up to it that had filled her mind. She had told herself in the early weeks that motherhood would come to her when it happened; now she was much more strongly aware that there would be a baby, another person, *her* child. It wriggled and prodded inside her, less balletic but more insistent as the available space decreased. It seemed to be growing almost visibly as the days succeeded each other.

Phil said thoughtfully, 'I should think so. Mind

you, it wouldn't be the first time that a summer team had had to overwinter because they got trapped. You know that.'

'Yes.'

'It'd be a nuisance, but on the other hand it wouldn't be the end of the world. Six months or so on short rations, that's all.'

'I'd prefer to go home,' Alice murmured. She made an effort to control her feelings, but a flutter of panic threatened to overtake her. They couldn't, must not, be caught here for a whole winter.

He shot a glance at her, not that it was possible to see anyone's face under the goggles and layers of hoods and balaclavas. 'Feeling trapped?'

'No. Well, yes. Just, you know, the idea of a winter here.'

'No bills, no car insurance, no parking meters. No ring tones, no queues, no muggers, no cold callers trying to sell you a new kitchen?'

This was the familiar litany that they often gleefully recited to each other. But Alice didn't add anything because she was thinking about medical advice, reassurance, Jo and Becky and her parents: all the things she needed in the next six months much more than she didn't need mobile phones or traffic wardens.

'No fuel, no food. Or not much.' There were emergency supplies, but it wasn't the discomfort she was concerned about.

Phil shrugged. 'Yeah, well. Don't worry. We'll be out of here somehow. Wouldn't look good for Sullavan otherwise, would it? He needs good news after the Thai business. You've just got third-quarter blues.'

'What's that?' She was panting a little in her

efforts to keep up as they clambered over the rough ice.

'It's a recognised symptom. Third month of a four-month stay, or whatever it is. You feel as though you've been here a long time, you've learned all the ropes, but it's still too soon to start counting the days to going home. So you get depressed. I've read the studies, Mood and Performance in Isolated Confined Environments, all that. Then when it does come to home time you get final-reaction syndrome, outbreaks of immature and emotional behaviour. Which translates mainly as wild partying, immoderate drinking and bouts of irresponsible sex. You heard it here first. So can I count you in?'

'We'll see, Phil. I make no promises.' The defensive bantering had become automatic.

That's all right, then, Alice thought. Just third-quarter blues. Nothing to do with being an indeterminate number of months pregnant and fearing having to give birth down here. Oh, God. The possibility had been in her mind since the bay had frozen, but this was the first time she had fully articulated it to herself.

Back in the hut, Richard called a meeting.

He looked around at all of them, his eyes slightly glassy. Since coming back from the last field trip he had withdrawn further into himself. He didn't make the same efforts to preside sociably over meals, often sitting in silence over his food, but he chivvied them ever more aggressively to get their work done.

He clapped his hands together now, too loudly for the quiet room. His handsome face looked stiff, making his smile appear fixed. 'Well, now. We've got less than one month left. We need some results to show for our first season. We need to publish, get ourselves talked about.'

Eight pairs of eyes were on him.

Without his usual beaming grin, Valentin said, 'I am not one of your graduate students. I work my own rate, and I do not discuss my findings and certainly do not publish until I am ready.'

Arturo nodded sulky agreement.

Richard inclined his head towards Alice, waiting for her comment.

'I think everyone is doing their best,' she ventured and he flinched. Rooker tilted his chair and raised one black eyebrow.

Richard collected himself and went on, 'We will be leaving here on 15 March, on schedule. I guarantee you that. In the meantime I ask you to give Kandahar your best effort.'

Russell and Phil exchanged sceptical glances. How could Richard guarantee a departure date? He was drifting away from logic into the realm of wishful thinking.

If anyone was depressed, Alice decided, it was the expedition leader. His polar expedition had not delivered any antidote to his self-doubt, or even any properly notable scientific discoveries. It was not exactly her field, but she was beginning to wonder if the gastropod was as important as he wanted it to be.

Without Jochen, the established structure of the group had changed. The hut was emptier and also oddly quiet, as if their number had diminished by more than one person. The big, noisy doctor hadn't been their scapegoat, exactly, but he had been thick-skinned enough to take some disapprobation without apparently suffering from it. Jochen could always be relied upon tediously to state the obvious or to crow about what the others were usually tactful enough to leave unsaid. If the room was overcrowded it was because of Jochen's sheer bulk and if there wasn't quite enough food to go round it was because of his excessive appetite. Now that he was gone, and was recovering in Santiago from his appendectomy, the ebbing and flowing tides of irritation were less predictable.

Russell and Valentin were experienced enough to be automatically loyal to Richard as the leader, and Alice had her own reasons, but the others hardly disguised their resentful dislike of him. Niki's Baltic melancholy cast a lengthening shadow, whereas Phil's constant flippancy grated in a different way. Rooker's sardonic silences were unnerving, and without Jochen to pay her attention Laure was becoming increasingly subdued. In the bunk room she talked more and more wistfully to Alice about Paul, and whether or not he would be waiting for her when she got back to Paris.

'I want to see him too much, I know you will say, Aleece, because your advice is always good. But this place, it is getting me down. Richard is not the leader, he is like a different person, without direction and with too many instructions to give.'

'A month goes quickly,' Alice murmured. 'We'll soon be home.'

Alice attracted her own share of disapproval. Pregnancy was beginning to make her physically clumsy and also forgetful. She forgot to write her name and destination on the board when she went out, and Rooker scolded her for her carelessness. When she tried to hide her lapses by making herself as inconspicuous as possible, she realised that everyone else thought she was just being lazy.

She had lost much of her appetite, but to provide an explanation for her increasing girth she tried to make it look as if she ate a lot. She loaded up her plate at every meal, then slipped the food back or scraped it away when no one was looking.

Arturo pursed his lips. 'Without Jochen, I thought all of us might eat too much food. But Alice is kind, she takes care of it all.'

Alice went red. This was exactly the observation she had hoped someone might make but she still wanted to escape from the table and hide in her bunk. She forced a smile instead. 'I'm always hungry at Kandahar. I'm getting as fat as a pig.'

Arturo smirked, delicately agreeing with her.

'The climate suits her. A bit of extra flesh suits her too. I like a woman I can get hold of,' Valentin countered.

When she looked in her tiny mirror Alice saw that her face had filled out. She even had the beginnings of a double chin.

Another dinner was eaten and cleared away, another day was greedily enveloped by the Antarctic night. The time passed slowly. Bad weather meant that outdoor work became more difficult. Inside the hut they waited, trying to contain their irritation with each other and their confined world.

Jochen was not going to be replaced. Richard discussed the possibilities with the Polar Office and with Beverley, and even spoke via satphone to Lewis. It seemed that it was not worth the expense of sending another medic all the way down to Kandahar for what would now be a stay of just over three weeks.

Richard repeated, '15 March'. Snow was driving against the dark windows. 'What do we need a doctor for between now and then? We can hardly get out of the hut door.'

When she did venture outside into the short-lived twilight, Alice stood on the sea ice and stared up at the hut. The lights made it look like a luminous golden shell, perched so precariously on the rocks that the smallest puff of wind might lift it and carry it away. Their existence here was so fragile. It was hubris, she thought, to imagine that they or anyone else could outwit the forces of Antarctica. They crouched here in their tiny wooden hut, scratching away at the rocks and ice, and making their small observations, and all it took to overthrow their elaborate plans was a few extra degrees of cold. The sea froze and they were potentially trapped.

Dusk lasted only a few minutes. Darkness fell like a curtain and the sky was thick with theatrically bright stars. The cold knifed through her parka, but it was not just the wind that made Alice shiver. No one had said yet that they might well have to overwinter at Kandahar, but the possibility drained most of the flavour from the endless conversations about what they were most looking forward to on returning to the world.

Arturo would lift his eyes to heaven. 'A double espresso, a barber shave, a concert.'

'A shag,' would be Phil's typical retaliation.

The claustrophobia of the hut and the predictability of her companions tempted Alice to linger outside, but the cold was too intense. She climbed the rock steps back to the hut, past

344

motionless ranks of Adélie penguins. They stood patiently, their sleek feathers now a tattered greying mess. During the annual moult the birds waited on the rocks, unable to swim or, therefore, to feed. This year the early freeze meant that the water margin had receded into the invisible distance. Once their moult was completed and before they could break their fast, the penguins would have to march upright or slither on their bellies all the way to the open sea.

The rising wind blew discarded feathers, making them whirl up into the air like tiny blizzards.

A weighty silence filled the hut. Richard was wearing headphones and scribbling in his notebook; Phil was at the computer. It was Rooker's duty day and he was washing up. Alice picked up the drying-up cloth.

'Don't bother,' he advised.

She ignored him. She polished a plate carefully on both sides and put it down, then did the same with the next one. The exaggerated normality of the business only emphasised the fact that her mouth was dry and her heart was fluttering with anxiety.

'What's going to happen?' she asked casually.

When he looked round his enigmatic gaze travelled all the way over her, from head to foot. The stretched skin on her stomach itched unbearably and it took all her willpower to resist the urge to scratch it. *He knows*, she thought. *He's guessed*. It didn't surprise her, not really. She had a feeling that Rooker saw much more than any of the others.

Then his eyes twitched away again. Relief flooded through her, weakening her knees. Of course he hadn't guessed.

'Losing your nerve?' He was half smiling.

'Um. I'd just . . . like to know.'

'We'll get away. If I have anything to do with it,' he said.

Alice went on drying plates. The air in the hut whispered with tension. It was like static electricity, stored in the door handles and metal surfaces, waiting to discharge itself at the lightest touch.

She wrote to Becky and Jo. She had decided that she should lessen the impact of the news when the time finally came to break it, so she told them first that she had changed her mind about travelling in South America and was planning to come straight home.

. . . Once we do get out of here. The bay has iced over very early so there's some doubt at the moment about exactly when that might be . . .

Becky responded at once. She had been sitting at her desk in London when Alice's mail appeared in her in-box.

Darling, the best news! Dying to see you. South America's always going to be there—quite understand you wanting to get straight back to civilisation. When are you getting here? V taking me for a quick w/e to New York some time in March but DON'T want to miss the big return. Let me know asap!

Jo's reply came two days later.

346

Al, so sorry for delay, everything seems to take twice as long to get done these days. Are you sure about coming straight back?? Are you just a bit homesick and fed up with being on the base? If I were you I'd take the op to go everywhere while you've got the chance: I'm really ENVIOUS. Isn't the house let until Sept? Are you sure you're okay? Tell all, please.

Neither of her friends had picked up on the significance of the sea freeze. There was no reason why they should—they were a long way away, in a temperate climate. They would imagine that a ship could smash the ice, or that a plane could descend from somewhere and lift them all away, and she hadn't tried to tell them otherwise—not yet.

Apart from that the difference in the responses made her smile, although it was a smile with an edge to it. Becky's pleasure in her freedom contrasted so sharply with Jo's wistful acknowledgement that her travelling days were over. Alice told herself that it was too late to make comparisons between her friends' lives, or to indulge herself with regrets. She was going home— if Rooker was correct and she wanted very much, *needed*, to believe him—to a life that would be completely different from her previous one. All being well, she would have a child to take care of.

All being well. First, to escape the ice and make her way back to Oxford.

On the same day as Jo's, some messages came from Peter. Typically, she hadn't heard from him since Christmas and now here was a flurry of three at once. They were all imploring.

*Are you going to be angry with me for ever? I
don't know what I can say or do to make it up,
Al, but the truth is that I love you. I don't
know why I didn't recognise this before: it's
like it was just too monolithic for me to see it
properly. I miss you. I'm waiting for you to
come home so that I can tell you in person.
Will you let me?*

  Please answer this.
  xxx always P

Alice stared at the screen. At least there was no
longer any risk of Jochen looming over her
shoulder pretending to check if she was surfing the
porn sites.

It was Pete's child she was carrying; did he have
a right to know what she was doing and the risks
she was running?

Considering what had happened—Georgia and
the woman in the pub and no doubt others—she
didn't think he did. After the accident of
conception, the baby was hers. When she got home
she would tell Pete what was happening and if he
wanted it they would negotiate for him to have
some share in its future, although it wasn't clear to
her yet what that role might be.

Her fingers rested on the keyboard while she
reflected on what to tell him now. She looked down
briefly at her bruised, chapped knuckles and the
broken nails. It was like seeing someone else's
hands grafted on to her own wrists, but when she
came to think about it the arms didn't feel like her
own either, nor did the rest of her heavy, pregnant
body. The other Alice, the familiar one who had

been a scientist and Peter's girlfriend and part of a trio with Jo and Becky, had gone and someone who would be a mother had crept into her skin in her place.

The floor, scuffed tiles gritty with dirt, suddenly seemed to drop away from under her feet.

Disorientation made her shiver. Home was far away and getting there was a series of obstacles. Nothing was ordinary any longer, none of the coarse or slippery textures of normality revealed themselves.

The only thing that was still real was Antarctica itself, that giant white mouth. She sensed it, outside the pathetic barrier of the hut walls, opening up to swallow her. She understood why the old explorers had found it so difficult to extricate themselves and why Margaret had never really escaped its thrall. Its raw power was such that it made the world beyond seem pale and slight.

She frowned now, trying to make herself focus on what she would say to Peter. It would be easy enough to spell out the words to tell him that she would come back and they could be together. The baby would have a father; she wouldn't have to face the decisions that lay ahead on her own.

But it would not be *right*, and she was as sure of that as she was sure of the ice outside the hut. To try to make it so would be like falsifying research results to prove a thesis. The solution might briefly hold, but it could not endure.

*Dear Pete, I was very glad to hear from you. I'm not angry, and I miss you too [*all this was the truth*].*
I'll be back in Oxford in about a month's

*time, earlier than I originally planned, and I'd
like to see you then, of course. I do know you
love me and I love you too, in a way, but it's
not enough on either side, nor in the right way,
for me to say what I think you want to hear.
I'm sorry if this hurts you, and I honestly wish
it were different [*how much easier the future
would be, if only*].*

*I'm not sure exactly when I'll be back
because of the weather conditions here. But I
will call you as soon as I am.*

Much love, Al

She read and reread this, wondering how to expand
on it, but she couldn't think of anything else that
wouldn't sound mysterious or offer him grounds
for false hope. In the end she pressed the send
button and the bleak message went on its way to
Peter just as it was.

The hut was quiet. In their room, Laure was
asleep. Alice took out the Polaroid of himself and
Desiderata that Pete had sent her and examined it
in the light of her head torch. She felt a
complicated mixture of affection and warmth
towards him, even though it was diluted by absence
and distance and disappointment. Loneliness and
regret wrapped round her as she reflected that they
wouldn't be bringing up their child together. She
thought of the holidays and Christmases and school
prize-givings and milestones they might all have
shared. That togetherness couldn't happen, she
was certain of that, but alone in the chilly darkness
she still yearned for it.

She couldn't go to bed yet. She needed to talk to
someone, not about Peter or home and certainly

not about the baby secretly unfurling inside her, but just to have the affirmation of human company. She put the photograph away and went to find Rooker.

Russell had taken her place at the computer and Phil was idly throwing darts at a picture of Lewis Sullavan that someone had pinned to the wall. There were dirty cups on the table and the CD of *Van Morrison's Greatest Hits* had been played so many times that no one heard it any more, it was just white noise. She put on her parka and ran the few steps across to Margaret Mather House. She found Rooker in the empty radio room. He was reading, rocking gently in Niki's chair. The little cubicle smelled of dust and heated metal, and in the background was the fluid, insistent pipping of Morse.

He looked up. 'Hi. Has something happened?'

'No. Do you have anything to drink?'

'Sure. Scotch or bourbon?'

'Doesn't matter. Scotch, then.'

He poured whisky from a flask into a cup and gave it to her. Alice sat down in the only other seat, a rickety typist's chair with brown rexine seat pads that looked as if it belonged in one of Pete's sculptures. With a certain effort she hooked her feet up on the bench and took a mouthful of whisky.

'Go on,' Rooker said after a minute.

'What?' Then she smiled. It was cosy in here, hemmed in by the winking dials and glowing lights of the radio equipment, and the clutter of logbooks and Niki's chessmen. 'I haven't come to say anything. You tell *me* something,' she added recklessly.

351

Rooker put down his book. It was a thriller he had borrowed from Phil and it wasn't very good. It occurred to him, startlingly, that talking to Dr Alice Peel—telling her something, even—was a much more appealing option than reading any more of it.

He started to speak but his voice dried up and he cleared his throat before taking a drink. 'Where shall I start?' The words came out without premeditation.

'What about . . . when you were growing up. In New Zealand, before you went to live with Uncle Henry Jerrold?'

He was utterly amazed that she remembered all this. He had almost forgotten that he had mentioned it, in the tent out at Wheeler's Bluff.

He began to tell her about the first thing that came into his head, his friend Gabby Macfarlane.

*   *   *

Gabby's home was a couple of miles outside town. His dad was a farmer and his mother was a small woman with a pursed mouth who wore a nylon scarf over her hair to do the housework, and who stuck the head of her dusting mop out of the open windows and twirled it to send the cobwebs spiralling away in the sharp wind. At Gabby's there were glasses of milk to drink and apples from a bowl on the kitchen sideboard. You weren't allowed to come inside with your boots on; you had to take them off and walk around in your socks. Mrs Macfarlane looked at Jimmy's black toenails sticking out of the ends of his and pursed her mouth even tighter.

It was a very clean and orderly house, Gabby's,

but it didn't feel all that comfortable. Mr Macfarlane was a square, blocky man with a red face like a slab of meat. When he came in, Mrs Macfarlane and the children would go quiet. Once, Jimmy saw Gabby pull his father's shotgun out of the cupboard beside the back door and take aim with it across the yard towards the orchard, thinking that his father was down at the barn. But he came out of the scullery and saw the boys with the gun. Gabby flung it down and tried to escape out of the door but he was too late. His father hoisted him by the neck and his socked feet dangled in the air. He hit Gabby in the face twice with the back of his hand, blows that made his head crack and jerk sideways as if his neck would snap, but Gabby never uttered a sound. He slipped back to the floor and staggered against the open door. Mr Macfarlane put his gun back in the cupboard and walked away.

Apart from when his father was around, Gabby was an inspired wrongdoer. Jimmy and he had recognised each other almost at first glance, and they fell into a life of crime. They stole sweets and toys from the shops in town, and sometimes things they didn't need or even want like tins of paint or nail brushes. Just because they were there and because they could. It was Gabby who decided in the end that this was stupid and they should plan their heists, and it was Jimmy who introduced him to the word.

'Heistmeisters, that's what we are,' Jimmy said.

'Yeah, that's what,' Gabby agreed without much interest.

So they graduated to records, targeting desirable singles in shiny sleeves from the Main Street

353

Record Barn. They took these home to play at Jimmy's house, and his mother would either try to dance with Gabby or she would waltz on her own, singing along with the words and laughing. 'Are You Lonesome Tonight?', that was one of their trophies. She loved Elvis Presley. She never once asked where they'd got the records from.

Gabby and he liked setting fires. A match tossed on rags soaked in petrol from the can that Mr Macfarlane kept in the tractor shed made a *whump* and a wall of pure flame out of a pile of rubbish or even a deserted garden shed.

Gabby had three older sisters. One day he and Jimmy squirmed on their stomachs through the toetoe grass to a place where the two bigger ones were sunbathing in their knickers. Jimmy gazed through the screen of grass stalks at Joyce's pale splayed legs and the way the bones of her hips poked up to make a kind of cradle of the flesh that spanned them. He thought how much he would like to rest his head in that cradle and then felt embarrassed to connect this hot unwieldy tenderness with Joyce Macfarlane, who had frizzy colourless hair and pink-framed spectacles.

That day, the same day, was the first time he went home and found Lester there.

'Jimmy,' she said to him, waving her glass and slopping some of the contents down the front of her silky blouse, 'this is my friend Lester Furneaux and he's a designer.'

He might well have been, but Jimmy never saw him design a thing in the whole of the year that followed.

'This is my son. Say hello, Jimmy,' she ordered.

He did as he was told, reluctantly poking out the

word with his tongue. The man looked coldly back at him and they both knew that they were rivals for her affection and attention.

Lester. There had been years when he had been able to stop every avenue of thought leading back to him, so why did he have to intrude now?

*   *   *

'What happened to Gabby Macfarlane?' Alice Peel asked.

In the light cast by the small desk lamp her face was luminous. She wasn't prying, she was just interested in his storytelling. He could see the faint down on her rounded cheek, the flat rose-pink cushion of her earlobe and a tendril of hair spun out by the lamplight into tiny metallic filaments. The memory of Joyce Macfarlane came back to him, and he felt the same unworded tenderness that was distinct from and much less resistible than lust. He was going to lift his hand and put it over hers, without making any calculation about what might happen next.

The radio gave out a loud burst of scrambled noise that made them both jump.

Instead of touching Alice's hand, Rook picked up Niki's headphones and pulled them over his head. The static shriek resolved itself into a human voice as he hastily adjusted the frequency.

'Vernadsky, Vernadsky, I read you. This is Kandahar. Over.'

Vernadsky was a Ukrainian station on the peninsula. Niki regularly played radio chess with his opposite number, and Phil and Russell were engaged in an honesty-darts tournament against the field assistants. 'Bloody amazing darts players, these Russkies, I can tell you,' Phil had said drily.

Tonight, though, there was no chess move or claim of a double top. Rooker listened intently to the torrent of Russian-English, then lifted the headset from one ear. 'Go and get Niki. Our leader will want to hear this as well.'

Alice knocked on the doors of the bunk rooms and woke the two men. They spilled blearily into their windproofs and she followed them back to the radio room.

Niki took his seat and the rest of them waited behind him. Richard frowned at the gabble of Russian.

'Ship? There's no ship. What are they talking about?'

But there was a ship.

When Niki flipped a switch and quiet flooded into the room, Richard was already shaking his head. He leaned over and took the handset from Niki, stretching the black snake of flex. Rooker was watching every move.

'Vernadsky, Vernadsky, this is Dr Shoesmith. Thanks for the kind offer. Much appreciated. But we'll stay on base until our scheduled departure day. Over.'

The radio operator's voice sounded startled in response. 'Weather conditions, Kandahar, and the latest forecast, indicate increasing difficulty . . .'

'Thanks again, Vernadsky. We have information. Out.'

Rook's hand shot out and grabbed Richard by the wrist. He dropped the handset and it plunged off the edge of the desk. They all winced at another burst of high-volume static.

'Call up again,' Rooker ordered.

'I beg your pardon?'

'You heard.' He stooped for the handset, picked it up and thrust it back into Richard's hand. 'You're the expedition leader. The Ukrainians are making room on their relief ship to take all your personnel to safety, leaving in two days' time. It's still a manageable trek out over the ice. Make the right decision.'

Richard was white to the lips. 'I have already made my decision. We stay here another nineteen days, until our scheduled departure. There's work to be done. We couldn't be ready to leave in forty-eight hours' time, in any case.'

'We could be ready in *four* if necessary. If it were a matter of life and death.'

Silence bled through the room. Niki's bony fingers lightly rested on the dials, waiting.

'It isn't. It's a matter of duty,' Richard said softly. 'And you'll do yours, Rooker, along with everyone else.'

'You are a fool,' Rook snapped.

'I'm the expedition leader,' he repeated.

Rooker got up and walked away. He left the door of the radio room swinging open and a shaft of chill air struck in.

Niki sat with his head down. Alice met Richard's eyes. There was a new narrowness that made him look cunning, even a little unbalanced.

'Why don't we leave with the Ukrainians, while we can?' she asked.

His lips tightened. 'I'd have thought *you'd* understand why not. You're not a time waster. It's what we have to do, Alice. It's our job to stay here, to deliver what Lewis expects, to finish our work, to close down the base properly when the time comes and not to run away at the first sign of difficulty like rats off a sinking ship.'

She held his gaze. 'It's an accident of the weather. You're not Captain Scott or Ernest Shackleton, or Mawson or Amundsen. You're not your grandfather, but that's because you don't have to be, not because you haven't got it in you. The pioneer days have long gone. We're just a party of scientists, with our bags of rock and tubes of penguins' blood, holed up in our lab on what was the seashore and is now ice. We could go home in two days' time, and do our analyses and write up our results. The business of science will either be infinitessimally advanced or it won't, but we'll have done all that anyone expects of us. Who's expecting so much anyway? Lewis?'

Richard slowly shook his head, staring at her as if he barely understood what she was saying. 'Who? Ourselves, of course. Oneself. Are you afraid of staying here, Alice?'

'No.'

It was a lie. As she stood there her stomach jutted out like the prow of a ship. In the corner of her mind she knew that she must be further along than she had calculated. She must have already been pregnant when she had spent her last night in Oxford with Pete. How many months? Two? Three, even?

She was thinking that she didn't care about duty or honour or science. She cared about life.

The life she was carrying inside her. She was afraid to put it in further jeopardy. 'I would like to leave on the Ukrainian ship.'

He brushed the words aside. 'We will all leave

together as planned on the *Polar Star*. We'll negotiate the ice by skidoo or be lifted out by helicopter, which contingency we have planned and paid for. It's a matter of routine.' He smiled at her without humour.

Niki carefully took off his headset and placed it on the hook above the bench.

Alice nodded. 'I see.' She hauled her parka round her shoulders and walked the bitterly cold steps back to the hut. The room was littered but empty. The only sound was the wind and in the distance, like a heartbeat, the steady pulse of the generator.

*　　　*　　　*

In the morning Rooker insisted that everyone convene round the mess table.

A low sun, tangerine-coloured, glowed through the snow-crusted windows and revealed indoor air thick with bluish smoke coils from the breakfast frying and Niki's cigarettes. There was a smell of old food and dirty clothes. Richard sat silently in his usual place at the head of the table, his hands pressed close together.

'You all know what this is about,' Rook said calmly. 'We can leave here on the Ukrainian ship. I think we should take a show of hands.'

A pulse twitched at the corner of Richard's mouth. 'I am the leader of this expedition,' he said again. There was a crack in his voice and his knuckles were as white as bone. Alice felt so much sympathy that she could hardly look at him.

Rook ignored him. 'Round the table, then. Russ?'

'Stay till *Polar Star* comes.' The base manager's dry Kiwi voice was unemphatic. Russell's loyalty to the expedition leader was unshaken.

'Arturo?'

'I am able to wind up my studies in time, I see no point in maybe spending a whole winter here. I go with Ukrainians.'

'Laure?'

Laure looked exhausted and faintly tearful. 'Me also.'

'Niki?'

'Ukrainians.'

'Four of us in favour so far, so . . .'

'Just wait a minute, mate.' It was Phil who interrupted him. There was no sign of his usual chirpy grin. 'It's eighteen days to finish the job, right? I don't like pulling out early. I'm for staying put until the fifteenth.'

'That's the considered view of our safety officer?' Rooker's voice grated with sarcasm.

'Yeah, it is. Who are you to appoint yourself vote taker, anyway?'

Hostility reared between them and seeped round the rest of the table. Everyone was fidgeting now, not looking at anyone else.

'Valentin?'

'I stay. Same reasons as Phil. I think there is no need to hurry away.'

Four all. It was Alice's turn and there was an uncomfortable silence.

'I vote to go out on the Ukrainian ship,' she said clearly.

Rooker leaned back in his chair. 'That's a majority,' he said to Richard.

It was as if there were only the two of them in

360

the room.

Very slowly, Richard got to his feet. He stood behind his chair, gripping the back. 'I remain the leader of this expedition and what I say goes. Lewis Sullavan has provided the funding, I control our budget. *Polar Star* is paid for, an entirely unnecessary Ukrainian evacuation is not. I remind you also that this is a team. We stay here as a group, regardless of your divisive *voting*, Rooker, until the agreed date for our departure.'

There was a stubbornness in him that Alice couldn't help but admire even now. But she was summoning up all her courage to tell them the truth, to blurt out why the Ukrainian ship would have to come. It shamed her to think that she hadn't even considered the cost implication.

Before she could open her mouth Rook sprang up and leaped across the room. They all saw what a big, coiled, dark, dangerous man he was. His hands went to Richard's throat and he shook him as if he were a child's doll. Russell and Valentin ran at him and tried to haul him off while Phil wrestled an outraged Arturo. Niki's fists swung. Suddenly there was a mêlée of men and overturning chairs. Alice and Laure stared at each other. This was what all their high-minded European collaboration and teamwork had come to—a brawl over the breakfast table.

The fight was over as quickly as it had begun. Rooker wiped his mouth with the back of his hand, with Russell and Valentin hanging on to his arms.

Richard spoke out of pinched lips. 'You're relieved of your duties, Rooker.'

Rooker laughed. He seemed genuinely amused.

Looking from one face to another, Alice found

361

that her confession had died in her mouth. She couldn't—*could not*—pipe up now and tell them that she was pregnant and needed to go home. That would be to place her concerns in direct opposition to Richard's. That would oblige him to choose publicly between her requirements and his own overwhelming need.

She would rather almost anything than have to witness his choice.

No. She would have to stay put and pray that her luck would hold. Maybe Phil and Russ and the others would be proved right after all, and they would steam away north on *Polar Star*.

Richard stalked out of the hut. In silence, the rest of them turned away from each other.

*   *   *

There was a wary stillness on the base for the two days until the Vernadsky ship left. Mealtimes were silent, outdoor work was done as the weather permitted. Niki reported eventually that the Ukrainians had closed their station for the season and were aboard ship en route for Ushuaia.

Richard acknowledged the information with a mechanical nod. The rest of them looked at each other, mutely reflecting on the extra degree of their isolation. They depended now on the possible arrival of their own ship, ice permitting, or on the air support of the Chileans at Santa Ana.

'Antarctic heroes, eh?' Phil tried to rouse them, but no one responded.

As soon as the Ukrainian ship was gone the weather deteriorated. There was still daylight because the sun climbed above the horizon for a few hours each day, but the sky was either dark with cloud or obscured by blizzards. The snow was so thick that there might just as well have been no light, because there was no visibility. Alice completely understood the old description of a serious blizzard as 'white darkness'.

The frozen bay lost its crests of ice and became a pearly blank plain with no beginning or end. Only the shawled berg stood out, intermittently visible during the ragged gaps in the weather as a reminder of the landscape's vanished scale. The penguins deserted the Kandahar rocks and began their exodus towards the distant sea margin. Without the little birds' constant bustle, or the glimpses of seals basking on the ice or whales blowing in the deeper water, the sense of isolation deepened further. The wildlife and the sun were retreating, leaving the human interlopers to the mercy of winter.

The baby moved around much less now. The walls of her womb were tightening around it, restricting its blind ballet. When Laure was out of the bunk room, Alice slid her hands over the mound of her stomach, feeling the pressure of a tiny heel or fist answering her touch.

Are you there? Can you hear me, baby?

She tried to make the monologue soothing and reassuring.

We're going to be fine, you and me. Wait and see. Wait quietly there until we're home.

Once, Laure opened the bunk-room door, startling her. Alice hunched her back and pulled more clothes round her body.

'What were you saying?' Laure asked, eyeing her doubtfully.

'Nothing,' Alice answered. She realised that she had been talking out loud. Now her room-mate thought that she rambled on to herself. It didn't matter. They were all retreating into eccentricity in their different ways, as the light dwindled. As the food supplies began to run low, meals became fragmentary, eaten at different times, and they passed by each other silently in the narrow confines of the hut.

One night, Alice was reading in her bunk by the light of her head torch. The little beam concentrated on the page gave her the illusion of cosiness, as if she were curled up with a book in her childhood bedroom at Boar's Hill. Then an awareness that something was not quite as usual intruded into her consciousness. She lay still for a moment, trying to fix on what it might be before she lifted her head off the pillow. When she did so, an icy draught of air bit at her bed-warmed neck. She could feel it on her face now, too. The room was unusually cold. She sat up and the torchlight showed her Laure rolled up and fast asleep in the opposite bunk. Laure slept more and more these days, retreating for twelve and fourteen hours at a time.

Alice pulled the covers up round her shoulders and tried to concentrate on her book again, but it was no use. She was shivering now. She swung her legs out of bed and padded in her thick socks to touch the electric wall heater. The panels were cold, with only a faint suggestion of warmth lingering in the lowest rib. She clicked on the main light switch, intending to check the controls in case the heater had been turned off by mistake. Nothing happened. She listened and realised that it was the absence of the generator's constant low murmur that had first caught her attention. There was no electrical power because the generator was off.

Quickly, she dragged on some more layers of clothes. She opened the bunk-room door and closed it behind her with a soft click.

Someone was moving around in the hut. The walls were flickering with a soft, unfamiliar light.

'Hello?' Alice said. She twisted the casing of her torch to widen the beam.

There were lit candles all around the room, on the shelves and windowsills, on the computer table and even on the monitor. Some of the candles tipped at an angle, already drooling wax.

A dark figure turned and his huge shadow reared up the wall. She knew who it was.

'Richard?'

Instinctively she switched off her torch so as not to dazzle him, then wished that she had not. Candlelight threw his features into exaggerated relief. His beard was black and she couldn't see his eyes, only the dark sockets.

'Richard, what are you doing?'

It was one o'clock in the morning. Everyone else on the base must be asleep.

'We have to economise on fuel, you know.'

On the table was a big box, a gross of candles. He took another and clicked Niki's cigarette lighter to it. A little teardrop of flame flared and steadied. Richard cupped a hand round it. His face was all raw bones and black hollows. The hair prickled at the nape of Alice's neck.

'Why is the generator not running?'

'I told you.' He was tetchy, not wanting to be distracted from his task. He put the new candle on a shelf close to the picture of Lewis Sullavan that Phil had pocked with darts.

Alice heard another footstep behind her and whirled round. She almost collided with Valentin.

'Val,' she breathed in relief. 'The generator.'

He dodged round her. He was frowning. 'It has broken down? We must fix. The freezer will be off. I have to preserve my ice core samples.' Valentin's first thought was for his glaciology study. The freezer in Margaret Mather House was full of the neat sections he had drilled out of the heart of the glacier. Alice remembered that Laure's penguin blood samples were stored there too.

'I switched off the generator to save fuel,' Richard murmured abstractedly. The lighter clicked again as he lit another candle.

The other men had woken up now and they came out of the bunk rooms. Their shadows swept over the walls as the candle flames shivered. The room was crowded with giant spectres.

Somebody shouted, 'Shoesmith, what in Christ's name d'you think you're doing?' Rooker was large, angry and reassuringly three-dimensional. He was already scrambling into his boots and weatherproofs. He and Phil headed outside, followed by Valentin. The blast of cold air made them all shiver.

Russell tried unthinkingly to switch on the electric kettle, then filled a pan with water and lit the gas under it instead. Niki thumbed a cigarette from his pack and took the lighter out of Richard's hand. Arturo held Richard by the arm and guided him to a chair. He gave no sign of a protest. He put his elbows on the table and rested his head in his hands.

No one looked at anyone else. Seconds crumbled away, the silence only broken by the wind and the hissing gas. After a few minutes they heard a stuttering roar that settled into a steady chugging as the generator fired up again. The lights blinked on and the candle flames paled. Alice went quietly round the room and blew them out one by one. The puddles of hot wax hardened instantly in the freezing air.

Richard lifted his head. 'I do apologise,' he said quietly. 'That was an overreaction. But it is important, you know, if we can't leave here. We must conserve fuel. An airdrop might not be possible for weeks.'

Alice stood at the end of the table and gazed at the dense blackness framed by the window. Blood pulsed noisily in her head and her scalp tightened as the realisation finally and properly dawned on her.

We may well be stranded here for the polar winter.

The Ukrainian ship had gone; miles of sea ice would separate them from *Polar Star* when it finally did arrive. Helicopters didn't take off in weather conditions like these. It wasn't that they might die or even go really hungry, because they had walls and a roof to shelter them, and fixed-wing flights from Santa Ana would drop fuel and food supplies on the ice even though they could not land. A few months of isolation would be a grand inconvenience for the other expedi tion members, but it would mean something entirely different for her.

Alice ran her tongue over her cracked lips and kept her head turned towards the window in case anyone should glimpse her face. Ripples of panic began to wash through her.

Russell was putting mugs of tea on the table. Valentin came banging back from the lab hut. 'No defrosting yet, lucky to say.' He drank a gulp of hot tea and scowled.

Rooker and Phil returned, stamping their feet and shaking snow off their protective clothes.

Richard repeated his apology. 'I should not have closed down the generator.'

'Does that really need *saying*?' Rooker snarled.

'Shut up, Rook.' It was Russell, startling them all with the crack in his usual mildness.

'Tomorrow, as a group, we will make contingency plans for rationing fuel and food,' Richard said.

Alice sat down at the edge of the circle, keeping as far as possible out of the lamplight. Richard looked almost himself again, although his face was drawn. She glanced in turn at each of the other bleary, bearded faces. She had felt safe, all through the past months, in the company of these men. She hadn't liked them all equally, or felt completely comfortable with some of them for the entire time, but she had trusted their decisions because their experience of everything in Antarctica was much greater than hers. Now the props were being removed, leaving each of them exposed. When it came down to it, she thought, when the collective strength was eroded by pressure of circumstances or failing leadership or just the expiry of mutual tolerance, then all you were left with was yourself.

Perhaps, after all, she had been too dependent on other people for too much of her life. On Trevor and Margaret; her friends; Peter. She had set too much store by their beliefs and trusted too little in her own instincts. Except for coming to Antarctica in the first place, that is, and then deciding to stay on even though she was pregnant. She had done *that* by following her own instincts.

A cough of self-mocking laughter almost broke out of her, but she managed to suppress it before any of the others turned to stare at her.

Right or wrong, foolish or criminally insane, she had brought herself to this point and all that mattered from now on was survival for her child's sake.

She lifted her head and straightened her spine. There was no question but that they would survive, the two of them. For now, there was no point in doing anything more than she had already done. She would wait quietly, to see if the ship or the helicopters came in good time.

You wait too, baby.

Richard concluded, 'Thank you for restoring the power tonight. Rooker, you've got your job back. Let's try to work together, shall we?'

Rook laughed again. 'Thanks a lot.' His levity was somehow shocking in the sombre atmosphere. Alice alone was glad of his shrugging carelessness. It meant—it must mean—that their plight wasn't serious.

They drifted back to their bunks, with the old refrain of the howling wind and the bass vibration of the generator to lull them to sleep. Laure had slept through the whole business.

*   *   *

When the next all-too-brief break in the succession

369

of blizzards came, Rooker and Phil took the skidoos across the sea ice to attempt to find the margin beyond which the water would be navigable. The rest of them waited in the huts, monitoring the threatening weather reports and listlessly arranging their belongings ready for packing. No one could believe that a day of departure would actually come, but the opposite was equally unimaginable.

The brief daylight subsided rapidly into darkness, and Phil and Rooker were still not back. Niki reported that they were in radio contact, but return progress in darkness over the snow-blanketed ice was painfully slow. Alice was tortured by anxiety. She reached a point when the only way to contain herself was by pacing slowly from the kitchen to the window overlooking the bay and back again.

Arturo jerked his head at her. 'What is the matter with you? Can you not sit still for one moment?'

'I'm sorry,' she murmured and slumped into a chair, but five minutes later she was on her feet again and staring through the snow-laced glass.

A smear of torchlight was visible in the distance, swaying in the blackness. 'They're back,' she cried.

The two men were exhausted. They stood blinking in the hut lights, clods of ice and driven snow thickening their beards. Phil's hands were so numb that he couldn't pull off his fur-lined gauntlets. When Russ did it for him they saw that his fingers were frozen into claws and the tips were blackening with frostbite. There were dead white patches on his cheeks too. Rooker sat down heavily and let Valentin unfasten and pull off his boots.

'How far is it?' Richard asked.

'Let them get warm first,' Russ said.

Warm drinks and food were produced. Neither of them could eat much, but they drank mug after mug of sweet tea.

It was nine miles over the ice to the closest point where they judged the ship might be able to follow leads inwards through the pack ice. These were conditions almost unheard-of for the early part of March. The frozen ice was extending fast. By the time the ship did arrive, navigable water might easily be twelve or fifteen miles distant.

'A day's travel,' Richard judged.

Phil said nothing. After a moment Rook told them, 'It doesn't sound far by skidoo. But it's uneven going all the way. With nine people and loaded sledges, I'd say more than a day.'

'So if we get a clear weather spell we'll do it by helicopter shuttle. It's only in the worst case that we'll have to go out over the ice. I'll talk to Santa Ana and I'll ask the Polar Office if they can get the ship in earlier.'

Phil and Rooker looked at each other. With her heightened awareness Alice saw the flicker of resigned disbelief that passed between them, but she didn't think any of the others did.

To save fuel, the main generator was turned off every night at 10 p.m. ('We're not short of freezer capacity,' Richard had said, jerking his chin at the white outdoors. The men had dug an ice cave behind the lab hut and consigned the lab freezer contents to it.) Everyone piled on extra layers of insulation and retired to their bunks to keep warm, but tonight Alice was too restless. She lit a couple of candles and paced the main room, wearing most of her clothes except her windproofs.

A man's shadow loomed over the wooden wall ahead of her. She turned with her heart leaping into her mouth and saw Rooker.

'So you can't sleep either,' he said. He produced the inevitable bottle and poured scotch into two mugs.

'Will you have enough whisky for the winter, if we get stuck?'

'No,' he said. 'This is the last. Cheers.'

She drank, then took a breath, with the spirit still scalding her throat. 'Rook, I've got to get back to England.'

'This is Antarctica, not Spain or somewhere. There's no *got* to. You'll get back if it's possible and if it isn't you'll stay here until the ice breaks up.'

'But . . . you said we'd get away, if you had anything to do with it.'

The look he gave her was pitying. 'You didn't see what I saw today. Outside this bay, the sea has frozen in broken waves. Can you imagine that? Crests and troughs of ice, choppy, either bare and slippery or piled with loose, soft snow. Every ridge has to be negotiated, up and down for miles. It's difficult and dangerous. And with nine people and heavy sledges?'

'There are two helicopters at Santa Ana. They'll come.'

'Yeah,' he said.

Shockingly, she felt her face begin to crumple. Tears burned at the back of her eyes. Rooker saw and put his hands on her shoulders. Very gently, he drew her close to him. She wanted more than anything to rest her head against his shoulder and tell him what was wrong. Instead, she arched her back and resisted his comfort, afraid that he would notice the swollen bulk of her stomach.

'What is it? Why does it matter so much?'

She only shook her head.

With his thumbs he stroked the tears away from under her eyes, surprising her with his gentleness. Then he took her face between his hands. 'I've watched you. You're strong and you're brave as well. It's only waiting. What do you fear?'

She was ashamed to tell him her secret, with all its soft womanishness and the attendant implications of wilful miscalculation. She stepped away from him instead. 'I'm sorry,' she said in a different voice. 'The uncertainty gets to us all in different ways, doesn't it? I think I'll go to bed. Thanks for the whisky.'

'Goodnight,' he said.

Alice lay in her bunk and listened to the familiar din of the night wind. None of them knew for sure yet that 15 March wouldn't see them on board the *Polar Star*.

*   *   *

Beverley Winston and the Polar Office responded to Richard's request that in view of the extreme weather conditions the relief ship might come to bring them out earlier than scheduled. Unfortunately, she noted, the ship's programme was already determined and to change its itinerary would be very expensive. It would cost an estimated mimimum of $25,000 to reroute the *Polar Star* and in view of the fact that it would only make a few days' difference to the planned date, Mr Sullavan judged that this would be an excessive expenditure.

When he gave them this news, Richard's face was creased with resignation.

Russ let his disgust show. 'A few days? Does he really not understand that a single day can make the difference down here?'

'We should have accepted the invitation of the Ukrainians,' Arturo complained.

'Too fucking right,' Phil groaned. He was angry with himself for having come down on the wrong side.

'Lewis Sullavan's an amateur. He wanted a polar station, but now he's finding out that his toy's too expensive.' Rooker was scathing and no one tried to contradict him.

*   *   *

The days passed, but every hour stretched out painfully.

The last week came. The base was stripped down ready to be closed up and most of the equipment was packed, although it seemed impossible that they would actually be leaving.

The weather reports were seized upon as soon as they arrived, but there was never an optimistic note. The helicopters had been on the ground at Santa Ana for more than two weeks, without flying a single excursion. The blizzards followed one upon the other with hardly a break between them, and fifty- and sixty-knot winds screamed down from the glacier.

The Kandahar personnel watched and waited. On 12 March the *Polar Star* left port to make its way across the Drake Passage and down to the peninsula.

The same night Alice was lying sleepless and cold in her bunk. There was a wind, but for once the sky was clear. She had seen the brilliant necklaces of stars when she took a last look out over the motionless bay.

She heard the small noises of someone moving around in the hut, but after a while everything went quiet again. But then she sensed something else. It was unidentifiable at first but it still made her heart leap and pound with fear. She sat upright, groping for her torch.

She couldn't see the window. It should have framed a velvet, starry square. Then she coughed.

Smoke. The room was full of smoke.

CHAPTER FOURTEEN

She couldn't see anything. She half fell out of bed, coughing and gulping for air, and flung herself in pitch darkness to try to find the light switch. Her hands clawed at the wall and then scraped over the switch, but no light answered the click.

No generator, of course.

'Laure,' she shouted, as she fell across her bunk. 'Laure, wake up.'

The other woman's body was warm under the covers. She stirred and groaned as Alice shook her. '*Qu'est-que c'est . . . ?*'

'Get up,' Alice yelled. 'Fire.'

They were both coughing in the rolling, blinding smoke.

Torch. Find the torch. Breathe some air. Low down. Disconnected imperatives swirled in Alice's head as Laure reared out of bed and stumbled against her, grabbing at her for support. Brutally Alice shook her off and dropped to her knees. Better. Air clearer down here. She groped and found the legs of her bunk, the coiled mass of covers, the pillow, yes—and here, her torch lying where she had dropped it. The yellow beam reassured her for only a split second. The wreathing, acrid smoke was so thick that the light was just a dim blur. Alice took two steps and heaved open the door of the bunk room.

The scene beyond brought a scream into her mouth. There was a wall of flame where the main room lay and there were figures silhouetted against it, spraying a fire extinguisher which even in her shock and panic Alice could see was useless. She slammed the door again. There was no escape that way.

'Quick, blankets. Here, seal the cracks.'

'*Comment? Je ne comprends . . .*'

They were both choking. Burning tears poured down Alice's face. The window, that was the only chance. She hauled the blankets off the bunk and wadded them against the crack under the door, then hunted wildly around the room for something with which to break the window.

Fighting for sight, she hammered with a shoe, then threw it aside when she realised that the thick glass would never shatter under the feeble impact. There was nothing else here . . .

'*Attends, j'ai mon piolet,*' Laure shrieked. Alice couldn't understand what she was saying, but Laure squirmed under her bunk and dragged out a kitbag. Inside, blessedly, there lay an ice axe. Alice grabbed the shaft, double-fisted, and swung the

376

adze at the glass. The first blow only cracked the pane but the second splintered a hole in it. Cold clean air flooded into the room.

'*Oh merci, merci*,' Laure sobbed.

Alice jumped on a chair. She chopped a bigger hole in the glass and then padded the jagged shards with the nearest clothes that came to hand. Now that they were about to escape the smoke and the flames, she was already aware of the intense cold waiting outside. 'Throw everything out. Anything warm.'

A cascade of blankets and clothes and towels rained down on the snow, followed by a shower of boots and shoes.

'*Vite, vite*,' Laure gabbled.

There was no time to rescue anything else. They perched on the chair together, and Alice held on to Laure's shoulders as she squirmed over the padded glass and dropped the few feet to the ground. It was lucky that the rocks were blanketed with thick snow. Alice swung her legs over the padding and launched herself forward. She felt a sharp scrape along her arm as she fell and a jarring crack as she hit the ground. Laure put an arm round what had once been her waist and helped her to her feet. Above their heads, dense billows of black smoke poured out of their bunk-room window. Louder than the wind, they could hear the greedy crackling of flames.

Already shivering, they picked up boots and pulled them on over their snowy socks, then fought their way into as many layers of clothing as they could pile on. Alice had no gloves and when she glanced down at her fingers she saw that there were black tributaries of blood running down her left wrist. She enveloped her hands within her sleeves and ran in Laure's wake round the corner of the hut.

Flames were dancing out of the hut door and as they stopped in their tracks to gaze in horror, the front windows blew out in the heat. A corner of the roof curled up like a stale sandwich and a fat column of fire escaped and leaped towards the sky. Sparks showered down around them and they had to stumble backwards as red diamonds of flame spat and died at their feet.

There were other figures, stumbling through the snow and waving their arms. Their shouts were swallowed by the roar of the fire.

Alice counted. Four . . . five. Where were the others?

Black smoke clouds were driven low over the base, fanned by the stiff wind. Flames roared out of the eyes and mouth of the hut, horizontal tongues licking towards the wooden walls of Margaret Mather House.

Only five of the men. Even with their hoods up the shapes and sizes of all her companions were so familiar to Alice that she didn't even have to think, she knew at once that it was Richard and Rooker who were missing.

She turned in a full circle. 'Rook?' she screamed.

No one could hear. Russell plunged past her with Phil at his shoulder. A glance flashed backwards showed her that a flower of fire was blooming round the nearest window of the lab hut. Laure was dragging on her arm, trying to pull her back, but she broke free and ran forward. The narrow neck of ground between the two huts was engulfed by a wall of flame as the dry wood of the

378

second structure caught in several places. There was no question of passing that way. She ran counter-clockwise, back in the direction she and Laure had come, to circumnavigate the inferno of the main hut. On the far side, furthest from the point where the blaze must have started, was the window of the scientists' bunk room. Smoke poured out but she couldn't see any flames. Alice ran forward and jumped to the nearest rocks. There were two heads at the window, still inside the hut but at least they were there.

'Rooker,' she yelled. 'Get out.'

It looked as if they were fighting. Richard's arms were raised, Rooker's were locked round him. They lurched and banged against the interior walls.

Alice lunged forward and hoisted herself so that she was leaning into the room through the broken window with her legs dangling. The wood of the sill felt hot under her hands. 'Climb out,' she screamed.

Rook was dragging Richard towards the window and the clearer air but Richard was pulling away. His head was down and he writhed like an animal being dragged to slaughter.

'*Richard.*'

Somehow, through the din, the sound of her voice registered on him. He swung his head in her direction and she saw the whites of his eyes, shocking in his smoke-blackened face.

The door of the bunk room dissolved in a blast of heat. A pall of smoke swept at them with a rectangle of fire at its heart. Richard gave a rending cry but he could only retreat from the blistering heat. The two men flung themselves at the window, their arms up to shield their faces.

Alice dropped to the ground and as she rolled aside Richard thudded down, pushed out of the window by Rooker. An instant later Rooker himself landed beside them. Richard hauled himself to his hands and knees and hung his head, panting like a dog.

Rooker was already on his feet. 'Move,' he ordered.

They were up and running, all three of them, out into the snow away from the fire. Flames forked through the window from which they had just escaped. There was an indrawn breath, an instant of silence when the air pressure seemed to lessen and the world hung motionless. Then there was an explosion that hurt their ears. The entire long side of the main hut blew out. For a second or two the familiar outlines of the interior—the metal-topped kitchen table, the wall cupboards, the door frames—stood out against the molten orange like shadows in a developing photograph. Then the fire wiped them out. The hut and everything in it was finished.

Richard and Rooker and Alice stopped running. They halted in the calf-deep snow and watched as the last roof supports frayed and collapsed inwards.

Richard gave another cry. 'The gastropod,' he said.

Alice licked her lips but her throat was heat-parched and sore with shouting, and she couldn't speak. A fossil? A *fossil* didn't matter.

She turned to Rook. He didn't move. His eyes were starting and his lips were drawn back from his teeth. He looked as if he was seeing a ghost.

The lab hut was properly on fire now too. Three figures were darting around it, aiming the jets of fire extinguishers at the blaze. Slowly, Rooker collected himself. He dragged a black hand over his sooty face and began to walk. He took long, unsteady strides, as if he were wading through water, towards the second fire. Alice moved to follow him but Richard dragged at her arm.

'It was in my locker,' he groaned. 'In *there*.'

Alice found her voice. 'I don't care. I care about . . . living things.'

She brushed off his hand and stumbled after Rook. But in the fear and heat and confusion, the crazy essence of this exchange shone at her like a blade of white light. It was people who were important, these dark stumbling victims of the fire and the others she loved who were asleep at home. Science didn't matter. History didn't matter. For all she cared, knowledge could vanish into swirling oblivion to save just *one* familiar and beloved face.

Suddenly she thought of Peter. She could remember him saying almost the same thing to her when they first met. 'What would you rather have, love or the theory of relativity? The human gene code mapped or one life saved that's precious to you?' Shocked by his lack of gravitas, she had claimed science every time. As he had known she would.

Breath snagged in her burning chest and something close to a sob rose in her throat. The white light went out as suddenly as it had come on. Alice shook her head and struggled through the snow to where the others were huddling upwind of the lab hut. Laure held out her arms and they clung to each other for comfort. For the first time in weeks Alice didn't try to hold her body apart. They were all together in this, whatever came; keeping

381

her secret wasn't important any longer.

The extinguishers had temporarily contained the blaze, but the wind and the tinder dryness of the wooden construction were against them. Sparks flew and were fanned into little red blossoms that darted petals of flame. They needed water, but for all the snow and ice that surrounded them there was none to be had. Niki broke away from the group. He ran to the rear of the lab hut and smashed the back window, then hauled himself inside. Everyone knew that he was going for the radio equipment. Without radio contact they were truly stranded. Phil darted after him.

'The pipeline,' Russell shouted.

The base water supply came via insulated piping from an as-yet unfrozen glacier lake high up the hill behind the huts. Russell and Rooker immediately began ransacking the generator hut for anything that would hold water while Arturo and Valentin dug frantically in the snow to uncover the buried piping. Richard fell to his knees beside them and hauled with his bare hands at loose rocks. The flames from the huts lit up the snow with lurid splashes of orange and crimson, and the smoky shadows of the diggers stretched away into the darkness.

The piping was disinterred and taken apart, and water trickled out. Seconds later they had formed a chain. Buckets and jerrycans and old paint tins were filled and thrust from hand to hand. Spilled water soaked their arms and feet, and froze in the wind. Their clothes turned stiff and their hands were numb. The volume of water reaching the eager flames was pitifully small. Each bucketful doused the flicker for an instant, then the flames re-emerged there and elsewhere, always bigger and greedier.

They worked like machines. Nobody spoke. In a pall of smoke Niki and Phil dragged and hauled metal boxes with trailing festoons of flex from the broken window and ran with them to the safety of the generator hut.

At first it seemed that the fire was steadily gaining on them. The front wall of the hut was a mass of flames and Margaret's brass name plaque fell inwards and vanished as its section of wooden planking collapsed. The lab room was full of curling smoke, and the reek of flaring chemicals and melting plastic made them choke and gag. Then slowly it became apparent that they were holding their own. There were no more little tongues of fresh flame and the hissing smoke turned black. Alice looked round once from the water chain and realised that they were only winning the battle because the wind had dropped.

'Keep at it,' Rooker yelled back up the line.

They worked grimly for another half-hour. Without the wind blowing sparks and fingers of fire across from the main hut, it seemed that the shell and the back half of the lab hut were safe. The procession of brimming receptacles going one way and the empty ones passing back slowed, then came to a halt. They stood in silence, soaked and shivering, and looked around them.

The wreckage of the main hut was still burning, but with a less ferocious appetite. The snow all around it was blackened, littered with charred embers and the belongings that had been salvaged and thrown clear of the blaze. Margaret Mather House loomed in a wreath of smoke, half

383

destroyed. A few snowflakes lazily descended.

Richard stood with an empty bucket hanging in one hand. Niki trudged past him with the radio-room manuals clasped in his arms. Alice searched for Rook. He was staring into the smouldering core of the old hut with horror in his eyes. A stab of cold prompted her to look down at her hands. They were stiff white claws and the left one was caked with black dried blood. As she gazed at it a dribble of fresh blood ran down from her sleeve.

The others stood in exhausted silence too, gazing at the devastation.

The blood dripped from Alice's fingertips and pocked the snow. 'We should try to get under cover,' she said. The thinness of her voice and the inadequacy of the suggestion surprised her, but still everyone started moving obediently.

They gathered up the scattered clothing and equipment salvaged from the two huts, and carried armfuls up to the generator hut. It was plain that there wasn't going to be enough room for everyone because the field supplies and camp equipment were also stored there. The only other intact structure was the new skidoo shelter, so Phil drove the skidoos out and they ducked inside. They squeezed together in a double row and sank down with their backs to the sloping walls. Russell lit a tilley lamp and suspended it from the roof. It shone on blackened faces, frozen or soaking ruined clothing, feet in a mixture of boots and shoes and even hut slippers. They huddled together, shivering, waiting to see if Richard would assume the leadership.

Richard raised his head. He said in a flat voice, 'Niki? Can we make radio contact?'

'I don't yet know. I must have daylight.'

The antennae that had cross-hatched the sky were lying in a tangle over the ruins.

Richard continued his muttering. 'Making contact with Santa Ana is the first priority. Until then, shelter, warmth, hot drinks, food.'

'There's the field supplies and Primus stoves,' Russell offered.

'All right. Yes. We'll use those. And we'll wait until daylight.'

It was as if, Alice thought, just as if none of this night's events had come as a surprise to him.

Dismay rushed down her spine.

It must have been Richard who had started the fire, accidentally or otherwise.

He had been lighting candles again, trying with his distorted logic to conserve fuel. What was Richard Shoesmith thinking? That this was what Antarctica did—it drove you to the edge of the ability to survive and then cruelly tipped you over?

Gregory Shoesmith had survived, just. Captain Scott and his companions had not. Was there some streak of fatalism buried in Richard that had drawn him to the point of disaster, so they now found themselves crouched in a tin shed, without heat or fresh food, without radio contact, with the frozen sea trapping them and winter closing in?

Perhaps Richard's present blank resignation was born out of some conviction—possibly intention— that this is exactly what *would* happen, even to twenty-first-century scientists who had the support and backing of one of the world's media moguls. Was this the catastrophe that he thought he owed to his history?

Anger surged through Alice. It heated up her

blood and brought sensation stinging and burning back to her frozen fingertips. It might be Richard's history but it wasn't hers and it wasn't going to touch her. *Never*.

'Why are we just *sitting* here? We've got gas and food.' She began to scramble to her feet.

Rooker had shaken off his reverie of horror, whatever had caused it. His glance leaped at hers and for an instant their eyes locked. 'I'm going for the supplies,' he said. The shed door opened on a hanging curtain of smoke.

'Look at you,' Laure cried. She grabbed at Alice's hand. The blood had dried again. Phil and Laure made her take off her filthy, ice-stiff parka. They eased back her sleeve and revealed a long gash in her forearm. Alice gazed at it in surprise.

'Needs a stitch or two, I'd say.' Phil's warm Welsh voice seemed to come from a distant place.

The medical supplies were all gone. They had been stored in the main hut.

'Is anyone else hurt?' Phil asked. No one spoke. Richard sat next to the door with his parka drawn round him, apparently studying the metal floor between his feet. The days of shed squash were a long way off, but a dented ping-pong ball lay like a broken eggshell close to the toe of his boot.

Rook came back with a Primus, a set of camping pans and some of the neat boxes of dried field rations. Russ crawled outside to the pipeline and a minute later there was the smell of gas and the hiss of blue flame. It made the cramped tin hut feel briefly like the haven of a tent out in the field.

'We've got fourteen two-man days,' Rooker reported.

Enough food, just about, for three days for all of

them.

'Gas?' Valentin asked. He had been raking through his pockets and now he brought a crushed pack of Marlboro out of the depths. There were two cigarettes left. He hesitated, then put the pack away.

'Four cylinders after this one.'

Russ and Phil exchanged looks. It would take a lot of gas to cook for nine people.

Arturo kneeled upright and began opening the ration boxes. He found a set of packet soups and poured the contents into the pan of water, then unfolded his pocket knife and began stirring. 'It will be enough,' he said calmly. 'And there's always penguin.'

Stranded on Elephant Island for four and a half winter months while their leader went for help, Shackleton's men had lived almost entirely on boiled or fried seal and penguin. No one spoke of this, but it was in all their minds. Their present situation, black as it might be, was a summer picnic by comparison. Only Alice shivered as she watched the blade of Arturo's knife swirling gobbets of soup powder on the surface of the water.

Laure tightened an arm round her shoulders. 'I will dress it for you in a moment,' she said, misunderstanding. 'I will make hot water next.'

Her concern made Alice's eyes burn with unexpected tears. 'It's all right,' she lied.

Gratefully, they drank the hot soup. Valentin and Niki morosely murmured to each other in Russian, Niki's hugely elongated shadow curving up over the corrugated wall with Valentin's big round head nodding next to it like a pumpkin. Russell was silent and sombre, and Phil rested his

387

chin on his drawn-up knees and gazed into space. It was Arturo who had tipped soup into tin mugs and handed them round with a smile of encouragement. Except for the soot blacking his face, Rooker looked just as if he were sitting at the mess table on any ordinary night. Alice reflected that his impassivity must have been developed in childhood as a form of self-defence. So what could he have seen in the hut flames that was powerful enough to have transfixed him with such horror, even for a moment?

She wanted to go and kneel beside him, to take his huge hands between hers and rub warmth into them both, but she couldn't do it with seven pairs of eyes on them. There wasn't room to move in the shelter in any case. The cramped floor space was a thicket of jammed-together limbs.

Food and relative warmth slowly thawed them. The immediate shock ebbed, and they looked into one another's smoke-streaked, exhausted faces and began to take stock.

A helicopter rescue was now their only hope and it would have to come quickly. But without radio communication there was no way of letting the outside world know of their plight and summoning that assistance.

Niki's hollow face looked even more gaunt. They all knew that what would happen next was dependent on his expertise. 'I shall try my best,' he said into the quiet of the tin shell, although no one had spoken a word. 'I will wait until the morning, when the light comes, and I will investigate what I can do. In the meantime'—he shrugged wearily—'the best thing is maybe sleep.'

Everyone else had hungrily finished their soup,

but Richard hadn't even picked up his.

'You do not want?' Arturo gently asked.

Seeming to rouse himself, Richard reached out one hand, but the fingers were tightly curled and he couldn't grasp the handle.

'Let's have a look,' Phil demanded. Richard made to withdraw but Phil caught his wrist and turned the hand palm-up. It was burned and blistered raw, soot-caked but weeping and with the seared flesh curling and hanging in loose shreds. Phil drew in a breath and reached for the other hand. It was the same.

Phil's own fingertips were black and hardened with frostbite from his trek to find the sea margin. Alice looked from one pair of damaged hands to the other.

'I was trying to save my gastropod,' Richard said in the strange flat voice. 'But Rooker came and dragged me out.'

They had looked as if they were fighting, Alice remembered. 'It's a fossil,' she repeated in a high, hard voice. 'It's not worth a life.'

Rooker had risked his for Richard. Awe and admiration and another feeling, hot and wild, flooded through her. She wanted to look at Rooker but she dared not.

'We'll have to try and dress those,' Phil muttered. He was staring around at the ruined clothes and the puddled floor and the crowded bodies. 'What's clean?'

There was nothing.

Arturo held the tin cup of soup to Richard's mouth. 'Drink this,' he said.

'I know,' Laure cried. She began pulling off her parka, then one by one the layers of down and fleece beneath. The innermost layer was a white long-sleeved vest with a tiny frill of lace and a ribbon bow at the neck. Without hesitation she stripped that off too. Her bra was underwired, pale-pink and lacy. Her exposed skin was ethereally white in the lamplight, the pallor intensified by the black of her throat and wrists.

'Christ. My first sight of a real live woman in her bra in five months and I'm busy ripping up her vest for bandages,' Phil said. Valentin laughed, and a second later they were all wildly giggling and coughing with the remnants of smoke in their throats. Richard only stared blankly at them.

Laure scrambled back into her outer clothes. Water was boiled and allowed to cool, and she and Russ did their best to clean Richard's burns and wind strips of bandage round them. While the attention was on this, Alice dared to turn her head and at once met Rooker's eyes. To her surprise he smiled, a smile full of warmth and understanding that was as relaxed as if they had been sitting on either side of the hearth in a safe and familiar home.

Rooker wasn't afraid. And if she was with him, she realised, she didn't fear anything either.

'Aleece, now you,' Laure said. They peeled back her sleeve again and while Russ held the edges of the wound together she dipped a fragment of white vest in the water and sponged away the blood and dirt. When it was as clean as they could make it, Laure tightly bound her arm.

'It should be stitched,' Phil fretted.

'Don't worry.'

'I think you will have a dramatic scar,' Laure said.

390

'If that's the worst thing that comes out of all this we'll count ourselves lucky, eh?'

Rooker was still watching her.

There was nothing left for them to do but try to sleep. The skidoo shelter didn't offer enough space for everyone to lie down so Niki had already gone to curl up next to the generator in the other hut. Alice felt the baby languorously move and then the sudden, vigorous digging of a small limb beneath her ribcage. Relief that it was unaffected by the night's exertions, and the belated realisation that for hours she had hardly even thought of her child, made her want to jump up and pace up and down to contain her racing thoughts. She clambered over the legs and torsos to reach the door and half fell out into the darkness. The sky was inky black and after the stuffy shelter the cold was like a bell ringing loud and painful inside her head.

She stood up, drawing her clothes round her. Her arm was throbbing.

The main hut was a mess of black wreckage from which a pillar of grey smoke rose like a lazy ghost, but the lab hut was less damaged than she had feared. Three walls and part of the roof were still standing, although they were black with smoke. Alice walked in a slow circle over the filthy snow. The water that they had poured and spilled had frozen into a sheet of ice as slippery as glass.

Russell and Phil had put a half-barrel in the loose snow a few yards past the shelter. As she used it she heard the start of a distant low moaning that steadily rose in volume. It was the wind getting up at the head of the glacier. Soon enough, she knew from experience, it would start gathering speed and howling dementedly as it rushed down the steep slopes towards the sea. Some bad weather was coming in the wake of the brief lull.

She plodded back towards the shelter with the wind already tugging at the loose flaps of her parka. Rooker was standing in her path.

'If you're looking for the bathroom . . .' She smiled, pointing back the way she had come to cover up the wild leap of her heart at the sight of him.

His answer was to put his hands inside her hood and cup her face. He stared down at her, with his mouth almost touching hers.

'You came for me. The hut was on fire and you came to look for me.'

So he knew she had been searching for him, not Richard. That was good.

'You did the same for him,' she said quietly.

He bent his head so that his mouth came even closer. His breath was warm on her cold-pinched face. He shielded her from the wind, and blotted out the sky and the iron-hard glitter of the stars. 'You can't know how much that means to me.'

'I was afraid . . . I was so fearful that you might be hurt.'

The truth of this seemed enormous, swelling up and washing over her. *I feared that the smallest part of you might be hurt or damaged, that you might be taken away before I had even the chance to tell you so.*

He kissed her. The kiss warmed the blood in her veins and she forgot the fire and the reek of smoke and tomorrow's difficulties. She forgot her pregnancy and the circumspection that had governed her ever since she first saw him. He held her in a tight lock, as if he expected her to run away. But Alice stood on tiptoe to reach closer to him, greedily and blindly kissing him back, digging her frozen fingers into the stiff carapace of his parka while the wind flapped and battered at them, and everything else in the frozen world stood still as if time itself had frozen too.

She didn't know how long they stayed locked together, buffered by all their clothes.

At last he raised his head, still holding her face between his warm hands. 'Thank you,' he said in a voice she had never heard him use before. His thumbs stroked the corners of her mouth and she didn't know or care if it was ice crystals or gritty dirt that minutely chafed there.

She suddenly remembered his exquisite driftwood carving of a baby. It had been in her locker, with the Polaroid of Pete and *Desiderata*. 'Your Christmas carving. It's gone.'

'I'll do you another,' he promised. They were only inanimate things.

He took her left hand, gently because of her gashed arm, and led her back to the tin shelter. There was nowhere else for them to go and the wind was already whipping the snow into the beginnings of a blizzard.

The tilley lamp had been turned out and as they squeezed inside there was a low rumble of complaint from the tangle of uncomfortable bodies. In the darkness Alice patted with her hand and discovered Laure's shoulder. She slid into a space alongside her and Laure sighed and rearranged herself with her head on Alice's shoulder. Rook folded himself into the draughty slot between Alice and the door. Warmth seemed to radiate out of him. They settled in a sitting position with their backs against the ridged wall, shoulders and hips touching, hand searching for, then clasping, the other's. Alice couldn't even think of sleep. Her heart was knocking too hard and disbelief and desire and wild excitement chased each other through her thoughts. They sat in the darkness, silently listening to the storm, feeling the rhythm of each other's breaths. She wished that she could hear what he was thinking. There would be time, she promised herself, when all this was over. There would be all the time they needed for him to tell her and for her to listen.

*   *   *

Alice opened her eyes. When she moved her head a stab of pain shot up her neck. Her mouth was dry and her throat was sore. She had drifted into sleep at some point in the long night and her head had awkwardly fallen against the end wall of the hut. Every inch of her body ached with cold and from lying on the hard floor, although someone had tucked a blanket round her.

Rook.

Wincing, she twisted her head to look for him but the only other person in the shelter was Laure. She lay fast asleep with her knees drawn up to her chest and her head in Alice's lap. Remembering the details of the night, Alice tried to catch her breath as it turned ragged in her chest. Where was he now? The wind was a constant roar around the tin walls.

Laure stirred as if Alice's wild thoughts had penetrated her sleep. Alice stroked matted locks of hair off the Frenchwoman's face.

Abruptly, Laure came to full consciousness. 'Aleece?' she breathed. She turned to gaze up and her ear was pressed hard against Alice's belly. Alice saw confusion, speculation and amazed certainty widening the other woman's eyes. Laure was a biologist; she had heard the rapid tick-tick of the baby's heartbeat. It was too late to push her away, too late to scramble to her feet or begin protesting. Instead, Alice sat calmly as Laure struggled upright, gaping in shock. Now she slipped her hand under Alice's parka and explored the taut dome of her belly. '*Ce n'est pas possible. Tu es . . . ?*'

Alice slowly nodded.

'*Mais, personne sait pas?*'

'No,' Alice agreed.

Laure's hand came up to her mouth. Her head was wobbling in astonishment. 'My God. *You* did not know?'

'Not when I arrived, no.'

'And now we are trapped, and there is no doctor and no medical supply and no good shelter, and what if we must stay here for the whole winter?'

It was Alice who took Laure's hand and reassuringly squeezed it. 'The baby won't come yet. They'll get the helo in in a couple of days and we'll be on the ship and back in the world in no time.' She believed her own words. A wild, reckless happiness was singing under her skin. With the memory of Rook and last night in her head it was as if she had found something she had searched for all her life.

Nothing could touch her now; there was no threat and no uncertainty.

Laure rocked back on her heels. She stared at Alice in utter disbelief. 'I thought you were cool and sensible. But you are not. You are a crazy, crazy madwoman.'

There was the sound of banging outside the tin door. It swung open and Phil and Russ crawled into the shelter. Alice just had time to raise one finger to her lips in a stern, forbidding gesture to Laure. It was a relief to share her secret with just one person, but none of the others need know. She would find a way to tell Rooker herself.

'He's lost it. Just totally lost it,' Phil was saying.

'Who?' Laure demanded. She was shaking her head as if she couldn't process any more surprises.

Russ lit the Primus. 'Could one of you fix some porridge? It's blowing a tenner out there. I don't reckon much of our chances of getting workable antennae up today.'

'*Who?*'

'Our leader.' Phil sighed. 'He's marching around like a robot, giving orders, listening to nobody, then dropping to his knees in the ashes and scrabbling with his bandaged hands for some fossil.'

'The gastropod,' Alice said.

'Russell?' Laure begged for more comprehensible information.

Russell's mouth set in a line. He considered for a second before he said, 'I reckon maybe Richard is having some kind of a mental breakdown?'

Alice set a pot of water on the gas. She thought that they had probably guessed as much, all of them, without having given voice to their suspicions. She tore open a sachet from the ration boxes and sprinkled porridge oats into the water.

'What shall we do?' Laure asked.

'Watch and wait,' Russ answered.

'And hope to get the fuck out of here asap,'

396

Phil added.

The next arrival was Richard himself. Snow and ash were mixed in his beard, and his lips were cracked and bloody under the soot. He lowered himself into his corner and wedged the mug of porridge that Alice gave him between his knees. He peeled off his mitts to reveal loops of filthy bandages. With the fingertips of his right hand he could just about manipulate a spoon.

'Shall I help?' she asked.

The look he gave her seemed to contain no element of recognition. 'Everyone must help, and more. We'll only get out of here if each one of us gives a hundred and ten per cent.'

Arturo came in. Snow and smuts blew in with him, and the tin door banged twice in the gale before he could secure it. 'It is not the best weather for putting up radio antennae,' he said. Of all of them, Alice thought, apart from Rook, Arturo was handling this best. He sat down in front of Richard and took the mug from him. As if it were the most natural thing in the world, he began to feed him spoonfuls of porridge. Richard tasted it, mistrustfully at first, then devoured it as fast as Arturo could spoon it into him. Afterwards Arturo wiped the remnants from his beard as if Richard were a child. 'You were awake all night. You should sleep now,' he advised him.

'Sleep? With everything to do here?'

'You will work better after sleep.'

Richard nodded his head. Obediently he turned sideways and curled himself up under a blanket. A few seconds later, it seemed, he was lost to the world.

The first batch of porridge was finished. To

escape the oppressive atmosphere of the shelter Alice went for more water, but as soon as she was outside the blizzard assaulted her. There was grey daylight but the air was a thick, filthy mixture of snow and ash and oily smuts. She saw the hut wreckage with drifts already piling against it, and could just discern the struggling shapes of Rook and Valentin. Bent almost double against the wind, they were fighting to re-erect a pole for the antennae. As soon as they raised it to the vertical and tried to anchor it with guy lines, the pegs tore loose and the pole toppled again.

Rooker didn't see Alice until she grabbed at his arm. 'Let me help,' she yelled.

'No. We'll have to wait until the wind drops.'

'Come and get some hot food.'

'Yeah.'

In the generator shed Niki was crouched with the radio components spread around him, working by the light of a head torch.

'Niki? Come and have breakfast.'

'In a few moments,' he answered, not even looking up.

Alice fought her way to the water pipe that already had a tap rigged to it. She filled the canisters and battled back to the skidoo shelter. The skidoos themselves were little more than white-and-black-speckled humps.

Laure had made more porridge, and Rooker and Valentin were eating. Alice let her hand drop for a second on Rook's shoulder, then sat where she could find a space. Richard was buried under his blanket and Arturo was nodding off too. There was a smell of bodies and burned fabric and grease, and the floor was gritty with dirt and puddled with water, but at least it was almost warm compared with outside. A heavy silence spread until Niki pushed his way in.

He took his mug of porridge and thoughtfully wrapped his frozen fingers round it. It was almost impossible to do intricate electronic work in the icy chamber of the generator hut, and the radio room itself was too wet and exposed to the wind through the burned wall and roof.

'What d'you reckon?' Russell asked.

'I think, maybe,' he answered. Phil gave a little whoop of satisfaction and Laure clapped her mittened hands. 'And since we have not made this morning's radio schedule with Santa Ana they will know now that we have some problem. But for making contact I must of course have antenna in place, and for now . . .' His shrug was expressive.

'Last night's forecast was only one to two days of wind. Not a full-blown storm,' Russ reminded them.

'Let's wait and see,' Rooker said coolly.

There was no point, yet, in even speculating about when or if they could expect to be rescued.

The time passed very slowly. Their cramped confinement was miserably uncomfortable, but the close press of bodies did keep the worst of the cold at bay. The wind showed no sign of slackening and the grey daylight quickly faded into blackness once again. They had no books, not even a pack of cards, and Phil's guitar had gone up in flames with everything else. At Russ's suggestion they sang a couple of songs, but the unaccompanied voices soon petered out.

'Then someone tell us a tale,' Russ insisted.

Arturo told them about the restaurant his

399

grandparents had owned, in one of the steep cobbled streets leading up to the hilltop magnificence of the Alhambra Palace. 'My grandmother's rabbit stew,' he murmured. 'With roasted potatoes flavoured with rosemary. That was marvellous.'

There were groans of longing. Between nine people, only two full days of field supplies now remained, so food was strictly rationed. They ate an evening meal of soup and two crackers apiece. They had to ration the gas too, but in the evening they allowed themselves a small pan of just-warm water each to wash the soot and grease off their faces and hands.

Alice sat quietly, occasionally shifting her weight on the hard floor. Laure kept looking speculatively at her, but she only smiled back. It was peculiar to think of happiness or even contentment in connection with their present plight, or to feel ambivalent about the idea of rescue, but each minute that slipped away brought closer the moment when she might have to part with Rook. Even though they hadn't exchanged a single private word throughout the whole drab, worrisome day he was still close enough to touch. His eyes were often on her and she knew that he was waiting too. She heard his voice and felt his nearness prickle her thin skin through the foul layers of her clothes.

Richard went outside before the light faded and in his absence they agreed in low voices that all they could do was keep a watch on him. Phil went out too, ostensibly to stretch his legs.

'Poor bastard,' Russ muttered. 'It's gone haywire all right, his big Sullavan–EU Antarctic enterprise.'

When he came back the state of his hands told

them that he had been sifting through the debris again.

Alice put her mouth close to his ear. 'There will be other fossil finds. There are seasons still to come.'

'I don't know.' There was such despair underlying his flat monotone that she wanted to take him in her arms and try to comfort him. Instead, she undid his ruined bandages and replaced them with the last two strips of Laure's vest.

The night was even longer and more painful than the day, but the tilley lamp was blown out and Alice and Rooker were able to sit with their hands linked. It was almost as if they *were* talking, she thought. In the endless hours their histories and hopes and confessions seemed to flow through their joined palms.

No one slept very much. The talk murmured between them.

'In the village where I come from, in the mountains in northern Bulgaria, the houses all are carved in wood,' Valentin said. 'It is a picture. The lakes are full of fish, and the wild honey . . . ah.' They heard him kiss the tips of his fingers.

Laure whispered, 'When I was a small girl, our family holidays were every year in Arcachon, near Bordeaux. In this place there is the biggest sand dune in the world. I remember slip-sliding from the top to the bottom, and near the foot of it there is a small seafood restaurant. Here you can eat *langoustines*, and *moules*, and *soupe de poisson* that is the best I have ever tasted.'

It wasn't surprising that the memories they chose to share were of food and summer's warmth.

401

Phil gave a deep sigh. 'A long day's climbing. The rock hot from the sun, jelly legs, a big thirst on. Sit down outside the pub and take the first pull on the first pint of the night. That's the best taste in the world, followed by a fry-up at Pete's Eats in Llanberis.'

'Rook?' Laure said out of the dark.

'No,' he said. Nothing else. Alice held on to his hand.

*   *   *

The second morning's weather was no improvement on the first. In the generator shed a makeshift radio table had been rigged up from salvaged planking and Niki had reassembled the radio components. After three missed schedules with Santa Ana there would now be concern about what was happening at Kandahar Station, but until the wind decreased and the visibility improved there was no chance that they would mount an air reconnaissance.

They ate the last of the porridge and some chocolate.

Apart from his nap after breakfast the previous day, Richard had not slept since the fire. He told them about his grandfather's march with Captain Scott and his raggle-taggle teams of ponies to the foot of the Beardmore Glacier, beneath Mount Shoesmith, where the ponies were finally butchered to feed the dogs on the onward journey. 'My grandfather shot his pony after a day on soft snow, when the beast had been sinking almost up to his hocks with every step. He wrote in his diary that Samuel enjoyed his last feed and, until the last days when the severity of the constant blizzards wore him out, he had pulled with all his heart.'

Most of them were familiar with the story but they all listened in silence. Richard sat with his head thrown back against the shed wall and his burned hands hanging loose between his knees. There were tears in his eyes.

As the light faded again, the wind seemed to give a sigh of exhaustion. The double row of dejected figures stirred and looked at each other. An hour after that there was no more banging and battering against the hut walls.

The men filed outside to try to erect the pole.

'Are you all right?' Laure demanded as soon as they were alone.

'I'm fine,' Alice said smoothly. There were strange ripples of pressure chasing across her belly. Braxton-Hicks practice contractions, she remembered from her website reading. It was very early to be having them. Even now she didn't want to leave, but she had to get out of here. To escape from Laure she scrambled outside to see if she could help.

They worked by torchlight, digging a pit for the pole and clearing snow for ice screws to secure the guy wires. Eddies of snow chased across the serene landscape, where all the blackness of the fire had now been rubbed out. The wreckage was all soft, voluptuous white hummocks. Another pole was raised against the generator hut. Phil and Rook climbed up on the hut roof and the remains of the lab building with coils of wire. With a pulse beating in her neck, Alice held a torch steady as they ravelled a cat's cradle of loops between the two poles. Niki was already at the table inside the hut

403

with headphones clamped to his ears. The tilley lamp overhead swayed as the roof sagged under Phil's tread.

There was a series of crackles interspersed with flat silences. Niki's long fingers minutely tuned the signal. The rest of them crowded into the hut and crammed the doorway. A loud burst of static made them all leap.

Niki clicked the hand mike and began calling, 'Santa Ana, Santa Ana, this is Kandahar Station. Do you read me? Over.'

The airwaves were a buzz of interference.

'Santa Ana, Santa Ana, Santa Ana. Kandahar Station, do you read me? Over.'

Nothing came back but scribbled noise.

Niki was patient. 'I will keep trying. What more can we do?'

Valentin and Russ and Phil hovered in the hut. Richard broke away as if he couldn't listen any longer. He blundered back to the skidoo shelter, and Arturo patiently followed him.

Alice and Rooker stood outside in the billowing snow. The half of Margaret Mather House left standing was wreathed in garlands of white.

Now that they had the opportunity, there was too much to say. The beam of Alice's torch made a pallid circle round their feet as they looked into each other's eyes.

Rooker was remembering the moment of trying to drag Shoesmith away from the fire as it galloped through the hut. His skin crawled with fear, and with the ancient layers of recollection and determined oblivion that accompanied it. Fire was the worst thing he could think of. Fire and Lester.

Then he had looked up and saw Alice at the

window, heard her shouting his name. She had come because of him, not Richard, and that flash of grateful recognition set off a chain of realisation.

He *wanted* her, this stocky, determined little English scientist with her quiet voice that made you listen. Not just her unseen body, although he desired that too. He wanted to touch her and learn about her and hear her talking just for him, and the wish had been in him from almost the beginning when she had stumbled over him out on the rocks. He had been drunk in an attempt to forget himself and her stillness had been like a cool hand on his burning head. She was courageous and stoical and clear-minded, and yet he sensed there were undercurrents of passion in her that ran like molten precious metal. Out of all the women he had known over all the years he had never met one like her.

He had been angry with Shoesmith partly because he was jealous.

It had seemed that she might favour *him*, of all people.

But she came back to the burning hut for his sake. She had kissed him, and he had tasted smoke and tears on her skin, and they had sat for two endless and still too-short nights with their hands joined.

Rooker smiled down into her eyes.

Alice saw his face with the frown and the cynical glare melted away. There was just him and she felt a beat of wondering love.

'I am afraid of fire,' he confessed.

She remembered the horror filling his eyes as he watched it. 'You don't fear anything else. What is it about fire?'

He was very still. After what seemed like a long time, he said, 'A friend of my mother's died in a fire.'

* * *

Jimmy came home from school one afternoon to find his mother and Lester both wearing bathing caps. The rubber caps were poked full of holes and there were hanks of gluey hair sticking out. They looked grotesque and they were drinking white wine from a two-litre flagon. They were even wearing the same lipstick, smudged from the boozing.

'We're highlighting our hair, darling. Blonde streaks,' she said.

Lester struck a pose, tilting his head on one side and kiss-pursing his lips. He rested his rubber-gloved fists on his snake hips. 'What do you think, darling?' he cooed.

He was always in the house nowadays. Every evening: watching TV, drinking and giggling, painting her toenails, dressing her up and pinching her flesh as if she were some oversized doll.

'Fuck off,' Jimmy spat at him.

'Oh, *dear*,' Lester said.

'Jimmy, don't be rude. Come on, sit down with us and have a chat. Tell me about . . .' her eyes flicked to Lester and back again '. . . school. How was school today?'

Lester was rubbing a lock of her hair between his fingers, squinting at it through the smoke of his cigarette. 'Nearly done, hon.'

'Is there anything to eat?' Jimmy asked.

'I expect so, darling. Have a look in the fridge,

eh?'

Jimmy knew that there was no point, but he went anyway. Then he sat in his bedroom, staring out of the window at the scrawny plum tree and the view of old Ma Douglas's backyard. She came out and pegged some dusters and cloths on the washing line. There was a science test tomorrow and he had other homework to do as well, but he made no attempt to open his school bag. After a while he stood up again and went along to the bathroom to pee. There were wet nylons dripping over the bath, and squeezed tubes of cream and face make-up in the cracked basin. He scooped up some orangey stuff on the tip of one finger and sniffed it.

Behind him, the door slid open. He looked into the mirror on the tin cabinet and saw Lester.

Lester was smiling, a big wet smile of pleading and fake friendliness that turned Jimmy's stomach. 'Hey, Jim. Hey, there?' he said softly. There was the funny look in his eyes that always came when he was drunk. Jimmy whirled round but as he tried to wriggle past, Lester caught hold of him. There was the sour-wine and Players stink of his breath and then his wet mouth was pressed to Jimmy's. His huge sloppy tongue probed between his teeth. Jimmy bit hard and then, as Lester recoiled, he brought his knee up between his legs. Lester folded up and slid to the floor, gasping.

Jimmy stepped over him and walked to the kitchen. There was no food in the house, but there was a two-thirds-full bottle of whisky next to the bread bin. He stuffed it into the pocket of his coat.

'Lester? Le-ess?' his mother called blurrily from the sofa. Jimmy walked out of the back door. There was a tight, hot feeling in his chest that made him want to kick the dog that was licking its own arse in the lane, or to smack his fist against the nearest fence. He slouched round to Gabby's house, thinking they might down the whisky together and that he would look at Joyce's underclothes strung out to dry amongst Mr Macfarlane's flannel work shirts. But when he opened the gate he saw Mr Macfarlane himself, standing in the doorway like a red-faced bull, and he slipped away again.

He walked down the river path and sat on a log. He unscrewed the cap of the whisky bottle and took a long swallow. Later he tried to cry, but his eyes stayed dry and prickly. He shouted 'fuck, fuck', over and over again, but the damp chilly air closed over the words. He sat there until it got dark, thinking of Lester in his house with his mother. They would be watching *Hawaiian Eye*— no, *Bonanza*—and giggling over how handsome Jess Cartwright was, and slopping wine whenever they moved.

Disgust at the memory of Lester's breath and tongue rose in his throat, fighting with the fumes of whisky. A hot wall of rage hemmed him in, shutting out the drearily familiar outlines of the trees on the opposite bank and the pewter glimmer of the water. Jimmy stood up abruptly. The path rose under his feet and tipped him sideways so that he almost fell into the river, but he staggered and managed to right himself.

Lester lived in a caravan that stood raised on blocks in a quiet cindery enclosure beyond a row of farm outbuildings at the edge of town. Jimmy had never actually been inside the van, but he and Gabby had played around outside when they knew Lester was out. There were thick curtains looped at the little windows, but when they stood on a couple of boxes from the rubbish tip they could peer inside at the cushions and framed photographs and the single armchair. They had also snooped through the outbuildings. There was an old petrol-driven lawnmower in one of them, and a mouldy shelf with jerrycans and tins and canisters on it.

One of the bigger cans was almost full of petrol.

Jimmy yanked the stuffing out of some old cushions that were piled in the corner of the end shed. He teased out the yellow fibrous material and gently, surprising himself with his gentleness, he fed all of it through the letter box low down in the door of Lester's caravan. Then he poured petrol in on top. He lit a match and poked that in as well.

There was an immediate huge *boom* followed by a whoosh of flame that came licking out of the slot. It was a cold night and Jimmy had his woolly gloves on. Feeling like one of the slick baddies in a TV show, he snapped off the gloves and hastily shoved them into the fire. As he walked away he heard the flames whipping and crackling.

He took the back route home, down the lanes, but there was no one about. He expected to find the two of them sitting where he had left them but the house was utterly silent.

'Mum?' He clicked the light on in the living room and saw her lying on the couch. She was asleep, her mouth hanging open and drool marking the cushion under her cheek.

'Lester?'

Lester wasn't anywhere in the house. Jimmy left his mother where she was and crept silently to bed.

There was a police investigation into Lester Furneaux's death, but no one was ever arrested for setting the fire. There was some question of whether the petrol had actually been stored in the caravan, and whether Lester might have fallen asleep and left a cigarette burning. He was known to drink heavily.

Queers like him were not popular or welcome in Turner, South Island, in the 1950s.

Two months later Mrs Annette Rooker committed suicide by pulling a one-bar electric fire into her bath. She left a short note saying that she felt too lonely to go on. She apologised to her son, Jimmy, and wrote that his uncle, Henry Jerrold, would look after him. He was to be a good boy in England.

*   *   *

Alice was looking at him. She was waiting and listening, but not wanting to force him to say something he preferred to keep back. Maybe some day he might even tell her a part of the truth, although the mere thought made his throat close up. 'Are you cold?' he asked, just to fill the moment.

She shook her head quickly. 'Rook, I want to tell you something.'

Her words seemed to mirror his thoughts and he frowned, trying to work it out. He was close enough to feel the warmth of her breath and he saw her eyes widen with uncertainty.

Then there was a huge yell from the generator hut. Someone banged triumphantly on the wall and the door flew open.

'We've got 'em!' Phil bawled.

Rook and Alice ran the few steps to the shed.

Niki's headset was clamped to his head and the

410

mike to his lips. Russ and Valentin were shaking fists in the air. They heard the tinny, distorted but still unmistakable voice of Miguel, Miggy, the radio op at Santa Ana.

'Kandahar, Kandahar. Come in, please. Repeat, Kandahar, come in please.'

CHAPTER FIFTEEN

Santa Ana had been trying to contact Kandahar for thirty-six hours. But the people there had assumed that the prolonged radio silence was due to a technical malfunction, never imagining a disaster on the scale of the fire.

Alice listened to the rapid radio exchanges.

'No major casualties,' Niki was repeating. 'Some minor injuries only. But the hut is gone. We are seriously short of food and gas. Shelter is limited. Over.'

They were going to be rescued.

Luck was with her after all. Everything would be all right in spite of the risks she had taken. They would be out of Kandahar and on to the ship, and she would be flying back to London and home in a matter of days. At first she felt a hot surge of relief, but after the first seconds her euphoria was dampened by a wave of sadness. She would be leaving the ice, probably for ever. To go home was to enter a world full of problems that hadn't even delineated themselves as yet. But the question that was troubling her most of all was what about Rooker? Where and how could they ever be together beyond Kandahar?

411

A swoop of anxiety unbalanced her so that she stumbled against him. He put out his arm to steady her and she resisted the impulse to cling on and never let go.

Richard and the others hurried in from the skidoo shelter. All nine of them crowded round the radio table. The voice of the Chilean expedition leader replaced that of Miguel the radio operator.

'Let me,' Richard ordered and with his burned hands seized the mike from Niki.

The first news was that *Polar Star* had arrived and was waiting for them out in open water. There was a cheer at this; Laure caught Alice's eye and gave her a meaningful thumbs-up signal. Richard impatiently gestured for quiet. He was telling the Chilean leader that he needed the helicopters to be ordered out as soon as possible, to lift the Kandahar personnel to a point out on the ice margin from which the *Polar Star*'s Zodiacs could reach them.

The Chilean leader's response was concerned but conservative. He was not prepared to risk both helicopters in a hazardous mission—one would have to remain at Santa Ana as a safety back-up. The Squirrel only carried four passengers so it would have to make three return journeys to the ship, unless some people made the difficult journey out over the ice by skidoo. The immediate weather forecast was bad, he said, so it was unlikely in any event that the pilots would be able to leave for at least another twenty-four hours.

'I am sorry, Kandahar, I know you are in trouble. We will get to you just as soon as possible.'

'We have field rations. We can hold out as necessary,' Richard rejoined, glaring at the circle of

412

intent faces pressing around him. 'Morale is excellent,' he added. Of course, he would not report anything else.

'Very good,' said the Chilean leader warmly.

It was arranged that they would maintain four-hourly radio contact.

'Good luck,' Santa Ana said in signing off.

Everyone was smiling and clasping hands, and patting Niki on the back. He had done a remarkable job to restore the radio equipment and get them back on air so quickly.

'Top man, Nik. Antarctic hero, in fact,' Phil crowed.

Richard nodded. 'It's good,' he kept repeating, but he was outside the group now. The ripples of their relief and elation didn't seem to touch him. Alice watched him duck outside and after a minute she followed. He was standing in the drifts of snow on the margins of the burned-out hut, with his hood pulled forward over his bent head. His damaged hands were muffled in torn mittens.

'Richard?'

He looked round briefly, then resumed his contemplation of the wreckage. 'I've failed,' he said.

'No, you haven't. No one's hurt, we did our work, we completed the full season. The fire was an accident, it's one of those things that just happen.'

If you light dozens of candles in a wooden hut where the atmosphere is so dry that it crackles with static electricity, she thought, and she knew he could hear her thinking it. Richard said no more, but as she studied his face she saw the depths of his misery and self-disgust.

413

She whispered fiercely, 'We're all alive. Lewis Sullavan's values don't matter, rock samples don't matter. All that matters is survival and the power of the human spirit. You of all people should know that. Scott and your grandfather and the others on that expedition were beaten to the Pole and five of them died, but their heroism and will to survive is what the world remembers.'

'Don't ever speak of this and my grandfather in the same breath,' Richard begged her.

It finally dawned on Alice that he never would escape from under the dead weight of his history. It had pressed on him for his entire life and now it was dragging him beneath the smooth surface of reason. She cast around for something positive she could offer him. All the scientists' notes and papers had been burned, their laptop computers and Arturo's weather records and Jochen's incomplete human physiological data. Valentin's ice-core sections had survived along with Laure's penguin samples, buried in the ice cave, but she felt that this comfort was too meagre to offer. Their own rock samples from the Bluff and elsewhere, left in Margaret Mather House, were unaffected by a mere fire, although they were of little scientific value since all the plastic sample bags and labels had melted.

Richard's hours of scratching through the debris had not uncovered the lost Gastropoda.

From the skidoo hut came the sound of Russ banging a spoon on a tin pot. The familiar noise conjured the best days at Kandahar and Alice's heart lurched with affection for the place and sorrow at its destruction. Richard had turned away to conceal his face, but she grabbed his arm and dragged him round to face her again. It suddenly came to her that there was one thing she could say that might make a difference. She stamped her feet and swung her arms, realising that cold had numbed her feet and fingers. 'You are still expedition leader. Lead us. Lead us out of here,' she challenged him.

For a moment it seemed that he hadn't heard.

But then he straightened up and lifted his head. He stood taller, closer, looming over her. An unfamiliar light suffused his cold-stiffened features and the sight of it chilled her. 'Yes,' Richard said.

Alice became aware that there was one other person loitering outside in the searing cold, while all the others had squeezed back into the shelter in search of hot food. It was Rooker. He would not deal well with being made to feel jealous, now or ever. The thought reassured her rather than the opposite. Richard swung past Rook without even looking at him.

'We should get some food while there's some left,' Alice said. The most trivial observations became significant because they were directed at him.

'You were going to tell me something.'

There were voices spilling out of the shelter and a triangular smear of dirty-yellow lamplight at the open door.

She took a breath, an opportunity to consider. 'I will,' she temporised.

The helicopter would lift them across the barrier of ice to the ship and safety. They could walk on the rimed decks together and stare ahead for the first glimpse of Cape Horn. That would be the time to tell him, not here and now outside a hut full of ears and eyes.

'Is that a promise?' He didn't smile and his expression was wary. He had been told too many things in his time that were not good news.

'Yes,' Alice said. She couldn't guess exactly how he would react, but all her senses told her that she could trust him.

They crammed themselves in at the end of one row of bodies. Valentin passed up two plates from which other people had already eaten. The food was a small helping of dried pasta cooked up with a soup cube, and a squeeze of tomato ketchup. It was still hot, that was all that mattered, and they crouched down and spooned it up in hungry silence until the plates were empty again. There was plenty of talk around them and even laughter, after the grimness of the last two days. The forecast for the next afternoon and evening was for light winds and improving visibility. *When*, everyone kept saying, when the chopper arrives, when we get back, instead of *if*. The loss of a season's work, and of the plans for the future based on that work, were briefly forgotten.

Niki had spoken by radio to the captain of *Polar Star*.

The ship lay fourteen miles north-west of Kandahar, in open water beyond the unseasonal ice. It was a short distance, but a serious obstacle as Rooker and Phil had already discovered. The frostbitten tips of Phil's fingers had turned black and hard. He drummed a staccato rhythm with them on the side of his tin mug, causing Laure to shudder and turn away. Phil grinned. He knew that in the end the dead tissue would drop off, leaving new pink skin underneath.

When the helicopter was ready to begin the evacuation, the ship would nose deeper into the pack to bring the Zodiacs within range of ice solid enough for the Squirrel to land on. There might be a few hundred yards of more hazardous ice to cross between helicopter and dinghies, but the Kandahar personnel would be able to deal with that. Alice thought she was the only one who was anticipating the flight and the scramble to the dinghies with a shiver of foreboding.

'They wait for us,' Niki confirmed, nodding in satisfaction over the rim of his tin mug.

To follow the pasta there was a spoonful of instant coffee and a half-mug of hot water for each of them. When he came back with refilled water canisters Russell announced that the supply was slowing to a trickle, either because the pipeline was freezing up or because the glacier lake itself was turning to ice.

'We've only got a few more hours to go,' Rook rallied them. The sky above the hut was black and starless, and a thin, keen wind sliced off the glacier. There were just two full camping canisters of gas left. Without running water, they would have to melt snow for drinking. The gas wouldn't last long under those circumstances.

Reluctantly, they settled as best they could for the third night in their cramped shelter. Niki and Arturo were taking the first radio shift in the generator hut, but even with only seven bodies there wasn't room for everyone to lie down properly. Alice half lay and half sat propped against the icy wall between Laure and Rooker. Rooker's arm came round her shoulders and she let her face rest against him. She pulled her parka

417

over her mouth and throat, and closed her eyes. If she concentrated hard she thought she could just hear his steady heartbeat.

An hour passed. Her feet and legs were cold, and her bones ached from lying on the hard floor. She listened to the sigh and scrape of the others' breathing, and the faint catch of a snore in the back of someone's throat.

How many more hours?

Rook's grip on her loosened and his heavy hand dropped from her arm. He had fallen asleep too.

Alice tried to relax her limbs but they were knotted with cold. She was shivering, and every involuntary tremor brought a fresh little shock of loneliness and fear.

She told herself: *Don't be afraid now, after all this time and when we are about to escape.*

A bigger shudder swept over her, crawled inwards from her knees and elbows, intensified and found a focus in her belly. It turned into a definite knot of pain that tightened and made her gasp. Her eyes widened in the absolute darkness. As abruptly as it had come, the pain faded away again.

No, she thought. This can't be.

Cramp. Indigestion. Food poisoning. Surely one of those?

Anything, please, let it be anything but what she feared.

She bit her lips until that different pain distracted her. Long minutes passed; she had no way of telling how many but it might have been ten or more. Her shoulders finally sagged and her clenched fists uncurled. Her palms were clammy with sweat.

Then it came again. An insistent wave that

418

tightened until she stared, then rolled away and left her prickling with sweat and horror.

Breathe. Think.

If this was the onset of labour, what did that mean?

The birth of a baby, several weeks premature, in this place?

No doctor, no medical supplies, no heat, severely limited water.

Alice levered herself to sit upright, away from the support of Rook's shoulder. *Polar Star* was just a dozen or so miles away. Wait, hope. Daylight and the helicopter would come.

Daylight, the helicopter, she repeated to herself. It became a mantra as she sat and stared at the whirling infinity of darkness.

Daylight, the helicopter.

The radio shift changed. Rooker and Valentin yawned and crawled out into the painful cold, Niki and Arturo bundled back in their place. When the others come back, she calculated, there will be just four more hours until dawn. Then she would beg Phil and Russ to radio Santa Ana and call for the helicopter to leave at first light. If the wind and weather were right. *Please.*

She went back to repeating her mantra. Next to her, Niki fell asleep as if he were curled up on a feather mattress under a quilt of goose down.

*   *   *

These were the longest hours Alice had ever known.

The contractions intensified by stealthy bounds. It became as much as she could do not to cry out as

419

the latest one reached its height. Instead, she gave a series of gasps that ended in a sharp hiss of exhaled breath. As the pain ebbed, her head fell back and hit the metal wall. Droplets of cold sweat stood out on her forehead.

The intervals were now much less than ten minutes.

She heard the sound of boots kicking the ice outside the door, then there was a shaft of bitter cold air striking her as Valentin's head appeared. The shift was changing.

Where was Rook?

Phil swore softly and hauled himself out of sleep, with Russell in his wake. They blundered over the recumbent bodies and made their exit. A big shadow, blacker than the night, slipped in after them. Rook, thank God. He was nestling into his old place, pushing the dormant Niki aside, reaching out for her.

Another contraction started. This time there was no beginning to it, no time to prepare herself. The pain caught her full on and she cried out. Rooker took hold of her shoulders and muttered some wordless question but it was Laure who reared up and snapped on her head torch. The beam shone full in Alice's face.

'*Aleece!*'

The other sleepers were muttering and stirring.

Alice realised how bad she must look from the way Laure sucked in her breath so sharply.

'What?' Rooker demanded in a new, raw voice. 'Alice?'

Laure's head jerked round. 'She is pregnant,' she hissed. 'That is *what. Dîtes-moi, Aleece. Vite.*'

'It has started,' Alice said wearily.

Through his hands that were still supporting her she felt the physical impact of these two pieces of information on Rooker. His body jolted as if he had been punched in the diaphragm. She had time to think *I wish it weren't like this for us* and to glimpse the ring of murky faces with staring eyes and mouths gaping at her in the torchlight. Then the claw of yet another contraction dug into her.

'What's that? She cannot be pregnant. It's not possible.' Richard's loud, shocked voice sawed through her head.

Laure was kneeling over her, gentle hands exploring the dome of her belly and trying to loosen her clothes. Rooker hadn't uttered a word but he drew her closer so that she rested against him. His elbow crooked under her chin and one huge hand cupped her cheek.

'She is,' Laure said curtly.

'Radio Santa Ana for help. Tell them just to get here,' Rooker said over her head. Niki was already moving, shouldering his way past Arturo who squatted against the shed wall.

'*Madre de dios*,' Arturo muttered. 'What will be next? What will the end of this be?' Laure glared at him, then bent over Alice again.

Richard spoke: 'Rooker, I suppose this is your doing, is it?'

Alice's head flopped back as the contraction ebbed away.

'Shoesmith.' Rooker's voice was low, but there was a note in it that made everyone in the shelter breathe in and lower their eyes. 'This is nothing to do with me, you piece of shit. Even if it were, it's none of your business. So keep the fuck out of it. Just stay away from her, and me. I'm telling you

421

now that if you interfere, if you so much as try to touch her, I will rip you to pieces.'

Richard seemed to shrivel, collapsing inside his layers of down clothing. 'You can't talk like that,' he babbled. 'She can't give birth to a baby here. This is Kandahar, it's a scientific research station.'

'Or was. Until you burned it down,' Rooker said.

Laure filled a mug of water and held it to Alice's parched mouth.

Phil bumped in through the doorway. The habitual merriment had drained from his face and his eyes were bulging in disbelief.

'Nik and Russ are trying to raise Santa Ana. Alice, can you . . . ?'

But the question faded away as he looked from her to Rooker and Laure. He whispered, 'I don't know what to do with her. What's a pregnant woman doing here? I've only got mountain first-aid training. I've never had anything to do with babies.'

'She is going to be fine,' Rooker said.

Phil was angry; concern and anxiety made him so. 'She shouldn't *be* here,' he repeated. His head shook from side to side.

Alice struggled to sit upright. She couldn't explain the complicated series of decisions and omissions that had brought her to this point. She wanted to move, the hut was so crowded and the smell of gas and bodies made her feel sick.

'Let me,' she muttered to Rook and he understood at once. Pushing Richard and Phil and the gaping Arturo aside, he helped her to roll on to all fours. The door of the shelter stood ajar and beyond it there was black emptiness. She crawled towards the ebony slice of pure air. Rooker's arm supported her and they broke out of the shelter

422

together. As she stood upright the cold seared her throat.

'What do you need?'

'I want to move around. It's . . .' Another contraction took all her attention. Her face screwed up in concentration and she gasped as it washed over her. But it was easier, better when she was moving around than lying inert and helpless in the smelly hut.

'I'm here,' he said calmly. 'Hold on to me.'

Laure materialised at her other side. Another arm came round her waist. They took one and then two small, delicate steps in the greasy snow.

A round head bobbed at the door of the generator shed. Russell called out, 'Santa Ana say that they'll be airborne as soon as they can. *Polar Star*'s standing by as well.'

Alice lifted her head and looked up. The eastern sky was faintly tinged with grey. It would get light soon.

'Aleece?' Laure urgently whispered. 'Can you tell me how many weeks you think you could be?'

'I worked it out. You know, when I realised. I thought by now, twenty-six. But I must have been wrong. Two months wrong, probably. It could be . . . Perhaps thirty-four weeks. *Oh . . .*'

They stopped their pacing and two pairs of arms supported her as the claws of pain dug in again. The receding wave left her gasping for breath.

'What does that mean, Laure?' Rook demanded.

'I am not certain. I am only a biologist, I know everything about avian embryology, not so much about human gestation. But I believe that a baby at thirty-four weeks has a chance to survive. It will be small, but if there are no breathing difficulties and it can be kept warm . . .'

There was a second's silence.

Rooker broke their slow stride and placed himself squarely in front of her. 'We'll get you out to the ship. There's a doctor on *Polar Star*, oxygen, everything. Alice, I promise.' Laure was still holding her on the other side. Rook took both Alice's hands in his. 'I promise that you and the baby will both be safe.'

The grey light of the rapid polar dawn was flooding towards them over the snow. The glacier and the peaks crowning it were draped with low cloud, but the sea ice and the trapped berg were illuminated, and beyond them, away to the north somewhere, *Polar Star* was riding on the ice margin.

Alice held on to Rooker's hands and looked into his eyes.

There was enough light for her to see the frown groove between his eyebrows, the dark mole on his forehead where the hood of his parka had pulled back. She could feel the slow vice grip of another contraction beginning and she opened her mouth to breathe. The need for reassurance, *his* reassurance, made her ask him in a voice that was hardly more than a gasp, 'How do you know?'

Rooker didn't move. He bent his head so he could see her better. Their mouths were almost touching. Laure was right next to them, Russell had come out of the generator shed, Arturo and Phil were close by with empty water containers. Either the piping or the lake itself was now completely frozen and the trickle of water had stopped. There was a ring of faces gazing at them; instead of tactful and obliterating darkness the daylight now seemed bright enough to dazzle him, yet he felt a pressure

424

to speak that was too strong to resist. The urgency of it filled his mouth. He had to tell her something he had never told anyone else.

He saw Alice's face beginning to screw up in a mask of concentration as the pain flowered yet again. If he didn't speak now, this minute, it might be too late and all the blocked avenues and dead ends of the past would come together to make one huge impenetrable dark obstacle, and that would be his life, and there would never be the light and the sunshine that he was stumbling towards in this polar dawn.

'I know, because I love you,' he said.

'Ah, *ah*.' Alice threw her head back and moaned aloud.

'Breathe, Aleece. Breathe big, like this, *whoo whooooo*,' Laure gabbled. The endless distorted seconds stretched and then Alice's shoulders slumped and her head came forward.

'Because I love you,' Rooker repeated slowly. The words were like a foreign language, scratchy and unwieldy on his tongue, but he had uttered them. Alice never took her eyes off his, she was smiling a wide, drunken smile and her face was wet with tears. There were tears in Laure's eyes, too, and the watching, dismayed men were stunned into a silent tableau with their jerrycans and their smoke-black ripped parkas and their huge mittened hands.

'Walk,' Alice begged. They resumed their slow, lurching steps.

'I love you too,' she whispered. 'Don't leave me.'

Warning recollections skewered Rooker's thoughts. Memories punctured his absorption in this shining moment and all the old black shadows

425

came flooding in on him. 'I won't leave you,' he murmured. 'Not until you and the baby are safe.'

Richard unfolded himself from the skidoo shelter. He moved like a marionette, legs and arms jerking and his head pecking backwards and forwards. 'What's happening? What's happening?' he demanded.

'What do you think? We are taking care of her,' Laure snapped.

'Out here? Shouldn't she lie down?'

'Not if she doesn't want to,' Laure shouted back.

Valentin came and draped his huge parka over the top of Alice's.

Phil brought his sheepskin hat, the warmest any of them owned, and awkwardly pulled it down over her fleece cap. He tucked her sweaty hair under the flaps and held a cup of water to her mouth. 'I don't know what to do,' he repeated. To be caught without practical resources was hard for him.

'Thank you, thank you,' Alice dazedly muttered. The familiar faces swam in and out of her sightline. She was grateful but her body was taking over; all her attention becoming fixed on the huge task at hand so that even Rooker and what he had just told her were pushed to the margins of her mind.

Breathe. Feel the muscular waves inside, wrenching and squeezing, opening up like a mouth to emit a yell of agony.

Niki burst out of the generator hut with his headset askew. 'They are airborne, just now,' he yelled.

'*Grâce à Dieu*,' Laure breathed.

Rooker only nodded. His face was impassive.

They went on walking, small shuffling steps with Alice supported between Rooker's and Laure's linked arms. With each contraction they stopped to let Alice breathe and cry out and roll her head against Rook's shoulder. Her hands clenched so tightly on theirs that it hurt them even through their mittens. There seemed almost no respite now between the gulfs of pain.

The time passed, a long unmeasured crawl, as the helicopter steadily flew south towards Kandahar.

Alice stared down through the fog of agony. Nothing could have prepared her for this, nothing would have convinced her that anything could hurt so much. Her vision blurred, then cleared again. She could suddenly see in minute detail. Between her feet there were snowflakes and crystals, tiny prisms and intricate facets more opulent than the most precious jewels, shirred ice and folds of pure snow, droplets of water that froze into diamonds, and silvery furrows that trapped blue and amethyst shadows. It was a miniature Antarctica that held all the variety and wonder of the harsh immensity that had seduced her.

Antarctica, Antarctica.

The syllables formed a new mantra, rolling and tapping in her head as she tried to breathe instead of drowning in the infinite sea of pain. Her knees were buckling, she could hardly lift her feet. Contraction had merged into contraction until it felt as if she would be torn in pieces. She was moaning and sobbing, beyond any shred of pride or dignity.

Once she caught sight of Valentin biting the knuckles of his own hand, and there was Arturo, watching with his arms wrapped round himself as if for protection against this raw femaleness. Russ

427

and Phil grimly waited with their faces turned to the pearl-grey sky. Niki was on the radio to the incoming pilot.

Richard stood to one side, alone, stiff-backed, his face unreadable.

'Listen,' Phil yelled.

Alice's head drooped but the others' jerked up in unison.

At first it seemed that they must have conjured the sound out of their collective longing, but then it steadied and swelled. It was the unmistakable distant buzz of the helicopter.

'Thank Christ,' Phil whispered.

Rooker allowed himself a backward glance, over his shoulder towards the sea ice and the distance that shrouded *Polar Star*.

What he saw, what he didn't see, almost stopped his heart.

There was no berg visible in the bay. There was no bay at all, no ice, no ragged glacier tongue or familiar line of serrated peaks. All there was was a wall of thick grey sea mist, stealthily rolling in on them. Moist, cold air that would condense and turn to a layer of ice on whatever it touched.

Ahead, in the direction of Santa Ana, the sky was clouded but the air was still clear. A black dot had materialised against the greyness. Russ and Phil were hastily laying out red canisters and parkas to give an improvised landing square some extra definition for the pilot.

'Just a few minutes now, darling,' Laure murmured to Alice. 'We will take you safe to the ship.'

The roar of the helicopter drowned out their voices. As they gazed upwards, their exposed faces stinging from the whirl of ice crystals whipped up by the blades, the mist was already billowing over the ruins of Kandahar. The machine hovered, then slowly sank to the ground. The others shielded their eyes from the blizzard; Alice's head was sunk on her chest; Laure and Rooker turned their faces aside as they supported her. The pilot cut the engines and the blades spun to a standstill. Silence descended.

The pilot leaped out in his red overalls and flying helmet, and ran towards their little group. 'How is she?'

'I think not long,' Laure said.

Rooker hoisted Alice towards the helicopter. He knew that there wasn't even one second to spare. She stumbled, hanging on to him but trying to help herself. 'Let's go,' he was shouting. 'Come on, get her in and get it off the ground.'

The pilot was Andy. He was shaking his head, shouting and pointing over Rooker's shoulders. Rook didn't try to catch the words, he already knew what he was saying. He lifted Alice off her feet and somehow ran the last few steps to the Squirrel with her in his arms. The Kandahar people were running in his wake, pushing Andy and Richard aside in the rush. Richard and the pilot were conferring, their heads bobbing and their hands waving as they looked out into the wall of mist and back at the helicopter.

Alice found herself in the rear seat of the Squirrel. Her head rolled on the seat back, then she shuddered and clenched her fists. A different feeling swept over her, not a pain any longer but an irresistible compulsion. 'Need to push.' She thought she was saying it aloud, but the words didn't escape her mouth. 'Help me.'

Andy shouted, 'I can't take off now. Look at the mist. Vis can't be more than sixty metres, it can't be done. It's too dangerous.'

Laure had had one foot on the door sill, ready to scramble in after Alice. Now she turned and looked back at the huddle of parkas and overalls. She hesitated, then slowly stepped back down to the ice. The Kandahar people milled around Richard and Andy. There was a blur of arms and faces and a babble of voices.

Rooker ran to Andy. He caught him by the shoulders and tried to propel him towards the Squirrel. 'Get in now. Fly it.'

Andy swept his hand towards the mist. 'Look at it. It would be suicide . . .'

Richard seemed to wake up. 'No one goes anywhere. No one flies in these conditions. I am the leader of this expedition and I *will* lead it. I forbid you to fly.'

If Alice had heard him she might have reflected that it was Richard's ironic destiny not to lead them anywhere, but to insist that they stayed put. But Alice was out of earshot and trying with shuddering breaths to control the imperatives of her body.

The pilot rubbed his beard with the back of his hand, clear regret in his eyes. 'He's right, mate. I'm sorry.'

'I'll fly it myself,' Rooker shouted.

He swung round and made for the Squirrel. Inside it he could see Alice's bent head. Richard and Andy grabbed his arms but he shook them off like flies. A second later he was buckling himself into the pilot's seat.

'Stop him,' Richard howled at the Kandahar

430

people. But without any conferring a collective impulse had taken hold of the team. It was Richard they moved in on. Valentin and Phil pinioned his arms, Russ took hold of the collar of his parka, the others blocked his path. Richard fought and struggled but he was outnumbered. The astonished pilot stood aside, his mouth hanging open.

Inside the Squirrel, Rooker deliberately slowed his mind to make a series of cold calculations.

Ice. It was ice that could kill them, just as always.

The helicopter had been on the ground for no more than three or four minutes but already the thick, wet mist was beginning to freeze on the fuselage and blades. Once the Squirrel was iced up, take-off would be impossible. They would all be trapped with no hope of escape until the mist lifted and the machine could be de-iced. There was no food on the base, practically no water, only the supplies that were loaded in the helicopter's stowage section.

There was no time to unload anything. He had to get airborne right now and up above the mist bank before the air intakes froze up and the engines lost power. He had to fly Alice to the ice margin and get her into the *Polar Star*'s Zodiac, then bring the Squirrel back to Kandahar. The mist was thickening, but he rated his chances higher than Andy's. He knew the terrain around the base more intimately, and he had already made the journey to the sea and back.

Fly. He could fly, it was in him, his first instructor had told him so.

'*Rook.*' There was raw desperation in her voice.

'I'm going to pilot us.'

'Do you know how to?'

431

'Of course I do.'

He ran his eyes over the unfamiliar instruments and controls in a deliberate slow sequence. Yes. Start it up: switch on batteries and fuel pump, check voltage, start up both engines. The blades shivered and obediently spun, and through the white murk Rooker saw the Kandahar people scatter backwards. Laure's hands were at her mouth. He gave the engines a thirty-second warm-up and accelerated towards flying speed. The Squirrel shivered on its skids. Even over the roar of the engines he heard Alice give a series of gasping cries. He raised the collective lever and the machine lifted as if it were tiptoeing on the snow. Thank God, the skids were free. Rooker accelerated and lifted into a low hover. They were airborne. Check temperature, pressure and power. Visibility was now down to about fifty metres.

Alice raised herself into a half-crouch. Her last glimpse of Kandahar was a semicircle of gaping, upturned, familiar faces. Their arms were raised and although she knew in one corner of her mind that they were protecting their eyes from the storm of snow, it looked as if they were waving in a salute or a blessing.

The helicopter swung in a tight circle and headed out over the sea ice.

Rooker needed every particle of concentration for flying and navigation by instruments alone. It was like being airborne in a bowl of milk. There was no room for even the faintest flicker of uncertainty or self-doubt. He eased the machine into a steady ascent and at 110 metres a dirty-yellow glimmer began to suffuse the milk. A few seconds later they rose out of the fog bank into thin

432

sunshine. The fog undulated beneath them, a billowing cloud that stretched to the lemon-yellow horizon. Fourteen miles to the north-east somewhere lay *Polar Star*.

Rooker lifted the pilot's headset and pulled it over his head. At once Niki's thick voice filled his ears with directions. It was good. He was dead on course for the ship. 'The Zodiac is launched. They look for you on the ice,' Niki said.

'Thank you, Kandahar.'

He had a second's respite now to look over his shoulder to Alice. Her eyes were starting, and her face was shiny with sweat and tears.

'It's coming. Help me.'

'Hold on.'

'I can't. Stop. Please, stop.'

The wind was getting up. Below them, the mist was now streaming in thin tatters. Rooker caught a glimpse of the ridged pack ice far beneath. Under his layers of matted clothing a cold sweat chilled his back. He swallowed and eased the Squirrel back into a descent. The ice loomed up to meet him. He glimpsed ragged frozen waves and searched desperately for a smoother trough between them. They were skimming over a solid blue-grey sea. Then he caught sight of a flat grey saucer that measured little more in diameter than the Squirrel itself. Sweating, hardly able to breathe, he hovered and with a wordless prayer put the helicopter down. It rocked alarmingly but the ice surface held.

Alice was making low noises in her throat. He told her to lie back across the rear seats and bend her knees. Struggling in the awkward space, they dragged down her torn windproofs and soaked underlayers.

Rooker shouted into the headset mouthpiece, *'Polar Star, Polar Star?'*

He could see the baby's head. It was wet and black, and netted with blood and mucus. Alice was staring and pushing and as she did so the oval of head swelled in the birth canal.

A Spanish voice broke in on him: 'NZ two-zero, do you read me?'

'I read you.'

'What is happening, please?'

'The baby is being born. I can see the head.'

'Okay. Listen to me. Let her push. Put your left hand on the baby's head, use your right hand to support the mother's tissues underneath.'

It was the *Polar Star*'s doctor. Rook did as he was told but he could see that Alice's body knew what to do. She had stopped groaning and the terror had faded out of her eyes. Now there was a fierce light of absolute determination. A contraction passed and she rested with her chin sunk on her chest. The doctor's voice crackled in his ear but Rooker ignored it.

'Good.' He smiled at her. 'I'm here. Wait for the next one, then push.'

She sucked in a deep breath. 'Here it comes.' Her jaw clenched and her eyes squeezed shut. Through his hands Rook felt the clench of muscles as the baby's head was born. He cupped his hand to support and protect it, gazing down in wonder at the tiny features. He had nothing within reach with which to wipe the blood and mucus from its nasal passages, so he gently did it with the tips of his fingers.

Here was a new person, a whole new life beginning in this instant.

He had never known anything so natural and simple, and yet so momentous. His heart was swelling and he had to stare even harder to keep his tears from blinding him.

'Is it there?' Alice whispered.

'I can see its face.'

'Again,' she panted, then gave a long wail of triumphant effort.

Gently, with his left hand, Rooker eased out the slippery hunched shoulders and the folded limbs. The baby lay in his two palms, wet with blood and amniotic fluid. She opened her deep, dark eyes and gave a tiny ragged cry.

'It's a girl.'

'Margaret,' Alice said.

They were both weeping.

'NZ two-zero, can you hear me?' the insistent voice went on. 'Come in, please.'

'Yes,' Rooker croaked. He lifted the tiny creature and laid her on Alice's belly.

Alice cupped her hands round her child's head and bottom, and cradled her close to her body's warmth, and he stripped off his parka and fleece jacket and tucked it over them. Alice was laughing as well as crying. 'Meg,' she was murmuring.

Beyond the windscreen of the Squirrel the mist rose like steam as the sun strengthened. The ice all around their small saucer and as far as he could see was chopped into frozen waves and crazily welded floes. But there was no time for more than the briefest glance to get his bearings. Rook looked for the helicopter's emergency survival kit and found it stored against the fuselage behind the rear seats. He broke the seal, tore off the lid and saw what he was looking for. He shook out the silvery folds of

435

an insulated bivouac shelter and wrapped that over and round the baby as well. 'The baby's born,' he said into the headset.

'Are they both all right?'

'Yes.' It felt like the most significant word he had ever uttered. 'What do I do now?'

He listened as the doctor advised him how to deliver the placenta and did exactly as he was told.

'Don't try to cut the cord,' the voice ordered. So he wrapped the baby and the cord and the afterbirth in a warm bloody muddle against Alice's body, and wound them in clothes and the folds of the shelter.

'Now you fly them out to us,' the doctor said. 'Good luck.'

Rooker quickly leaned over Alice and looked into her eyes. 'You did well. Are you ready now?'

'I'm ready.' Her face was soft and beautiful, and full of trust.

'Good. Let's go.'

Anxiety about what he had to do next was rising in his mouth like bile. He swung across into the pilot's seat and opened the door to clamber down on to the pack. He couldn't even try to lift off again without checking to see how much ice had formed on the Squirrel. And what he saw next made his throat close and his hands shake. There was a dark, serpentine thread winding through the ivory and grey monotony of the pack ice. It was a polynya, a little crack through which water came welling up. The weight of the Squirrel had depressed the flat floe and the sea water had flooded up over the skids. And now it had frozen over them in a thin, glassy layer of pure menace.

Mist drifted gently over the world of ice like a

legion of ghosts.

He climbed back into the pilot's seat, shivering without his outer clothes. He started up the engines and uttered a soundless, wordless prayer. All he could do was use the engine power to break the seal of ice and pray to God that both skids came free at the same time. If one came loose before the other and the machine tilted by more than fifteen degrees, the blades would strike the ice and send them all cartwheeling into oblivion.

Rook pulled on the headset once again. Alice lay wrapped in her silver cocoon behind him.

'Preparing for take-off, *Polar Star*,' he said through clenched teeth.

Here we go.

He raised the collective lever and the machine trembled and tried to lift off. At once it began to list to the left and he hastily lowered the lever again. The right skid was now free but the left was still solid. The only option left to him was to try again with less power but more yaw. He swallowed hard and gave the left pedal almost full deflection as the engine screamed and the machine juddered and vibrated. Alice said something in a voice sharp with alarm. Suddenly the trapped skid tore free of the ice, and the machine soared into the air and spun through 180 degrees to face in the direction they had come. It lurched and tilted crazily as Rooker fought the yaw pedals to regain control, but now they were airborne.

'What's happening?' Alice screamed.

It was another five seconds before he could answer her. He gripped the stick and they rose steadily through the wreaths of mist.

When he did speak his voice was almost steady.

437

'Nothing to worry about. Not the easiest take-off.'

He flew onwards. Then suddenly there was grey water in the distance, flecked with ice like foam, and dead ahead through the screen he saw the paler grey superstructure and red funnels of the *Polar Star*. There was a black smudge down on the ice margin, surrounded by half a dozen tiny orange specks.

'Look,' he said and pointed.

*   *   *

He set the Squirrel down for the second time, a safe distance from the open water. The sailors were already running towards them across the waves of ice. Two of them were carrying the poles of a stretcher. They reached the helicopter and there was a babble of Spanish voices giving orders. Big gloved hands lifted Alice and the baby in their silver blanket, and laid them gently on the unfurled canvas of the stretcher.

'Rook,' she called, twisting her head to see him.

He rested his hand on her head as the phalanx hurried over the ice. 'I'm here.'

'Come back quickly.'

He couldn't meet her eyes. 'You'll be safe now.'

Another sailor was standing in the stern of the Zodiac. The big outboard motor was already revving and churning the iron-grey water of a lead in the ice. They reached the black rubber side of the dinghy. Sailors in float suits stepped and balanced all round them as they prepared to lift the stretcher. Alice fought to free one arm and caught Rooker's wrist. She pulled his hand to her mouth and kissed it.

438

A wave of terrible emotion flooded over him.

He remembered the moment of purity and innocence amidst the panic as the baby was born. He wanted to sink down next to her stretcher and pull her into his arms, and tell her the truth and never have to run or hide or fight ever again. He wanted to hold her and the baby, and keep them safe from whatever the world could do. Most of all he wanted to tell her the truth.

He stood stock-still, ignoring the precarious ice and the jostling sailors and their imprecations, not even noticing the cold any more. There were tears in his eyes and on his cheeks.

'You will come as soon as you can? Rook? *Answer me.*'

He took a deep, burning, painful breath. 'Alice. I can't follow you. It isn't right. I am not right.'

Sailors' arms and legs kept getting in the way, blocking their sight.

'You must.'

He lowered his voice. 'You don't know me. You don't know what I've done. A man died because of me. I am a murderer.'

There wasn't even a beat. 'I don't care,' she screamed. 'I don't care what or who you are. I love you.'

But it was too late. They prised her hands away from him and folded her into her coverings. Rook stepped back and watched the sailors lifting her stretcher and placing it in the bottom of the Zodiac. She was sobbing and trying to sit up, clutching Meg, and there were huge boots clumping around her as the men clawed their way off the ice and perched themselves on the pontoon, until only one remained on the ice.

439

He put his arm across Rooker's shoulders. *'Adiós,'* he said, not unkindly, and pushed him back towards the helicopter. Then without another glance he leaped to join his companions. The boatman immediately opened the throttle and the Zodiac nosed away through the ice-thick water. Rooker couldn't see anything of her, but he didn't take his eyes off the dinghy until it reached the ship's side. The seamen clambered up the metal stairway, a line of fat orange matchstick men, but the dinghy itself and the boatman and their cargo were winched straight up on to the deck of *Polar Star*. Only then did Rooker finally, slowly, turn away.

He strapped himself into the pilot's seat and pulled on the headset. With absolute brutality he made himself think of nothing but what must be done to make a safe return to Kandahar. Batteries, fuel pump. Start up both engines. The Squirrel's blades spun again. 'NZ two-zero, airborne,' he muttered.

The voice of *Polar Star*'s radio operator came right back at him. 'Good luck,' he repeated.

Alice saw the ship's mast and funnels looming crazily over her, and there were faces and the backs of heads, then the cream-painted walls and booming stairways of the interior. Meg's tiny wet body lay in a sticky morass on her belly but she was alive, stirring, and her cry was a bleat that sounded louder in her mother's head than all the shouting in Spanish and the racing footsteps and banging of heavy steel doors.

An indoor draught of hot air hit Alice full in the face. It stank of oil and paint and food and disinfectant, so much stronger than anything she

440

had smelled in months that she almost retched. Another door opened ahead of her and she was borne into a clean, quiet white space. Spanish voices told her to be ready and then she was lifted on to a bed. A man's face came into view. He looked odd until she realised that it was only because he was soap-pink, and plump, and clean-shaven.

'You have given us quite a big surprise,' the doctor said.

* * *

When the cord was tied and cut, and Alice had been stitched, and Meg had been examined and warmed on a heated pad, and wrapped in linen cloths and warm towels, the doctor gave her back to Alice to hold. She was entirely swaddled except for her small, composed face. For what seemed a very long time, suspended between awe and amazement, Alice studied her stipple of black eyelashes and the scoop of flesh that formed her nose and the precise bud of her mouth. A jerky tape of the helicopter and Rook's stricken face played inside her head, and shock and relief made the breath catch in her throat as she held the white bundle close.

'I think all right, both of you, to put you on the aeroplane,' the doctor pronounced at last.

Alice lifted her head to stare at him. Pieces of the world, little fragments of awareness, were sliding back into place. She realised that she could hear the throb of the ship's engines. 'Where are we going?'

'To Santa Ana,' the doctor said, staring a little.

441

'And then, I think they make you a flight to Santiago. We have no facility on the ship . . .'

She looked around her with a sudden falling-away sensation. *'Santiago?'* Wait. The pilot . . . the helicopter pilot. Where is he? I have to speak to him. I thought the ship would wait for the other people to come aboard from Kandahar . . .'

The doctor shook his head.

Alice grabbed at his wrist. 'Why not?'

Her vehemence made him demur, 'I am only the medical man. I will find someone to tell you.'

The ship's first officer knocked and came in. He wore a white shirt with epaulettes, the buttons straining over his generous paunch. He told Alice that the helicopter had landed again at Kandahar.

'Thank you,' she managed to whisper, over the disablement of relief.

The man twinkled at her. 'You are VIP, I think.'

'What do you mean?'

'We have already urgent radio instructions from the big man, we are straight to Santa Ana and a special plane for you and the baby, all the way to hospital in Santiago.'

The big man.

Alice struggled to tease some sense out of the tide of bewilderment. It must be Lewis Sullavan. 'And the others?'

The officer almost shrugged. 'Another ship. Maybe one, two days. But by then you will be in a safe place. By order.' He patted her hand and turned down a corner of the wrappings in order to gaze benignly at Meg's sleeping face.

Alice let her head rest against the pillows. She stared unseeingly at the metal cupboards that lined the walls of the ship's clinic, the stainless-steel sinks

442

and the square of colourless Antarctic sky beyond the square porthole.

'Please will you thank everyone for me? The sailors on the Zodiac and the radio operator and the captain. Everyone,' she repeated.

The officer patted her hand again. 'It is not every day,' he murmured.

When he had gone and the doctor was at his desk in the corner writing notes, Alice shut her eyes. The tape instantly started playing its jerky scenes again and she knew that she would be living with them for a long time yet.

She could hear his voice too, a desperate low exclamation, *I am a murderer.*

She had answered, *I don't care what or who you are. I love you.*

That was the simple truth.

CHAPTER SIXTEEN

Midway through the flight from Madrid to Heathrow the Sullavanco PR woman turned to Alice. 'There may be some press at the airport. You don't have to say anything, of course. But there will be photographers. Just so you're ready, okay?'

'I see,' Alice replied.

The PR woman, who introduced herself as Lisa, had met them off the plane from Santiago and escorted them to the London flight. She offered to carry Meg to the departure gate, but Alice declined.

In the five days since they had flown out of

443

Antarctica she had never let the baby out of her sight and most of the time she had held her in her arms. Meg slept and cried her small mewing cry, and Alice watched her and fed her, realising in bewilderment that she had hardly unwrapped the first layer of the package that she and Rook had delivered into the world. Sometimes, in the hazy midday sunshine of her room at the Clinica Providencia in Santiago, she felt confident that they would come to know each other in good time. At others, mostly in the lonely small hours when Meg was asleep and she lay staring at the small picture of the Virgin on the wall opposite her bed, she wondered in terror how she would ever find a mother's instincts within herself after the way it had all begun.

The ship had taken her to Santa Ana and as the second day of Meg's life dawned they went ashore in the Zodiac again. This time she carried the baby wrapped in layers of ship's blankets. She refused a stretcher, but most of the Chilean personnel came out anyway to help her walk the few metres up to the base. When she was ensconced in the living area one or two of them shyly asked if they could take photographs of her holding Meg. Alice nodded distractedly; all she could think of was how to contact Rooker back at Kandahar.

'Please try to raise them for me,' she begged Miguel, the radio operator. 'Please? Now?'

The Chilean leader was explaining that a Dash-7 chartered by Lewis Sullavan was on its way from Punta Arenas to collect her and would land at the permanent ski-way in about two hours' time. Sullavan had sent a radio message, would she like to read it?

444

Alice was amazed. Less than twenty-four hours had elapsed since Meg's arrival, but from wherever he was in the world Lewis was already dealing with matters. Or his people were. All this would be for Margaret's sake, she guessed, and long-ago memories.

He sent his congratulations, adding that they were no less warm for being unexpected, and his best wishes for both Alice's good health and the baby's, following the dramatic circumstances of her arrival. (Lewis evidently knew all the details.) She was to allow him the privilege of making arrangements for them from now on. Professor Peel and Dr Mather were being informed of her whereabouts, and she would of course be able to speak to them from Santiago. In the meantime, so that she could rest and recover, it would be simpler if she were to let Sullavanco do any talking that might be necessary.

What talking? Alice wondered in surprise, before she put the message aside. She wasn't thinking properly yet even about Trevor and Margaret. All that mattered were her daughter and the radio connection to Kandahar.

The minutes crawled while she drank tea and waited. The Santa Ana people had improvised a cradle for Meg out of a cardboard carton lined with towels and in order not to seem ungrateful she laid the baby in it. Her sleeping face was a pucker of closed-up features with one fist pressed against her mouth. The men gathered round and peered at her, awkwardly smiling. Mike, the second helicopter pilot, Miguel and the leader were the only ones who spoke English.

Miguel's head came round the connecting door

445

to the radio room. 'If you like to talk . . .'

Alice stumbled forward.

Niki's voice greeted her. 'You are well, and lucky, I hear.'

She gasped, 'Nik . . . oh, Nik, are you all right, all of you?'

'A little cold, a little hungry, but not so bad. *Polar Star* will come back or maybe another ship, but first we must have no mist in order to fly.'

Alice tripped over the words in her anxiety. 'That's good, I mean, not good that you're still there. I'm sorry I took the ship away and everything. Nik, please, I need to speak to Rooker. Is he there? Over.'

'He is waiting here.'

In her mind's eye she saw the generator hut and the improvised table and the tilley lamp hanging from the hook overhead. And Rook's face.

'Alice. Can you hear me?' His familiar voice sounded remote.

'I'm here. Tell me. I know you landed, but the flight back, was it all right? Over.'

'It was less eventful.'

'Rook. Thank you for everything you did.'

The words were so dry and colourless. She could only pray that he knew what lay behind them. She closed her eyes on a sudden rush of tears, then opened them again to see the blurred clutter of the Chilean radio room. Two hundred miles of ice already separated them, and soon the distance would stretch to thousands more.

She said urgently, 'When you get out of there, will you come to England?'

There was a static silence and she glanced in dismay at Miguel before Rook's voice finally cut in again. 'I told you something, do you remember?'

'I don't care, it doesn't matter, all that matters is now. *Please.*' She couldn't contain the explosion of sobs. Tears ran down her face as a flood of exhaustion and confusion and grief swept through her.

'It matters to me. Look after Meg, and yourself. Goodbye, Alice.'

'*No,*' she howled. Miguel's hand descended and uncertainly patted her shoulder.

A second later Niki's voice came back again. 'Santa Ana, Santa Ana. Weather report, please.'

She handed over the mike and pressed the flat of her hands into her eyes. The dressing that the *Polar Star* doctor had put on her arm must be too tight because the veins throbbed in her wrist. Someone came and led her away from the radio room and someone else gave her another mug of sweet hot tea.

Two hours later they were in the air. The plane swept her away from Rooker and Antarctica.

*   *   *

Her room in the private hospital was full of flowers. There were scarlet and flame lilies with fiercely speckled throats, lush purple orchid stems and the spiky black and orange heads of birds-of-paradise, all from Sullavanco. In the car from the airport she had seen huge trees in the city parks, their leaves beginning to turn with autumn colours. There were skyscraper buildings all shining with glass and steel, lines of traffic steaming in the heat, shop windows crowded with goods. She had forgotten that the ordinary world held so much variety, and noise and

447

relentless activity. There was too much *detail*, and she turned her head from it and looked down at Meg instead.

Her doctor at the Clinica was a young woman called Cecilia Vicente. She had thick, glossy black hair held back with tortoiseshell combs, and serious brown eyes. She gave Meg a thorough examination. She weighed only just over four pounds but she was having no problems with her breathing, she was alert and she would soon begin to gain weight. The baby was in good health, considering the circumstances of her birth. It was Dr Vicente's opinion that she had been delivered about five or six weeks before full term.

'We will watch her carefully for one or two days. But I am not very worried about this little girl,' she announced. 'Now let us take a look at her mother. Would you like to tell me the details about how you came to give birth in Antarctica?'

Alice did her best to explain. The doctor listened as she examined her, nodding once in a while. At the end she said, 'I see. I suppose this makes some just-about sense. I had thought at first that you must be a kind of a crazy person.' The doctor had a smile like the sun coming out and Alice found herself smiling back at her. It was the first time in days that she hadn't immediately winced with the pain of cold-cracked lips.

It was, Dr Vicente explained, not quite the only time in history that a woman had miscalculated her dates by as much as two months. The first time Alice had bled might have been caused by the implantation of the embryo, and the second much heavier loss a little more than a month later had almost certainly been a threatened miscarriage.

'But here we are. Your daughter is a determined creature. She is born with determination in her bones, a true survivor.' Yes, Alice thought. She will be Margaret's granddaughter in all that.

The doctor stripped off her rubber gloves but instead of putting her hands into the pockets of her white coat and bustling away to the next patient, she sat down on the end of Alice's bed. For a minute they both looked out in silence at the opposite wing of the Spanish colonial clinic building.

'How do you feel?' Cecilia asked.

Once, before Antarctica, Alice might have answered that she was fine. And as far as her body and her immediate circumstances were concerned it was the case. She was exhausted and the cut on her arm was slightly infected. She had perineal stitches that made it agony to sit down and her breasts ached and leaked with milk, but she was alive and the wounds would heal. Meg was going to be all right and they were lying in a warm sunny room banked with flowers sent by Lewis Sullavan. She had much to be grateful for, but she was not all right.

The loop of images from the helicopter journey and the birth and the events before and after kept going round and round in her head. The more they repeated themselves the more she realised how desperate it had all been, and the faster the what-if scenarios multiplied. These thoughts made her shudder with delayed terrors.

Meg might have been born dead, or strangled by the cord, or she herself might have haemorrhaged. They might have crashed in the mist, or overturned on the ice, and all three of them would have died.

449

She was only just comprehending the risks Rooker had taken for her sake. The more she thought about it the more she longed for him and the bigger the vacuum of his absence became. She had to learn to be a mother and go home to a life that could never be the same as the one she had known, and she didn't know how she was going to do any of this without him.

It became important to try to answer Cecilia Vicente's question without the old automatic defensiveness, but Alice was afraid that if she talked too much she would cry and never be able to stop. Whenever she was alone tears that tasted of longing filled her eyes.

'Bewildered' was what she finally said.

The doctor put her hand over Alice's. It was smooth, lightly tanned, with short oval nails and a thin gold wedding band, and her own was rough and chapped, with the torn nails surrounded by half-healed fissures from working in the ice.

'Where is the baby's father?'

'He is in England. But we are not together.'

'Does that mean you are alone?'

'I have parents, good friends.' She paused. How to tell anyone, who had not been with them in Antarctica, about Rooker?

Her heart contracted with a beat of longing for Kandahar and the realms of ice, and all the people who had been there. For all of them, even poor Richard. Perhaps for Richard even more than the others, except for Rooker, because she knew and understood the heat and despair within his own layers of ice.

'There is someone, the man who flew us out to the ship and delivered my baby. But he is not a

450

person you can . . . put reins on.'

The doctor nodded her head. 'I want you to remember that you have had a shock. A physical shock, yes, of course, but also an emotional one. You are too suddenly a mother but I believe there has always been a denial in you about this child, or you would not have been able to keep it so far to the back of your mind that you allowed yourself to become trapped on your base. Am I right, Alice?'

She thought about the past.

Pete, Margaret, Oxford. Science, the vast but measurable geological aeons, thesis and proof, self-control, quiet acceptance of her mother's power. Trevor's awareness, passed on to her, of how small individual human concerns appeared when you set them against the immensities of time and nature.

Now there was Rooker; passion that was held somewhere at bay but which still had the power to overwhelm her and a hunger in her that she hadn't yet learned how to assuage.

Finally, in a burst of terror and wonder, the birth of her child. She had felt the absolutely imperative and uncontrollable impulses of her own womb. The unexpected birth of an unplanned baby was the antithesis of everything that had happened in her life before and nothing would be the same again.

Alice automatically turned her head to gaze at Meg, asleep in the crib beside the bed. Devotion shone through her confusion and the doctor saw all this.

Alice said, 'Yes. You are right.'

'And so it will take a little time for you to adjust and accept that this is what has happened to you. You will feel panic and fear that you cannot do what you know you must.'

451

'I suppose so.'

'I have seen many, many mothers with their newborn babies. I think, I believe, all will be well for the two of you.'

'Thank you,' Alice said.

'Try to sleep, or at least to rest. I would like you to stay here maybe for three or four days, while we observe your Margaret. Is that possible?'

'Of course, if that's what is best for her,' she answered unhesitatingly.

Later that day the telephone rang beside her bed.

'Alice? Is that you?' From halfway across the world her mother's crisp voice was instantly recognisable. 'I must say, I would have preferred a little more warning before becoming a grandmother.'

'I know. You'll have some knitting to catch up on.'

This was such an outlandish idea that they both burst into laughter and everything was all right. Margaret wanted her daughter to come home, and she was deeply excited about her granddaughter and namesake, and her voice gave as much away even though she couldn't quite frame the words.

Then Trevor came on. 'Ali, I am concerned about you,' he said.

'Don't be. Meg is beautiful and I'm longing to show her to you. I'll be home soon and we can talk then until we're hoarse.'

'What about Peter? He rang this morning, he was frantic for news of you.'

'He's her father. We'll have to work out between us what that means.'

There was so much to tell Trevor, all of it

impossible on the telephone. Then a thought struck her. 'How does Pete know? Did you tell him?'

Trevor said, 'Your mother and I haven't spoken to anybody. A young woman from Mr Lewis Sullavan's organisation telephoned to advise us against it. But, darling, it's not a secret. In fact, you should get ready to be famous.'

'*What?*'

'You're in Sullavan's paper this morning. The rest of 'em'll be following suit. The baby's hit the headlines as the First European Citizen of Antarctica and you are Dramatic Snow Birth Heroine. Or some such,' he concluded drily. 'There are even pictures of you and Meg on the Internet.'

Alice fell back against her pillows. She hadn't reckoned with this, but now she realised her naivety. Of course Lewis's generosity with chartered planes and private clinics would have a double edge, and that edge was forthcoming publicity for Kandahar and the joint European Antarctic programme. The first season had ended in disaster, which meant there would be no scientific discoveries, glamorous or even routine. A heart-warming human-interest story laced with helicopter action and heroism was exactly and perfectly what Lewis needed. It was providence.

'Oh, God,' she said faintly. The pictures taken by the Chileans while she was dazedly waiting at Santa Ana must be the ones that had found their way on to the net.

'Mmm. But don't worry too much, old thing. Next week's chip wrappings, you know.'

'Let's hope so.'

Later, when Alice was dozing after Meg had

453

finally fed herself into milky tranquillity, the phone rang again. She snatched it up, hoping against the odds. But this time she heard a voice that had the colour and consistency of golden syrup; a familiar voice although not the one she longed to hear.

'This is Beverley Winston.'

'Yes.'

Don't even think about jealousy. To be jealous of other women where Rooker was concerned would be to condemn herself to a life of agony. How had she described him to Cecilia? As a man you can't put reins on.

And that was if she were ever to see him again. *I will*, somehow, she resolved, as she did over and over in her waking hours. When she slept he filled her dreams.

Beverley wanted to know whether she was comfortable, whether she had everything she wanted, that the medical attention was good enough, how the baby was getting on. Alice thanked her and insisted that all was well and then thanked her again. Beverley asked in a friendly, concerned way about the flight from Kandahar and the birth. Alice thought for a second, then answered her questions. If there were going to be stories about her in Lewis's newspapers and magazines, they might as well be factually accurate. Her voice only grew warmer, and she couldn't help it, when she described what Rooker had done.

'Yes. Very daring, but perhaps not the most advisable course of action, on the face of it. To make off with a company-leased helicopter in weather conditions considered too dangerous by the authorised pilot.'

This time Alice didn't think. 'To hell with the

company,' she said.

'Did you like the flowers, by the way?' Beverley asked after only a second's delay.

'Wonderfully gaudy. After the visual purity of Antarctica, you know.'

'That's good. Well, now, I won't disturb you any more. If I might just beg you to let us take all the responsibility for dealing with media requests. It is a lovely story, of course. Everyone will want to know about you.'

Will they? Or will Sullavanco just make sure that they do know?

'It's no big deal, surely? She's by no means the first baby to be born inside the Antarctic circle.' It was true that Argentinian and Chilean babies had been born in remote southern communities, partly as a form of territorial marker.

'She is the first European on a European base, and she is Margaret Mather's grandchild.'

Of course.

'Beverley, there is something I would really like you to help me with.'

The suggestion of a bargain to be struck quivered between them.

'What's that?'

'Where is Rooker now? And the others? Where can I reach him and how can I speak to him?'

She would trade her story for information. Beverley briefly weighed this up, then murmured, 'Of course, you don't know, do you? They were all finally lifted out of Kandahar this morning and transferred to another ship. They are at sea now, I gather.'

So they were all safe. And what remained of Kandahar lay deserted, under the pristine blanket of fresh winter snow.

'The ship's name? And I'm sure that the Polar Office must have an address where he can be reached?'

'The best way to handle it would be an exclusive interview with a young journalist, the one I am thinking of is very good and totally sympathetic, and some lovely mother and baby pictures.'

'The ship? And an address?'

'It's the *Southern Mariner*. And I do believe Rooker gave us an address down in Ushuaia, and a reference from, ah, a building company. I don't have either to hand, I'm afraid.'

Alice smiled, even though her jaw ached with the tension of this exchange.

'I'd be so glad if you could get them for me. And then I don't see why there should be a problem about an interview and a couple of pictures. If you think anyone is likely to be that interested?'

'Excellent,' Beverley said quickly and rang off.

For two days Alice struggled to establish ship-to-shore contact with the *Southern Mariner*, but it was a ramshackle-sounding cargo vessel registered in Liberia and it didn't include a satellite telephone amongst its amenities.

On the third day Alice and Meg were discharged from the Clinica Providencia. Cecilia Vicente and Alice's two special nurses came out on to the steps to wave them off in a car with a Sullavanco escort.

Cecilia said, 'I will not wish you luck because I do not think you need it. But I do wish you happiness.'

Their eyes met. 'Thank you,' Alice said. She didn't think Dr Vicente could even guess how grateful she was. They hugged each other, quickly

456

and wordlessly.

Santiago International Airport was crowded and the temperature outside was thirty-two degrees. Alice stood with Meg in her arms, obsessively watching the departure boards even though the escort wanted them to sit down in a lounge.

The *Southern Mariner* must be putting into port very soon, if it hadn't done so already. There was an obscure flight scheduled to Trelew in Patagonia, and Alice was certain that she would be able to take a connecting flight from there to Ushuaia. She could go right now and search until she found Rooker.

But Meg gave a small snuffling whimper and nuzzled against her neck. Alice massaged the tiny back with the flat of her hand. To go looking for him would mean flying her premature baby to distant places, in a chase that might not even lead her to him.

She hesitated for one long, painful moment.

Then she turned round and boarded the overnight LanChile flight to Madrid. At the end of it she found Lisa waiting to whisk them through to London.

*   *   *

There was a thick blanket of cloud all the way from the Bay of Biscay. Meg woke up and wailed and wouldn't be pacified, and although Lisa looked at her in the expectation that she would know what to do, Alice had no more real idea than she did. A suited man sitting next to them sighed and irritably refolded his newspaper. Only the thought that she was almost home kept her from howling louder

457

than Meg.

At last they were walking down the endless carpeted tunnels at Heathrow.

There was no wait for luggage. Alice had nothing but what she stood up in: a tracksuit, trainers and underwear that had been brought to her in the clinic (there had been an invitation from Sullavanco to buy whatever she wanted, but she had refused all except the minimum), some toiletries in a plastic zipper bag, and another bag of nappies and a change of clothes for Meg. She cupped the back of Meg's bonneted head and held her own head high as they walked through the customs hall towards Arrivals.

'Ready?' Lisa smiled.

As they emerged the sudden blaze of camera flashes almost blinded her.

There was a babble of voices shouting out her name, Lisa's hand firmly propelling her forward, a television crew, the staring faces of other travellers, and in the midst of it all a brief glimpse of Trevor and Margaret. Alice's eyes filled with tears at the sight of them. Her mother looked stooped, but she was wearing a new red hat and Trevor's hair fluffed out round the dome of his head like half a dandelion clock.

Before she had a chance to see properly, Lisa's hand dug into her arm and expertly swivelled her to face the cameras. There was another storm of flashes.

'Dr Peel is very pleased and relieved to be home,' Lisa called out. 'Nothing else at this time. Thank you.'

'Let's see the baby!'

'Alice, did you plan to do this?'

'What's her name?'

Lisa wheeled them away from the press again. 'That's all,' she said firmly.

The crowd fell aside and Trevor and Margaret emerged. Margaret was surging forward like a small, fierce hound on the scent. She scooped Meg out of Alice's arms and gazed down into the puckered crimson face. Then she lifted her up to the cameramen and the passing Heathrow crowds and the invisible, clouded, English March skies.

'Her name is Margaret.' She beamed.

A big man in a dark jacket fell in beside them and with Lisa leading the way they were swept quickly to the nearest exit and a waiting limo. Margaret and Trevor and Alice breathlessly toppled into the back with Meg somewhere between them, Lisa beamed as the doors closed and assured them she'd be in touch later, and the car accelerated. A last long lens homed in on Alice's stunned face as they sped away.

The three of them clutched hands and blinked at each other. Tears of relief and exhaustion and confusion ran down Alice's face. Margaret gave her a folded handkerchief and Trevor massaged the hand that wasn't holding Meg.

'Meg has had quite an introduction to the world,' he said mildly as they swept into the airport tunnel. 'Let me have a look at her.'

Almost blinded by her tears, Alice put the bundle into his arms. He peeled back the white blanket to look at the baby and Meg's bottomless stare met his.

'I want to go home,' Alice sobbed, as if she were a child again herself.

'That's just where we're going,' Margaret said

firmly.

Alice sat wedged between her parents, holding on to both of them.

There was much to say, but not yet.

*　　　*　　　*

The bare twigs of the trees on Boar's Hill were thickening with buds and the hawthorn hedges showed a wispy veil of green. The damp, smoky air and the glistening tarmac and the tedium of the morning traffic were so familiar, yet Alice felt utterly disorientated. She could still feel the thick heat of Santiago in her veins and behind her eyes lay the contradictory white vistas of Antarctica. As they drove up the lane she saw Roger Armstrong at the wheel of his Volvo and Felicity Armstrong in the passenger seat craning her head to get a look at them all.

Trevor murmured, 'I told you, you're famous. Felicity dropped in yesterday just to catch up, as she put it. To nose around for information, actually.'

'That woman is a terrible bore,' Margaret pronounced.

Alice carried Meg for the last five steps of the crazy journey, across the path to the front door and into the house. There was the sound of a clock ticking and the white cat lay licking his hind parts in a warm spot under a radiator. Nothing, and everything, had changed.

'I'll make a cup of tea,' Trevor said. Alice and Margaret went upstairs together.

In Alice's bedroom lay a Moses basket with a blue quilted lining, a pile of tiny folded garments

460

and four packs of newborn Pampers, and a stuffed penguin made of black and white plush with an improbable bright-orange beak.

'Jo brought the baby things over. She sends her love. And Peter came with the penguin. To make her feel at home, he said.'

'Oh,' Alice said uncertainly. Another wave of utter bewilderment threatened to overwhelm her. Her body felt cumbersome and not fully under her control, as if it belonged to someone else and she was only exercising squatter's rights.

She put Meg down in the basket. Margaret held out her arms and suddenly they were clinging together, swaying a little, making small noises of comfort. It was rare for them to hug each other, but now it seemed not so fraught with risk. They stood for a long time, just holding on.

In the end Alice laid her cheek on the red felt crown of her mother's hat and Margaret told her not to crush it, and then she said that with the windburn and the white goggle marks Alice looked like a real polar explorer. She put her hands up to cup Alice's face and asked her why she hadn't come home as soon as she knew that she was pregnant.

Alice met her eyes. Margaret should know at least part of the reason. 'I wanted to finish what I had started. That is something I learned from you.'

'And why didn't you tell anyone?'

'Because I didn't know what to say. And because I thought the only person to take responsibility for what I *had* decided should be me.'

Margaret frowned and swallowed hard. She let go of Alice. She sniffed and took a paper tissue out of the sleeve of her cardigan and blew her nose. 'I am not sure that was entirely logical. But ordinary logic doesn't work down south, does it? I remember that.'

There was a store of memory; maybe now they could begin to tap it together.

'Mum, how are you?'

'I've got arthritis. I'm as good as you could expect, at my age. I'm a grandmother, you know.' Her sharp expression softened. 'Just look at her, Alice. Did you ever see anything so perfect?'

'I know. I'm amazed, too.'

They gazed into the basket until Margaret collected herself. She said with a show of briskness, 'Now then, I suppose we'd better go down and get our cup of tea before it goes cold. Leave her there to sleep; she's been dragged around quite enough already. You'll hear her if the door's open. I'll shut the cat out in the garden until you get a cat net, although he won't be interested in her anyway.'

The doorbell was ringing. Trevor puffed along the hallway to answer it and take delivery of the first cellophane sheaf of pink-ribbon-puffed flowers.

Later Alice took a nap in her own bed, with Meg in her basket alongside, but she woke up again the instant the baby began to whimper. She undid her dressing gown to start feeding her again. She gazed around her old bedroom with the netball team photographs and her girlhood books on the shelf, as if she had never seen it before. It felt utterly strange to be back here after so much had happened.

She thought about Rook and the words he had blurted out as the sailors carried her away. I am a murderer. What did he mean by that? He *wasn't* a

462

murderer, she would have wagered her own life on it, but what was it that lay in his past like a dark obstacle between them?

Every mile that separated her from Rook was painful. All her instincts still told her to fly south and search, and go on searching until she found him and uncovered the truth. But she couldn't any longer do whatever she wanted whenever she wanted it, because her rhythms must now become the baby's. She began to understand why Jo had been hit so hard by motherhood and she longed to talk to her, but there was another call that had to be made first.

When Meg fell asleep again, she called him on the number he had left with Trevor. 'Pete?'

There was a silence, then his words rushed at her. 'You're home. Al, my God, Al. Why didn't you tell me about this? Why? She is mine, isn't she?'

'Yes, she's yours.'

'My God,' he said again, now in a whisper. 'How is she?'

'She is perfect.'

'I'm on my way. I'll be there in half an hour.'

'Pete, I . . . it's not . . .'

'I will be there in half an hour.'

It would have been more in character for him to appear anything up to half a day later, but he was as good as his word. Trevor opened the front door to him and he whirled in with his camera bag and a bunch of tulips spilling out of a sheaf of tissue paper.

'Hello. Come on in. I'll, ah, make some coffee,' Trevor muttered.

Alice hadn't wanted to see him in her bedroom, and the big living room downstairs doubled as

Margaret's study. By some unlikely leap of empathy Margaret had said that she thought she would go out for a little walk and leave Alice to talk to 'that boy', as she usually referred to him. She was putting on her green padded jacket and tying a scarf as Peter juggled his flowers and camera in the hallway.

'You look rather discombobulated,' she observed.

'I've never become a father before. And certainly not at three days' notice.'

'You'll get used to it.' Margaret patted her headscarf. 'They're in there.'

Peter nudged open the door with his toe.

Alice was sitting on the sofa with Meg at her breast.

Peter stopped short, the tulips drooping in his hand. For once, he couldn't find a word.

He had chunks of plaster sticking to his jeans and his hair was thick with plaster dust. He was wearing a loose-knit jersey with an unravelling neckline and his hands were grimy from the studio. Alice felt her heart quicken with affection at the sight of him, but that was all. The knowledge that here was Meg's father didn't make her want to try to love him again. She saw that he was just Pete; he was a good man, but he wasn't the one she wanted.

He came awkwardly and half kneeled in front of her. He touched one fingertip to Meg's nearest cheek and the baby sighed. She stopped sucking and gave a tiny theatrical yawn.

'My God.' Pete breathed again. 'I can't believe it.'

'I know. A whole person, not me, not you, but

464

herself.'

It was this individuality that struck Alice most of all. There was a whole separate future within the baby, like a long message written in tiny handwriting and hidden inside a nutshell. She was so small and fragile compared with the world, with the majestic and fearful backdrop of the ice where her life had started, but there was a spark in her, a continuation of a long, long story, that somehow held its own with all the vast perspectives of Antarctica.

Pete found a seat beside them. He sat with his long arms and legs folded, the fingers of one hand pinching the bridge of his nose, his eyes screwed shut.

'What do you want?' he asked at length. 'I'm here, you know. I'll do whatever you like.'

She knew what he was offering. She took his other hand and held it against her cheek. 'I don't want anything,' she whispered. 'But thank you.'

'Marry me.'

'No. I can't do that. But it means so much that you asked me.'

Pete shouted now. '*Shit*. And *fuck*, and all that, and I swear right now that she'll never hear me swear again. D'you know what you're saying, Alice? *I* am her father. *Me*.'

'I know you are. Nothing's going to change that. You can see her whenever you like, share her with me, take responsibility for her sometimes if that's what you want. But asking me to marry you involves me as well, and I don't want to.'

A tap on the door announced Trevor with the coffee tray. He put it on the table, glanced sharply at Alice, then vaguely nodded and smiled his way out of the room again.

Knowing the Peels' coffee from past experience Peter didn't leap to the pot. He studied Alice's face instead, revealed by the thin spring sunshine. He looked at the lines round her eyes and the fading white mask in the windburn, and the expression in her eyes. They could hear the clock ticking in the hallway and the baby's soft snuffling. 'You have changed,' he said slowly.

Alice didn't look away.

'What has happened? It's something big, isn't it?'

'Having a baby is big.' She was trying to soften the impact.

But Pete wouldn't be deflected. 'I think you should tell me.'

He was right. She detached Meg and rearranged her clothes, then cupped the warmth of her up against her bare neck. The baby gave a triumphant belch. Peter watched and waited.

Alice searched for words. 'Pete . . . I honestly didn't know I was pregnant when I went south. But we'd both realised that it was finished between us, hadn't we?'

'You decided that.'

'Whatever you were saying differently, you *acted* that,' she began, then stopped herself. She took his hand instead and held it, rubbing the prominent knucklebones with her thumb. 'I'm sorry, that came out wrong. I didn't mean to sound accusing. Down south, when I worked out what was happening, I intended—what we intend never quite comes to pass, does it?—to come back here in good time for the baby to be born. To tell you about it, if I could, before anyone else, give you time to prepare

466

yourself, to decide how much or how little you wanted to be involved. To let you know that I was happy. That was the plan.'

'Instead?'

'I miscalculated. I took a gamble, which I shouldn't have done. The ice came early, I missed a chance to leave when I probably could have done if I'd had the courage to insist, then there was a fire on the base. It seemed that in a matter of hours every way out was closed and the safety I'd relied on just melted away. It was stupid of me. I'd been there all those weeks and seen the weather, and lived with the cold like an affliction, and I *still* hadn't understood how quickly and how close you can come to the edge. Then the baby came.' Peter was looking intently at her. 'A man called Rooker flew us out. She was born halfway between the base and the ship.'

'I read about it, yes. My daughter, the first European citizen of Antarctica.'

There was an edge in his voice that gave away much more than his words. He was hurt and she understood that, and as he always did and probably always would do, he thought of the world as it related to himself.

'I'm sorry,' she whispered again. 'It's not how it was meant to happen. There was a chain of circumstances. And I was selfish, and I did put her and other people in danger. It wasn't until . . . until I stood holding her in the airport in Santiago that I began to understand what *a mother* means.' She chose her words with care, knowing that they must be the truth. 'I promise you that from now on she is and always will be the most important person in the world to me.'

467

Not the only person.

The image and the absence of Rooker filled all her waking thoughts, but the decision at the airport in Santiago had been the first uncertain step in what she understood would be the longest journey. She would be Meg's mother until her dying day, whatever else came.

Pete's head was bent and she couldn't see his face.

'I don't know how much danger you were in, Al. I don't think I even want to know. What matters is that you are both safe and well now. But that's not all, is it?'

The clock ticked steadily.

'No. I fell in love.'

Peter exhaled a long breath. 'I thought that must be it.'

He let go of her hand, stood up and went to the window, where he stared into the garden over the piles of Margaret's papers and books. When he turned round again it was Meg he looked at. 'Let me hold her.'

Alice passed the baby into his hands. He cradled her tenderly and awkwardly, as if she might break.

'A man called Rooker?'

It was Alice's turn to breathe harder now. 'Yes.'

Meg moved her head, seeming to focus on her father's face. Her tiny features puckered on the edge of breaking into a wail, but the impulse passed and she settled again. Peter began to hum a tune to her. When he stopped and spoke again it was as if he was thinking aloud. 'You know what? I always guessed that when you did fall in love properly it would transform you. And it has.'

'I loved you,' Alice said humbly. Peter was a very

good man, a better man than she had understood him to be.

'In a way, yes.' He tucked Meg's blanket round her and handed her back. He added abruptly, 'I've got to go now. There's always going to be a connection between you and me, Al. It's here. She's here, between us.'

The tulips lay on a chair, a painterly splash of colour, with the camera bag on the floor beside them.

'You sent me a picture of *Desiderata*,' Alice remembered sadly. 'It got burned in the fire.'

'I'll take another. And I'll come back to take a picture of Meg. I don't think I can actually do it today.'

He gathered up his bag, hesitating as if he were being pulled in two directions. Then he stumbled for the door. 'I'll see you soon,' he called over his shoulder and went without looking back.

Trevor came and found the coffee untouched. He poured a cup and gave it to Alice, and she took it unseeingly.

'I've made him unhappy.'

'It will pass,' Trevor observed. 'He's quite robust.'

'Have I made a mess of everything?'

'I don't think so. It depends rather on what happens next.'

'Can I tell you about something?'

'I hope you will.' Trevor ran his hand over his thistledown hair and sat down in Pete's place.

Beginning at the beginning, she told him the story of Kandahar and Rook. Trevor didn't distract her or try to interrupt. He had always been a good listener. The only thing Alice didn't mention was what Rooker had told her at the end.

'Now I've got to take care of Meg. I have to be strong and help her to grow up strong, haven't I? But I also know that Rooker and I belong together. It's elemental. It's like chipping open a chunk of Jurassic limestone and finding an ammonite. One embedded within the other.' She lifted her eyes and searched her father's face. 'Does that make any sense?'

He nodded. 'I understand. I know what it's like to feel the way you do now.'

She thought of Margaret with Lewis Sullavan, and probably others too, and yet Trevor and Margaret had made it through their painful times. You couldn't harness Rook or subdue him, but there were many different ways of being together, as many ways as there were people, and maybe Rooker and she could find their own.

At the thought of him impatience flooded through her again, and her feet itched and her heart thumped.

She *had* to find him and tell him that whatever was in his past they could confront it together. How long before she could go to him? Where could she begin the search? What if she couldn't find him— how could she live with that?

Trevor's hand was resting on her arm and he felt the electric impulses flickering under her skin. This burning, passionate creature was a different daughter from the cautious, reflective one he had known. He was happy that she had caught fire and he was full of apprehension for her.

'I know. I know you do,' Alice was saying to him.

The front door slammed and Margaret marched into the room. 'Well, then. Has he gone? What are

470

you two talking about?'

Trevor smiled. 'Antarctica,' he said.

CHAPTER SEVENTEEN

Rooker glanced briefly around the bare room. There wasn't much to see. The bookcase was empty and there was nothing in the cupboard except a few twisted coathangers. It was already dark outside and in any case the view from the window was of the same old rocky slope, now crusty with snow. He hoisted his two bags and tramped down the stairs.

Marta was waiting for him, her bulk almost blocking the hallway. She was smiling but her eyes were sad. 'Rooker, you know, I am sorry you leave.'

Her hand grabbed his sleeve and the sudden movement set the carved wooden hatstand teetering. He caught and steadied it.

'Maybe I'll be back.'

'Maybe, eh? We don't know anything in this world. You have time for a little drink before you go?'

He didn't care where he was going and time stretched shapelessly ahead of him, but he shook his head just the same. 'Better be getting to the airport.'

She nodded quickly, her smile still in place. 'So, where you heading?'

'North. Somewhere warm. I've seen enough snow for a while. Marta, thanks for looking after my stuff and for the room.'

She had stored his few surplus belongings while

471

he was at Kandahar, collected half a dozen items of mail, none of them personal, and let him have his old room back for two nights after the *Southern Mariner* docked in Ushuaia.

'*De nada*. As you can see, there is no people fighting for it.'

Winter was closing in on the town. The tourist restaurants were shutting down, Guillermo, the chef, had already moved on and Marta had no other lodgers. For three or four months the flame of life would barely glimmer down here.

'Are you staying?' he asked.

Marta regarded him. 'Where else I go?'

'I don't know. Stupid question, I'm sorry.' Anywhere and precisely nowhere, he thought. Just where he was going himself.

'*Adiós*, Rook,' Marta said.

He leaned down and kissed her, and for a second she pressed her broad cheek against his.

'I'll send you an address, when I've got myself fixed up somewhere,' he promised.

'Sure,' she agreed.

It was bitterly cold outside, too dark to see the sea, but he knew that it would be greasy with plate ice. Rooker carried one bag on his back and lifted the other on to his shoulder. He walked quickly downhill, over the hard ridges of frozen dirt and away from Marta's house, his breath clouding round his head. Once he hit the main street he would thumb a ride out to the airport, or he might even take a five-dollar ride in a cab if there was one waiting at the rank down the side of the Hotel Albatross. He had money, a whole season's money from working at Kandahar, and a seat booked on the evening flight up to Buenos Aires.

The other Kandahar personnel would all have left town by now, heading back to their homes and families. Rooker wanted and needed to travel alone.

A truck stopped for him and dropped him off at the airport. The flight when he boarded it was half empty.

The plane banked sharply after take-off and the bitter-orange and pale-green lights of Ushuaia tilted briefly beneath them before they were blotted out by low cloud. Rooker remembered the sea mist and the desperate helicopter journey across the ice from Kandahar. He reached quickly into the pocket of his coat, slid out his flask and took a long swallow of whisky. The seatbelt sign winked off over his head.

He made a silent tribute. To you, Alice Peel. Then he drank again.

His thoughts resumed the course they had been following for days.

The birth of a baby. He had never seen such a thing, had never dreamed that it could be so profound and so pure, and that a tiny, wet, hot body delivered into his hands, and a woman's face contorted with pain and then elation, could etch themselves so deeply into his mind. He remembered every detail of those minutes and he heard all over again Alice shouting and gasping, and then the first tiny fluttering cry from the baby. He knew that what he had witnessed was as timeless and elemental as the slow glaciers, the mercurial shifts of the weather and the ice itself.

Rook closed his eyes. He was glad of the whisky; the bottle was a better companion tonight than Niki or Phil.

Meg was another man's child. Apart from the accident of her birth he hadn't the remotest claim on her. This was a new life and he couldn't contaminate her absolute innocence with his presence, let alone his history. No: Alice and Meg belonged together, in a safe place, a long way from the marginal territories that he occupied. Rooker had never been to Oxford but he made a picture in his mind of calm grey stone and green lawns and lamplit college rooms with their walls lined with books.

He loved Alice but he must let her go.

She had said things to him that he would treasure—*I love you, don't leave me*—but he understood now, with distance widening between them and Kandahar, that she had spoken under pressure of danger and isolation. It was enough, he tried to tell himself, that she had turned to him in those circumstances. It would be too much to expect her to look at him in the same way once she was safely back in England and amongst friends. What could Alice Peel want, or need, from him?

The memories were what he had; he didn't want to diminish them by demanding more and being refused, however gently. She would do it gently, of course.

'*Señor?*'

The cabin attendant had appeared with a plastic tray of food. Rooker shook his head and his fingers closed on the flask in his pocket. He was hungry, but he didn't want to eat anything. The attendant passed on down the aisle and Rooker turned his head to the window. There was nothing to see; only impenetrable blackness.

The birth of a baby. Alice's lovely face, as no

474

other man had ever seen her, burned into his consciousness. He loved her but he must let her go.

His thoughts went on, round and round, following the same course.

In Buenos Aires it was hot and at first Rooker felt his bones ease in the benign warmth. He walked beside the broad reach of the Río Plata and watched the fishermen with their lines arcing into the khaki water. But after Antarctica the air tasted acrid with pollution and his hotel room was so noisy with traffic that he couldn't sleep. He flew on up to Cuba and sat for three days in a bar in Havana Vieja, drinking *mojitos* and avoiding the attentions of the *jineteras*. There was the same aimlessness with which he had originally drifted south, but the emptiness was far harder to bear. Time weighed heavily on him and the future stretched away like a parabola that finally dipped out of sight beyond an uninviting horizon.

In the end he moved on to Mexico City, where he rented a room and looked half-heartedly for some casual work in the construction business, just to give himself something to do. But he felt too withdrawn to put much effort into the search and nothing came of it. In yet another bar one night a young girl slid into the seat beside him and rested her hand on his thigh.

She greeted him in Spanish and asked if he was looking for a friend.

He answered in English, 'Yes, but not the kind of friend that you mean.'

The girl smiled. There were tiny gems of sweat on her top lip. She reminded him of Edith in one of her taunting, bar-room moods. '*Americano?*'

'No.' He didn't want to talk but the girl was still

475

looking expectantly at him, with her head tilted to one side. '*Inglés*,' he said, surprising himself. It had been a long time since he had admitted to any nationality except for official purposes.

'English. I like,' she said. 'I speak very good.'

'Yes.'

'Me drink?'

He had a bottle on the table beside him. Rooker shrugged and poured whisky into a second glass. They sat for a few minutes in oddly companionable silence, watching the eddying of the crowds.

'You like to?' the girl asked after a while, making a small suggestive movement.

'No,' Rook said shortly. She was pretty and she looked clean enough, but he couldn't imagine touching her. He couldn't imagine anything except Alice.

The girl looked over her shoulder, checking for her pimp. She understood that she wasn't going to get anywhere with Rook, so she hitched her bag over her skinny arm and prepared to move on. But before she went she leaned across him, giving him a good look down the front of her blouse. Her breath fanned his face. 'You know, everyone have friend some place. Even you, mister.'

Immediately, Rook thought of Frankie.

'*Chao*.' The girl nodded, pleasantly enough, and wandered away.

*　　　*　　　*

The morning after her return to Boar's Hill, Alice was woken at five in the morning by Meg's crying. She sat groggily up in bed and fed her. Afterwards she stumbled between her bedroom and the bathroom, fumbling with the nappy tags that wouldn't stick and making lists in her head of all the equipment that she would need to buy. Changing mat. Wipes. Nappy disposal bags. Zinc cream. Baby bath. Some kind of sling to carry her around in. Breast pads. The practical implications of motherhood were dawning on her.

The dawn probed between the folds of her old curtains. The stripe of light bisecting the wallpaper moved slowly leftwards, turning from grey fuzzed with pale-lemon to bright gold. Meg slept again, wrapped in a white cellular blanket, her mouth fallen open in a moist triangle. Alice studied the light on the blanket's satin binding. The way that suggestions of colour were locked into the whiteness made her think of the ice, and a wave of longing for Antarctica and for Rooker swept through her. She ached with loneliness for him and for what she had left behind.

Later, Trevor came in with a pot of tea on a tray. He brought the newspapers too. Alice thirstily drank her tea and they sat on her bed looking at the *Oxford Mail* together. There was a big picture of their arrival at Heathrow, with Meg's face just visible and Alice herself looking shellshocked in the camera's flash. *South Pole Mum home* the subhead read inaccurately. There were pictures and brief stories in the national tabloids too. *Ice cool, baby. Antarctic drama Mum. Snow place like home for polar birth scientist.* Most of the papers mentioned the joint European Antarctic initiative and two described Meg as the first European citizen of Antarctica. Lewis would be pleased with that, anyway.

'Fifteen minutes of fame.' She smiled wryly at

477

Trevor.

'More tea?' he asked.

Between feeds, Alice managed to telephone the Polar Office. She remembered the sleek curve of the receptionist's desk and the arrangement of hot-orange flowers, rather like those in her room in the clinic. Alice identified herself and heard the note of avid curiosity in the woman's voice as she answered, 'Oh *yes*. Dr Peel. How can I help you?'

Alice said quickly, 'I would very much like to speak to Mr Sullavan, if possible. To thank him.'

'Of course, Dr Peel. I know that he's eager to speak to you too, but he *is* involved in a series of meetings in Toronto today.'

'I understand. Perhaps you could just leave that message? Oh, and one other small thing. May I have James Rooker's contact details, please? His telephone number, in particular?'

'I'm *so* sorry. We can't give out . . .'

'You see, I didn't have a chance to thank him properly. For what he did,' she added delicately.

'Yes.' There was a pause. 'Dr Peel, I know that Mr Sullavan is *particularly* hoping that you'll want to tell your story personally. So many people will be interested to hear it. I know I will.'

'We-ll,' Alice said, trying to sound as if she might countenance the idea but was too preoccupied at the moment to give it proper consideration. 'Beverley Winston did mention it,' she added vaguely. Another meaningful silence ensued.

'So maybe I could just make an appointment for the journalist to pop in to see you and the babe, and have a chat about it all?'

'Perhaps, if I could clear my mind first, you know? I owe such a debt to James Rooker.'

478

'I *could* just take a very quick peek at the records. For the interview, though, shall we say tomorrow at 2 p.m. ?'

'All right. Yes.'

'And a photographer? Just a couple of lovely informal snaps, you know, mum-and-baby?'

'All right.'

'Perfect, Dr Peel.'

A moment later she was noting down a telephone number and an address in Ushuaia. She replaced the receiver, took a breath, then lifted it again and dialled. She listened to a foreign ring tone for what seemed like a very long time and at length a woman's voice answered. With her heart hammering in her chest Alice asked to speak to him.

'Rooker? No.' She couldn't properly decipher the rapid Spanish that followed but the meaning was clear enough.

'But he must have left a forwarding address, surely? He can't have just gone.'

She heard the other woman's laugh, a wheezy exhalation of breath without merriment in it. 'I think you don't know Rooker,' she said in English.

You don't know me. You don't know what I've done. I am a murderer.

The last words he had spoken to her face-to-face echoed in her head yet again.

But she *did* know him. She knew him better than she had ever known anyone, as if their hands matched palm to palm at this very moment and their eyes met and saw right inside the other's head. She didn't know any of the ordinary things, like who his friends were, or exactly how old he was, or his birthday, or his mother's name, or

479

where he might be heading right now, but she knew in every fibre of herself that he was not what he claimed. He had a black place in his past and he believed it must be hidden from her. To disappear was his solution.

'There must be something.'

'I am sorry. He say that he will send address when he fixes up somewhere.'

Alice understood that this woman, whoever she was, would very much like there to have been more. She was obviously telling the truth and Rooker had left without giving any indication of where he was going, yet she didn't want to hang up and sever even this tenuous connection. She was thinking that she didn't have so much as a snapshot of him. The fire had consumed her exposed film, her diary, the Christmas wood carving, every scrap of physical evidence that he had ever existed. She had a brief horrible feeling that it was licking at her memories too, torching the margins with a ribbon of blue flame that would burn faster until even these shrivelled and she would be left with nothing at all.

She gave her name and her telephone number to the Argentinian woman, biting her lip and waiting while she shuffled away in search of a pencil and paper, and then asking her to read back what she had written down. She tried to picture the woman's face—a landlady? A friend? More or less than that?—and her surroundings, but the fog of language and distance got in the way, and she could see nothing.

When she had to hang up she felt as if a lifeline had snapped.

From upstairs, as she tended to Meg for the rest of the day, she heard the phone continually ringing. Margaret and Trevor fielded the calls, not even bothering to relay messages up the stairs to her because they could hear her footsteps as she walked up and down with the baby in her arms to soothe her crying, or because she was feeding her, or changing her, or just in case they had both fallen into a doze.

I'll get a routine organised, Alice thought, remembering that Jo had somehow managed all this with *two* of them. She found herself shaking her head in empathetic astonishment.

So far, the evenings had seemed to be Meg's quietest time. Alice carried her downstairs in the Moses basket and put her in the corner of the dining room. A one-bar electric fire burned with a dry glow, taking the chill off the air within three feet of it. There were flowers everywhere, stripped of their cellophane sheaths and wedged at random into whatever receptacle would hold water. Margaret ran her finger down a list of telephone messages while Trevor served up portions of grey-knobbed cauliflower cheese, the sauce torched to black blisters over the uplands of the dish.

'Good nourishing cheese and fresh vegetable for you,' Margaret helpfully elaborated. 'Now then. Jo called twice, Becky called once. They're going to come and see you tomorrow. Er, let's see, Peter rang yet again. And Dr Davey's going to drop in; he says he and the practice nurse will be here in the morning to look at you and Meg. One of your colleagues from Kandahar rang.' Alice's head

481

jerked up. 'A Frenchwoman. I wrote down her name and number, here it is. Laure Heber. I haven't bothered listing the journalists. I put most of the flowers in water, there are a couple of those basket arrangements in the kitchen. You won't be wanting them in your room, will you?' She paused to eat a forkful of cauliflower before adding, 'You could do with a secretary. Oh, and there was a call from Lewis Sullavan. I think you were sleeping.'

Alice put down her knife and fork. 'What did he say?'

'Best wishes and so on. Sorry not to have spoken in person yet. Hopes to be able to see you before too long.'

'To see me?'

Lewis had instinctively liked Rooker, he had recognised him in the way that she had recognised Richard Shoesmith. Surely Lewis would help her to find him?

'Where was he calling from?' He had been in Toronto earlier, but that didn't mean he mightn't be in Los Angeles or London by now.

'I don't know. I didn't ask,' Margaret answered.

Alice glanced at her father. Silvery fronds of fine hair rose vertically from his pink scalp. With his napkin tucked into his shirtfront he was eating his dinner with apparent appetite, unconcerned at the mention of Sullavan's name.

This is what time and age do, she thought. Passion and pain are both dulled, then they fade away altogether and leave acceptance in their place. Habit and familiarity knot round each other like the dry balled roots of an ancient tree. The contrasting urgency of her need for Rooker, the white-hot importance of finding him before too many precious days could trickle away, made her shift and double up in her chair as if she were in pain.

Margaret stared at her over the top of her glasses. 'Are you all right?'

'Yes, thank you,' Alice made herself answer.

Trevor was watching her now too, but he didn't say anything.

A small experimental cry rose from the Moses basket. I am home, Alice was thinking. But I don't belong here any longer. Everything has shifted and I don't recognise the perspectives. Her parents were two tired old people, rattling around in a dilapidated house that was too big for their needs. There were too many books, the layers of dust were steadily thickening, there were memories and regrets blown into all the corners like drifts of fine sand.

'Finish your food, before you pick her up,' Margaret advised. 'Babies have to learn who's boss.'

'I think things are done differently nowadays,' Alice replied.

*   *   *

Jo and Becky arrived in the middle of the following morning. Alice got as far as the front step to greet them as they whirled at her. They enveloped her in hugs and questions and exclamations, and as they swept into the house she laughed wildly with the joy of being with her friends again. 'I missed you,' she gasped. 'I *really* missed you.'

'Where is she? Let's have a look at her.'

Up in Alice's bedroom where they had confided

about boys, and chopped each other's hair, and shared their first spliff one evening when Margaret was away, they leaned over the Moses basket.

'Pete!' they exclaimed in unison.

Alice pressed her head between them. 'I don't think she looks like anyone, just herself.'

Becky gripped Alice's wrists, held her at arm's length and studied her face. 'You look tired, but more or less all right. How do you feel? And why didn't you tell anyone about all this, not even Jo and me?'

'Yes, why didn't you?' Jo demanded. 'We're your friends, aren't we?'

'You are. I didn't know, I didn't realise until weeks after I got there. And then it . . . seemed both too late and too soon to leave, and so I decided just to stay and to deal with everything to do with being pregnant once I got back home. I thought there was plenty of time. It sounds strange now, but can you understand how I felt?'

Jo shook her head, Becky nodded.

'How are the twins?'

'They're with Harry. They're almost walking. Don't try to change the subject, I still think you could have told us. I didn't even realise why you were e-mailing me with questions about babies.'

'It wouldn't have been fair to tell you, for one thing.'

As she explained that once she had made the decision to stay on the ice it had seemed essential to take the entire responsibility herself, Alice had the strange sensation that there were two separate worlds spinning around her, both containing parallel places that she and Meg could occupy. There was Oxford; that took in the Department of

Geology and her students, her house once she had retrieved it from the tenants, Jo and Becky and her parents, Pete, all their friends and the rhythms of a life that had once seemed to offer everything she wanted. And there was another world, a much hollower and emptier place where the wind blew and the horizons were cracked with ice, but it was where Rooker was.

The two places would never merge.

She could choose one or the other, but not both.

Jo and Becky were both staring at her.

'Ali?'

She blinked, realising that she had stopped talking. 'Sorry. I can't seem to make my brain work properly.'

Jo took her by the arm and steered her to the bed. They sat down, Alice propping herself against the wooden headboard and Jo perching on the end as they had often done before. But now the Moses basket lay between them. Becky leaned against the chest of drawers, listening, a frown line showing between her groomed eyebrows.

Jo said, 'I know how you feel. Just a few days ago you owned yourself and your body, and you slept when you were tired and talked joined-up sense to other sensible people, and you imagined that when the baby came life might be disrupted a bit but it wouldn't change completely. And now it's as if your entire existence has been whisked away. You can't finish a sentence, you can't even get dressed in the mornings. You're exhausted and bewildered, and in your case you haven't even got Pete around. That's not to say he wouldn't be with you if he could, by the way. He's been on the phone non-stop to Harry and me. "I'm the father, I ought to be there." Et cetera. Listen. It may feel like it, but it's not going to be this way for ever. Remember what I was like? And now'—she shrugged, then smiled—'I can get out of the house on my own for two whole hours at a time. Look, Beck and I bought you some things.'

In the carrier bags that Becky had brought upstairs there were candy-striped Babygros and tiny pink socks and a hat like a strawberry, and a white toy polar bear.

Alice had tears in her eyes as she unwrapped them. 'Polar bears live in the Arctic,' she sniffed.

'Don't be so bloody pedantic. And Al, you know what? It's okay to have a good cry if you want to.'

Noisy, racking sobs suddenly burst out of her.

Her friends exchanged anxious glances. Jo held Alice's shoulders and Becky put a clump of tissues into her hand.

'It's all right,' Jo soothed, but tears ran down Alice's chin and she gasped and hiccuped with grief, shaking her head because she couldn't get out the words to say that it wasn't all right at all. Meg snuffled and began to howl too.

Jo turned aside and scooped up the baby. She nestled her against her shoulder and rubbed the tiny bent back, murmuring, 'There, little girl. Hush now.'

Becky kneeled and gripped Alice's hands. 'Tell us what's wrong,' she murmured.

Looking down through the blur of tears Alice saw the pastel flowers on the duvet cover and the little pile of baby clothes, and bright frills of tissue paper and ribbon, and all the dense furnishings and memories accumulated in her room. She remembered the searing brilliance of the flowers in the clinic, and how Santiago had seemed so hot and crowded and complicated, and the noise and hectic speed of the flight from Santa Ana, and the close air of the medical room on the *Polar Star*, and all the way back to the utterly contrasting unlimited whiteness of the ice.

She couldn't speak. Jo rocked Meg to soothe her and Becky massaged Alice's hands while she cried and cried.

Kandahar had been a life stripped bare, reduced to a matter of survival that was too stark and too engrossing to require any embellishment or decoration. The grandeur of Antarctica didn't account for detail, or call for any refinement. Rook was part of that; that was what he was for her. He was elemental and essential. It didn't matter what he did or had done, or what he looked like or how he spoke. The only thing that mattered was where he was now, because she was beginning to believe that she couldn't live without him.

Gregory Shoesmith's famous poem came into her head, 'Remember This, When I Am Best Forgotten'. She had known it by heart, but exhaustion and the confusion of hormones had broken the lines into elusive fragments. How did it go? . . . *no human ornament, only the day's luminous aisles, night's rafters . . .*

The white pillars and flutings, and the massive blackness of the endless polar night were so vivid in her mind that the absence at the centre, of Rooker himself, was almost unbearable.

At last, the sobs came with less violence. Alice gasped for breath and lifted her head. She held the wadded tissues to her swollen eyes and looked away from the colours lapping over her bed. Then she took Meg gently out of Jo's arms and held her against her heart.

Jo stood up. 'Pete's said he's sorry. You think he doesn't mean it but he does. Let him take care of you both. You can move back into the house together, make it home again, be a proper family.'

Becky shook her head at her, but Alice knew that Jo was offering her her own version of happiness. 'No,' she murmured. 'I can't do that.'

'So who is he?' Becky asked.

Becky had understood what Jo had missed.

There was a small, weighted silence.

Then Alice said, 'Rooker.'

It made her happy and at the same time it pierced her heart just to speak his name. There was a pause while the other two placed him amongst the jumble of names and anecdotes that Alice had included in her e-mails, and in the garbled press reports of the birth and rescue.

'The pilot?'

'Yes.'

'Who took you out in the helicopter? Delivered Meg on the way?'

'Yes.'

Jo whistled. 'That's quite a story. You fell in love with him.'

In spite of everything Alice smiled. Her nose was streaming and her eyes stung. 'It's not a story. It's the truest thing I've ever known. I fell in love with him without realising it and then there was a fire and everything suddenly got very dangerous and difficult, and I understood that he is the most important person in the world for me. Then Meg started to come and he did everything he could. Somehow he saved us.'

'Does he love you?' It was Becky who asked this.

488

The frown line creasing her forehead was easing.

'He did then.'

'Where is he now?'

Alice's eyes met hers. 'I don't know. He seems to have disappeared. And I don't know how to find him.'

'That's it?'

'Yes.'

There was an ache and an emptiness in Alice's voice that discouraged any more questions for the time being. Meg was whimpering and nuzzling. Alice sat down and undid her shirt, and as the three women sat and looked at each other there were the small ticking sounds as the baby latched on.

'Antarctic Drama Mum,' Jo said in a bemused voice.

'Fifteen minutes,' Alice dismissed Lewis's PR machine as she concentrated on feeding.

'You are famous today.' Becky nudged the heap of newsprint with her toe.

Alice's free hand suddenly flew up to her mouth. 'Oh, my God. The journalist. And the photographer. Two o'clock. What time is it now?'

Jo looked at her watch. 'Coming up to one.'

'What journalist?' Becky demanded.

'*quoted* magazine. Writer and photographer. Coming here. Heart-warming exclusive story. Mum-and-baby pics. I promised Lewis Sullavan's people. If I do this garbage for him he'll have to help me to find Rooker, won't he?'

'*quoted*? You're going to be in a photo spread in *quoted*?'

It was Lewis's most popular and successful news and gossip title. Even Alice had occasionally leafed through it.

'And look at you.'

'What do you mean?'

'I mean that Lewis Sullavan won't want Antarctic Drama Mum actually *looking* as if she's just spent six months in somewhere godforsaken like Antarctica and then given birth in a helicopter, will he?'

'Before crying for a solid hour.'

'He'll want you in full slap and straight from a blow-dry at Nicky Clarke's. Are they sending hair and make-up?'

'I don't think so.'

'What kind of a magazine is this? I'll just have to do what I can. Let's get going.'

They set to work. Jo ran downstairs for ice for an eye mask and Becky began tugging at her hair. Alice submitted, the way she had done when the three of them first became friends, and Becky and Jo had propelled her away from her books and into a world that contained mascara and David Bowie. She didn't care about how she looked for *quoted*'s photographer, but it was a way for her old friends to draw her temporarily back into the circle.

They were not ready yet to acknowledge that she might not be the same old Alice any longer, and it was too soon for her to try to explain what had changed her. Perhaps no one would ever fully understand that, except Rooker himself. And Margaret. She suspected that Margaret did, somewhere in her heart.

The photo shoot gave them something to fix on.

Becky blotted out the windburn with matte foundation and erased the black lines under Alice's eyes with Touche Eclat. They plucked and gelled

490

her eyebrows, and applied coats of lash thickener and a hint of kohl. Jo squeezed something from a tube and scrubbed it over her mouth.

'Ouch. Mind the baby. What's that stuff?'

'Lip exfoliant. Your mouth's all chapped.'

'I know that. *Ow.*'

'Give me my goddaughter.'

'What?'

'Well, aren't I? Isn't she?'

'Beck, of course you are, if you want to be. Wait, though. We'd better ask Pete what he thinks.'

They stopped for a moment, with Meg and the lipgloss and the mirror suspended between them, acknowledging that there were currents here that would require careful navigation.

Becky quickly nodded. 'Of course. You're right.'

Jo said briskly, 'What shall we dress the First European Citizen in? The stripes? And a clean nappy, to start with. I'll do it.'

At five minutes to two Becky held up the mirror. 'What do you think?'

Alice stared at her glossed and tweezed reflection. 'Who am I?'

They held each other's hands and laughed. 'Drama Mum.'

Jo peered out of the window. 'They're here. They both look about fourteen. And the photographer's unloading a silver lighting umbrella. Maybe he'll shoot you through a soft-focus lens.'

'Go away, both of you,' Alice begged. 'And leave me to my fate.'

'Another car's just arrived,' Jo said.

A moment later they heard a voice at the front door. 'Hi. We met at the airport. I'm Lisa.'

491

'Won't you come in?' Trevor said.

Alice hugged Jo and Becky. 'Thank you. Thank you for everything and I'll call later, and . . . I'm glad you're here. Now *go*.'

*   *   *

Margaret's wobbly gateleg table was pushed aside to make room for the photographer to set up his lights. The journalist was dressed in black from head to toe, and when she settled on a chair a greyish mat of cat hair instantly attached itself to her back. Alice sat on the sofa with Meg in her arms, and Lisa perched on an ottoman after pushing aside a pile of Royal Zoological Society papers.

'Don't pay any attention to me,' she ordered. 'I'm just here to look after everything. You look so rested, Alice, you really do.'

Trevor and Margaret went and sat at the kitchen table.

'Alice is a scientist, not a . . . *pop star*,' Margaret sniffed.

'I know that, dear. Maybe you should tell Lewis Sullavan.'

The journalist turned on her recorder and set it in front of Alice. 'What was it like to be a woman in Antarctica?'

Alice smiled. 'You should really ask my mother that, she was one of the very first.'

The other woman took this at face value. 'I hope to be able to have a couple of words with Dr Mather afterwards. And we'd love a picture of the three generations of polar women, if that would be possible.'

'If Dr Mather agrees,' Lisa chirped.

'You can ask her,' Alice conceded.

'Ready,' the photographer announced. The lights flashed in Meg's eyes and set off a wail.

'What was it like to be a *pregnant* woman in Antarctica?'

Alice sighed. If this was going to be the price she would pay it.

*   *   *

When her turn came, Margaret dealt with *quoted* in crisp style. She gave a rapid résumé of her seal and penguin work, smiling patiently as the journalist struggled a little with the scientific language. She dismissed the suggestion that she had been a pioneering female by saying that everyone had been on the ice to do their work and that gender was an irrelevance.

'But sometimes gender does raise its head, doesn't it?' the journalist pointedly put in. Lisa sat upright on her ottoman and gently cleared her throat.

Alice held up her hand. 'I should answer that. I am a woman, but I went south as a scientist. I made a mistake, two mistakes if you like, in not knowing that I was pregnant in the first place and in staying on at Kandahar once I discovered it instead of coming home immediately. But anyone, woman or man, can make a wrong decision. All I can tell you is the truth. I stayed because I was proud to be part of the EU team at Kandahar, and Dr Shoesmith and I were doing useful work. So were all the other scientists. We made a good beginning and then lost some of the ground we made, but it *was* only a

493

beginning and there are many more seasons to come. I was very lucky to be with everyone who was there, both as professionals and as people. More than lucky at the end. Blessed. Now I'm very relieved that we are all safely home again.'

Or safe somewhere, wherever he is.

'Antarctica was the most beautiful place I've ever seen, but I'm more than happy to be back now. And I'm very proud of my daughter.' Alice held up her head and Meg's black eyes opened wide. The photographer clicked again and the lights flashed.

'Very nice, Alice,' Lisa said approvingly.

*　　　*　　　*

Two weeks went by. At the end of that time the issue of *quoted* magazine appeared with its upbeat version of Meg's birth and the European scientists' eventual escape from the burned-out shell of their base. The fire was described as a dramatic accident and the survivors as polar heroes. The loss of most of a season's data and samples was compensated for by Meg herself, as a perfect symbol of a successful European birth and flowering against all the natural odds of Antarctica, and as the latest addition to what the journalist chose to call a polar dynasty. The helicopter episode was played down and the only mention of Rooker was as 'brave stand-in pilot'.

Beverley Winston and Lisa telephoned to offer their congratulations and thanks, and another vast floral arrangement arrived from Lewis Sullavan. The Polar Office sent word that the story and pictures would be widely syndicated across Sullavanco media worldwide and that there had been some talk of a feature film of the events.

'We weren't heroes,' Alice said with a sigh when she read the article. 'Except for Rooker.'

'Yes, maybe that Rooker. Any news of him?' Margaret asked.

'No. None.'

Trevor's concerned gaze rested on his daughter.

The main picture, covering almost an entire double spread of the magazine, was of the three of them. Margaret stood up fierce and straight-backed in spite of her arthritis, with an emerald-green turban pulled down over her hair and one hand resting on Alice's shoulder. Alice sat on the arm of the sofa, her face made neutral with make-up, and Meg lay in her arms, swathed in a blanket except for her little round red face with dark unwinking eyes.

'How absurd,' Margaret protested when she saw it. But she framed the copy that the Polar Office sent her and propped it on the windowsill in front of her work table, next to the pictures of what had, briefly, been Margaret Mather House.

'That's all that over with,' Alice said with relief. It had lasted longer than fifteen minutes, but not much.

The end of April came, and then it was early May and the weeping willows along the river in the University Parks were in leaf, dipping green wands into the water. Meg steadily gained weight, and small windows of space began to open up between feeding and nappy changing. When she was just over a month old, Alice looked into the Moses basket and was sure that she glimpsed the beginnings of a smile, but Jo insisted that it was much more likely to be wind.

After some negotiations Alice's tenants agreed to move out of the Jericho house a month early. It would be a relief to be able to take Meg home, along with the small mountain of baby equipment that they had already accumulated. The Boar's Hill house had begun to seem very crowded, and too small for Margaret and Alice to occupy together.

'I need to get on with work. But I do need to see my granddaughter at least every other day,' Margaret fretted.

'You will see her. She *is* your granddaughter,' Trevor soothed her.

Every day, in whatever spare time she could capture for herself, Alice did everything she could think of to locate Rook.

The Polar Office grew resistant to her calls for more information. In the end they simply gave her all the contact details they had, for all the expedition members. There was nothing in Rooker's file except the Ushuaia address and a reference from an Argentinian building company. She spoke to an uncomprehending personnel officer in Buenos Aires and an unhelpful American architect, neither of whom could tell her anything except that Rooker had worked last winter as site manager at a hotel development in Ushuaia.

Rooker had worked at McMurdo, too. After much effort she got through to an official at the American Office of Polar Programs in Arlington, Virginia. Yes, a James J. Rooker had been employed on the base in the 1970s. There was no further data now available.

Russell was at home with his wife and children in Dunedin, New Zealand.

'Christ, Alice, how are *you*? And the baby? My

God, when I think of it . . .'

It was an effort to keep the tremor of urgency out of her voice as she asked the question.

'Rook? Nah. Haven't a clue. He disappeared pretty much straight off the boat. That's the way he is, isn't it? . . . Yeah, I understand, Alice, I understand it's important. But the way Rooker is, I don't want to get your hopes up. I know he lived up in Christchurch, though. I'll ask around a bit, see if anyone knows anything.'

'Thank you, Russ. *Thank you.*'

Laure was back in her lab. She was working on the penguin blood samples that they had managed to salvage from the snow cave. 'Yes, I am working, of course. I am lucky, to have this. Oh, Paul and I are still together, but nothing has changed. *Phh.* No, I am so sorry I have no contact for Rook. I think if he wants, he will know where to find you. Now, tell me some things about the little one? *What* a time that was.'

Valentin was in Sofia, Jochen was in Den Haag and Arturo was in Barcelona. They were all eager to hear news and exchange reminiscences but none of them had any information about Rooker. Niki was still travelling somewhere in South America. Phil was in North Wales, teaching climbing.

'Jesus. That was an epic and a half. I'll remember the way that bloody helicopter lifted off in a white-out until my dying day. Eh? Yeah, I'm sure you do. But if Rooker's such a fucking mix-up that he doesn't want to be found, what's there to say? I liked him, yeah, 'course I did. But I'm not sure that he's a prospect, if you want the truth. You've got the baby to think of. What? Yeah, 'course I will. Whatever I can.'

'Thanks, Phil.'

Richard, she learned, was away in Greece. He was said to be resting and recuperating, and had not left a contact address.

Through a local history society she established that there had been a Northumberland family called Jerrold and eventually she tracked down a young solicitor in Morpeth whose father had looked after their affairs. In a brief telephone conversation he told her that Henry Jerrold had died in the 1980s and his wife ten years later. There were no living relatives, and although he believed there had been a sister who had emigrated to New Zealand in the Fifties she had predeceased her brother and he had no record of her having had a child. His father was now also dead.

She trawled the Internet for possible polar or Patagonian or New Zealand connections, but nothing ever came up linked to any version of his name. She fed all the combinations of key words that she could think of into Google, but still came up with nothing.

She replayed their conversations, trying to pick out clues as to where he might have gone. The last words rang in her head.

I am a murderer.

He was not a murderer. That much she knew.

Her eerie sense that he might never have existed was intensifying. The trail had gone dead and she had only one prospect left.

*   *   *

Two days before Alice was due to move back into her own house, Margaret took a telephone call in the early morning. Three hours later a big car turned in at the gate and the chauffeur made the tight turn round the overgrown central flowerbed to the front door. Lewis Sullavan stepped out.

Against the crumbling house he looked even more buffed and polished than he had done at Kandahar. His handmade suit fitted every contour of his compact body, his shoes and leather attaché case and cropped silvery hair all gleamed in the May sunshine. When Margaret came out to greet him he held her knotty hands in his and kissed her.

'Come in, then. You'll have to take us as you find us, you know.' She smiled at him. Lewis was not much taller than she was but beside him she was like a bird, a tropical bird with very bright plumage. She had put on a red tweed skirt and a jumper that almost matched it, and draped a multicoloured silk scarf round her shoulders.

'It's good to see you, Maggie. You don't look any different.'

Her face glowed. Apart from Trevor, Lewis Sullavan was the only person who had ever called her Maggie. 'It's twenty years, my dear. Of course I look different. Here's Trevor, now.'

The two men shook hands. Trevor quickly removed his from Lewis's grasp and replaced it in his cardigan pocket, but otherwise he was affable. There was nothing in the air except sunshine and the scent of early mown grass. The two old people limped ahead down the hallway and showed Lewis into the living room. A tray of coffee was already waiting.

'Would your driver like a cup?' Trevor asked.

'What's that? No. He'll be fine, thank you.'

Trevor sat down firmly in Margaret's desk chair,

opposite Lewis and Margaret on the sofa.

'I wanted to come in person.' Lewis smiled. 'I see you've got some photographs, Maggie. That's good. It was a rather remarkable season. And I've come to tell you, promise you, that next season both the main house and Margaret Mather House will be entirely rebuilt. Out of the ashes a new lab building will rise. Bigger and better, improved facilities. I think we shall get extra funding from Brussels to support the work.'

That was how he would present it. There was no fading or failure in Lewis's world. If human error or fallibility or awkward truth didn't fit into his picture, the image could be adjusted or rubbed out altogether. The line was that Kandahar had survived both ice and fire. Everything moved forward, gathering momentum, growing and flourishing. The two old people sat and took this in.

'And of course there is the miracle of your granddaughter. I wouldn't have chosen such a thing to happen to one of my scientists . . .'

'Yours?' Trevor murmured, but neither of the others seemed to hear him.

'. . . But they are both safe, thank God, and it's a story that has appealed to thousands of people. A new birth, a rebirth for a science station, a growing community. It's rather marvellously appropriate, when you think of it.'

'Thank you for putting it like that.' That was Trevor again.

'Where are they?' Lewis asked, his smile widening.

'I'll call Alice.'

Alice came down the stairs with Meg in her

arms. She presented the baby to Lewis.

He peered down at her, adopting the right genial expression. 'She is almost as beautiful as her mother and grandmother.'

'Thank you,' Alice said.

'I have brought you a small present.'

In Lewis's briefcase there were two identically sized gift-wrapped packages. One was an album into which someone had pasted all the Sullavanco press cuttings relating to Meg's birth.

'Thank you. That's very kind.'

In the second album there were photographs.

'The cameraman who came with us was a good stills photographer too,' Lewis said.

Alice slowly turned the pages. There was the old hut, with its walls glowing fire-red in the low sunlight. There was a slice of lemon-yellow dawn, and clouds hanging over the glacier, and a pair of Adélie penguins amongst the ice debris on the frozen shore. The pictures lifted a blindfold. Everything, every detail, far more than a set of photographs could ever contain, spread out again in her mind's eye.

Their tiny camps out at the Bluff and the vast desert of whiteness with vortices of spindrift dancing across it. The blue cathedrals in the heart of icebergs, the countless shirred and grained and polished textures of the snow.

There were pictures of the expedition members, too.

Phil sitting astride a skidoo. Laure, with a hundred penguins standing sentinel at her feet. Richard, with the shadow from the hood of his parka slicing his face but still with the ghost of his grandfather in his features. And Rook. He was standing bareheaded at the door of the lab hut with a corner of Margaret's plaque showing behind him. He wasn't smiling, but there was the premonition of a smile round his eyes and mouth. Alice wanted to touch her fingertip to the dark mole at the centre of his forehead. Of course he existed. Here he was, whole and complete.

'I didn't have a single picture. They were all burned,' she managed to say.

'I know,' Lewis answered.

Trevor saw her delight at having these two-dozen coloured images to hold and for a moment he looked differently at Lewis.

For the rest of the short visit, Lewis talked about his plans for the next Antarctic season and the personnel he hoped to attract.

'No use asking a new mother.' He laughed.

'No. What about Richard?'

'I don't know that he would want to lead another expedition.' That was all.

'And Rooker?'

Lewis laughed again. 'That would be to repeat himself. It would go against all the man's instincts. Some of the other personnel may rejoin.'

Five minutes later a mobile phone purred discreetly. Lewis looked at his watch. The visit to Boar's Hill was over. 'I'm proud that you allowed us to use your name,' he said to Margaret. And added, including Trevor in his smile, 'And grateful for the contribution your daughter and granddaughter made to Kandahar.' They shook hands and Lewis kissed Margaret once more. 'Look after her,' he said to Trevor.

'I believe I always have done.'

It was Alice alone who followed him to his car.

The chauffeur stepped out to open the door.

'Do you know where he is?'

Lewis was too all-knowing even to miss a beat. 'No, I don't.'

'Will you help me to find him?'

The car door was open. The chauffeur took the attaché case and stowed it inside.

'That was the bargain, I think? Your co-operation with a little publicity, our co-operation over addresses and other details?'

Alice met his eye. 'That's right.'

He smiled once more, fine wrinkles showing in the tanned skin round his eyes. 'I remember the crevasse, Alice. It's me who owes you the favour, rather than vice versa. I'll do what I can.'

She hadn't thought of that.

He eased himself into the black leather cocoon of the back seat. The driver patted the door shut, climbed into his own seat and swung the car past the flowerbed. Alice stood with her hand raised in a wave, watching it edge out of sight.

In the house, Margaret was irritably gathering up coffee cups. 'Well, that's a whole morning gone. And now I suppose it's time to think about lunch.'

*   *   *

The next day another package arrived for Alice. She glanced at the foreign stamps and the unfamiliar handwriting and quickly opened it.

Inside was a card with an illustration of a fluffy stork holding a pink baby bundle in its beak, clipped to her old copy of *The Rime of the Ancient Mariner*. Jochen had written, 'I think you will like to have this book from your childhood to give to

503

your own daughter. With warm wishes from your colleague.'

Most of Alice's belongings were packed ready to go back to the house in Jericho, but the album of photographs lay on her bed. She placed the old book next to it and opened the album to look into the heart of the ice yet again.

CHAPTER EIGHTEEN

There was no sign of him, no way to reach him. The photographs were all she had.

Alice contemplated the two worlds. She lived in one, going through the motions of her old life. The other was dark and deserted but it still called to her day and night.

June came, and the Oxford streets turned black and white with students in exam clothes. Two weeks later it was party dresses and champagne bottles for the week of the summer balls. And then, as the incoming tide of tourists and summer-school students swelled, the University sank into the torpor of the long vacation. Most of her colleagues from the Department were heading out and scattering around the world for a summer of field studies, but Alice and the baby were staying in Oxford. There were no rock samples from Kandahar to work on; she struggled to rekindle enthusiasm for the research projects that had seemed worthwhile before she went out to Antarctica.

One day Alice put Meg into her new super-buggy, which Pete had insisted on buying, and pushed her through the streets towards the Parks. This morning Jo and the twins were waiting for her at the café where all those months ago she had had tea with Pete and Mark the sculptor, and had listened to the men debating art.

Charlie and Leo were almost a year old now. They were sturdy babies, already walking, with tiny sandals buckled on their feet. They pottered between the chair legs, picking up the chunky educational toys that Jo had thoughtfully brought along.

Afterwards they steered the babies under the trees beside the river. Jo's face and bare arms were dappled with shadows. She was talking about pre-school learning and she was earnest and smiling at the same time. Meg had fallen asleep. Alice tried hard to listen and make the right responses, but Jo suddenly stopped and faced her. 'You're not listening.'

They were at the curve in the river where Pete had leaped out of the punt and swum ashore. She remembered his dripping, gangling figure wading up on to the path just ahead of where they were now and she smiled.

In the past weeks he had often looked in to see Meg. He was generous with presents and offers of money, although Alice insisted that she could manage. He told her that *Desiderata* was now the centrepiece of an exhibition of his work at a London gallery and she read a couple of favourable notices of the show. And from another of their friends Alice heard that very recently he had begun to console himself with a girl with long red hair. He's a good man, she judged, as she always did at this point. He just doesn't have the longest attention span.

'I am listening,' Alice protested. 'You were saying . . .'

'It doesn't matter.' Jo sighed.

'Of course it does. It's important to give them a good start. But—music and movement? Isn't it a bit early?'

Jo had settled. Once she had forgiven her boys and Harry for the loss of her freedom, she began to turn into a committed mother. From now on there would be no investment in the twins' future that she would not make if it lay within her power. Meanwhile, Becky was taking the challenge of finding the right husband more seriously than even a year ago. She had confided to Alice that if she and Vijay weren't going to get married soon, she would have to start looking for a replacement.

'I don't think it *can* be too early, do you?' Jo was saying. They walked on, through the tunnel of trees. When she lifted her head, Alice saw jigsaw pieces of blue sky between the leaves.

Here were safety and caution, and somewhere beyond here there was freedom as well as fear. She felt as if the tendrils of familiarity were reaching out and wrapping round her ankles and calves, like vines, growing and thickening and anchoring her in this place that had once been hers and no longer was. Trapping her.

The roots of her dissatisfaction didn't just lie in her longing for Rooker. If he had sent her a single word, just a sign, she could have gone on waiting. Maybe Rook was fading into his own photograph, reality becoming a memory. Perhaps he had just been the agent of change, a way of knocking the scales from her eyes that was almost as cruel as it had been wonderful.

But I *can* see now, she thought. All my life I have been bending and conforming, doing what I ought rather than what I could. I've applied myself to science and closed my eyes to art; I have rejected fantasy and adopted reason. What was I afraid of?

I can't do it any longer.

This sudden certainty was the awkward, half-unwelcome, non-returnable gift that Antarctica had given her. No one who goes to the ice comes back the same person.

What can I do instead? A vertiginous space opened at her feet and she almost stumbled before tightening her grip on the moulded handles of the buggy.

They turned to walk towards the gates again. Keble Chapel held up black filigree fingers against the sky.

'Have you put her name down for the nursery?' Jo was asking.

'Not yet.'

'You must. The waiting list's endless and you'll need some childcare, won't you, when next term starts?'

'Yes.' Or no.

At the gates, where traffic slowly rolled past towards the science labs in South Parks Road, they stood for five more minutes chatting until Jo suddenly looked at her watch. 'Oh, God. I've got to get the car or they'll ticket me.'

They hugged each other and Alice stood for a minute to watch her old friend as she walked away, leaning forward to give the proper momentum to the cumbersome double buggy, her head down and her hips outlined by the folds of her summer skirt.

Then she crossed the road in the opposite direction and walked the familiar route back to the house in Jericho; so familiar that she could have done it blindfold.

The house was sunny and silent. From inside the front door she could see straight through to the crab-apple tree in the back garden. Her first action after settling Meg was to check her voice-mail. She always did it, always hoping.

The first of the two new messages was from Margaret, wanting to know if she was bringing Meg up to see them later that day. Margaret's arthritis had been troubling her and recently she had been having problems with her eyesight, which meant that she couldn't read as much as she wanted or even keep up with her e-mails. She was irritable and found fault with everything Trevor and Alice did, but she was always eager to see her granddaughter. Alice skipped to the second message, resolving to call her mother later.

The next voice was familiar, but it wasn't the one she was listening for.

'Hello, Alice. This is Richard Shoesmith.'

He gave the date, and the exact time of his call, as precise as always. He said that he was back in the country and was coming to Oxford on a brief visit. He hoped to look her up, if she could spare the time.

'Time is no problem,' Alice said aloud. She wrote down the number he had given and dialled it. She left a message, as instructed, saying that she would look forward to seeing him.

It was time to feed Meg. Alice lifted her out of the buggy and was rewarded by the flash of a moist, gummy smile.

508

'That's my girl,' Alice murmured, smiling back and holding her up so their eyes were level. What shall we do, eh? Where shall we head for, the two of us, in this wide world?

Meg's smile widened, turning her features into one ecstatic beam of delight while her eyes focused on the sun and moon of her mother's face. Alice swung her higher. They were both laughing now, lost in the moment. The baby kicked and squirmed until Alice swung her down again and hugged her. 'That's my girl. Are you hungry?' Meg's head lolled, soothed by the vibration of her mother's voice.

Alice carried her out into the garden and sat down on the bench. Out here in the sunshine was a good place to feed her.

Jo had said that she should start her on solids, but she thought that she would leave it for a week or so. From an open window further down the street came the sound of someone practising the flute.

*　　　*　　　*

Richard was wearing a tie and carrying a briefcase. For a moment she thought of Lewis Sullavan. It was a hot day, and she was in a loose blue cotton dress that showed her arms and wasn't properly done up at the front from Meg's last feed. Her hand came up to the buttons and Richard's eyes went straight to the rough pink-purple scar that jagged her forearm, a visible reminder of the fire.

'Come in,' Alice said quickly and stood back to make room. The hallway was narrow and they awkwardly skirted each other.

He followed her into the living room. Her computer screen in the corner workspace was blank, the desk space was bare of books and papers, and Meg sat in her chair in the middle of the floor, clutching an orange rubber rattle that was liberally smeared with drool.

'So. Here she is,' Richard said. He lowered himself into an awkward crouch beside Meg, as if to shake hands with her. She gave him a stare and then, predictably, her face screwed up and she opened her mouth to wail.

Alice stooped too. 'Hey. It's all right. This is Richard. Hmm? He knows all about the snow and the ice.' She unbuckled the seat straps and swung the baby on to her hip. She was used to this now, to moving two-headed around their domain and doing everything one-handed.

'Would you like a cup of tea, or maybe a glass of wine?'

'Oh, just tea. Tea would be perfect.'

He followed her into the kitchen and watched her fill the kettle. 'How are you?'

'I'm fine,' Alice said. In a way. In an everyday, don't-mind-the-tendrils way. Her scar throbbed as it hadn't done for weeks.

The last time we saw each other, she thought.

The blur of pain and panic, Rook's voice in her ear, his arms lifting her and carrying her to the helicopter. Then somehow the view backwards, into a wall of mist. Just enough visibility for her to see Richard with Valentin and Phil holding his arms, Russ grabbing his collar, the others scrambling in his path.

Stop him, Richard had shouted.

The spectres of what-if rose in front of her all

over again. The fire might have trapped some or all of them, or they might have been badly burned and then slowly frozen to death in their meagre shelter. They could have been imprisoned by the ice for six months. Meg might have died as she was being born, or later from exposure. The helicopter might have crashed into the frozen bay.

In retrospect, her own rashness was the most fearful spectre of all.

Gratitude for their escape and her extra good fortune flooded through Alice. She felt weak with it. She put her free hand out and caught Richard's arm, searching his face for a sign of what he might be feeling. She longed to talk, now, about what they had been through together.

But his handsome face was stiff, closed, with only a flicker of wariness in the corners of his eyes.

'Good. That's good. It was quite an escape we had, wasn't it? You especially. Extraordinary. But here we are. What about your work and so on?'

Alice blinked, but already she understood.

Richard's recuperation in Greece had been a process of sweeping up, tidying away broken glass and ashes, and locking away chunks of bleeding memory. It was all out of sight now and he would bend his attention back to a rigidly ordered world. Palaeontology, mild academic disagreements, university and departmental administration. He wouldn't dream any longer of living up to his grandfather, even of being his father's suitable son, because he couldn't. That dream lay in pieces.

Her heart lurched with sympathy for him, but she withdrew her hand. 'I'm not doing much work at the moment, because of Meg. And how are you?' she asked gently.

'I'm pretty well. Needed a rest, you know.'

'Of course.' It was the opposite of what she wanted but she found herself playing his game, nodding and not probing. She wondered why he had come here. They took their tea into the garden and Richard sat down on the rustic bench.

'Do you want to go back to the ice?' she asked at last, looking at Meg rather than at him. There was a silence, in which they heard the flautist practising scales.

'I do regret the loss of the Gastropoda. We were on to something there, you know.'

'There are others, probably. Waiting to be found.'

'That will be good. For Kandahar.'

The question burst out of her. 'What about *you*, Richard?'

With an effort, and almost inaudibly, he answered, 'I did my best. I . . . wish it had turned out otherwise, of course. No. I won't be doing another season.'

'That's a shame.'

'Ah. Yes. Well, there it is. Now, I've got a little present to give the baby.'

'That's very kind.'

He went off to retrieve his briefcase and brought out a rectangular box. Alice opened it and found a kaleidoscope with heavy metal cylinders and glass eyepiece, more like a proper instrument than a toy. She put it to her eye and turned the drum. The beads were chips of blue and silvery glass, and the mirrors multiplied them into the form of a snowflake.

'Thank you, it's beautiful. I'll keep it safe until she's old enough to appreciate it.'

Now he looked at his watch.

'Richard, do you remember the camp out at the Bluff? The first one?'

Not the second, when Rook had been with them.

He answered warily, 'Of course.'

'We talked a lot, then.' Exchanging histories, recognising one another in the straitjackets the past imposed.

'Yes.'

'If you want to talk any more, about Kandahar or anything else, I am here.'

'Thank you,' Richard said. She knew that he wouldn't talk to her. It was quite likely that they would never see each other again.

He began to gather himself together. He was going to meet an American palaeontologist, he said, who was briefly in Oxford. He mentioned the man's name and asked if she knew him. Alice shook her head.

All the way to the front door she didn't ask what was uppermost in her mind, but then as he was mumbling a formal goodbye she caught his arm again. 'Have you heard anything from Rook? Have you any idea where he might have gone?'

She saw the flash of pain in his eyes clearly enough now, and realised why he had come. It had been in order to find out if she was still wearing her straitjacket. Maybe he wanted to make her his co-conspirator, sweeping up the memory of a failed season together and locking it into a cupboard. This was so like him, and the woman she had once been understood the impulse perfectly.

Sadness and sympathy bled through her once more. What had happened was partly her fault. In the ice-bright, thin-skinned hyper-reality of

Antarctica she had begun to be attracted to him and then the avalanche of events and emotions had carried her onwards, and she had rejected him. He had been hurt, she now understood, more deeply than she had realised.

'I don't know anything about Rooker,' he said.

'I'm sorry,' she blurted out. 'I'm sorry for everything that happened.'

He frowned. 'The fire was an accident, you know.'

'Of course it was.'

'And the weather was . . . what it is. Of all people, I should have been better prepared. "Remember This"'—he smiled—'"When I Am Best Forgotten."' He swept up his briefcase, holding it against himself like a shield. Alice made a clumsy move to kiss his cheek but his formality obstructed her. Their hands met instead and he shook hers.

'I hope you find what you're looking for,' he said.

'And you,' she called after him as he headed down the path past her roses. If he heard, he didn't look back.

Alice sank down on the bottom stair and rested her chin in her hands.

Richard and she were moving in opposite directions. He was retreating and she was admitting to herself what a different world really meant. She wanted to be the person she had been at Kandahar.

She studied the worn patch of carpet at the bottom of the stairs, where everyone who descended placed their right foot. She knew for certain now that Meg and she would have to leave Oxford. The first imperative was to try to find

514

Rooker; after that she had no idea. Nor did she have any idea where to begin her search. All she did know was that she must do something, very soon, or the tendrils would wrap round her and hold her for ever. She would be like Richard, always keeping a version of herself hidden in case the daylight fell on it.

A similarity struck her. Rooker had his cupboard too, with painful truth swept up and locked away inside. The truth had something to do with *I am a murderer*, of course. Would he have told her even that, she wondered, if they had been in an ordinary place at an ordinary time?

Left alone in her baby seat in the garden, Meg began to cry and Alice stood up at once. Rooker's claim, that was the place to start. Exactly how to go about it was still a mystery.

*   *   *

In the end it was Russell who gave her the answer.

He telephoned one morning at 6 a.m. Alice was in the little box room that had become Meg's bedroom, changing the baby's nappy and talking to her. Meg always listened in apparent fascination, her eyes fixed on her mother's face.

'Alice? Sorry if it's the middle of the night or something.'

'This is fine, Russ.'

'Got a bit of info for you.'

'Go on.'

'There's a little place called Turner, between here and Christchurch. I've got a mate here in Dunedin who's interested in genealogy, family history, all that kind of stuff? Does a lot of his research on the Internet, but also searches in local records, death certificates, that kind of thing?'

'I know the kind of thing.' She bit back hard on her impatience.

'Well, he grew up about twenty miles from Turner. I was round there a few days ago, taking back a cement mixer I'd borrowed because I'm doing a bit of work on extending the deck out back here, Kathy's idea. I was asking him about how you set about finding a person's history, just out of interest more than anything, and he asked me for a name. I gave him Rook's, since I'd been talking to you. Seemed to ring a bell with him, although he couldn't place it then. Anyway, to cut a long story short . . .'

Please, Alice silently begged.

'. . . he came up with something. Sad story, in the local paper. He'd seen it in the archives when he was hunting up something to do with his own relatives. Woman called Rooker, committed suicide, not long after a friend of hers died in a fire. The friend was a bit of a boozer . . . I'm reading between the lines here . . . lived in a caravan and it was burned out one night with him inside it. She'd been questioned, but it doesn't sound as though she was a suspect. Quite a big story, for this part of the world.'

The hair stood up on the nape of Alice's neck. Fire. *A friend of my mother's died in a fire.*

'My mate even sent me a photocopy of a newspaper article. Here it is, 1967. It mentions that she had one son. Must be our Rooker, by my calculations.'

'Could you scan it and e-mail it to me, Russ? Everything you've got?'

'Will do.'

By that evening she had it in her hand. Almost a full page of the *Turner & Medfield Clarion*, smudged from the photocopier of Russ's friend, but still legible. There was a posed photograph of a woman, looking back at the camera lens over her shoulder, an actress's pose with one eyebrow raised and her dark-painted lips parted. *Tragic suicide*. There was another photograph, much less clear, of the fire victim. Lester Furneaux seemed to have a soft, elongated face and a scarf at his throat.

By coincidence almost the same information reached her two days later, in a fax marked 'From the office of Lewis Sullavan'.

There it was. The other side of the world. She and Meg would go to Turner, New Zealand, and try to find out what had happened long ago to the child, James Rooker. There was only the smallest chance that any thread would lead onwards from there, let alone to wherever Rook was now, but Alice was sure that this was where the key to the cupboard lay.

*　　　*　　　*

Rooker and Frankie drove in her battered VW up to the lake shore. It was a two-hour journey and the three children in the back seat were sticky and squabbling. Every so often she half turned from the wheel and swiped at them. The car swerved briefly.

'Stop that, Jackson. Leave your sister alone. If you want to go in a boat you better sit up and quit fighting.'

Jackson folded his arms and sulked. Frankie's daughter Corinna caught Rooker's eye and gave him a sly, turned-in smile exactly like her mother's.

'When will we be there?' the little girl asked.

'Twenty minutes.' Frankie sighed. 'Please God. Jackson, will you *stop* that.'

At last they turned into the parking lot.

They set off down a track, the two older children racing ahead. Rooker carried the folding chairs and the cold box and a plaid blanket. Frankie was holding Sammy the baby's hand, her head bent as she listened to whatever he was urgently telling her. Rooker wondered what it would be like to be locked into a family like this, instead of just visiting. There were houses on either side of this track, with sandboxes in their yards and bicycles propped against fences. What would it be like to live in a house like one of these, to go to work every day and come home every night? It was her only just-offbeam version of this, wasn't it, that Edith had offered him down in Ushuaia?

They reached the shore. It was a wide crescent of shingly sand backed by rough grass. There was a stone jetty with boats moored along its length, a converted boathouse calling itself the Coffee Plantation and sunlight winking on the water. After the nomadic weeks he had just spent, this vista looked so ordinary that it became hyper-real in every detail, like a Rockwell picture. He stared at the painted sign on the roof of the coffee shop and the way the flat primary colours of the lettering stood out against the azure depth of the sky.

Frankie stood with her fists on her hips, her head on one side, smiling at him. She wore a bandanna over her long straight hair, a Sixties chick born twenty years too late.

'You don't say much, Rook, do you? But you

know, I'm still pretty pleased you came by.'

Jackson clamoured, 'Can we go in a sailboat now, Rook? You said we could.'

'I need a beer first.'

'Awww.' But all three children were already running towards the water. Rook unfolded the chairs and set them in place.

Frankie took a can of beer out of the cooler and put it into his hand. 'What's with you?' she asked, her tolerance shaded by exasperation. Rook sat down, burrowing his feet into the pebbly sand. In the two days since he had arrived at the house in upstate New York, this was about the first word that he and Frankie had had alone together. There had always been Ross, or some permutation of kids hanging off her arms, or a neighbour dropping in and staying. Frankie was like that. 'How bad is it?' she pressed him.

Frankie had seen some bad times, that was true. There were times when he had been drinking, with Edith and before Edith came along, that he was glad he couldn't recall himself.

'It isn't bad.'

'It doesn't look good to me.'

The children were silhouetted against the glittering water. Jackson and Corinna were walking in the wet sand, and the baby was trying to stretch his legs to match his brother's footprints. Rooker closed his eyes on a sudden clutch of pain and greenish suns swam and merged behind his eyelids. He heard Frankie pop the ring on a can of beer for herself and take a long swallow.

'What happened to you, down at the South Pole?'

Automatically he corrected her, 'We weren't

519

anywhere near the Pole.' Then he added, 'A woman had a baby down there, can you imagine that? I delivered it.'

He was surprised. Once the first words were out, he felt a dam ready to break behind his tongue. There was a huge weight of water, words, history, waiting to pour out of him.

'Go on,' Frankie said softly.

He told her what had happened. He tried to explain about the innocence and how amazed he had been to hold it in his hands. Meg's birth had made him feel used up and polluted, with the dirt of a lifetime ingrained in the pores of his skin and the furls of his brain. It was too late to clean up. All he could do was keep away from them. Stay away from them.

'Rooker, you aren't seeing straight. You've lived tough, but you're no worse than most people who've been in this world four decades or more. What's so bad in the past that you think you're going to pollute a newborn just by being near to her?'

He wouldn't tell Frankie what. There was only one person he might have told—he had already blurted out the words, so he could have filled in the details—but she was nowhere near this sunny-day picture of a lake shore. He held up his hands instead, cupping them round empty air. 'She was so tiny. Folded, crimson, wet. And yet as soon as she took a breath she was a complete being. It was as though I had never seen anything in my life before, never opened my eyes on anything that mattered. And after I had seen it nothing really mattered except the two of them. Look at me. In the long term, how much better will it be for Alice and Meg if I'm not there? I can give up anything in the world for them, easily. Even the chance of being with them.'

They were both watching the two bigger children as they ran into the shallow water, sending up glittering cages of spray. Sammy hesitated, wobbling as the wavelets ran around his ankles.

'But children don't judge you, or ask for your history. They take you as you are. Mine do, don't they, and you let them? Tell me how you know that you *are* doing the right thing by giving these people up, if that's what drifting around the world like this means. Did you ask the mother—Alice—if she wanted you to be quite so nobly considerate? Or are you just being selfish and listening to your own inside voice?'

Jackson waded deeper, holding up his skinny arms like chicken wings to keep them out of the cold water for as long as possible, and Corinna shivered on his heels so as not to be left behind or outdone.

It was more than two years since he had last seen Frankie, but even so he counted her as his closest friend. He had come up here to find her, hadn't he, in the end? He had told her some of the truth; he should listen to her now. He guessed that if he didn't there was nothing left for him to do and nowhere else to turn.

'No, I didn't ask.'

'Do you love her?'

'Jesus, Frankie. I don't know. It doesn't matter now.'

'I think it does matter. Maybe it matters more than anything. Do you?'

'Yes.'

'Does she know?'

'Yes.'

Frankie tipped her head back to drain her beer. Then she stood up and walked almost to the water's edge where she scraped up a mound of gritty sand around the can. She stooped to collect a handful of pebbles, then came back to give half of them to Rooker. They took it in turns to aim at the can. Four out of five of Rook's pebbles pinged, and all five of Frankie's.

'Does she love you?' she asked at last.

'Perhaps.'

'What's that supposed to mean?'

'She's English.'

Frankie laughed. 'So are you.'

'Not in quite the same way, Frank. I'm just passport-English, she's Oxford and educated and classy, and she doesn't say much, but when she does believe me it counts. The answer to your question is I would have to find that out.'

Frankie let her long arms hang over the arms of the chair. She had a tattoo on her right bicep, a rose with an exaggeratedly thorny stem.

'Then *find* out.'

'I might discover she's gone back to Meg's father. I might screw things up for her in a hundred different ways. Or she might see things differently, now we're not on the ice any longer.'

'Is that how little you think of her?'

Shamed, Rook murmured, 'No.'

Frankie picked out another fistful of pebbles, this time keeping them all for herself. She sat up very straight and aimed a savage volley at the beer can. She didn't trust herself to look at him.

Jackson and Corinna were trying to coax Sammy

522

into the water. They each took one of his hands and swung him between them so his feet churned the surface while he yelled with the pleasure of fear.

Frankie snapped, 'Go to England, Rook. You think you're strong but you're not; you've got more cracks in you than grandaddy's whip. You never will be really strong either, not until you've had the courage to make yourself vulnerable, and if you don't do it soon you'll be so stiffened up that you'll never be able to. Fuck. *Listen to me*, you asshole.'

She shouted these last words, making him jump. She leaped to her feet and pushed him so hard that his flimsy chair overbalanced and sent him sprawling in the sand. Corinna let go of Sam's hand and he clawed briefly at his brother, then slid into the water. Frankie was already sprinting across the strip of sand as Rooker sat up. She ploughed straight into the water and swept Sammy into her arms, and the other two children clung to her as she waded out again. They lurched back together, a misshapen eight-legged creature that spattered the sand with drips. Frankie's long skirt clung to her legs.

Corinna was blue-lipped and her teeth were chattering. Rooker wrapped a towel round her and rubbed her dry. 'Corinna Corinna,' he sang as he did it.

'I hate that tune. Everyone always sings it when I'm around. It sucks.'

'Why's that?'

She shrugged and he saw the way her skin slid so smoothly over the planes of her shoulder blades. A kind of pain that was now knotted with anticipation suddenly gathered in him again.

523

'Be*cause*.' Corinna put her head on one side and he saw her mother in her once more. He couldn't detect much of Ross.

'Rook, c'n we go in a boat now? You said,' Jackson called out from inside his towel.

'Sure. You coming, Frankie?'

'No.' She shook her head, still not looking at him. 'Sammy and I'll stay here. Eh, Sam? You and me?'

They stayed late at the shore and it was already dark as they made their way home. All three children were asleep in the back and Frankie stared into the oncoming lights as Rook drove. She had been quiet all afternoon and he had left her to herself. There was enough talk from the kids.

But now she put her hand on his arm. 'Rooker?'

'Yeah.'

'Are you going?'

He sighed. 'I don't know.'

'Are you scared to? You could phone first or mail her or something.'

'Yes, I'm scared. And if I'm going to see her I'd rather it was face to face to start with. It's easier to see the truth that way.'

There was a silence.

After a while Frankie said, 'Edith called me last week.'

'What did she want?'

'To find out where you were.'

'What did you tell her?'

'That I had no more idea than she did. It was true, then.'

'Yeah,' Rooker said.

*   *   *

Two days later he was still at Frankie's place. A weight of uncertainty and indecision pressed on him, and he tried to work it off by painting the yard fences and taking down the storm shutters to replace the old frames.

He watched the patients coming and going from Frankie's husband's chiropractic clinic adjoining the house, and in the evenings he shared a beer with Ross while he talked about the Iraq war. On the third evening he helped Frankie to carry in the grocery bags after she came back from the store.

'I've got something to show you,' she said.

'What's that?'

She took the rolled-up baton of a magazine out of one of the bags and pitched it at him. The glossy pages flipped in a coloured blur. Rook bent slowly and picked it up, and it fell open at a big picture. He stared down into Alice's face. She was holding Meg on her lap and a fierce-looking old woman stood very straight beside them.

'That's her, isn't it?'

Rook felt a hammering inside him. 'Yes.' He couldn't read the text. The words jumped around in front of his eyes.

'So, are you going to England?'

All he could see was Alice's face, he could hear nothing but her voice in his ears. 'No,' he said wretchedly. 'How can I?'

Ross went out that evening to a football game. Once the children were in bed, Frankie and Rooker sat on the sofa together in front of the television. She curled up with her feet tucked under the folds of her skirt, her head resting on his chest. Rooker lightly stroked her hair, disentangling loose strands from her long earring and tucking them behind her ear. A glint of light on her cheek caught his eye and he saw that she was crying.

'Frank?' He drew her upright and cupped her face in his hands. She sniffed and tried to smile. 'What's the matter?'

'I want . . .' she began. 'Well, shit, it doesn't matter what I want. I want you to be happy. Go to England, find your Alice. Why can't you? Why are you so . . . so rigid? It's as if you've made up your mind not to be happy. If she loves you, what right do you have to make *her* miserable?'

Frankie's wet face was flushed. He looked into her eyes. Was that true? he wondered. Had he decided on the day that Lester died that happiness was not for him?

'You saw the picture. Her mother, her child. A whole life that I don't know, don't belong to. How can I walk into that?'

She stared at him. '*How*? By putting one foot in front of the other.'

Rooker let his head sink forward until their foreheads and noses touched. Frankie's hot tears ran over his thumbs.

'I love you,' she whispered.

He nodded slowly. Their faces were pressed together, his eyes were closed now. The dam holding back the buried words was close to breaking. Tears forced themselves between his eyelids and he clenched his teeth to hold everything in place. He loved Frankie too. Like a sister.

'Go to England,' she begged him. 'Do it for me.'

That she should be so generous, so full of concern for him and not herself, made him cry properly. He kissed her forehead and she clung to him. It was a moment before he could speak.

'I'll go,' he promised her at last.

*   *   *

'You're crazy,' Jo protested.

'Or else I'm totally sane.'

'What about Meg?'

'All Meg needs is me. And I will be there with her.'

Alice spoke with confidence. In the months since she had brought her home Meg had grown. She was still small compared with full-term babies of her age, but she was healthy and making good progress. Travelling with her now would be nothing like flying from Santiago to Patagonia in the first precarious week of her life.

They were in the house in Jericho and Jo was helping Alice to clear cupboards ready for it to be let yet again.

'Where will you live?'

'I don't know yet. I don't know how long I'll be there. I can rent a house like this one, can't I?'

'What about the Department? Your research, your students? They used to mean everything to you and now it's as if nothing except Rooker means anything at all. You're uprooting your baby, carting her off to the middle of nowhere . . .'

'It's New Zealand,' Alice said mildly, 'to begin with. Not Outer Mongolia. Of course what I'm leaving here is still important to me. But I have to do my best to find him; if I sit and do nothing my life here will be diminished by more than I'm prepared to accept.'

They came to a set of china. 'Pack or leave?' Jo asked.

'Leave. People might as well use it, mightn't they?'

Enough foreign academics visited Oxford to make letting a house easy. The chairs, pictures, china that furnished hers were just things, now. She had no anxieties about leaving them. There were infinitely more important assets that couldn't be stored in cupboards.

'Jo? When I left for the south, I thought you were jealous of my freedom.'

Jo stood upright. She brushed back her hair, ready to make a serious statement, the way she had been doing since they were fourteen years old. 'I was, of course. Our situations were completely different then and what you were doing showed up my dissatisfaction with mine. But now we are in the same place.'

'Not really. You have Harry, a family, you've made a set of commitments and it isn't a capitulation to be here. It's a promise.'

'You could have Pete. You could be a family.'

Alice closed a cupboard door with a small, decisive click. 'That isn't what I want,' she said.

*   *   *

Margaret was much more difficult to deal with.

'New *Zealand*? For how long?'

'I don't know yet.'

'You can't, Alice, and that's flat. Not running after some safety officer who . . .'

'Would it be different if he were a scientist?' Alice asked.

528

'Not at all.' Although Alice didn't think that was quite the truth. 'You've got a child now, you have responsibilities.'

Didn't you? Alice wanted to ask. But that would not have been fair. As a child she had had Trevor, they both had. Always: Trevor had always been the given in Margaret's life as well as in her own. He sat on the sofa now, with the cat beside him. He was rubbing the worn corduroy of his trouser legs, massaging warmth into his thin legs even though it was a balmy, still evening. It was Trevor's constancy that had enabled Margaret's unpredictability and without him she would have been half the person. Marriages were infinitely complex, Alice thought. Aspects of her parents' could still take her by surprise. She saw their partnership now as if it were a rock specimen, revolving on a display plinth, presenting her with new facets as it rotated.

'I'm not abandoning her,' she said quietly. 'Where I go, she goes.'

'What will you do about money?' Margaret asked. She was always frugal. Money was for saving, not spending.

Alice had resigned her teaching and research post. 'I've got the rent from the house. Some savings. I'll have to be careful, that's all.'

Trevor looked straight at her. 'I've got a bit put by. You can have that.'

Margaret cried, 'No. She can't. That's not the way to handle this.'

But Trevor held up his hand. He said in a tone that Alice had never heard him use before, 'Be quiet, Margaret.'

Margaret shrank. Tears came into her eyes. 'I'm not that well, Alice. You know I'm not. When am I

529

ever going to see Meg?'

Alice put her arms round her mother's shoulders and kissed the top of her head where the strands of thin hair parted to reveal pink scalp. 'Often,' she comforted her. 'I'll make sure of it.'

*   *   *

Pete tried cajoling, then anger and outrage, and finally threats. 'You can't take her without my consent. I won't let you do it.'

Alice took his two hands and turned them over in hers, looking at the nailbeds with purple hammer bruises and cuticles rimmed with plaster dust. 'Don't do this to us,' she begged at last. 'Not when we could stay friends.'

They were in the Jericho house where the last few boxes of Alice's clothes and books were waiting to be taken back to store. He broke away from her and leaned his forehead against the wall, beating at the paintwork with his clenched fist. 'This is our home,' he groaned.

'It was. Everything changes, Pete. You can't fix life like . . . like a sample catalogued in a drawer. All you can do is move with it.'

'Oh, Christ,' he mumbled, and there was real pain in his voice. 'She's my daughter.'

'Pete, she will always be your daughter. For the rest of your life and hers.'

He lifted his head. 'Yes.' He sighed then. 'Make sure you bring her back to me.'

'Of course I will.'

*   *   *

530

Becky said, 'I think you are doing the right thing. I don't want you to go, but that's for selfish reasons.'

'It is the right thing,' Alice agreed.

CHAPTER NINETEEN

'I would like Alice Peel's address, please.'

'I'm afraid we can't give out expedition members' personal details, Mr Rooker. The Polar Office will forward any communications, of course.'

He was standing in a mid-town phone booth, his bag at his feet, waiting to pick up the express bus for JFK. A hooting stream of yellow cabs and buses and cars poured past him, cruelly glittering in the low sunshine. Rooker frowned into the glare. He still wasn't sure whether or not to go to England. Prickles of indecision ran down his spine like beads of sweat. In spite of his promise to Frankie it would be easy—too easy—to find a way not to do it.

'Could I speak to Beverley Winston?'

'Just a moment, please.'

The line went dead and he thought the transatlantic connection had failed, but at last the woman's voice came back. 'You could try her on this number.'

Rooker crooked the receiver to his ear and scribbled the digits on the reverse of his air ticket folder. He pressed the disconnect button and rapidly dialled again.

'Hello.' The low voice was warm, and sweet as molasses.

'Hello, Beverley. This is James Rooker.'

'This is a surprise.'

'I might be going to London.'

Beverley laughed. 'And?'

'I'm thinking of looking some people up.'

The laugh again. 'You already have my number, apparently.'

'I'll call you. Can you help me with something else? I'd like to see Alice Peel, but the Polar Office won't bend the rules. It's like dealing with some Brit secret society that I'm not eligible to join.'

That touched a chord, as he had intended it to do. After a fractional hesitation she said, 'I know. It's comical, isn't it? Wait a minute.'

Rooker leaned against the glass, breathing in the scent of dirt. He heard a keyboard clicking.

'I've got it.'

The only telephone number listed belonged to Alice's parents, but the address was hers: 32 Cranbrook Street, Oxford. He wrote that down too, although he didn't need to because it had already stamped itself in his mind. He said goodbye to Beverley.

The bus was waiting in its bay, sweating people milling around it with their suitcases. Rooker lifted his single bag. He was travelling light now. His feet carried him forward. Ten minutes later the bus swung out into the late-afternoon Manhattan traffic.

At the airport, while he tried to decide whether or not to board the London flight, he went to a bar and bought a whisky that he didn't want.

He stared down into the glass. After the lonely weeks of travelling, Frankie's generous goodwill had unshackled him. Frankie liked him, loved him, even, and she trusted him to be around her kids. Meg would grow up, like Corinna was growing. He wanted to see that happening and he wanted to share it with Alice.

For how many years, Rooker thought, had he hated the sound of *we*, for all the obligations and restrictions and the potential for disloyalty and bitterness that could be contained in a single syllable?

Ever since she had failed him, he supposed. It hadn't been her fault, he didn't blame her. All he felt now was the soft ache of sympathy. But aversion was what there had been, ever since *we* hadn't meant the trust or security of a real family.

But now there was a chance that *we* might mean himself and Alice and her daughter. If Alice would allow it. If he hadn't already spent too long wandering the world, ruled by fear and self-disgust, instead of believing that love might take root and flourish, even for him.

Outside the windows of the terminal the jets took off in a steady stream, lights blinking in the thickening sky, chains of them linking all the airports and all the people who were waiting and watching. When the 'Boarding' sign flickered against his flight, Rooker got up and walked uncertainly to the gate.

*   *   *

Alice sat upright in bed. She looked at her travel clock and saw that it was only 2.15. Her heart was thumping but she couldn't recall the details of her dream, only that it had been to do with hurrying and missing something that was terribly urgent.

It's all right, she told herself.

She was ready. Everything was packed and ready

533

to go. Her luggage stood out as a dark hump on the bedroom floor. Meg was asleep. Trevor would drive them to Heathrow again in time for the evening's flight, London to Auckland, via Singapore. Twenty-five hours of travelling and then a stopover in Auckland before flying on to Christchurch.

She lay down and settled herself for sleep once more.

In the morning, Trevor arrived in good time. 'All set?' he asked. Meg's carry-seat was strapped in the back of the car, their two suitcases were loaded in the boot.

Alice stood back and looked up at her house. It was clean, closed up, waiting for the new tenants. The sun reflected back from the windows, making her shield her eyes. 'All set,' she answered. She put the keys in her pocket. They would drop them off at the lettings agency on their way out of town.

They headed east and the homebound traffic whirled past them in the opposite direction.

*　　　*　　　*

The centre of Oxford, when Rooker finally reached it, was a tangle of one-way streets and pedestrian zones. He fumed in his hire car as another massed party of Japanese blocked the road. He wound down the window and asked for directions, only to be told that he shouldn't really have come this way because the bypass would have been much easier. At last he was turning into Cranbrook Street. He saw a row of rosy brick houses, all with pointed gables and recessed porches with stone-lined arches. He could smell roses and fresh paint.

His chest felt hollow round the drumbeat of his heart. His mouth was dry with anxiety as he counted off the house numbers: 26, 28, 30.

This was the one. He checked in his inner pocket for a curled scrap of Velcro fabric that he had carried with him since they half dragged him out of the Squirrel at Kandahar. It was still there.

There was someone standing on the path in front of number 32.

Not Alice.

Rooker stepped stiffly out of the car. The young man outside Alice's front door glanced incuriously at him, then with more attention as he unlatched the little gate.

'I'm looking for Dr Peel.'

The man had spiky gelled hair, unhealthy skin. He was wearing a suit and tie. 'I'm afraid you've missed her.' He stepped hastily back as Rooker advanced on him.

'What do you mean?'

'She is travelling abroad. I'm just the letting agent.' He glanced down for reassurance at the inventory sheet in his hand. 'We have tenants coming in . . .'

His back was against the porch now. He shrank as Rooker loomed over him, black-faced. 'I have to know where she has gone. It's very urgent.'

The man faltered, 'New Zealand, I believe. But . . .'

Where? The white light of instant comprehension exploded painfully behind Rooker's eyes. Their paths had crossed. He had arrived just too late because she had set off to look for him. It dawned on him in the same second that he must reach her. He knew with absolute certainty

535

that without her there was less than nothing in the world.

'When?'

'An . . . hour or so. She dropped these keys in . . .'

Rooker's mind was tearing away, leapfrogging hours and miles. Wait. He had her parents' telephone number somewhere, scribbled in New York on the back of an airline ticket wallet. He held the alarmed agent pinned against the porch while he searched his pockets. The creased folder was still there, with the stub of his boarding card.

'Phone. I need to telephone.'

The man swallowed. 'There's a call box . . . no, you can use my mobile.'

Rooker took the miniature device and stabbed out the numbers. A woman's voice answered.

'My name is James Rooker. I need to speak to Alice.'

There was a beat and then, 'I am afraid she's gone. She's at the airport.'

Unrelated impressions worked at the margins of his mind. Her voice reminded him of long ago. Way back. The divorcée he had lodged with after leaving the Jerrolds, she had come from Yorkshire too, like Alice's mother. The tiny phone felt slippery, he was afraid of crushing it between his fingers.

'Do you have the flight number?'

'Wait a moment.' The voice was cold. Alice's mother didn't approve of him. It didn't matter now. He could pick up on all this later, stitch all the contexts and memories back together, try to reintroduce himself. The only thing that mattered at this instant was reaching her.

'Here it is. Singapore Airlines. SQ 328. Terminal Three. Ten p.m.'

Rooker waved his hand at the agent. The man was sweating, he noticed, but he obligingly produced a pen from his pocket.

'Thank you. Does she have a mobile with her?'

'No. Not for New Zealand.' The voice turned sharper still. Of course, because he was at the root of all this. 'Her father is driving her. But I see his telephone is still here.'

'Thank you.' There was no time for anything else. He would just have to retrace his steps to Heathrow. Rooker tossed the little phone back to its owner.

As he accelerated away, he saw the agent mopping his face in relief.

*   *   *

Alice and Trevor were at the check-in desk as it opened. Alice was assigned a bulkhead seat and promised a sky cot for Meg. They watched the suitcases as they travelled along the belt and disappeared. Afterwards they went and drank tea at the same food court as when they were waiting for her flight to Antarctica. They didn't talk very much, but the silence between them was comfortable.

When they had finished their tea Trevor put his hand over hers. 'This is what you want, isn't it?'

Alice nodded. Not the flying and the lonely distance and the weight of uncertainty, but to be doing something that would connect her to him instead of waiting and fading in a life that no longer fitted her.

'You will come home if you can't find what you're looking for?'

'Of course I will.' But she didn't want even to consider that possibility, because it left too much aching space that didn't have Rooker in it.

Trevor blew his nose. 'I think I'll get back to your mother. Do you mind if I don't wait until the last moment?'

'Of course not.'

He pushed Meg towards the exit and Alice linked her arm through his.

'I love you,' they told each other at the terminal doors. Trevor tried to smile, then smoothed his hair over the dome of his head and turned abruptly away. Alice watched him go, one hand raised and the other gripping the handle of the buggy, torn between the old familiar and the new desire.

When she could no longer see him she turned back into the endless cycle of the airport.

* * *

Rooker weaved his way through the fast traffic. The road signs and the miles flashed past. 'Wait for me, wait for me,' he muttered. The first sign for Heathrow whirled at him and then the second. The daylight was turning blue-purple as the sun sank.

He was almost there. A plane rose on his right hand, its nose lifting towards the sky. Wait for me, wait for me. Fifteen minutes later he was at the airport turn-off. He hunched forward over the wheel, searching for signs to guide him through the unfamiliar layout of flyovers and underpasses. There was no time to return the hire car. He slammed it into the terminal car park and ran.

The airport was packed. Queues stretched from the check-in desks for all the overnight long-haul destinations. He stood at the top of an escalator and scanned the crowds. She was here. She was here *somewhere*.

He ran to the enquiries desk. A plump woman in a uniform blinked at his gabbled request.

'Could you repeat that?'

He repeated himself, wrote down her name, begged for help.

'I'll see if we can do that for you.'

He tore himself away from the desk and ran again. 'Departures' a sign informed him.

*   *   *

Alice changed some money, bought herself a magazine, wondered if she had the right clothes for Meg. There would be shops in New Zealand, she reminded herself. She went into a cloakroom and changed Meg's nappy. There would be time to find a quiet corner to feed her and change her once more before they boarded. Her head was bent over Meg and a distant tannoy announcement was no more than a scramble of words.

She put the baby back into the buggy and slowly wheeled her towards the 'Departures' barrier. There was a long crowded slope, divided into aisles by chrome handrails. An electric zigzag of carpet led to boarding controls, and beyond that she could see baggage scanning machines and the white glitter of duty-free shops. The buggy was rolling down the slope, drawing her with it. There were people flowing around her, some of them walking backwards, in tears, eyes fixed on those they were leaving behind. There was a bored man behind a tall desk, holding out his hand for her boarding card.

*　　*　　*

Rooker pushed through the crowds and sprinted past shops. The aimless surges became a steady slow tide, creeping towards 'Departures'. He scanned the backs of heads as they bobbed in front of him. He reached a chrome rail and a slope leading downwards. The press was thickest here. People leaned over the rail with their hands to their mouths or stretched out in a final wave. He stared down at the sea of heads.

She was there. *There she was*. He could see her dark head, held upright.

She was at the desk, boarding card in hand.

'Alice,' he roared. 'Alice, Alice.'

The airport stilled for a second.

He was aware of a flowering of faces as the people all turned to stare at him.

*　　*　　*

Someone was calling her name. She froze, with her hand raised to take back her boarding card.

It was his voice.

Her head turned, the eyes of strangers catching the corner of hers.

It was Rook. Blood rushed to her head, hammered in the chambers of her ears. He vaulted over a rail, stumbled and pushed his way through the crowd as the slow tide crept forward again.

'Could you stand aside, please?' an official

540

voice ordered.

But she couldn't move in case something might break and admit reality again.

It *was* him. He reached her and caught her in his arms and held her against him. She could hear his heart, feel the pulse in his neck. Their mouths met blindly.

'Stand *aside*, please.'

The current was flowing around them as if they were two rocks standing up against a lee shore. His mouth moved against hers, shaping her name. She tasted and smelled the familiarity, the strangeness, the solid manifest reality of him, after months of waiting and wishing.

'It is really you, isn't it?' Her mouth suddenly curved against his, warm with amazement and delight.

Over their heads a disembodied voice spoke her name, advising her to contact the information desk.

'It is. You can't escape,' he answered. He held on to her and to Meg's buggy as they pushed their way back up the ramp, against the endless outwards current.

When they reached a quieter place he propelled her aside and took her face between his hands. 'Why are you going to New Zealand?'

He had to hear it from her, spoken in her voice.

She looked down, seeing the top of Meg's head. 'I'm going to Turner. Russ found a newspaper report from the *Turner & Medfield Clarion*.' She had the printout of it in her hand luggage along with the picture of him standing outside Margaret Mather House. 'It's your family, isn't it?'

'Yes.'

'I tried everything else, Rook. I couldn't think of

541

any other way to find you. I thought if I went there I might find a link and I could follow the chain and in the end it would have to lead me to you.'

There wasn't a shiver of unhappiness in her but her eyes filled with tears. They ran down her face and he tried to smooth them away, wordless, amazed that she was prepared to do this much.

'Where have you been?' she whispered.

He was looking down too, at Meg asleep between them.

'Cuba. Mexico. New York State. Oxford. It doesn't matter where. Forgive me. Running away, then running to get here.'

'Oxford?'

'I flew in this morning, drove straight to your house. I missed you by about an hour.'

She was shaking her head, gazing at him through her tears. 'You have to tell me the truth.'

'I've never told you a lie, Alice. I swear. I swear on her life.' He kneeled down then in front of Meg. She was transformed from the tiny, blood-smeared grey-pink fragment of humanity he had seen in the Zodiac on the frozen shore. Meg was round-cheeked now, with a crescent of dark eyelashes showing against her translucent skin. Her hand was curled on the blanket. The fingernails were perfect, the colour of rosy shells.

Alice said in a quiet clear voice, 'You told me that you are a murderer. What does that mean?'

Rooker stood up, the terminal briefly swimming around him. The time had come to tell the secret that he had never confessed to another living soul.

He looked blankly at the throngs of people. 'Can we go somewhere?'

'There's a place just up here.'

542

The tables were crowded and messy with spilled drinks and food debris. They found one as two people stood up to go. Alice moved aside two tall paper cups, a plate of cold chips smeared with ketchup. They sat down close together, their heads almost touching, Meg's buggy drawn up beside them. He held her wrists in his hands, one thumb resting on the puckered skin of the long scar, as if to restrain her when she tried to run away.

'Tell me now.'

He closed his eyes. It was hot and Tannoy announcements boomed over their heads.

'Fire' was the first word he managed to say. They both remembered the smoke and the flames, and the roar as the walls of the old hut were engulfed.

Alice waited, but he seemed lost for what to say next.

'Why did your mother do what she did?' she gently prompted.

He took a deep breath. Close, grease-tainted air filled his chest.

'She was an alcoholic. I was used to that; we could have managed between us. I looked after her when she needed it; she was a good mother in the in-between times. She was funny and clever and good company. I didn't feel deprived, you know. I was luckier than some of my friends.' Gabby Macfarlane, for instance. 'Then Lester arrived.'

'Was he her lover?'

'No.' Rooker turned his head away. She studied his quarter-profile, still only just able to believe that he was really here. 'He tried to be mine.'

'How old were you?'

'Twelve.' The dam was cracking. Words started to spill out of him. They were ugly in his mouth,

543

but relief was already flooding in after them. 'I didn't know he was there, Alice. I swear to you. He was at our house, drinking. He'd just come on to me, not for the first time, and I was disgusted. I hated him and I wanted to hurt him, but I didn't want him to *die*. I stole a bottle of scotch and ran out of the house. I drank as much of it as I could, then I went round to his caravan and set fire to it.'

The flood broke loose now. He talked faster and faster. Alice leaned forward, holding his hands. Her eyes never left his face.

'I didn't know he was in there. I didn't mean to kill him. And after he was found dead, no one had seen me, my mother couldn't remember anything. I just told everyone flatly that I'd been at home in bed all the time. Then I waited, wanting them to find out the truth, because it was too much of a secret to keep. But no one tried very hard. He drank, he was a queer, he was a misfit in Turner anyway. The police probably thought it was no more than he deserved. But what it meant, as well as a man being dead because of me, was that my mother lost her friend. He was grown up, he was someone to tease her and keep her company and listen to her grief. I didn't understand that, I thought she shouldn't need anyone but me. She didn't survive very long after Lester died. I suppose she felt too lonely. In the end she just got into the bath and pulled the electric fire in after her.' He hesitated, but only for a second. 'I came home from school and found her.'

A group of big men in football shirts noisily pushed past their table, beer slopping from their full pints. Rooker stared straight ahead, not seeing Alice or the crowds. He only saw his mother now,

544

the last image he had suppressed. Tears ran out of his eyes and down his cheeks.

Alice stood up and went round the table to him. She wrapped her arms protectively round him and cupped his head against her ribs. She stroked his hair and leaned down so that her mouth was against his ear. 'You are not a murderer,' she whispered. 'You never were a murderer.'

They stayed still. Rooker wept openly and Alice held him close. They created an eye of motionless silence together, in the midst of the airport's turbulence. And because it was an airport, where tears and delight were ordinary currency, nobody spared them more than a glance.

At last he was able to speak again. He felt empty, but calm. If Alice were to reject him now, he thought, it would hurt him deeply. But it would not be the end of him.

'Now you know,' he said simply. 'What shall we do?'

They looked into each other's eyes for a long moment. The airport noise swirled around them, but they were deaf to everything. Alice found that she was smiling. 'I don't care. As long as we are together.'

His grasp tightened. 'Don't go to New Zealand.'

'Come with me,' she countered.

The flight wasn't quite full, they had told her that at check-in. 'We can go back to Turner together. The three of us.'

She didn't think for a moment that what Rook had just told her would be the end of the darkness for him. But if they went back together and turned over the stones of his memories, maybe they could lay a solid foundation for the future.

Because her future, and Meg's, did lie with Rooker. She was as certain of that as anything she had ever known, and the travel and the distance and what lay beyond the gates of the airports was only so much detail by comparison.

He said, 'I haven't been back there since they took me to the children's home.'

'We should go now.'

Light suddenly kindled in Rooker's eyes. It was simple.

Everything was simple. They had each other.

'Wait here.' He grinned.

'Oh, no. Wherever you go, I'm coming with you.'

They leaped up. Hand in hand, propelling Meg in front of them, they ran like the wind back through the tide of travellers.

*　　　*　　　*

A flight attendant walked down the aisle. He leaned over the occupant of the seat next to Alice's. 'I wonder', he murmured to the gap-year backpacker, 'if you would be willing to exchange seats so that this family can travel together?'

Rooker felt a jolt of amazement at the word, then a sense of happiness taking root that he had never known before.

'Sure.' The boy shrugged indifferently.

*　　　*　　　*

The plane took off and London dwindled beneath them. Alice and Rooker sat with their hands linked, not speaking, knowing how much talking there was still to do. Rags of cloud blotted out the orange bloom of the city as they climbed. Ties and memories and fears dropped behind them.

They were airborne, in their jet capsule, suspended between what had been and whatever was to come.

Rooker released Alice's hand for a moment and fumbled in his pocket. He brought out a small curl of red Velcro fabric and dropped it into her palm.

One-handed, because Meg lay in her other arm, Alice unfurled it. It was a name label from an EU Antarctic Expedition parka.

Peel, it said.